OXFORD WORLD'S CLASSICS

CONFESSIONS OF AN ENGLISH OPIUM-EATER
AND OTHER WRITINGS

THOMAS DE QUINCEY (1785–1859) was born in Manchester to a prosperous linen merchant. As a young boy he read widely and acquired a reputation as a brilliant classicist. At 17, he ran away from Manchester Grammar School and spent four harrowing months penniless and hungry on the streets of London. Reconciled with his family, he entered Oxford in 1803, but left five years later without taking his degree and moved to the English Lake District to be near his two literary idols, William Wordsworth and Samuel Taylor Coleridge. In 1813 he became dependent on opium, a drug he began experimenting with during his days at Oxford, and over the next few years he slid deeper into debt and addiction. His most famous work, *Confessions of an English Opium-Eater*, appeared in the *London Magazine* in 1821. It was the first detailed account of drug use and abuse in English, and initiated the tradition of the modern artist as exile and prophet. Thereafter De Quincey wrote in the *London* and other leading magazines of the day on a wide variety of topics, including politics, literature, history, philosophy, aesthetics, and economics. In 1827, he published in *Blackwood's Magazine* the first of his three brilliant essays 'On Murder Considered as One of the Fine Arts', and in the 1830s he achieved further notoriety in *Tait's Magazine* with his scandalously informative biographical assessments of Coleridge (1834–5) and Wordsworth (1839). De Quincey published a sequel to *Confessions*, *Suspiria de Profundis*, in *Blackwood's* in 1845, and four years later for the same magazine he produced 'The English Mail-Coach', an essay that he originally intended to form part of *Suspiria*. De Quincey spent much of his life battling poverty, debt, and addiction, but his work was widely admired, and British and American editions of his writings began to appear in the 1850s. He died in Edinburgh in 1859.

ROBERT MORRISON is Queen's National Scholar at Queen's University, Kingston, Ontario. He is the author of *The English Opium-Eater: A Biography of Thomas De Quincey*, which was a finalist for the James Tait Black Prize. For Oxford World's Classics, he has edited Thomas De Quincey, *On Murder*, and (with Chris Baldick) *The Vampyre and Other Tales of the Macabre* and *Tales of Terror from Blackwood's Magazine*.

OXFORD WORLD'S CLASSICS

*For over 100 years Oxford World's Classics have brought
readers closer to the world's great literature. Now with over 700
titles—from the 4,000-year-old myths of Mesopotamia to the
twentieth century's greatest novels—the series makes available
lesser-known as well as celebrated writing.*

*The pocket-sized hardbacks of the early years contained
introductions by Virginia Woolf, T. S. Eliot, Graham Greene,
and other literary figures which enriched the experience of reading.
Today the series is recognized for its fine scholarship and
reliability in texts that span world literature, drama and poetry,
religion, philosophy, and politics. Each edition includes perceptive
commentary and essential background information to meet the
changing needs of readers.*

OXFORD WORLD'S CLASSICS

THOMAS DE QUINCEY

Confessions of an English Opium-Eater

and Other Writings

Edited with an Introduction and Notes by
ROBERT MORRISON

OXFORD
UNIVERSITY PRESS

OXFORD
UNIVERSITY PRESS

Great Clarendon Street, Oxford OX2 6DP
United Kingdom

Oxford University Press is a department of the University of Oxford.
It furthers the University's objective of excellence in research, scholarship,
and education by publishing worldwide. Oxford is a registered trade mark of
Oxford University Press in the UK and in certain other countries

Editorial material © Robert Morrison 2013

The moral rights of the author have been asserted

Confessions of an English Opium-Eater first published as a World's Classics paperback 1985
Reissued as an Oxford World's Classics paperback 1998, 2008
New edition 2013

Impression: 1

British Library Cataloguing in Publication Data

Data available

ISBN 978–0–19–960061–8

Printed in Great Britain by
Clays Ltd, St Ives plc

ACKNOWLEDGEMENTS

I would like to thank Judith Luna for inviting me to undertake this edition, and for her long-standing enthusiasm and support. For expertise and advice of all kinds, I am grateful to Jeff Cowton, James Crowden, Michael Cummings, Kory French, Anne Garner, Stephen Jacyna, Kaveh Khanverdi, Larry Krupp, Charles Mahoney, David Morrell, Christopher Ricks, Beert Verstraete, and Romira Worvill. Like all editors, I am indebted to those scholars who have produced previous editions of the texts in this volume, and I would especially like to acknowledge the work of Arthur Beatty, John Downie, Alethea Hayter, John E. Jordan, and Barry Milligan. For many years, Grevel Lindop, Daniel Sanjiv Roberts, and Barry Symonds have been my best De Quinceyean guides. They have all had an enormous impact on my understanding of De Quincey, and I would like to thank them for their friendship, confidence, and encouragement. The Social Sciences and Humanities Research Council of Canada has awarded me generous grants to pursue my research on De Quincey and the British periodical press. I am deeply grateful for the Council's continuing support.

For permission to publish manuscript material in their collections, I would like to thank the Wordsworth Library, Grasmere; the Berg Collection, New York Public Library; the Rosenbach Museum and Library; and the National Library of Scotland.

My greatest debt is to Carole, Zachary, and Alastair.

This edition is dedicated to Ian Reed.

CONTENTS

INTRODUCTION

'NOBODY who knows the nineteenth-century literature can fail to notice that there was a curious effort, under the surface, to make . . . Asiatic drugs as normal as European drinks,' G. K. Chesterton remarked in his essay on Samuel Taylor Coleridge (1936). 'It is a sort of subterranean conspiracy that ranges from the *Confessions* of De Quincey to the *Moonstone* of Wilkie Collins.'[1] Chesterton is right to emphasize the link between Thomas De Quincey and Wilkie Collins, but their shared preoccupation with drugs was far more than a 'subterranean conspiracy'. Asiatic drugs—specifically opium—are everywhere in nineteenth-century literature, not just under the surface but flowing openly through daily life, for De Quincey's *Confessions of an English Opium-Eater* (1821) launched a fascination with drug use and abuse that passed up through Edgar Allan Poe, Charles Baudelaire, Charles Dickens, and Collins to encompass Francis Thompson, Robert Louis Stevenson, Oscar Wilde, Ernest Dowson, and Arthur Conan Doyle in the later nineteenth century, and that was vigorously extended across the twentieth by Jean Cocteau, Aleister Crowley, William Burroughs, Aldous Huxley, Hunter S. Thompson, Ann Marlowe, and many others.

In 'The Crawling Chaos' (1921), H. P. Lovecraft saw much further than Chesterton when he observed that 'of the pleasures and pains of opium much has been written. The ecstasies and horrors of De Quincey . . . are preserved and interpreted with an art which makes them immortal, and the world knows well the beauty, the terror, and the mystery of those obscure realms into which the inspired dreamer is transported.'[2] In the *Confessions*, De Quincey reconceived the confessional genre and transformed our perception of drugs in ways that continue to inform current debates, not only by inventing recreational drug taking, but by putting in place two other formidable narratives of drug experience: the inexorable decline and collapse of the addict, and 'that other, even more pathos-ridden narrative called

---

[1] G. K. Chesterton, 'About S. T. C.', in *As I was Saying* (London: Methuen, 1936), 90.
[2] H. P. Lovecraft, 'The Crawling Chaos', in *The Doom that Came to Sarnath* (New York: Ballantine Books, 1971), 132. Lovecraft wrote this tale with Elizabeth Berkeley.

kicking the habit', as Eve Sedgwick observes.[3] Further, in *Suspiria de Profundis* (1845), De Quincey's 'sequel' to the *Confessions*, he expands his consideration of opium to comment incisively on issues ranging from the Industrial Revolution to the deep traumas of his childhood, though he also explicitly shifts his focus from the powers of the drug to the powers of the dreamer. Finally, in 'The English Mail-Coach', an essay that at one point formed part of *Suspiria*, De Quincey opens with engaging and nostalgic banter that steadily gives way to nightmare worlds of personal tragedy and apocalypse played out with horrifying repetitiveness in the tortured mind of the dreamer, as he relives again and again his opium-saturated self seated atop a mail-coach as it thunders down upon a young couple huddled in a small gig. Taken together, the essays in this volume constitute one of the most innovative autobiographical expressions of the nineteenth century, and one that has had a profound impact on our understanding of memory, addiction, creativity, and desire.

De Quincey was not the first to publish his confession. 'Since the Middle Ages at least,' observes Michel Foucault, 'Western societies have established the confession as one of the main rituals we rely on for the production of truth', and he proceeds to examine its central role in the administration of religious and legal power.[4] De Quincey's two key predecessors in the confessional mode are St Augustine, who wrote his *Confessions* from 397 to 400, and Jean-Jacques Rousseau, whose *Confessions* were posthumously published in 1782 and 1789. De Quincey was also acutely aware of the voracious popular appetite for criminal confessions such as Thomas Purney's *Account of the behaviour, last dying speeches and confessions of the 4 malefactors who were executed at Tyburn* (1725), Henry James's *The confessions and behaviour of H. James and C. Griffiths* (1791), William Henry Ireland's *The Confessions of William Henry Ireland* (1805), Thomas Ashe's *Memoirs and Confessions of Captain Ashe* (1815), and the anonymous *Authentic Memoirs, Memorandums, and Confessions: Taken from the journal of his Predatorial Majesty, the King of the Swindlers* (1820). De Quincey, too, was fascinated by the Gothic, and undoubtedly recognized the ways in which the confessional mode had been exploited

---

[3] Eve Sedgwick, 'Epidemics of the Will', in *Tendencies* (Durham, NC: Duke University Press, 1993), 131 (Sedgwick's italics).

[4] Michel Foucault, *The History of Sexuality*, vol. i, trans. Robert Hurley (New York: Vintage Books, 1990), 58.

in recent novels such as Ann Radcliffe's *The Italian; or the Confessional of the Black Penitents* (1797), Charlotte Dacre's *Confessions of the Nun of St Omer* (1805), and Robert Pearse Gillies's *Confessions of Sir Henry Longueville* (1814).

When De Quincey stepped forward with his *Confessions*, he made it plain that he knew the history of the genre but also that he intended to transform it. In his opening paragraph he refers to the confessions of English 'demireps, adventurers, or swindlers', as well as to the *Confessions* of Rousseau, but only to distance himself from these precedents (p. 3). He acknowledges the religious and legal dimensions of the genre, but with irony and bravado. 'This is the doctrine of the true church on the subject of opium: of which church I acknowledge myself to be the only member', he proclaims during his enthusiastic exploration of the 'Pleasures of Opium' (p. 42). And when he introduces the 'Pains of Opium', he asks mischievously whether the reader by this point regards him as 'the hero of the piece, or . . . the criminal at the bar'? (pp. 60–1). Above all, De Quincey turns the confession into a mode that is fundamentally concerned, not with crime or sin, but with the subjectivity of the confessor, and with those powerful moments of experience and feeling that inform his understanding of himself and the world around him. In De Quincey's hands, the confession was extended to include medicine, education, and relationships. It became a form that centred on personal desire rather than on institutions of power that wanted—or forced—confession from us. We now confessed willingly, and for reasons that reached from money to peace of mind. 'We have . . . become a singularly confessing society,' Foucault contends. 'One confesses in public and in private, to one's parents, one's educators, one's doctor, to those one loves; one admits to oneself, in pleasure and in pain, things it would be impossible to tell to anyone else, the things people write books about.'[5]

Yet at the same time—and like many before him and since—De Quincey also compromised the notion of the confession as a ritual for the 'production of truth' by lacing his own with self-interest, tergiversation, duplicity, and overstatement. He emphasizes that his *Confessions* are centrally concerned with the truth and 'nothing *but* the truth', yet he concedes that 'regards of delicacy towards some who are yet living, and of just tenderness to the memory of others

[5] Ibid. 59.

who are dead' has prevented him from telling 'the *whole* truth' (Appendix A, p. 228). He equivocates, half accepting what he is bent on denying: 'Guilt, therefore, I do not acknowledge: and, if I did, it is possible that I might still resolve on the present act of confession' (p. 4). In several instances he contradicts himself. '[O]n all occasions when I had an opportunity, I never failed to drink wine', he announces, only to declare a few pages later that he has 'never been a great wine-drinker' (pp. 33, 42). Or he states that he will not embark on any 'desperate adventures of morality', and then concludes his narrative with 'the moral': if the opium-eater 'is taught to fear and tremble, enough has been effected' (pp. 54, 78). Virginia Woolf once astutely observed of De Quincey that in his many pieces of autobiography he tells us only what he wishes us to know, and 'even that has been chosen for the sake of some adventitious quality—as that it fitted in here, or was the right colour to go there—never for its truth'.[6] In the *Confessions*, De Quincey confesses his desire to confess, but that is not the same thing as telling the truth. For him self-representation was often the subtlest form of self-concealment.

Opium was the central fact of De Quincey's experience, and for over fifty years he celebrated, denied, and renounced his relationship with it. He was, however, far from the first to write about it. Opium is perhaps the oldest drug known to humankind, and is derived from the milky sap found within the unripe seedpod of the poppy plant, *Papaver somniferum*. The ancient Greek poet Homer almost certainly refers to it in the *Odyssey* when he describes 'a drug to quiet all pain and strife, and bring forgetfulness of every ill'.[7] For centuries opium was the principal analgesic known to medicine, and consumed in various forms and under various names. In the 1660s, the English physician Thomas Sydenham introduced laudanum, which is Latin for 'praiseworthy', and which is prepared by dissolving opium in alcohol. Sydenham was an enthusiastic exponent of its use: 'Here I cannot but break out in praise of the great God, the giver of all good things, who hath granted to the human race, as a comfort in their afflictions, no medicine of the value of opium.'[8]

---

[6] *The Essays of Virginia Woolf*, ed. Andrew McNeillie and Stuart N. Clarke, 6 vols. (London: The Hogarth Press, 1986–2011), iv. 366.

[7] Homer, *The Odyssey*, ed. A. T. Murray and George E. Dimock (Cambridge, Mass.: Harvard University Press, 1995), 135.

[8] Cited in Martin Booth, *Opium: A History* (New York: St Martin's Press, 1998), 27.

Leading eighteenth-century medical discussions included Philippe Hecquet's *Reflexions sur l'usage de l'opium* (1726), George Young's *A Treatise on Opium* (1753), and Robert Hamilton's *Practical Hints on Opium Considered as a Poison* (1790). Samuel Crumpe gives a balanced account of the drug's effects in *An Inquiry into the Nature and Properties of Opium* (1793): 'I have myself, frequently and uniformly, experienced from large doses an increased flow of spirits, an observable gaiety, cheerfulness, and alertness, which, subsiding into a state of pleasing languor, terminated ultimately in a degree of drowsiness, stupor, and disinclination to motion.'[9] Other users, however, raised more serious concerns about the drug. In *The Mysteries of Opium Reveal'd* (1700), John Jones reported that someone who took opium habitually and then stopped invariably brought on 'great, and even intolerable Distresses, Anxieties and Depressions of Spirits, which in a few days commonly end in a most miserable Death, attended with strange Agonies'.[10] Horace Walpole put the same case rather more mildly in 1771 when he observed that 'opium is a very false friend'.[11] On balance, though, the medical community regarded the drug as a crucially important painkiller and tranquillizer, and saw its various side effects as regrettable but relatively infrequent consequences.[12]

At the turn of the nineteenth century opium was consumed ubiquitously by people of every class and age for self-medication in much the same way as aspirin is used today. Robert Southey took it for hay fever; Jane Austen's mother took it for travel sickness; Charles Lamb took it for a bad cold.[13] It was cheap: people who could not afford ale or spirits could afford the drug. It was legal: there was no effort to limit its sale until the Pharmacy Act of 1868. It could be purchased in a vast range of commercial cure-alls: Batley's Sedative Solution, Collis Browne's Chlorodyne, Godfrey's Cordial, the Kendal Black Drop, and Mother Bailey's Quieting Syrup, to name only a few. It was used to treat all manner of major and minor ailments: cancer,

[9] Samuel Crumpe, *An Inquiry into the Nature and Properties of Opium* (London: Robinson, 1793), 45–6.

[10] Cited in Booth, *Opium: A History*, 31.

[11] *The Yale Edition of Horace Walpole's Correspondence*, ed. W. S. Lewis et al., 48 vols. (New Haven: Yale University Press, 1937–83), xxxix. 149.

[12] Terry M. Parssinen, *Secret Passions, Secret Remedies: Narcotic Drugs in British Society, 1820–1930* (Manchester: University of Manchester Press, 1983), 8.

[13] Cited in Alethea Hayter, *Opium and the Romantic Imagination* (London: Faber, 1968), 30–1.

cholera, depression, diabetes, gout, pneumonia, tetanus, ulcers, and much else. It was available everywhere: chemists and pharmacists sold it, as did grocers, tailors, rent collectors, and street vendors. In the early nineteenth century, Britain imported almost all of its opium from Turkey. Morphine, which is the principal active agent in opium, was isolated in 1803, and commercially available by the early 1820s. With the introduction of the hypodermic syringe in the mid-1850s, the 'morphia solution' became widely known for its unparalleled efficacy in dealing with severe pain. Since the beginning of the twentieth century, the drug has been better known in the form of one of its chief derivatives: heroin. De Quincey was unquestionably what we would call an 'opium addict', but in the terminology of his day he had an 'opium habit', for medical professionals did not begin to develop modern ideas of drug 'addiction' until the second half of the nineteenth century. Two hundred years ago, it was a moral issue, a question of character. Today, the moral argument persists, but it is vigorously challenged by those who see addiction as a medical concern, a 'disease of the brain' rather than a 'disease of the will'.[14]

De Quincey published the vast majority of what he wrote in the leading magazines of his day. For many years he clung to the notion of himself as a leisured gentleman pursuing his scholarship in a rural retreat, and declared indignantly that he was thoroughly indisposed to sell his knowledge for money, and to 'commence trading author'.[15] But by 1818—with a young family, an exhausted patrimony, burgeoning debts, and his grander intellectual aspirations frozen by opium—the periodical press had come to seem his best option. In late 1820 De Quincey journeyed to Edinburgh, where his closest friend John Wilson was one of the mainstays of *Blackwood's Edinburgh Magazine*, which had been launched in 1817, and which had quickly established itself as the most original, exuberant, vicious, and unpredictable publication of the day, thanks in large measure to contributions from Wilson, John Gibson Lockhart, James Hogg, and William Maginn. De Quincey soon offered an 'Opium article' to the magazine.

---

[14] See Louise Foxcroft, *The Making of Addiction: The 'Use and Abuse' of Opium in Nineteenth-Century Britain* (Aldershot: Ashgate, 2007); and Barry Milligan, *Pleasures and Pains: Opium and the Orient in Nineteenth-Century British Culture* (Charlottesville: University Press of Virginia, 1995).

[15] Cited in Robert Morrison, *The English Opium-Eater: A Biography of Thomas De Quincey* (London: Weidenfeld and Nicolson, 2009), 184.

The drug had reduced him for several years 'to one general discour-
tesy of utter silence', he told its editor William Blackwood. 'But this
I shall think of with not so much pain, if this same Opium enables me
(as I think it will) to send you an article not unserviceable to your
Magazine.'[16] Before De Quincey could complete the essay, however,
he and Blackwood quarrelled, and six months later De Quincey went
to work for *Blackwood's* chief rival, the *London*, which was patterned
on *Blackwood's* but much more polished, dispassionate, and liberal
in tone, and which under the editorship of John Taylor and James
Hessey became one of the finest literary magazines of nineteenth-
century Britain. 'Certainly', De Quincey later observed, 'a literary
Pleiad might have been gathered out of the stars connected with this
journal', and from 1821 to 1825 he published almost exclusively in its
pages, alongside Thomas Carlyle, John Clare, William Hazlitt, Charles
Lamb, Walter Savage Landor, Mary Shelley, and many others.[17]

Confessions of an English Opium-Eater

In his *Confessions*, De Quincey offers an intimate, if highly selective,
exploration of his past life in which he presents himself as a philosopher and solitary who has endured extraordinary experience in both
urban and rural scenes. He discusses his boyhood and education, but
in this account the teenager is father of the man, and De Quincey
concentrates on his sorrows as a runaway in Wales and especially
London, where his relationship with the young prostitute Ann of
Oxford Street forms 'the most memorable and the most suggestively
pathetic incident' (Appendix A, p. 241). The circumstantial evidence
suggests that—despite De Quincey's explicit denials—he was
involved in a sexual relationship with Ann, and that his inability to
trace her may not have been an accident, for 'where he was going',
notes Charles Rzepka, 'whether it was to the relatively more upscale
and independent life of a gentleman-scholar in London or matricula-
tion at Worcester College in Oxford, Ann simply could not follow'.[18]

[16] 'De Quincey and His Publishers: The Letters of Thomas De Quincey to His
Publishers', ed. Barry Symonds (unpublished Ph.D. thesis, University of Edinburgh,
1994), 57, 56.
[17] *The Works of Thomas De Quincey*, vol. xi, ed. Julian North (London: Pickering and
Chatto, 2003), 273.
[18] Charles Rzepka, *Sacramental Commodities: Gift, Text, and the Sublime in De Quincey*
(Amherst: University of Massachusetts Press, 1995), 147.

Yet at the same time De Quincey idealizes Ann as his 'benefactress'
and 'saviour', and invests her with a nobility that transcends class
(pp. 23, 28). When he collapses in Soho Square, her generosity and
presence of mind save him, and though his future holds severe trials,
losing her is his 'heaviest affliction' (p. 34). These two sharply differing attitudes towards Ann—one carnal, the other protective—go a
long way towards explaining the deep feelings of remorse and anxiety
that he so clearly associates with her. Lamb—who once apostrophized
London as 'O City abounding in whores'—teased De Quincey one
evening about his experiences with Ann.[19] De Quincey did not find
it funny.

'There are,' said he, 'certain places & events & circumstances, which have
been mixed up or connected with parts of my life which have been very
unfortunate, and these, from constant meditation & reflection upon them,
have obtained with me a sort of sacredness, & become associated with
solemn feelings so that I cannot bear without the greatest mental agony to
advert to the subject, or to hear it adverted to by others in any tone of levity
or witticism. It seems to me a sort of desecration & unhallowing analogous
to the profanation of a temple'.[20]

The *Confessions* are a commercial venture in which De Quincey
exploits the circumstances of his past in order to engage a mass magazine readership. But they are also a sincere if partial record of his
teenage sorrows, and they powerfully commemorate his deep personal sadness over the loss of Ann.

The notion of being an 'English opium-eater' creates a series of
paradoxes that run throughout the narrative. Consuming the drug
for non-medical reasons was supposed to be an exclusively oriental
practice, and one that led directly to oblivion.[21] De Quincey dramatically overturned that view. Mounting his argument along racial lines,
he sneeringly remarks that the Turks who took opium usually sat
'like so many equestrian statues, on logs of wood as stupid as themselves'. De Quincey, on the other hand, is emphatically an *English*
opium-eater, which means that the drug produces a very different
effect on his refined faculties and profound sensibilities. 'I question

---

[19] *The Letters of Charles Lamb*, ed. E. V. Lucas, 3 vols. (London: Dent, 1935), i. 224.
[20] 'Richard Woodhouse's *Cause Book*: The Opium-Eater, the Magazine Wars, and the
London Literary Scene in 1821', ed. Robert Morrison, *Harvard Library Bulletin*, 9
(1998), 22.
[21] Barry Milligan, *Pleasures and Pains*, 25–7.

whether any Turk, of all that ever entered the Paradise of opium-eaters, can have had half the pleasure I had,' he observes. 'But, indeed, I honour the Barbarians too much by supposing them capable of any pleasures approaching to the intellectual ones of an Englishman' (p. 44–5). By ingesting vast quantities of an Eastern drug, however, De Quincey undermines the very Englishness he is intent on extolling. He is an uneasy hybrid, at once domestic and foreign, familiar and exotic, clean and contaminated, Eastern and English.

Equally paradoxical are the politics of the *Confessions*. De Quincey presents himself as a conservative and a traditionalist. He fraternizes with Etonians and Oxonians. He knows eminent men in the government, the church, and the law. He is on friendly terms with members of the aristocracy, including Lord Altamont and his son Lord Westport. He quotes the arch-conservative Edmund Burke. He comments rather glibly on the pleasures of his opiated wanderings among London's working classes: 'If wages were a little higher ... I was glad: yet, if the contrary were true, I drew from opium some means of consoling myself' (p. 47). At the same time, however, De Quincey defies parental and educational authority and lives outside traditional social structures. He is an exile, a recluse, a sinner. He draws on the work of the abolitionist William Roscoe. He lauds David Ricardo for his revolutionary economic doctrines. The radical poet Percy Bysshe Shelley is quoted on three occasions, while the radical essayist William Hazlitt is the third finest analytic thinker in England. Indeed, De Quincey himself sounds remarkably democratic when he maintains that he sees himself 'in an equal relation to high and low—to educated and uneducated, to the guilty and the innocent', and stresses that 'at no time' in his life has he been a person to hold himself 'polluted by the touch or approach of any creature that wore a human shape' (p. 21). His fierce xenophobia, though, soon subverts such claims: 'I have often thought that if I were compelled to forego England, and to live in China, and among Chinese manners and modes of life and scenery, I should go mad' (p. 72). In the *Confessions*, De Quincey is both humane and bigoted, an insider and an outsider, a reactionary and a rebel.

The writings of some of De Quincey's most important contemporaries give further shape to the work. Charles Lamb's 'Confessions of a Drunkard' appeared in 1813, and while much shorter than De Quincey's *Confessions*, it clearly anticipates them in its concern

with despair, addiction, and moral disorder: 'Life itself, my waking
life, has much of the confusion, the trouble, and obscure perplexity,
of an ill dream,' Lamb writes. 'In the day time I stumble upon
dark mountains.'[22] Samuel Taylor Coleridge's public persona was
by 1821 closely associated with opium dependence, unfulfilled potential, Gothic imaginings, the Lake District, the poetry of William
Wordsworth, and the philosophy of Immanuel Kant. De Quincey
seizes on these circumstances, modifies them to suit his own experience, and then markets them in the *Confessions* with a savvy that
Coleridge could not match. De Quincey is a scholar and drug addict
besieged by intellectual torpor. He lives in the Lake District and
studies German metaphysics, but has collapsed under the weight
of trying to complete his great philosophical treatise. Further, as
Grevel Lindop notes, 'the most intense accounts of De Quincey's
opium-induced nightmares in the *Confessions* seem to emulate the
visionary Orientalism of *Kubla Khan* but render it horrible by
organizing it around the self-tormenting psychic divisions of *The
Pains of Sleep*'.[23] Wordsworth too is central to the *Confessions*. When
De Quincey flees from Manchester Grammar School, he has a
copy of Wordsworth's *Lyrical Ballads* in his pocket, and in the
Confessions he transposes its descriptions of the rural poor into vivid
accounts of urban despair. Wordsworth's autobiographical master-
work *The Prelude* informs De Quincey's discussions of the growth of
his dreaming mind, and the ways in which his reading has come to
infuse and complicate his dreams. In the 'Pains of Opium' section,
De Quincey describes how his imagination is haunted by a power of
infinite growth and self-reproduction that he finds mirrored in a passage from Wordsworth's 1814 poem *The Excursion*, where a 'mighty
city' appears in the clouds, its 'towers begirt | With battlements that
on their restless fronts | Bore stars'. The 'sublime circumstance'
of those '*restless* fronts', De Quincey explains, 'might have been copied from my architectural dreams' (pp. 70–1).

What do we hold against drug addicts? It is not their desire for
transcendence—we all share that—but their taste for simulacra,

[22] Charles Lamb, *Elia and the Last Essays of Elia*, ed. Jonathan Bate (Oxford: Oxford
University Press, 1987), 319.

[23] Grevel Lindop, 'Lamb, Hazlitt, and De Quincey', in Richard Gravil and Molly
Lefebure (eds.), *The Coleridge Connection: Essays for Thomas McFarland* (New York:
St Martin's, 1990), 129.

hallucination, oblivion. 'Drugs in general are not condemned for the pleasure they bring, but rather because this aphrodisiac is not the right one,' Jacques Derrida argues. The 'hierarchy of pleasures goes together' with the 'metaphysics of work', and 'a poem ought to be the product of *real* work, even if the traces of that work should be washed away'. It is, he concludes, 'always nonwork that is stigmatized'.[24] In the *Confessions*, De Quincey charts both the pleasures and the pains of his drug use, passing inexorably from euphoria through stupor to dysphoric misery and deadlock, and mapping in the central narratives of the literature of addiction. His first dose of laudanum changed everything. 'I took it,' De Quincey recalls: 'and in an hour, oh! Heavens! what a revulsion! what an upheaving, from its lowest depths, of the inner spirit! what an apocalypse of the world within me! . . . Here was a panacea . . . for all human woes: here was the secret of happiness' (p. 39). De Quincey had many pleasurable experiences on opium, but no high seems ever to have matched this first one. In a marked degree, he was hooked from the start, and in the years that followed he took the drug recreationally on many occasions as a way of intensifying the pleasure of music, conversation, books, and solitude. Yet before long De Quincey came also to know the agonies of opium, and the devastating ways in which it eroded his judgement and determination. 'The opium-eater loses none of his moral sensibilities, or aspirations,' he states: 'he wishes and longs, as earnestly as ever, to realize what he believes possible, and feels to be exacted by duty; but his intellectual apprehension of what is possible infinitely outruns his power, not of execution only, but even of power to attempt. He lies under the weight of incubus and nightmare' (p. 66). On countless occasions De Quincey resolved to rise above these circumstances—to pull himself together, kick his laudanum habit, and fulfil his many responsibilities. Typically, these attempts met initially with success. 'I went off under easy sail— 130 drops a day for 3 days: on the 4th I plunged at once to 80 . . . and for about a month I continued off and on about this mark: then I sunk to 60: and the next day to —— none at all' (Appendix A, p. 232). In the end, though, De Quincey always returned to the drug: the effects of abstinence were 'so dreadful and utterly unconjectured by

[24] Jacques Derrida, 'The Rhetoric of Drugs', in Anna Alexander and Mark S. Roberts (eds.), *High Culture: Reflections on Addiction and Modernity* (Albany: State University of New York Press, 2003), 25, 37, 30 (Derrida's italics).

medical men' that he was 'glad to get back under shelter'.[25] Opium
inspired De Quincey, and gave him his most famous subject matter.
But for nearly fifty years it also wedged him between 'the collision
of both evils—that from the laudanum, and that from the want of
laudanum'.[26]

The impact of the *Confessions* was enormous. Some of the early
reviewers faulted De Quincey for disorganization, vanity, and moral
laxity, but most were enthusiastic. The *Imperial Magazine* described
the *Confessions* as produced by a 'mind gifted with first-rate talents'.
The *United States Literary Gazette* found that De Quincey's language
was 'always exquisitely felicitous . . . and sometimes powerful and
magnificent in the extreme'. Declared *The Album*, 'We thought it one
of the most interesting, and certainly the very most extraordinary,
production that we had ever seen.'[27] De Quincey published the work
anonymously, and while Edgar Allan Poe insisted that it was 'composed by my pet baboon, Juniper, over a rummer of Hollands and
water', Henry Crabb Robinson recognized that it was 'a fragment of
autobiography in emulation of Coleridge's diseased egotism', and
that it 'must be by De Quincey'.[28] For some readers, the *Confessions*
were a warning. 'Better, a thousand times better, *die* than have anything to do with such a Devil's own drug!', Thomas Carlyle exclaimed
after reading the work.[29] But for scores of others, De Quincey's
account of his experience was almost as seductive as the drug itself,
and his *Confessions* were embraced as an invitation to experimenta-
tion. In 1823, one doctor reported an alarming increase in the number
of people dying from an overdose of opium, 'in consequence of a little
book that has been published by a man of literature'. Southey cited

---

[25] Cited in Morrison, *The English Opium-Eater*, 344.

[26] *The Works of Thomas De Quincey*, vol. x, ed. Alina Clej (London: Pickering and
Chatto, 2003), 263.

[27] Anonymous, 'Confessions of an English Opium Eater', *Imperial Magazine*, 5
(1823), 89; Anonymous, 'Confessions of an English Opium Eater', *United States Literary
Gazette*, 1 (1825), 40; Anonymous, 'Confessions of an English Opium Eater', *The Album*,
2 (1822), 177.

[28] Edgar Allan Poe, 'How to Write a Blackwood Article', in *The Collected Works*, ed.
T. O. Mabbott, 3 vols. (Cambridge, Mass.: Harvard University Press, 1969–78), ii. 340;
Henry Crabb Robinson On Books and Their Writers, ed. Edith J. Morley, 3 vols. (London:
Dent, 1938), i. 267.

[29] David Alec Wilson, *Carlyle Till Marriage* (London: Kegan Paul, 1923), 250
(Carlyle's italics).

'one who had never taken a dose of opium before', but 'took so large a one for the sake of experiencing the sensation which had made De Quincey a slave to it, that a very little addition to the dose might have proved fatal'. The painter and poet William Bell Scott recalled the time when he and a fellow student took opium in 'imitation' of De Quincey, 'till my friend went into a comatose state, out of which he could not be roused. All night long I sat by him, and into the next day, when he came to himself.'[30]

For his part, De Quincey was characteristically divided on the influence of his *Confessions*. In the work itself he declares that his primary objective is to reveal the powers of the drug: opium is 'the true hero of the tale', and 'the legitimate centre on which the interest revolves' (p. 77). Yet later he sought to dodge the charge that his writing had encouraged drug abuse: 'Teach opium-eating!—Did I teach wine-drinking? Did I reveal the mystery of sleeping? Did I inaugurate the infirmity of laughter? . . . My faith is—that no man is likely to adopt opium or to lay it aside in consequence of anything he may read in a book' (Appendix B, pp. 250–1). De Quincey did not resolve this tension in his own response to the *Confessions*, and modern commentators continue to grapple with his legacy, for his name is still routinely invoked in debates about drug cultures but there is no agreement on whether he should be blamed, or absolved, or praised. Theodore Dalrymple, for example, states flatly that '[I]n modern society the main cause of drug addiction . . . is a literary tradition of romantic claptrap, started by Coleridge and De Quincey, and continued without serious interruption ever since'. Will Self, however, argues vigorously against such a view. 'The truth is that books like . . . De Quincey's *Confessions* no more create drug addicts than video nasties engender prepubescent murderers,' he asserts. 'Rather, culture, in this wider sense, is a hall of mirrors in which cause and effect endlessly reciprocate one another in a diminuendo that tends ineluctably towards the trivial.' Ann Marlowe takes yet another position on De Quincey, aligning herself with the earliest enthusiasts of the *Confessions*, and decisively setting herself apart from both Dalrymple and Self. 'Ever since

[30] Anonymous, *Advice to Opium Eaters* (London: Goodluck, 1823), p. iv; *New Letters of Robert Southey*, ed. Kenneth Curry, 2 vols. (Columbia: Columbia University Press, 1965), ii. 450; William Bell Scott, *Autobiographical Notes*, ed. W. Minto, 2 vols. (London: Osgood, McIlvaine, and Company, 1892), i. 98–9.

I read De Quincey in my early teens,' she declares, 'I'd planned to try opium.'[31]

Suspiria de Profundis

De Quincey's exploration of the drug continued in *Suspiria de Profundis*, which he published in 1845 in *Blackwood's* at a time when the magazine regularly featured the work of Edward Bulwer-Lytton, Catherine Gore, Walter Savage Landor, George Henry Lewes, Samuel Warren, and John Wilson. Opium, De Quincey stresses in *Suspiria*, offers great spiritual consolations to a population struggling to cope with the 'colossal pace' of industrialization and urbanization, and 'the continual development of vast physical agencies' such as steam. Some minds have been reduced to 'lunacy', others to 'a reagency of fleshly torpor'. Forces of 'corresponding magnitude' are needed 'that shall radiate centrifugally against this storm of life so perilously centripetal towards the vortex of the merely human', forces such as religion, philosophy, literature, and pre-eminently 'the power of dreaming', which De Quincey describes as 'the one great tube through which man communicates with the shadowy', and which at its noblest 'forces the infinite into the chambers of a human brain'. Solitude used to assist the faculties of the dreaming mind, but it is now 'becoming a visionary idea' amongst the many stresses of modern life. Opium, however, is everywhere, and it has a critical role to play, for it 'seems to possess a *specific* power . . . not merely for exalting the colours of dream-scenery, but for deepening its shadows; and, above all, for strengthening the sense of its fearful *realities*' (pp. 81–2).

Yet as the drug is to De Quincey both poison and cure, both without and within his body, both a natural and an artificial paradise, so it simultaneously exalts and eviscerates his private sense of the sublime.[32] Twice, he maintains, he has fought the 'dark idol' of opium, and twice he has emerged victorious, though on both occasions he

---

[31] Theodore Dalrymple, *Romancing Opiates: Pharmacological Lies and the Addiction Bureaucracy* (New York: Encounter Books, 2006), 61; Will Self, *Junk Mail* (London: Bloomsbury, 1995), 59; Ann Marlowe, *How to Stop Time: Heroin from A to Z* (New York: Basic Books, 1999), 239.

[32] See Natalie Ford, 'Beyond Opium: De Quincey's Range of Reveries', *Cambridge Quarterly*, 36 (2007), 229–49.

has relapsed because of his failure to undertake rigorous exercise as 'the one sole resource' for making withdrawal endurable. On a third occasion he falls, but this time he knows almost instinctively that there is no possibility of re-ascent. The 'dreadful symptoms' of his addiction have been 'moving forward for ever, by a pace steadily, solemnly, and equably increasing', and now at last they have run him down (p. 83). 'Were the ruin conditional, or were it in any point doubtful, it would be natural to utter ejaculations, and to seek sympathy,' De Quincey observes. 'But where the ruin is understood to be absolute, where sympathy cannot be consolation, and counsel cannot be hope,' the case is otherwise. When De Quincey realizes that there is no way back, that 'those awful gates' are 'closed and hung with draperies of woe, as for a death already past', he is unable even to protest or groan (p. 85). In *Suspiria*, as in the *Confessions*, opium is inspiration and annihilation, at once enriching and silencing the self.

How did De Quincey manage to surmount this devastation? The answer in many instances is that 'the true hero' of his tale is not opium but the powers of his imaginative—and especially of his dreaming—mind. In the *Confessions*, De Quincey foregrounds the powers of the drug but the dream finale reveals just how fully he was able to transform his experience into art with an explicitly poetic prose that captures the intensely associative qualities of his dreaming mind, and the tremendous energy and gloom of his nightmares. In *Suspiria*, however, he rewrites his intentions in the *Confessions* and maintains that the dream finale had been his objective all along, and that the primary purpose of the work had been to reveal the powers, not of opium, but of the Opium-Eater. The *Confessions*, De Quincey contends in *Suspiria*, 'were written with some slight secondary purpose of exposing this specific power of opium upon the faculty of dreaming, but much more with the purpose of displaying the faculty itself' (p. 82). Indeed, De Quincey makes this point at the start of both the *Confessions* and *Suspiria* when he notes that '[h]e whose talk is of oxen, will probably dream of oxen', by which he means that, for all its enormous power, opium cannot make a dullard interesting (pp. 81, 6). It can only darken and distend materials that already lie within the mind of the dreamer, and in *Suspiria* he makes it plain that the most crucial of these materials are found in his childhood. Charles Baudelaire, who deeply admired De Quincey, and who translated large passages from *Suspiria* in *Les Paradis artificiels* (1860), once observed that 'genius is no more than childhood recaptured at will, childhood equipped now with man's physical means to express itself'.[33] *Suspiria* is not in fact a 'sequel' to the *Confessions*, but a 'prequel' in which De Quincey pushes back past Ann of Oxford Street and Manchester Grammar School into the tragedies of his childhood.

The death of his beloved sister Elizabeth when he was only 6 years old was the most traumatic event in De Quincey's life, and *Suspiria* is dedicated to exploring his deep grief over her loss. De Quincey had what he described in *Suspiria* as 'a constitutional determination to reverie', and long before he tampered with opium he experienced intense visions and hallucinations (p. 81). Most poignantly, on the day following Elizabeth's death, De Quincey determined to see her again and slipped quietly up to her bedside. People in the house said that her features had not changed, 'but the frozen eyelids, the darkness that seemed to steal from beneath them, the marble lips, the stiffening hands, laid palm to palm, as if repeating the supplications of closing anguish, could these be mistaken for life?' (p. 98). De Quincey felt awe take hold of him. A 'solemn wind began to blow'. He fell into a trance.

A vault seemed to open in the zenith of the far blue sky, a shaft which ran up for ever. I in spirit rose as if on billows that also ran up the shaft for ever; and the billows seemed to pursue the throne of God; but *that* also ran before us and fled away continually. The flight and the pursuit seemed to go on for ever and ever. Frost, gathering frost, some Sarsar wind of death, seemed to repel me; I slept—for how long I cannot say; slowly I recovered my self-possession, and found myself standing, as before, close to my sister's bed. (pp. 98–9)

De Quincey experienced other visions in the days and weeks that followed Elizabeth's death, as he fought to comprehend her loss, and tormented the heavens with 'obstinate scrutiny, sweeping them with my eyes and searching them for ever after one angelic face that might perhaps have permission to reveal itself for a moment' (p. 104). Eventually his grief died down, but twelve years later when he was an Oxford undergraduate and regularly tasting opium, the memories of Elizabeth's death began to co-operate with the drug to produce a 'tremendous result', and De Quincey found himself once again beset by 'the trance in my sister's chamber,—the blue heavens, the everlasting vault, the soaring billows, the throne steeped in the thought (but not the sight) of "Him that sate thereon;" the flight, the pursuit, the irrecoverable steps of my return to earth' (pp. 129–30).

Elizabeth haunts De Quincey's autobiography. She is not mentioned explicitly in the *Confessions*, but her presence can be felt in De Quincey's observation that he loved Ann 'as affectionately as if she had been my sister', or his apostrophe to 'just, subtle, and mighty opium' for its power to restore 'blessed household countenances, cleansed from the "dishonours of the grave"' (pp. 28, 49–50). Similarly, Elizabeth is not named in the prose poems that close 'Part I' of *Suspiria*, but her death echoes powerfully through them. De Quincey argues in 'Savannah-la-Mar', for example, that God 'works by earthquake', and that '[u]pon the sorrow of an infant, he raises oftentimes from human intellects glorious vintages that could not else have been' (p. 150). 'The Apparition of the Brocken' is highlighted by a dialogue between De Quincey and his 6-year-old self: 'your heart was deeper than the Danube; and, as was your love, so was your grief,' he writes. 'Many years are gone since that darkness settled on your head; many summers, many winters; yet still its shadows wheel round upon you at intervals' (p. 147). In 'The Palimpsest', De Quincey develops a highly suggestive metaphor of the human brain, where '[e]verlasting layers' of ideas, images, and feelings fall upon one another as 'softly as light', effacing what was transient for the 'young man' or the 'boy', but unable to obscure 'the deep deep tragedies of infancy, as when the child's hands were unlinked for ever from his mother's neck, or his lips for ever from his sister's kisses'. These griefs, De Quincey states, 'remain lurking below all, and these lurk to the last' (pp. 135, 137).

'Levana and our Ladies of Sorrow', however, is the most compelling of these prose poems, and is suffused with both the tragedy of Elizabeth's death and the blight of the opium addiction that follows. Levana is the Roman goddess of early childhood, and she 'controls the education of the nursery', by which De Quincey means 'not the poor machinery that moves by spelling-books and grammars, but that mighty system of central forces hidden in the deep bosom of human life, which by passion, by strife, by temptation, by the energies of resistance, works for ever upon children' (pp. 138–9). Levana is assisted in her labours by three sisters. The first, Mater Lachrymarum, is 'Our Lady of Tears'. 'She it is that night and day raves and moans, calling for vanished faces'. De Quincey enters her kingdom when Elizabeth dies, as he hopes fervently to see her face again, and cries so often that he is 'told insultingly' to cease his 'girlish tears' (pp. 141, 103). The second sister, Mater Suspiriorum, is 'Our Lady of Sighs'. 'She weeps not. She groans not. . . . She is humble to abjectness. Hers is the meekness that belongs to the hopeless.' De Quincey is within her kingdom in *Suspiria* when he realizes that he will never escape the bondage of his drug addiction: 'One profound sigh ascended from my heart, and I was silent for days' (pp. 142, 85). The third sister, Mater Tenebrarum, is 'Our Lady of Darkness'. She is 'the mother of lunacies, and the suggestress of suicides'. In the *Confessions*, De Quincey moves within her kingdom when a change takes place in his dreams and he seems 'literally to descend, into chasms and sunless abysses' from which he cannot reascend. This 'state of gloom', he remarks, 'amounting at last to utter darkness, as of some suicidal despondency, cannot be approached by words' (pp. 143, 67–8). Over the course of *Suspiria* and then the *Confessions*, De Quincey's moral and spiritual education is profoundly shaped by these three sisters, and yet much of their work remains to be done. 'So shall he read elder truths, sad truths, grand truths, fearful truths,' avers Mater Lachrymarum. 'So shall he rise again *before* he dies. And so shall our commission be accomplished which from God we had—to plague his heart until we had unfolded the capacities of his spirit' (p. 144).

'Part II' of *Suspiria* eloquently expands upon the belief that underwrites much of 'Part I'. The 'rapture of life', affirms De Quincey, '. . . does not arise, unless as perfect music arises—music of Mozart or Beethoven—by the confluence of the mighty and terrific discords with the subtle concords. Not by contrast, or as reciprocal foils do these elements act, which is the feeble conception of many, but by union' (p. 151). Yet 'Part II' is most notable for a sentimental vignette that is only tangentially related to the concerns of 'Part I', and that features a young girl named Grace, who is 'of pure English blood' but who 'speaks very little English', for she was born and raised in India and converses fluently in Bengali with her Indian nurse (p. 170). Much critical attention has been paid to De Quincey as a 'furious jingoist', yet his attitude towards the East was much more complicated than is often allowed.[34] Daniel Sanjiv Roberts, for example, notes that in the *Confessions* the 'fear and loathing' of 'all things Chinese and Indian' in the Malay dream 'is followed by a dream of a different character wherein the Hebraic or Biblical orient promises a salvific and regenerative potential'.[35] Likewise, in *Suspiria*, De Quincey's sympathetic portrait of Grace is a remarkable blend of East and West, and while she comes from a family that has been ravaged by afflictions, there may still be hope in her future. De Quincey did not complete 'Part II' and his grander designs for *Suspiria* were never realized. Yet even in its fragmentary form it remains one of his most powerful pieces of autobiography, in its treatment not only of his childhood grief, but in its searching attempts to assess the variable effects of opium, dreams, industrialism, imperialism, and addiction. 'My heart trembled through from end to end,' wrote De Quincey's fellow opium addict Elizabeth Barrett Browning after reading *Suspiria*. 'What a poet that man is! how he vivifies words, & deepens them, & gives them profound significance.'[36]

'The English Mail-Coach'

De Quincey published 'The English Mail-Coach' in *Blackwood's* in 1849 as his final contribution to the magazine. At one point it was an extended section within *Suspiria*, but De Quincey 'did not scruple to detach it, and to publish it apart, as sufficiently intelligible even when dislocated from its place in a larger whole' (Appendix C, p. 258). De Quincey structured 'The Mail-Coach' around what he called an 'involute', an imaginative concept that he introduced in *Suspiria*. '[O]ften I have been struck with the important truth', he asserts, '—that far more of our deepest thoughts and feelings pass to us through perplexed combinations of *concrete* objects, pass to us as *involutes* (if I may coin that word) in compound experiences incapable of being disentangled, than ever reach us *directly*, and in their own abstract shapes' (p. 97). The definition is as evocative as it is misleading.

---

[34] John Barrell, *The Infection of Thomas De Quincey: A Psychopathology of Imperialism* (New Haven: Yale University Press, 1991), 50.

[35] Daniel Sanjiv Roberts, '"Mix(ing) a Little with Alien Natures": Biblical Orientalism in De Quincey', in Robert Morrison and Daniel Sanjiv Roberts (eds.), *Thomas De Quincey: New Theoretical and Critical Directions* (London: Routledge, 2008), 31.

[36] *The Brownings' Correspondence*, ed. Philip Kelley, Scott Lewis, et al., 19 vols. (Winfield, Kans.: Wedgestone Press, 1984–), x. 125.

Involutes, in fact, *are* capable of being disentangled partially or perhaps even fully, a point De Quincey himself makes in the fourth instalment of his *Blackwood's* essay on 'Style', which he published in 1841, four years before the appearance of *Suspiria*. '[T]he problem before the writer is—to project his own inner mind,' he explains; 'to bring out consciously what yet lurks by involution in many unanalysed feelings; in short, to pass through a prism, and radiate into distinct elements, what previously had been even to himself but dim and confused ideas, intermixed with each other.'[37] In *Suspiria*, De Quincey explores feelings that had long lain 'unanalysed' and 'intermixed' in his 'inner mind', a process that enables him to identify the five 'distinct elements'—summer sunlight, the grave, the Bible, a solemn wind, and a gathering frost—that are at the core of his experience in the bedchamber of his dead sister, and that he then weaves together to communicate his 'deepest thought and feelings' about the event. He adopts a similar strategy in 'The Mail-Coach', though on a far more elaborate scale. He begins the essay with a list of the five factors that he associates with these vehicles, and then steadily broadens and distorts them into impassioned strains of resurrection and grief.

Speed tops De Quincey's list. On the mail-coaches, he states, 'the vital experience of the glad animal sensibilities made doubts impossible on the question of our speed; we heard our speed, we saw it, we felt it as a thrilling' (p. 183). Second on his list is the 'grand effects for the eye between lamp-light and the darkness' as the mail-coaches journey through the night 'under accidents of mists that hid, or sudden blazes that revealed' (pp. 173, 184). The third factor is the power of the horses. The fourth is the role of these coaches as agents of the British government. And the fifth is the central part they play in distributing news of the great battles of the Napoleonic Wars: 'The mail-coach, as the national organ for publishing these mighty events,' De Quincey announces, 'became itself a spiritualised and glorified object to an impassioned heart' (p. 174). In the opening two sections of the essay—'The Glory of Motion' and 'Going Down with Victory'—De Quincey elaborates upon and illustrates these five factors with meandering badinage, anecdotal humour, and impassioned reminiscences of the beautiful Fanny of the Bath Road, the 'loveliest

---

[37] *The Works of Thomas De Quincey*, vol. xii, ed. Grevel Lindop (London: Pickering and Chatto, 2001), 71.

young woman for face and person that perhaps in my whole life I
have beheld' (p. 184). Yet as is so often the case in his writings, terror
resides just below the polished wit and nostalgia, and the most trivial
incident or association brings it surging to the surface. In the lurid
nightmares that close 'The Glory of Motion', De Quincey calls up
the face of Fanny, which in turn invokes a rose in June, and these two
images proliferate until he sees 'roses and Fannies, Fannies and roses,
without end'. Then come thoughts of Fanny's grandfather, a coachman whose inability to turn round reminds De Quincey of a crocodile, an association which immediately calls forth a 'dreadful host
of wild semi-legendary animals', including griffins, dragons, and
sphinxes. At length the whole vision of these 'fighting images' crowds
together 'into one towering armorial shield', and De Quincey is
brought face to face with his deepest fear. 'The dreamer finds housed
within himself', he trembles, '. . . some horrid alien nature.'

What if it were his own nature repeated,—still, if the duality were distinctly perceptible, even *that*—even this mere numerical double of his own
consciousness—might be a curse too mighty to be sustained. But how, if
the alien nature contradicts his own, fights with it, perplexes, and confounds it? How, again, if not one alien nature, but two, but three, but four,
but five, are introduced within what once he thought the inviolable sanctuary of himself? (pp. 188, 190)

De Quincey's sense of alienation and self-rupture was strong even in
childhood, as *Suspiria* makes plain. But in detailing these dream
horrors he is undoubtedly speaking too about his experience of addiction, and how he has fractured under the pressure of it. In Derrida's
formulation, a drug such as opium 'desocializes', it leads 'to the dis-
integration of the self'.[38]

De Quincey centres the second half of the essay on his memory of
the night when the mail-coach on which he was riding was involved
in the near-fatal collision with a small gig. He builds on key features
of the involute already introduced, such as the ways in which the
mail-coach's speed and power sometimes lead it to 'trample on
humanity' (p. 181). But he also compounds the involute with features
from the accident scene, such as the umbrageous isle formed by the
trees, and more crucially the image of the innocent young woman
terrified by the possibility of her own sudden death, 'as she rose and

[38] Derrida, 'The Rhetoric of Drugs', 37.

sank upon her seat, sank and rose, threw up her arms wildly to heaven, clutched at some visionary object in the air, fainting, praying, raving, despairing!' (p. 213). Then, in the closing dream fugue, De Quincey exalts and vastly expands all the various features of the involute into kaleidoscopic nightmares in which the political mission of the mail-coach and the accident scene are assimilated within a broader myth of Britain as a righteous colonial power charged by God with the task of preserving Christian civilization.

In the opening two movements, De Quincey transposes the collision scene onto the ocean, where 'the unknown lady from the dreadful vision and I myself are floating: she upon a fairy pinnace, and I upon an English three-decker' (p. 214). In the third movement, the young woman runs ashore and is trapped in quicksand, where De Quincey watches helplessly as God leaves her to die: 'I saw by the early twilight this fair young head, as it was sinking down to darkness—saw this marble arm, as it rose above her head and her treacherous grave, tossing, faultering, rising, clutching as at some false deceiving hand stretched out from the clouds' (p. 216). The scene changes again, and now in the fourth movement of the fugue a celestial mail-coach carrying the words 'Waterloo and Recovered Christendom' flies headlong down the grand aisle of a cathedral towards a frail gig carrying a female infant who is at once the goddess Britannia, the young woman aboard the gig, and—inevitably—Elizabeth: 'Ah! Pariah heart within me, that couldst never hear the sound of joy without sullen whispers of treachery in ambush,' De Quincey laments; 'that, from six years old, didst never hear the promise of perfect love, without seeing aloft amongst the stars fingers as of a man's hand writing the secret legend—"*ashes to ashes, dust to dust!*"—wherefore shouldst *thou* not fear though all men should rejoice?' (p. 221). A fatal collision between the coach and the gig seems unavoidable, and yet in this fourth movement death is cheated. For 'at the last, with one motion of his victorious arm', God sweeps the girl, now grown to a woman's height, far upwards to an altar, where she stands 'sinking, rising, trembling, fainting', but safe (pp. 222, 220). In the fifth and final movement, De Quincey and all the 'children of the grave' emerge through the eastern gates of the mighty cathedral, 'rendering thanks to God in the highest—that, having hid his face through one generation behind thick clouds of War, once again was ascending—was ascending from Waterloo—in the visions of Peace' (p. 221). It is perhaps the most astonishing moment in all of De Quincey, a moment in which he exploits in full the imaginative potential he associates with the mail-coach to produce an intense amalgamation of Protestantism, patriotism, history, and the self in which innocence is redeemed and God's ways are justified. In her essay on 'The English Mail-Coach', Virginia Woolf remarks that 'De Quincey's writing at its best has the effect of rings of sound which break into each other and widen out and out till the brain can hardly expand far enough to realise the last remote vibrations which spend themselves on the verge of everything where speech melts into silence'.[39]

De Quincey ranked the *Confessions* and the various parts of *Suspiria* as his finest work, and for two reasons. One, 'the perilous difficulty besieging all attempts to clothe in words the visionary scenes derived from the world of dreams, where a single false note, a single word in a wrong key, ruins the whole music'. And two, 'the utter sterility of universal literature in this one department of impassioned prose' (Appendix A, p. 238). De Quincey was not the first to write about opiates, and he was far from the first to consume them for non-medical purposes. But he was the first to memorialize his experience of drugs in a compelling confession that was aimed at a broad commercial audience, and that greatly increased the range and emotional intensity of the confessional genre. Opium battered De Quincey, but it did not finally defeat his creativity or his resolve. In the *Confessions*, *Suspiria*, and 'The Mail-Coach' he produced a pioneering autobiography that continues to illuminate our fascination with drugs, imagination, addiction, and desire. 'Of course it was stupor that he wanted', C. H. Sisson observes in 'Thomas De Quincey', 'But his mind would work. | He followed the eloquence whose end is silence | Into the dark.'[40]

---

[39] *The Essays of Virginia Woolf*, i. 367.
[40] C. H. Sisson, 'Thomas De Quincey', in *Collected Poems, 1943–1983* (Manchester: Carcanet, 1984), 86.

NOTE ON THE TEXT

Confessions of an English Opium-Eater was first published anonymously in the *London Magazine* in two instalments for September and October 1821 (vol. 4, pp. 293–312 and vol. 4, pp. 353–79). The owners and editors of the *London*, John Taylor and James Hessey, then published it in book form in 1822, with very minor revisions and an appendix. The print run was 1,000 copies. A second edition appeared late in 1822, and a third in 1823. In 1856, De Quincey published a revised and expanded version of the *Confessions* as volume v of *Selections Grave and Gay*, his own edition of his works. The 1856 version of the *Confessions* is two and a half times the length of the original, and modern critical opinion has been almost unanimous in judging it inferior to the original *London* version, which is the copytext for this edition. The differences between the two versions are thoroughly examined in Ian Jack, 'De Quincey Revises his *Confessions*', *PMLA* 72 (1957), 122–46. The Explanatory Notes refer to the 1856 version of the *Confessions* when it illuminates the 1821 text.

Suspiria de Profundis was first published in *Blackwood's Edinburgh Magazine* in four instalments for March, April, June, and July 1845 (vol. 57, pp. 269–85; vol. 57, pp. 489–502; vol. 57, pp. 739–51; and vol. 58, pp. 43–55). The articles were published anonymously but subtitled 'Being a Sequel to the Confessions of an English Opium-Eater', so that their authorship was immediately known. Throughout the publication of the articles, however, De Quincey was involved in a running dispute with his editor, and it is clear that *Suspiria* was not published in the form he desired, and that it was discontinued before he had finished. Remarkably, though, when De Quincey had the chance to revise and expand it for inclusion in *Selections Grave and Gay*, he decided instead to pillage various sections of it for inclusion in volume i of his *Autobiographic Sketches*. His plans to publish a revised version of the *Confessions* together with a completed text of *Suspiria* never materialized. The *Blackwood's* text is thus the only legitimate version, and the copytext for this edition.

'The English Mail-Coach' was first published anonymously in two parts in *Blackwood's Edinburgh Magazine*. The first instalment,

'The English Mail-Coach, or the Glory of Motion', appeared in October 1849, and the second, 'The Vision of Sudden Death', in December 1849 (vol. 66, pp. 485–500 and vol. 66, pp. 741–55). The two instalments, though obviously related, did not appear under their present title until 1854, when De Quincey revised the essay for inclusion in volume iv of *Selections Grave and Gay*. Like the 1856 version of the *Confessions*, however, the 1854 text of 'The English Mail-Coach' is generally considered inferior to the original *Blackwood's* version, which is the copytext for this edition. The Explanatory Notes refer to the 1854 version of 'The Mail-Coach' when it illuminates the 1849 text.

The copytext has been standardized in a number of ways: double quotation marks have been changed to single; full stops have been removed from terms of address (Mrs, Mr, Dr, St) and kings' numbers (Charles II or George III, for example); a standard format has been adopted for the headings; ligatures have been removed; and square brackets have been changed to round. Inconsistencies in punctuation, capitalization, and spelling have been retained. Obvious typographical errors have been silently corrected (in the fourth instalment of *Suspiria*, for example, 'the progress of of his head form' appears as 'the progress of his head form'). Possible misprints are cited in the Explanatory Notes.

The appendices in this volume contain a variety of published and unpublished material related to the three main texts. Headnotes to material published by De Quincey give full bibliographic information. Headnotes to manuscript material unpublished by De Quincey give details on manuscript location, and any distinctive or anomalous features. In the manuscript transcriptions, I have included only material that is significantly different from the published versions of the *Confessions*, *Suspiria*, or 'The Mail-Coach', and that is directly related to them. I have aimed to produce a readable text that renders De Quincey's intentions as clearly as possible. I have written out his abbreviations; thus, his 'hor.—so prof^d' appears as 'horror—so profound'. I have retained deleted words, sentences, and paragraphs when legibility permits and they bear directly on the works in this volume; thus, in one of the most important manuscripts related to *Suspiria*, I have retained De Quincey's list of three titles—'The Dark Interpreter, the Apparition of the Brocken, and Savannah-la-mar'— though he himself crosses this list out. I have, however, followed

De Quincey when he deletes words or phrases that disrupt the sentence or confuse the sense; thus his 'In after life when at from 20 to 24' appears as 'In after life from 20 to 24'.

Throughout the volume, De Quincey's footnotes are cued by superior figures and explanatory notes are cued by asterisks.

SELECT BIBLIOGRAPHY

Bibliographies

Dendurent, H. O., *Thomas De Quincey: A Reference Guide* (Boston: Hall, 1978).

Morrison, Robert, 'Essayists of the Romantic Period: De Quincey, Hazlitt, Hunt, and Lamb', in Michael O'Neill (ed.), *Literature of the Romantic Period: A Bibliographical Guide* (Oxford: Clarendon Press, 1998), 341–63.

Biographies

Eaton, Horace, *Thomas De Quincey: A Biography* (New York: Oxford University Press, 1936).

Lindop, Grevel, *The Opium-Eater: A Life of Thomas De Quincey* (London: Dent, 1981).

Morrison, Robert, *The English Opium-Eater: A Biography of Thomas De Quincey* (London: Weidenfeld and Nicolson, 2009).

Sackville-West, Edward, *A Flame in Sunlight: The Life and Works of Thomas De Quincey* (London: Cassell, 1936).

Standard Edition

The Works of Thomas De Quincey, gen. ed. Grevel Lindop, 21 vols. (London: Pickering and Chatto, 2000–3).

Letters

De Quincey at Work, ed. W. H. Bonner (Buffalo: Airport, 1936).

De Quincey to Wordsworth, ed. John Jordan (Berkeley: University of California Press, 1963).

'De Quincey and His Publishers: The Letters of Thomas De Quincey to His Publishers, and Other Letters, 1819–1832', ed. Barry Symonds (unpublished Ph.D. thesis, University of Edinburgh, 1994).

Criticism

Abrams, M. H., *The Milk of Paradise: The Effect of Opium on the Works of De Quincey, Crabbe, Francis Thompson, and Coleridge* (Cambridge, Mass.: Harvard University Press, 1934).

Balfour, Ian, 'On the Language of the Sublime and the Sublime Nation in De Quincey: Toward a Reading of "The English Mail-Coach" ', in Robert Morrison and Daniel Sanjiv Roberts (eds.), *Thomas De Quincey: New Theoretical and Critical Directions* (New York: Routledge, 2008), 165–86.

Barrell, John, *The Infection of Thomas De Quincey* (New Haven: Yale University Press, 1991).

Baxter, Edmund, *De Quincey's Art of Autobiography* (Edinburgh: Edinburgh University Press, 1990).

Black, Joel, 'National Bad Habits: Thomas De Quincey's Geography of Addiction', in Robert Morrison and Daniel Sanjiv Roberts (eds.), *Thomas De Quincey: New Theoretical and Critical Directions* (New York: Routledge, 2008), 143–64.

Blakemore, Steven, 'De Quincey's Transubstantiation of Opium in the *Confessions*', *Massachusetts Studies in English*, 9 (1984), 32–41.

Bridgwater, Patrick, *De Quincey's Gothic Masquerade* (New York: Rodopi, 2004).

Bruss, Elizabeth, 'Thomas De Quincey: Sketches and Sighs', in *Autobiographical Acts: The Changing Situation of a Literary Genre* (Baltimore: John Hopkins University Press, 1976), 93–126.

Burt, E. S., *Regard for the Other: Autothanatography in Rousseau, De Quincey, Baudelaire, and Wilde* (New York: Fordham University Press, 2009).

Burwick, Frederick, 'De Quincey as Autobiographer', in Eugene Stelzig (ed.), *Romantic Autobiography in England* (Farnham: Ashgate, 2009), 117–29.

—— 'Motion and Paralysis in "The English Mail-Coach"', *Wordsworth Circle*, 26 (1995), 66–77.

Clej, Alina, *A Genealogy of the Modern Self: Thomas De Quincey and the Intoxication of Writing* (Stanford: Stanford University Press, 1995).

Crawford, Joseph, 'The Haunting of Thomas De Quincey', *Cambridge Quarterly*, 40 (2011), 224–42.

Davis, Mary, 'De Quincey's *Confessions*: A Strategy for Salvation', *Christianity and Literature*, 38/3 (1989), 33–44.

De Luca, V. A., *Thomas De Quincey: The Prose of Vision* (Toronto: University of Toronto Press, 1980).

Dillon, Sarah, 'Reinscribing De Quincey's Palimpsest: The Significance of the Palimpsest in Contemporary Literary and Cultural Studies', *Textual Practice*, 19 (2005), 243–63.

Favret, Mary, 'Conclusion, or the Death of the Letter: Fiction, the Post Office, and "The English Mail-Coach"', in *Romantic Correspondence: Women, Politics, and the Fiction of Letters* (Cambridge: Cambridge University Press, 1993), 197–213.

Fay, Elizabeth, 'Hallucinogenesis: Thomas De Quincey's Mind Trips', *Studies in Romanticism*, 49 (2010), 293–312.

Ford, Natalie, 'Beyond Opium: De Quincey's Range of Reveries', *Cambridge Quarterly*, 36 (2007), 229–49.

Franta, Andrew, 'Publication and Mediation in "The English Mail-Coach"', *European Romantic Review*, 22 (2011), 323–30.

Garcia, Humberto, 'In the Name of the "Incestuous Mother": Islam and Excremental Protestantism in De Quincey's Infidel Book', *Journal for Early Modern Cultural Studies*, 7 (2007), 57–87.

Higgins, David, 'Imaging the Exotic: De Quincey and Lamb in the *London Magazine*', *Romanticism*, 17 (2011), 288–98.

Holstein, Michael, ' "An Apocalypse of the World Within": Autobiographical Exegesis in De Quincey's *Confessions of an English Opium-Eater*', *Prose Studies*, 2 (1979), 88–102.

Hopkins, Robert, 'De Quincey on War and the Pastoral Design of "The English Mail-Coach" ', *Studies in Romanticism*, 6 (1967), 129–51.

Jarvis, Robin, 'The Glory of Motion: De Quincey, Travel, and Romanticism', *Yearbook of English Studies*, 34 (2004), 74–87.

Krishnan, Sanjay, 'Opium and Empire: The Transports of Thomas De Quincey', *Boundary 2*, 33 (2006), 203–34.

Leask, Nigel, 'Murdering One's Double: Thomas De Quincey and S. T. Coleridge. Autobiography, Opium, and Empire in *Confessions of an English Opium-Eater* and *Biographia Literaria*', in *British Romantic Writers and the East: Anxieties of Empire* (Cambridge: Cambridge University Press, 1992), 170–228.

Lever, Karen, 'De Quincey as Gothic Hero: A Perspective on *Confessions of an English Opium-Eater* and *Suspiria de Profundis*', *Texas Studies in Literature and Language*, 21 (1979), 332–46.

Lindop, Grevel, 'De Quincey's *Confessions* in Context', in *Confessions of an English Opium-Eater: Thomas De Quincey*, ed. Jean Pierre Naugrette (Nantes: Éditions du Temps, 2003), 7–20.

—— 'De Quincey and the Cursed Crocodile', *Essays in Criticism*, 45 (1995), 121–40.

—— 'Pursuing the Throne of God: De Quincey and the Evangelical Revival', *Charles Lamb Bulletin*, 52 (1985), 97–111.

Logan, Peter Melville, 'Suspiria de Machina: De Quincey's Body and the *Confessions of an English Opium-Eater*', in *Nerves and Narratives: A Cultural History of Hysteria in Nineteenth-Century Britain* (Berkeley: University of California Press, 1997), 73–108.

Maa, Gerald, 'Keeping Time with the Mail-Coach: Anachronism and De Quincey's "The English Mail-Coach" ', *Studies in Romanticism*, 50 (2011), 125–43.

McDonagh, Josephine, *De Quincey's Disciplines* (Oxford: Clarendon Press, 1994).

McFarland, Thomas, 'De Quincey's Journey to the End of Night', in *Romantic Cruxes: The English Essayists and the Spirit of the Age* (Oxford: Clarendon Press, 1987), 90–122.

Maniquis, Robert, 'De Quincey, Varieties of the Palimpsest, and the Unconscious', *Romanticism*, 17 (2011), 309–18.

—— 'The Dark Interpreter and the Palimpsest of Violence: De Quincey and the Unconscious', in Robert Lance Snyder (ed.), *Thomas De Quincey: Bicentenary Studies* (Norman: University of Oklahoma Press, 1985), 109–39.

—— 'Lonely Empires: Personal and Public Visions of Thomas De Quincey', in *Literary Monographs*, vol. viii, eds. Eric Rothstein and Joseph Anthony Wittreich (Madison: University of Wisconsin Press, 1976), 47–127.

Miller, J. Hillis, 'Thomas De Quincey', in *The Disappearance of God: Five Nineteenth-Century Writers* (Cambridge, Mass.: Harvard University Press, 1963), 17–80.

Milligan, Barry, 'Morphine-Addicted Doctors, the English Opium-Eater, and Embattled Medical Authority', *Victorian Literature and Culture*, 33 (2005), 541–53.

—— *Pleasures and Pains: Opium and the Orient in Nineteenth-Century British Culture* (Charlottesville: University Press of Virginia, 1995).

Morrison, Robert, 'De Quincey's Addiction', *Romanticism*, 17 (2011), 270–7.

—— 'Earthquake and Eclipse: Radical Energies and De Quincey's 1821 *Confessions*', in Robert Morrison and Daniel Sanjiv Roberts (eds.), *Thomas De Quincey: New Theoretical and Critical Directions* (New York: Routledge, 2008), 63–79.

—— (ed.), 'Richard Woodhouse's *Cause Book*: The Opium-Eater, the Magazine Wars, and the London Literary Scene in 1821', *Harvard Library Bulletin*, 9 (1998), pp. i–xxiv, 1–43.

North, Julian, *De Quincey Reviewed: Thomas De Quincey's Critical Reception, 1821–1994* (Columbia: Camden House, 1997).

—— 'Opium and the Romantic Imagination: The Creation of a Myth', in Sue Vice, Matthew Campbell, and Tim Armstrong (eds.), *Beyond the Pleasure Dome: Writing and Addiction from the Romantics* (Sheffield: Sheffield Academic Press, 1994), 109–17.

O'Quinn, Daniel, 'Ravishment Twice Weekly: De Quincey's Opera Pleasures', *Romanticism on the Net*, 34–5 (2004).

—— 'Who Owns What: Slavery, Property, and Eschatological Compensation in Thomas De Quincey's Opium Writings', *Texas Studies in Literature and Language*, 45 (2003), 362–92.

Perry, Curtis, 'Piranesi's Prison: Thomas De Quincey and the Failure of Autobiography', *SEL*, 33 (1993), 809–24.

Porter, Roger, 'The Demon Past: De Quincey and the Autobiographer's Dilemma', *SEL*, 20 (1980), 591–609.

Reed, Arden, '"Booked for Utter Perplexity" on De Quincey's "English Mail-Coach"', in Robert Lance Snyder (ed.), *Thomas De Quincey: Bicentenary Studies* (Norman: University of Oklahoma Press, 1985), 279–307.

Roberts, Daniel Sanjiv, 'The Janus-face of Romantic Modernity: Thomas De Quincey's Metropolitan Imagination', *Romanticism*, 17 (2011), 299–308.

——'"Mix(ing) a Little with Alien Natures": Biblical Orientalism in De Quincey', in Robert Morrison and Daniel Sanjiv Roberts (eds.), *Thomas De Quincey: New Theoretical and Critical Directions* (New York: Routledge, 2008), 19–43.

—— *Revisionary Gleam: De Quincey, Coleridge, and the High Romantic Argument* (Liverpool: Liverpool University Press, 2000).

Russett, Margaret, *De Quincey's Romanticism: Canonical Minority and the Forms of Transmission* (Cambridge: Cambridge University Press, 1997).

Rzepka, Charles, 'Bang Up! Theatricality and the "Diphrelatic Art" in De Quincey's "English Mail-Coach"', *Nineteenth-Century Prose*, 28 (2001), 75–101.

—— *Sacramental Commodities: Gift, Text, and the Sublime in De Quincey* (Amherst: University of Massachusetts Press, 1995).

Schmid, Thomas, 'Crocodiles and "Inoculation" Reconsidered: De Quincey, Opium, and the Dream Object', *Wordsworth Circle*, 39 (2008), 35–38.

Schmitt, Cannon, 'Narrating National Addictions: De Quincey, Opium, and Tea', in Janet Farrell Brodie and Marc Redfield (eds.), *High Anxieties: Cultural Studies in Addiction* (Berkeley: University of California Press, 2002), 63–84.

Slusser, George, 'Breaking the Mind Circle: De Quincey's "The English Mail-Coach" and the Origins of Science Fiction', *Extrapolation: A Journal of Science Fiction and Fantasy*, 42 (2001), 111–23.

Spector, Stephen, 'Thomas De Quincey: Self-Effacing Autobiographer', *Studies in Romanticism*, 18 (1979), 501–20.

Stapleton, Laurence, 'The Virtù of De Quincey', in *The Elected Circle: Studies in the Art of Prose* (Princeton: Princeton University Press, 1973), 119–66.

Sudan, Rajani, 'Englishness "A'muck": De Quincey's *Confessions*', *Genre: Forms of Discourse and Culture*, 27 (1994), 377–94.

Whale, John, *Thomas De Quincey's Reluctant Autobiography* (London: Croom Helm, 1984).

Wilner, Joshua, 'Autobiography and Addiction: The Case of De Quincey', *Genre: Forms of Discourse and Culture*, 14 (1981), 493–503.

Wordsworth, Jonathan, 'The Dark Interpreters: Wordsworth and De Quincey', *Wordsworth Circle*, 17 (1986), 40–50.

Young, Michael, '"The True Hero of the Tale": De Quincey's *Confessions* and Affective Autobiographical Theory', in Robert Lance Snyder (ed.), *Thomas De Quincey: Bicentenary Studies* (Norman: University of Oklahoma Press, 1985), 54–71.

Youngquist, Paul, 'De Quincey's Crazy Body', *PMLA* 114 (1999), 346–58.

Ziegenhagen, Timothy, 'War Addiction in Thomas De Quincey's "The English Mail-Coach" ', *Wordsworth Circle*, 35 (2004), 93–8.

Further Reading in Oxford World's Classics

Baudelaire, Charles, *The Flowers of Evil*, trans. and ed. James McGowan, introd. Jonathan Culler.

Coleridge, Samuel Taylor, *Selected Poetry*, ed. H. J. Jackson.

Collins, Wilkie, *The Moonstone*, ed. John Sutherland.

De Quincey, Thomas, *On Murder*, ed. Robert Morrison.

Rousseau, Jean-Jacques, *Confessions*, trans. Angela Scholar, ed. Patrick Coleman.

Wordsworth, William, *Selected Poetry*, ed. Stephen Gill and Duncan Wu.

A CHRONOLOGY OF THOMAS DE QUINCEY

1785 Born (15 August) in Manchester, son of Thomas Quincey, textile importer, and Elizabeth Penson.

1790 Death of his sister Jane, age 3.

1792 Death of his sister Elizabeth, age 9.

1793 Death of his father.

1796 Moves to Bath and enters Bath Grammar School. His mother takes the name 'De Quincey'.

1799 Enters Winkfield School, Wiltshire. Reads Wordsworth and Coleridge's *Lyrical Ballads*, which he later describes as 'the greatest event in the unfolding of my own mind'.

1800 Translation from Horace's Twenty-Second Ode wins third prize in a contest, and is published in the *Monthly Preceptor*. Accidentally meets George III at Frogmore. Summer holiday in Ireland with Lord Westport. Enters Manchester Grammar School.

1801 Spends summer in Everton, near Liverpool, where he meets William Roscoe, James Currie, and other Whig intellectuals.

1802 Flees from Manchester Grammar School. Wanders in North Wales and then spends four months penniless and hungry on the streets of London.

1803 Reconciled with his mother and guardians. Spends another summer in Everton. Reads Gothic fiction voraciously. Plans literary career: 'I have besides always intended of course that *poems* should form the corner-stones of my fame'. Deepening admiration for Coleridge, whom he begins to think 'the greatest man that has ever appeared'. Writes fan letter to Wordsworth, and the two begin a correspondence. Enters Worcester College, Oxford.

1804 Begins occasional use of opium. Meets Charles Lamb.

1805 Travels to the Lake District at the invitation of Wordsworth, but loses his nerve and turns back without meeting the poet.

1806 Travels again to the Lake District to meet Wordsworth, and again loses his nerve. He writes his 'Constituents of Happiness', a list of twelve items that includes 'some great intellectual project', 'health and vigour', and 'the education of a child'.

1807 Meets Coleridge. Gives him £300 under the polite pretence of a 'loan'. Escorts Coleridge's family to the Lake District and meets Wordsworth at Grasmere.

1808 Sees Coleridge daily and assists him with his lectures for the Royal Institution on Poetry and Principles of Taste. Bolts from Oxford midway through his final examinations and does not receive his degree. Introduced to John Wilson, the future 'Christopher North' of *Blackwood's Magazine*. The two become close friends.

1809 Supervises the printing of Wordsworth's political pamphlet on *The Convention of Cintra*, and contributes a lengthy 'Postscript on Sir John Moore's Letters'. Moves to Grasmere, where he rents Dove Cottage, the former home of the Wordsworths. With Wilson and Alexander Blair, publishes 'The Letter of Mathetes' in Coleridge's metaphysical newspaper *The Friend*.

1810 Enters period of greatest intimacy with Wordsworth and Coleridge. Reads manuscript of Wordsworth's *Prelude*.

1812 Enters the Middle Temple briefly to read for the Bar. Grief-stricken by the death of Wordsworth's 3-year-old daughter Catharine.

1813 Becomes addicted to opium. Strained relations with the Wordsworths. Begins to court Margaret Simpson, the daughter of a Lake District farmer.

1814 Visits Edinburgh with Wilson, where he meets leading members of the Scottish literary scene, including John Gibson Lockhart, the future biographer of Walter Scott, and James Hogg, the 'Ettrick Shepherd'.

1816 Birth of son, William Penson, by Margaret Simpson. Estranged from the Wordsworths.

1817 Marries Margaret Simpson. William Blackwood founds and edits *Blackwood's Edinburgh Magazine*, with Wilson, Lockhart, and Hogg as major contributors.

1818 Publishes the Tory jeremiad *Close Comments Upon a Straggling Speech*, a denunciation of Henry Brougham, Independent Whig candidate in the parliamentary election campaign in Westmorland. Appointed editor of the local Tory newspaper, the *Westmorland Gazette*. Battles debt and addiction. Lucid opium nightmares.

1819 Dismissed from editorship of the *Westmorland Gazette*. With Wilson and Lockhart, writes review of Percy Bysshe Shelley's *The Revolt of Islam* for *Blackwood's Magazine*.

1821 Translation of Friedrich Schiller's 'The Sport of Fortune' published in *Blackwood's Magazine*. Quarrels with William Blackwood. Publishes *Confessions of an English Opium-Eater* in the rival *London Magazine*. Conversations with John Keats's friend Richard Woodhouse.

1822 First publication of the *Confessions* in book form, with a new appendix. Projects a work entitled *Confessions of a Murderer* but it does not appear.

1823 'Notes from the Pocket Book of a Late Opium-Eater', including 'On the Knocking at the Gate in Macbeth', in the *London Magazine*. Appears as 'The English Opium-Eater' in the *Noctes Ambrosianae*, a series of raucous and wide-ranging dialogues published in *Blackwood's Magazine* (completed 1835), and written in the main by John Wilson.

1824 Unfavourable review of Thomas Carlyle's translation of Goethe's *Wilhelm Meister's Apprenticeship* in the *London Magazine*.

1825 Translates and abridges the German pseudo-Waverley novel *Walladmor*. Leaves the *London Magazine*.

1826 Rejoins *Blackwood's Magazine*, where he publishes his review of Robert Pearse Gillies's *German Stories*, and begins his 'Gallery of German Prose Classics' (completed 1827), which includes portraits of Gotthold Ephraim Lessing and Immanuel Kant.

1827 The first instalment of 'On Murder Considered as One of the Fine Arts' in *Blackwood's Magazine*. Begins to write for the *Edinburgh Saturday Post*. Meets Carlyle and an intimacy develops.

1828 'Toilette of the Hebrew Lady' and 'Elements of Rhetoric' in *Blackwood's Magazine*.

1829 'Sketch of Professor Wilson' in the *Edinburgh Literary Gazette*.

1830 'Kant in his Miscellaneous Essays', 'Richard Bentley', and a series of heated Tory diatribes, including 'French Revolution' and 'Political Anticipations', in *Blackwood's Magazine*. Moves permanently to Edinburgh.

1831 'Dr Parr and his Contemporaries' in *Blackwood's Magazine*. Prosecuted for debt.

1832 *Klosterheim: or, the Masque*, a one-volume Gothic romance, published by Blackwood. 'In purity of style and idiom' the novel reaches 'an excellence' to which Walter Scott 'appears never to have aspired', Coleridge observes. Briefly imprisoned twice for debt. Death of son Julius, age 3.

1833 Contributes a translation of Kant's 'Age of the Earth' and an assessment of 'Mrs Hannah More' to *Tait's Magazine*, the leading Scottish rival of *Blackwood's Magazine*. Prosecuted for debt four times. Takes refuge in the debtors' sanctuary at Holyrood.

1834 'Samuel Taylor Coleridge' (completed 1835) and 'Sketches of Life and Manners from the Autobiography of a Late Opium-Eater' (completed 1841) in *Tait's Magazine*. Five times prosecuted for debt. Death of eldest son William—'the crown and glory of my life'—from acute leukaemia. Death of Samuel Taylor Coleridge, William Blackwood, and Charles Lamb. Blackwood's sons Robert and Alexander take over the management of the magazine.

1835 'Oxford' and 'A Tory's Account of Toryism, Whiggism, and Radicalism' (completed 1836) in *Tait's Magazine*.

1837 'The Revolt of the Tartars' in *Blackwood's Magazine*. Prosecuted for debt on ten occasions. Grief-stricken by the death of his wife Margaret.

1838 Two tales of terror, 'The Household Wreck' and 'The Avenger', in *Blackwood's Magazine*. 'Recollections of Charles Lamb' in *Tait's Magazine*.

1839 'Second Paper on Murder Considered as One of the Fine Arts' in *Blackwood's Magazine*. 'William Wordsworth' in *Tait's Magazine*.

1840 'The Opium and the China Question' in *Blackwood's Magazine*. Prosecuted for debt. Flees Edinburgh for Glasgow.

1843 Moves to Mavis Bush Cottage, Lasswade, outside Edinburgh.

1844 Publishes one-volume treatise on *The Logic of Political Economy* with Blackwood.

1845 'Coleridge and Opium-Eating' and *Suspiria de Profundis* in *Blackwood's Magazine*. John Blackwood becomes editor of *Blackwood's Magazine*. 'On Wordsworth's Poetry' and 'Notes on Gilfillan's "Gallery of Literary Portraits"': Godwin, Foster, Hazlitt, Shelley, Keats' (completed 1846) in *Tait's Magazine*.

1846 'System of the Heavens as Revealed by Lord Rosse's Telescope' in *Tait's Magazine*.

1847 'Joan of Arc' and 'The Nautico-Military Nun of Spain' in *Tait's Magazine*.

1848 'Final Memorials of Charles Lamb' in *North British Review*. Meets Ralph Waldo Emerson.

1849 Briefly imprisoned for debt. 'The English Mail-Coach', his last essay for *Blackwood's Magazine*.

1850 Contributes several essays to *The Instructor*, a weekly magazine issued by the Edinburgh publisher James Hogg. Ticknor, Reed, and Fields of Boston begin publication of *De Quincey's Writings* (twenty-two volumes, completed 1856). Death of Wordsworth.

1851 'Lord Carlisle on Pope', his last essay for *Tait's Magazine*.

1853 Begins sometimes extensive revision of his work for *Selections Grave and Gay*, an edition published by Hogg (fourteen volumes, completed 1860). *Autobiographic Sketches* appear as volumes i and ii. Much of *Suspiria de Profundis* is folded into volume i.

1854 Takes lodgings at 42 Lothian Street, Edinburgh. Publishes 'The English Mail-Coach' and the 'Postscript' to 'On Murder Considered as One of the Fine Arts' in volume iv of *Selections Grave and Gay*. Death of Wilson.

1856 *Confessions of an English Opium-Eater*, revised and greatly expanded, appears as volume v of *Selections Grave and Gay*. Begins to contribute to Hogg's monthly magazine, *The Titan*.

1857 Publishes pamphlet on *China* with Hogg. Articles on the Indian Mutiny for *The Titan* (completed 1858).

1859 Dies (8 December) in Edinburgh. Buried beside Margaret in St Cuthbert's Churchyard. Hearing of the death, Charles Baudelaire spoke of De Quincey as having 'one of the most original' minds in 'all of England'.

CONFESSIONS OF AN ENGLISH OPIUM-EATER
AND OTHER WRITINGS

CONFESSIONS OF AN ENGLISH OPIUM-EATER:

BEING AN EXTRACT FROM THE LIFE OF A SCHOLAR

To the Reader.—I here present you, courteous reader, with the record of a remarkable period in my life: according to my application of it, I trust that it will prove, not merely an interesting record, but, in a considerable degree, useful and instructive. In *that* hope it is, that I have drawn it up: and *that* must be my apology for breaking through that delicate and honourable reserve, which, for the most part, restrains us from the public exposure of our own errors and infirmities. Nothing, indeed, is more revolting to English feelings, than the spectacle of a human being obtruding on our notice his moral ulcers or scars, and tearing away that 'decent drapery,'* which time, or indulgence to human frailty, may have drawn over them: accordingly, the greater part of *our* confessions (that is, spontaneous and extra-judicial confessions) proceed from demireps,* adventurers, or swindlers: and for any such acts of gratuitous self-humiliation from those who can be supposed in sympathy with the decent and self-respecting part of society, we must look to French literature,* or to that part of the German,* which is tainted with the spurious and defective sensibility of the French. All this I feel so forcibly, and so nervously am I alive to reproach of this tendency, that I have for many months hesitated about the propriety of allowing this, or any part of my narrative, to come before the public eye, until after my death (when, for many reasons, the whole will be published): and it is not without an anxious review of the reasons, for and against this step, that I have, at last, concluded on taking it.*

Guilt and misery shrink, by a natural instinct, from public notice: they court privacy and solitude: and, even in their choice of a grave, will sometimes sequester themselves from the general population of the church-yard, as if declining to claim fellowship with the great family of man, and wishing (in the affecting language of Mr Wordsworth)

> —— Humbly to express
> A penitential loneliness.*

It is well, upon the whole, and for the interest of us all, that it should be so: nor would I willingly, in my own person, manifest a disregard of such salutary feelings; nor in act or word do anything to weaken them. But, on the one hand, as my self-accusation does not amount to a confession of guilt, so, on the other, it is possible that, if it *did*, the benefit resulting to others, from the record of an experience purchased at so heavy a price, might compensate, by a vast overbalance, for any violence done to the feelings I have noticed, and justify a breach of the general rule. Infirmity and misery do not, of necessity, imply guilt. They approach, or recede from, the shades of that dark alliance, in proportion to the probable motives and prospects of the offender, and the palliations, known or secret, of the offence: in proportion as the temptations to it were potent from the first, and the resistance to it, in act or in effort, was earnest to the last. For my own part, without breach of truth or modesty, I may affirm, that my life has been, on the whole, the life of a philosopher: from my birth I was made an intellectual creature: and intellectual in the highest sense my pursuits and pleasures have been, even from my school-boy days. If opium-eating be a sensual pleasure, and if I am bound to confess that I have indulged in it to an excess, not yet *recorded*[1] of any other man, it is no less true, that I have struggled against this fascinating enthral-ment with a religious zeal, and have, at length, accomplished what I never yet heard attributed to any other man—have untwisted, almost to its final links, the accursed chain which fettered me.* Such a self-conquest may reasonably be set off in counterbalance to any kind or degree of self-indulgence. Not to insist, that in my case, the self-conquest was unquestionable, the self-indulgence open to doubts of casuistry,* according as that name shall be extended to acts aiming at the bare relief of pain, or shall be restricted to such as aim at the excitement of positive pleasure.

Guilt, therefore, I do not acknowledge: and, if I did, it is possible that I might still resolve on the present act of confession, in consideration of the service which I may thereby render to the whole class of opium-eaters. But who are they? Reader, I am sorry to say, a very numerous class indeed. Of this I became convinced some years ago, by computing, at that time, the number of those in one small class of English society (the class of men distinguished for talents, or of

---

[1] 'Not yet *recorded*,' I say: for there is one celebrated man of the present day, who, if all be true which is reported of him, has greatly exceeded me in quantity.*

eminent station), who were known to me, directly or indirectly, as opium-eaters; such for instance, as the eloquent and benevolent ——, the late dean of ——; Lord ——; Mr ——, the philosopher; a late under-secretary of state* (who described to me the sensation which first drove him to the use of opium, in the very same words as the dean of ——, viz. 'that he felt as though rats were gnawing and abrading the coats of his stomach'); Mr ——;* and many others, hardly less known, whom it would be tedious to mention. Now, if one class, comparatively so limited, could furnish so many scores of cases (and *that* within the knowledge of one single inquirer), it was a natural inference, that the entire population of England would furnish a proportionable number. The soundness of this inference, however, I doubted, until some facts became known to me, which satisfied me, that it was not incorrect. I will mention two: 1. Three respectable London druggists, in widely remote quarters of London, from whom I happened lately to be purchasing small quantities of opium,* assured me, that the number of *amateur* opium-eaters (as I may term them) was, at this time, immense; and that the difficulty of distinguishing these persons, to whom habit had rendered opium necessary, from such as were purchasing it with a view to suicide,* occasioned them daily trouble and disputes. This evidence respected London only. But, 2. (which will possibly surprise the reader more,) some years ago, on passing through Manchester, I was informed by several cotton-manufacturers, that their work-people were rapidly getting into the practice of opium-eating; so much so, that on a Saturday afternoon the counters of the druggists were strewed with pills of one, two, or three grains, in preparation for the known demand of the evening.* The immediate occasion of this practice was the lowness of wages, which, at that time, would not allow them to indulge in ale or spirits:* and, wages rising, it may be thought that this practice would cease: but, as I do not readily believe that any man, having once tasted the divine luxuries of opium, will afterwards descend to the gross and mortal enjoyments of alcohol, I take it for granted,

> That those eat now, who never ate before;
> And those who always ate, now eat the more.*

Indeed the fascinating powers of opium are admitted, even by medical writers, who are its greatest enemies: thus, for instance, Awsiter,* apothecary to Greenwich-hospital, in his 'Essay on the

Effects of Opium' (published in the year 1763), when attempting to explain, why Mead* had not been sufficiently explicit on the properties, counteragents, &c. of this drug, expresses himself in the following mysterious terms (φωναντα συνετοισι):* 'perhaps he thought the subject of too delicate a nature to be made common; and as many people might then indiscriminately use it, it would take from that necessary fear and caution, which should prevent their experiencing the extensive power of this drug: *for there are many properties in it, if universally known, that would habituate the use, and make it more in request with us than the Turks themselves*: the result of which knowledge,' he adds, 'must prove a general misfortune.' In the necessity of this conclusion I do not altogether concur: but upon that point I shall have occasion to speak at the close of my confessions, where I shall present the reader with the *moral* of my narrative.

PRELIMINARY CONFESSIONS

These preliminary confessions, or introductory narrative of the youthful adventures which laid the foundation of the writer's habit of opium-eating in after-life, it has been judged proper to premise, for three several reasons:

1. As forestalling that question, and giving it a satisfactory answer, which else would painfully obtrude itself in the course of the Opium-Confessions—'How came any reasonable being to subject himself to such a yoke of misery, voluntarily to incur a captivity so servile, and knowingly to fetter himself with such a seven-fold chain?'—a question which, if not somewhere plausibly resolved, could hardly fail, by the indignation which it would be apt to raise as against an act of wanton folly, to interfere with that degree of sympathy which is necessary in any case to an author's purposes.

2. As furnishing a key to some parts of that tremendous scenery which afterwards peopled the dreams of the Opium-eater.

3. As creating some previous interest of a personal sort in the confessing subject, apart from the matter of the confessions, which cannot fail to render the confessions themselves more interesting. If a man 'whose talk is of oxen,'* should become an Opium-eater, the probability is, that (if he is not too dull to dream at all)—he will dream about oxen: whereas, in the case before him, the reader will find that the Opium-eater boasteth himself to be a philosopher; and accordingly,

that the phantasmagoria of *his* dreams (waking or sleeping, day-dreams or night-dreams) is suitable to one who in that character,

Humani nihil a se alienum putat.*

For amongst the conditions which he deems indispensable to the sustaining of any claim to the title of philosopher, is not merely the possession of a superb intellect in its *analytic* functions (in which part of the pretension, however, England can for some generations show but few claimants; at least, he is not aware of any known candidate for this honour who can be styled emphatically *a subtle thinker*, with the exception of *Samuel Taylor Coleridge*, and in a narrower department of thought, with the recent illustrious exception[1] of *David Ricardo*)*—but also on such a constitution of the *moral* faculties, as shall give him an inner eye* and power of intuition for the vision and the mysteries of our human nature: *that* constitution of faculties, in short, which (amongst all the generations of men that from the beginning of time have deployed into life, as it were, upon this planet) our English poets have possessed in the highest degree—and Scottish[2] Professors* in the lowest.

I have often been asked, how I first came to be a regular opium-eater; and have suffered, very unjustly, in the opinion of my acquaintance, from being reputed to have brought upon myself all the sufferings which I shall have to record, by a long course of indulgence in this practice purely for the sake of creating an artificial state of pleasurable excitement. This, however, is a misrepresentation of my case. True it is, that for nearly ten years I did occasionally take opium, for the sake of the exquisite pleasure it gave me: but, so long as I took it with this view, I was effectually protected from all material bad consequences, by the necessity of interposing long intervals between the several acts of indulgence, in order to renew the

[1] A third exception* might perhaps have been added: and my reason for not adding that exception is chiefly because it was only in his juvenile efforts that the writer whom I allude to, expressly addressed himself to philosophical themes; his riper powers having been all dedicated (on very excusable and very intelligible grounds, under the present direction of the popular mind in England) to criticism and the Fine Arts.* This reason apart, however, I doubt whether he is not rather to be considered an acute thinker than a subtle one. It is, besides, a great drawback on his mastery over philosophical subjects, that he has obviously not had the advantage of a regular scholastic education: he has not read Plato in his youth (which most likely was only his misfortune); but neither has he read Kant* in his manhood (which is his fault).

[2] I disclaim any allusion to *existing* professors, of whom indeed I know only one.*

pleasurable sensations. It was not for the purpose of creating pleasure, but of mitigating pain in the severest degree, that I first began to use opium as an article of daily diet. In the twenty-eighth year of my age, a most painful affection of the stomach, which I had first experienced about ten years before, attacked me in great strength. This affection had originally been caused by extremities of hunger, suffered in my boyish days. During the season of hope and redundant happiness which succeeded (that is, from eighteen to twenty-four) it had slumbered: for the three following years it had revived at intervals: and now, under unfavourable circumstances, from depression of spirits, it attacked me with a violence that yielded to no remedies but opium. As the youthful sufferings, which first produced this derangement of the stomach, were interesting in themselves, and in the circumstances that attended them, I shall here briefly retrace them.

My father died, when I was about seven years old, and left me to the care of four guardians.* I was sent to various schools, great and small; and was very early distinguished for my classical attainments, especially for my knowledge of Greek. At thirteen, I wrote Greek with ease; and at fifteen my command of that language was so great, that I not only composed Greek verses in lyric metres, but could converse in Greek fluently, and without embarrassment—an accomplishment which I have not since met with in any scholar of my times, and which, in my case, was owing to the practice of daily reading off the newspapers into the best Greek I could furnish *extempore*: for the necessity of ransacking my memory and invention, for all sorts and combinations of periphrastic expressions, as equivalents for modern ideas, images, relations of things, &c. gave me a compass of diction which would never have been called out by a dull translation of moral essays, &c. 'That boy,' said one of my masters,* pointing the attention of a stranger to me, 'that boy could harangue an Athenian mob, better than you or I could address an English one.' He who honoured me with this eulogy, was a scholar, 'and a ripe and good one:'* and of all my tutors, was the only one whom I loved or reverenced. Unfortunately for me (and, as I afterwards learned, to this worthy man's great indignation), I was transferred to the care, first of a blockhead,* who was in a perpetual panic, lest I should expose his ignorance; and finally, to that of a respectable scholar, at the head of a great school on an ancient foundation.* This man had been appointed to his situation by ———— College, Oxford;* and was a sound, well-built scholar, but (like most men, whom I have known from that college) coarse, clumsy, and inelegant. A miserable contrast he presented, in my eyes, to the Etonian brilliancy of my favourite master: and besides, he could not disguise from my hourly notice, the poverty and meagreness of his understanding. It is a bad thing for a boy to be, and to know himself, far beyond his tutors, whether in knowledge or in power of mind. This was the case, so far as regarded knowledge at least, not with myself only: for the two boys, who jointly with myself composed the first form, were better Grecians than the head-master, though not more elegant scholars, nor at all more accustomed to sacrifice to the graces.* When I first entered, I remember that we read Sophocles;* and it was a constant matter of triumph to us, the learned triumvirate of the first form, to see our 'Archididascalus'* (as he loved to be called) conning our lesson before we went up, and laying a regular train, with lexicon and grammar, for blowing up and blasting (as it were) any difficulties he found in the choruses; whilst *we* never condescended to open our books, until the moment of going up, and were generally employed in writing epigrams upon his wig, or some such important matter. My two class-fellows were poor, and dependant for their future prospects at the university, on the recommendation of the head-master: but I, who had a small patrimonial property, the income of which was sufficient to support me at college, wished to be sent thither immediately.* I made earnest representations on the subject to my guardians, but all to no purpose. One, who was more reasonable, and had more knowledge of the world than the rest, lived at a distance: two of the other three resigned all their authority into the hands of the fourth; and this fourth with whom I had to negotiate, was a worthy man, in his way, but haughty, obstinate, and intolerant of all opposition to his will.* After a certain number of letters and personal interviews, I found that I had nothing to hope for, not even a compromise of the matter, from my guardian: unconditional submission was what he demanded: and I prepared myself, therefore, for other measures. Summer was now coming on with hasty steps, and my seventeenth birth-day was fast approaching; after which day I had sworn within myself, that I would no longer be numbered amongst school-boys. Money being what I chiefly wanted, I wrote to a woman of high rank,* who, though young herself, had known me from a child, and had latterly treated me with great distinction, requesting that she would 'lend' me five guineas. For upwards of a week no answer came; and I was beginning to despond, when, at length, a servant put into my hands a double letter,* with a coronet on the seal. The letter was kind and obliging: the fair writer was on the sea-coast, and in that way the delay had arisen: she inclosed double of what I had asked, and good-naturedly hinted, that if I should *never* repay her, it would not absolutely ruin her. Now then, I was prepared for my scheme: ten guineas, added to about two which I had remaining from my pocket money, seemed to me sufficient for an indefinite length of time: and at that happy age, if no *definite* boundary can be assigned to one's power, the spirit of hope and pleasure makes it virtually infinite.

It is a just remark of Dr Johnson's (and what cannot often be said of his remarks, it is a very feeling one), that we never do any thing consciously for the last time (of things, that is, which we have long been in the habit of doing) without sadness of heart.* This truth I felt deeply, when I came to leave ——, a place which I did not love, and where I had not been happy. On the evening before I left —— for ever, I grieved when the ancient and lofty school-room resounded with the evening service, performed for the last time in my hearing; and at night, when the muster-roll of names was called over, and mine (as usual) was called first, I stepped forward, and, passing the head-master, who was standing by, I bowed to him, and looked earnestly in his face, thinking to myself, 'He is old and infirm, and in this world I shall not see him again.' I was right: I never *did* see him again, nor ever shall. He looked at me complacently, smiled goodnaturedly, returned my salutation (or rather, my valediction), and we parted (though he knew it not) for ever. I could not reverence him intellectually: but he had been uniformly kind to me, and had allowed me many indulgencies: and I grieved at the thought of the mortification I should inflict upon him.

The morning came, which was to launch me into the world, and from which my whole succeeding life has, in many important points, taken its colouring. I lodged in the head-master's house,* and had been allowed, from my first entrance, the indulgence of a private room, which I used both as a sleeping room and as a study. At half after three I rose, and gazed with deep emotion at the ancient towers of ——,* 'drest in earliest light,'* and beginning to crimson with the radiant lustre of a cloudless July morning. I was firm and immoveable in my purpose: but yet agitated by anticipation of uncertain danger and troubles; and, if I could have foreseen the hurricane, and perfect hail-storm of affliction which soon fell upon me, well might I have been agitated. To this agitation the deep peace of the morning presented an affecting contrast, and in some degree a medicine. The silence was more profound than that of midnight: and to me the silence of a summer morning is more touching than all other silence, because, the light being broad and strong, as that of noon-day at other seasons of the year, it seems to differ from perfect day, chiefly because man is not yet abroad; and thus, the peace of nature, and of the innocent creatures of God, seems to be secure and deep, only so long as the presence of man, and his restless and unquiet spirit, are not there to trouble its sanctity. I dressed myself, took my hat and gloves, and lingered a little in the room. For the last year and a half this room had been my 'pensive citadel:'* here I had read and studied through all the hours of night: and, though true it was, that for the latter part of this time I, who was framed for love and gentle affections, had lost my gaiety and happiness, during the strife and fever of contention with my guardian; yet, on the other hand, as a boy, so passionately fond of books, and dedicated to intellectual pursuits, I could not fail to have enjoyed many happy hours in the midst of general dejection. I wept as I looked round on the chair, hearth, writing-table, and other familiar objects, knowing too certainly, that I looked upon them for the last time. Whilst I write this, it is eighteen years ago:* and yet, at this moment, I see distinctly as if it were yesterday, the lineaments and expression of the object on which I fixed my parting gaze: it was a picture of the lovely ————,* which hung over the mantle-piece; the eyes and mouth of which were so beautiful, and the whole countenance so radiant with benignity, and divine tranquillity, that I had a thousand times laid down my pen, or my book, to gather consolation from it, as a devotee from his patron saint. Whilst I was yet gazing upon it, the deep tones of ———— clock proclaimed that it was four o'clock. I went up to the picture, kissed it, and then gently walked out, and closed the door for ever!

—— —— —— —— —— ——

So blended and intertwisted in this life are occasions of laughter and of tears, that I cannot yet recal, without smiling, an incident which occurred at that time, and which had nearly put a stop to the immediate execution of my plan. I had a trunk of immense weight; for, besides my clothes, it contained nearly all my library. The difficulty was to get this removed to a carrier's: my room was at an aërial elevation in the house, and (what was worse) the stair-case, which communicated with this angle of the building, was accessible only by a gallery, which passed the head-master's chamber-door. I was a favourite with all the servants; and, knowing that any of them would screen me, and act confidentially, I communicated my embarrassment to a groom of the head-master's. The groom swore he would do any thing I wished; and, when the time arrived, went up stairs to bring the trunk down. This I feared was beyond the strength of any one man: however, the groom was a man—

> Of Atlantean shoulders, fit to bear
> The weight of mightiest monarchies;*

and had a back as spacious as Salisbury plain.* Accordingly he persisted in bringing down the trunk alone, whilst I stood waiting at the foot of the last flight, in anxiety for the event. For some time I heard him descending with slow and firm steps: but, unfortunately, from his trepidation, as he drew near the dangerous quarter, within a few steps of the gallery, his foot slipped; and the mighty burden falling from his shoulders, gained such increase of impetus at each step of the descent, that, on reaching the bottom, it trundled, or rather leaped, right across, with the noise of twenty devils, against the very bed-room door of the archididascalus. My first thought was, that all was lost; and that my only chance for executing a retreat was to sacrifice my baggage. However, on reflection, I determined to abide the issue. The groom was in the utmost alarm, both on his own account and on mine: but, in spite of this, so irresistibly had the sense of the ludicrous, in this unhappy *contretems*,* taken possession of his fancy, that he sang out a long, loud, and canorous peal of laughter, that might have wakened the Seven Sleepers.* At the sound of this resonant merriment, within the very ears of insulted authority, I could not myself forbear joining in it: subdued to this, not so much by the unhappy *étourderie** of the trunk, as by the effect it had upon the groom. We both expected, as a matter of course, that Dr ——— would sally out of his room: for, in general, if but a mouse stirred, he sprang out like a mastiff from his kennel. Strange to say, however, on this occasion, when the noise of laughter had ceased, no sound, or rustling even, was to be heard in the bed-room. Dr ——— had a painful complaint, which, sometimes keeping him awake, made his sleep, perhaps, when it *did* come, the deeper. Gathering courage from the silence, the groom hoisted his burden again, and accomplished the remainder of his descent without accident. I waited until I saw the trunk placed on a wheel-barrow, and on its road to the carrier's: then, 'with Providence my guide,'* I set off on foot,—carrying a small parcel, with some articles of dress, under my arm; a favourite English poet* in one pocket; and a small 12mo. volume, containing about nine plays of Euripides,* in the other.

It had been my intention originally to proceed to Westmoreland, both from the love I bore to that county, and on other personal accounts.* Accident, however, gave a different direction to my wanderings, and I bent my steps towards North Wales.

After wandering about for some time in Denbighshire, Merionethshire, and Caernarvonshire, I took lodgings in a small neat house in B———.* Here I might have staid with great comfort for many weeks; for, provisions were cheap at B———, from the scarcity of other markets for the surplus produce of a wide agricultural district. An accident, however, in which, perhaps, no offence was designed, drove me out to wander again. I know not whether my reader may have remarked, but *I* have often remarked, that the proudest class of people in England (or at any rate, the class whose pride is most apparent) are the families of bishops. Noblemen, and their children, carry about with them, in their very titles, a sufficient notification of their rank. Nay, their very names (and this applies also to the children of many untitled houses) are often, to the English ear, adequate exponents of high birth, or descent. Sackville, Manners, Fitzroy, Paulet, Cavendish, and scores of others, tell their own tale. Such persons, therefore, find every where a due sense of their claims already established, except among those who are ignorant of the world, by virtue of their own obscurity: 'Not to know *them*, argues one's self unknown.'* Their manners take a suitable tone and colouring; and, for once that they find it necessary to impress a sense of their consequence upon others, they meet with a thousand occasions for moderating and tempering this sense by acts of courteous condescension. With the families of bishops it is otherwise: with them it is all up-hill work, to make known their pretensions: for the proportion of the episcopal bench, taken from noble families, is not at any time very large; and the succession to these dignities is so rapid, that the public ear seldom has time to become familiar with them, unless where they are connected with some literary reputation. Hence it is, that the children of bishops carry about with them an austere and repulsive air, indicative of claims not generally acknowledged, a sort of *noli me tangere** manner, nervously apprehensive of too familiar approach, and shrinking with the sensitiveness of a gouty man, from all contact with the ὁι πολλοι.* Doubtless, a powerful understanding, or unusual goodness of nature, will preserve a man from such weakness: but, in general, the truth of my representation will be acknowledged: pride, if not of deeper root in such families, appears, at least, more upon the surface of their manners. This spirit of manners naturally communicates itself to their domestics, and other dependants. Now, my landlady had been a lady's maid, or a nurse, in the family of the Bishop of ———;* and had but lately married away and 'settled' (as such people express it) for life. In a little town like B———, merely to have lived in the bishop's family, conferred some distinction: and my good landlady had rather more than her share of the pride I have noticed on that score. What 'my lord' said, and what 'my lord' did, how useful he was in parliament, and how indispensable at Oxford, formed the daily burden of her talk. All this I bore very well: for I was too good-natured to laugh in any body's face, and I could make an ample allowance for the garrulity of an old servant. Of necessity, however, I must have appeared in her eyes very inadequately impressed with the bishop's importance: and, perhaps, to punish me for my indifference, or possibly by accident, she one day repeated to me a conversation in which I was indirectly a party concerned. She had been to the palace to pay her respects to the family; and, dinner being over, was summoned into the dining-room. In giving an account of her household economy, she happened to mention, that she had let her apartments. Thereupon the good bishop (it seemed) had taken occasion to caution her as to her selection of inmates: 'for,' said he, 'you must recollect, Betty, that this place is in the high road to the Head*; so that multitudes of Irish swindlers, running away from their debts into England—and of English swindlers, running away from their debts to the Isle of Man,* are likely to take this place in their route.' This advice was certainly not without reasonable grounds: but rather fitted to be stored up for Mrs Betty's private meditations, than specially reported to me. What followed, however, was somewhat worse:—'Oh, my lord,' answered my landlady (according to her own

representation of the matter), 'I really don't think this young gentleman is a swindler; because ———:' 'You don't *think* me a swindler?'
said I, interrupting her, in a tumult of indignation: 'for the future
I shall spare you the trouble of thinking about it.' And without delay
I prepared for my departure. Some concessions the good woman
seemed disposed to make: but a harsh and contemptuous expression,
which I fear that I applied to the learned dignitary himself, roused
her indignation in turn: and reconciliation then became impossible.
I was, indeed, greatly irritated at the bishop's having suggested any
grounds of suspicion, however remotely, against a person whom he
had never seen: and I thought of letting him know my mind in Greek:
which, at the same time that it would furnish some presumption that
I was no swindler, would also (I hoped) compel the bishop to reply in
the same language; in which case, I doubted not to make it appear,
that if I was not so rich as his lordship, I was a far better Grecian.
Calmer thoughts, however, drove this boyish design out of my mind:
for I considered, that the bishop was in the right to counsel an old
servant; that he could not have designed that his advice should be
reported to me; and that the same coarseness of mind, which had led
Mrs Betty to repeat the advice at all, might have coloured it in a way
more agreeable to her own style of thinking, than to the actual expressions of the worthy bishop.

I left the lodgings the very same hour; and this turned out a very
unfortunate occurrence for me: because, living henceforward at inns,
I was drained of my money very rapidly. In a fortnight I was reduced
to short allowance; that is, I could allow myself only one meal a-day.
From the keen appetite produced by constant exercise, and mountain
air, acting on a youthful stomach, I soon began to suffer greatly on
this slender regimen; for the single meal, which I could venture to
order, was coffee or tea. Even this, however, was at length withdrawn:
and afterwards, so long as I remained in Wales, I subsisted either on
blackberries, hips, haws,* &c. or on the casual hospitalities which
I now and then received, in return for such little services as I had an
opportunity of rendering. Sometimes I wrote letters of business for
cottagers, who happened to have relatives in Liverpool, or in London:
more often I wrote love-letters to their sweethearts for young women
who had lived as servants in Shrewsbury,* or other towns on the
English border. On all such occasions I gave great satisfaction to my
humble friends, and was generally treated with hospitality: and once,

in particular, near the village of Llan-y-styndw (or some such name),* in a sequestered part of Merionethshire, I was entertained for upwards of three days by a family of young people, with an affectionate and fraternal kindness that left an impression upon my heart not yet impaired. The family consisted, at that time, of four sisters, and three brothers, all grown up, and all remarkable for elegance and delicacy of manners. So much beauty, and so much native good-breeding and refinement, I do not remember to have seen before or since in any cottage, except once or twice in Westmorland and Devonshire. They spoke English: an accomplishment not often met with in so many members of one family, especially in villages remote from the high-road. Here I wrote, on my first introduction, a letter about prize-money, for one of the brothers, who had served on board an English man of war;* and more privately, two love-letters for two of the sisters. They were both interesting looking girls, and one of uncommon loveliness. In the midst of their confusion and blushes, whilst dictating, or rather giving me general instructions, it did not require any great penetration to discover that what they wished was, that their letters should be as kind as was consistent with proper maidenly pride. I contrived so to temper my expressions, as to reconcile the gratification of both feelings: and they were as much pleased with the way in which I had expressed their thoughts, as (in their simplicity) they were astonished at my having so readily discovered them. The reception one meets with from the women of a family, generally determines the tenor of one's whole entertainment. In this case, I had discharged my confidential duties as secretary, so much to the general satisfaction, perhaps also amusing them with my conversation, that I was pressed to stay with a cordiality which I had little inclination to resist. I slept with the brothers, the only unoccupied bed standing in the apartment of the young women: but in all other points, they treated me with a respect not usually paid to purses as light as mine; as if my scholarship were sufficient evidence, that I was of 'gentle blood.'* Thus I lived with them for three days, and great part of a fourth: and, from the undiminished kindness which they continued to show me, I believe I might have staid with them up to this time, if their power had corresponded with their wishes. On the last morning, however, I perceived upon their countenances, as they sate at breakfast, the expression of some unpleasant communication which was at hand; and soon after one of the brothers explained to me, that

their parents had gone, the day before my arrival, to an annual meeting of Methodists,* held at Caernarvon,* and were that day expected
to return; 'and if they should not be so civil as they ought to be,' he
begged, on the part of all the young people, that I would not take it
amiss. The parents returned, with churlish faces, and '*Dym Sassenach*'
(*no English*), in answer to all my addresses. I saw how matters stood;
and so, taking an affectionate leave of my kind and interesting young
hosts, I went my way. For, though they spoke warmly to their parents
in my behalf, and often excused the manner of the old people, by saying, that it was 'only their way,' yet I easily understood that my talent
for writing love-letters would do as little to recommend me, with two
grave sexagenarian Welsh Methodists, as my Greek Sapphics or
Alcaics:* and what had been hospitality, when offered to me with the
gracious courtesy of my young friends, would become charity, when
connected with the harsh demeanour of these old people. Certainly,
Mr Shelley is right in his notions about old age:* unless powerfully
counteracted by all sorts of opposite agencies, it is a miserable
corrupter and blighter to the genial charities of the human heart.

Soon after this, I contrived, by means which I must omit for want
of room, to transfer myself to London. And now began the latter and
fiercer stage of my long-sufferings; without using a disproportionate
expression I might say, of my agony. For I now suffered, for upwards
of sixteen weeks,* the physical anguish of hunger in various degrees
of intensity; but as bitter, perhaps, as ever any human being can
have suffered who has survived it. I would not needlessly harass my
reader's feelings, by a detail of all that I endured: for extremities such
as these, under any circumstances of heaviest misconduct or guilt,
cannot be contemplated, even in description, without a rueful pity
that is painful to the natural goodness of the human heart. Let it suffice, at least on this occasion, to say, that a few fragments of bread
from the breakfast-table of one individual (who supposed me to be ill,
but did not know of my being in utter want), and these at uncertain
intervals, constituted my whole support. During the former part of
my sufferings (that is, generally in Wales, and always for the first
two months in London) I was houseless, and very seldom slept under
a roof. To this constant exposure to the open air I ascribe it mainly,
that I did not sink under my torments. Latterly, however, when
colder and more inclement weather came on, and when, from the
length of my sufferings, I had begun to sink into a more languishing

condition, it was, no doubt, fortunate for me, that the same person to whose breakfast-table I had access, allowed me to sleep in a large unoccupied house, of which he was tenant. Unoccupied, I call it, for there was no household or establishment in it; nor any furniture, indeed, except a table, and a few chairs. But I found, on taking possession of my new quarters, that the house already contained one single inmate, a poor friendless child, apparently ten years old; but she seemed hunger-bitten;* and sufferings of that sort often make children look older than they are. From this forlorn child I learned, that she had slept and lived there alone, for some time before I came: and great joy the poor creature expressed, when she found that I was, in future, to be her companion through the hours of darkness. The house was large; and, from the want of furniture, the noise of the rats made a prodigious echoing on the spacious stair-case and hall; and, amidst the real fleshly ills of cold, and, I fear, hunger, the forsaken child had found leisure to suffer still more (it appeared) from the self-created one of ghosts. I promised her protection against all ghosts whatsoever: but, alas! I could offer her no other assistance. We lay upon the floor, with a bundle of cursed law papers for a pillow: but with no other covering than a sort of large horseman's cloak: afterwards, however, we discovered, in a garret, an old sopha-cover, a small piece of rug, and some fragments of other articles, which added a little to our warmth. The poor child crept close to me for warmth, and for security against her ghostly enemies. When I was not more than usually ill, I took her into my arms, so that, in general, she was tolerably warm, and often slept when I could not: for, during the last two months of my sufferings, I slept much in the day-time, and was apt to fall into transient dozings at all hours. But my sleep distressed me more than my watching: for, besides the tumultuousness of my dreams (which were only not so awful as those which I shall have to describe hereafter as produced by opium), my sleep was never more than what is called *dog-sleep*; so that I could hear myself moaning, and was often, as it seemed to me, wakened suddenly by my own voice; and, about this time, a hideous sensation began to haunt me as soon as I fell into a slumber, which has since returned upon me, at different periods of my life, viz. a sort of twitching (I know not where, but apparently about the region of the stomach), which compelled me violently to throw out my feet for the sake of relieving it. This sensation coming on as soon as I began to sleep, and the effort to relieve it constantly awaking me, at length I slept only from exhaustion; and from increasing weakness (as I said before) I was constantly falling asleep, and constantly awaking. Meantime, the master of the house sometimes came in upon us suddenly, and very early, sometimes not till ten o'clock, sometimes not at all. He was in constant fear of bailiffs: improving on the plan of Cromwell, every night he slept in a different quarter of London;* and I observed that he never failed to examine, through a private window, the appearance of those who knocked at the door, before he would allow it to be opened. He breakfasted alone: indeed, his tea equipage would hardly have admitted of his hazarding an invitation to a second person— any more than the quantity of esculent* *matériel*, which, for the most part, was little more than a roll, or a few biscuits, which he had bought on his road from the place where he had slept. Or, if he *had* asked a party, as I once learnedly and facetiously observed to him—the several members of it must have *stood* in the relation to each other (not *sate* in any relation whatever) of succession, as the metaphysicians have it, and not of co-existence; in the relation of the parts of time, and not of the parts of space. During his breakfast, I generally contrived a reason for lounging in; and, with an air of as much indifference as I could assume, took up such fragments as he had left— sometimes, indeed, there were none at all. In doing this, I committed no robbery except upon the man himself, who was thus obliged (I believe) now and then to send out at noon for an extra biscuit; for, as to the poor child, *she* was never admitted into his study (if I may give that name to his chief depositary of parchments, law writings, &c.); that room was to her the Blue-beard room of the house,* being regularly locked on his departure to dinner, about six o'clock, which usually was his final departure for the night. Whether this child were an illegitimate daughter of Mr ———,* or only a servant, I could not ascertain; she did not herself know; but certainly she was treated altogether as a menial servant. No sooner did Mr ——— make his appearance, than she went below stairs, brushed his shoes, coat, &c.; and, except when she was summoned to run an errand, she never emerged from the dismal Tartarus* of the kitchens, &c. to the upper air, until my welcome knock at night called up her little trembling footsteps to the front door. Of her life during the day-time, however, I knew little but what I gathered from her own account at night; for, as soon as the hours of business commenced, I saw that my absence would be acceptable; and, in general, therefore, I went off and sate in the parks, or elsewhere, until night-fall.

But who, and what, meantime, was the master of the house himself? Reader, he was one of those anomalous practitioners in lower departments of the law, who—what shall I say?—who, on prudential reasons, or from necessity, deny themselves all indulgence in the luxury of too delicate a conscience: (a periphrasis which might be abridged considerably, but *that* I leave to the reader's taste:)* in many walks of life, a conscience is a more expensive incumbrance, than a wife or a carriage; and just as people talk of 'laying down'* their carriages, so I suppose my friend, Mr —— had 'laid down' his conscience for a time; meaning, doubtless, to resume it as soon as he could afford it. The inner economy of such a man's daily life would present a most strange picture, if I could allow myself to amuse the reader at his expense. Even with my limited opportunities for observing what went on, I saw many scenes of London intrigues, and complex chicanery, 'cycle and epicycle, orb in orb,'* at which I sometimes smile to this day—and at which I smiled then, in spite of my misery. My situation, however, at that time, gave me little experience, in my own person, of any qualities in Mr ——'s character but such as did him honour; and of his whole strange composition, I must forget every thing but that towards me he was obliging, and, to the extent of his power, generous.

That power was not, indeed, very extensive; however, in common with the rats, I sate rent free; and, as Dr Johnson has recorded, that he never but once in his life had as much wall-fruit as he could eat,* so let me be grateful, that on that single occasion I had as large a choice of apartments in a London mansion as I could possibly desire. Except the Blue-beard room, which the poor child believed to be haunted, all others, from the attics to the cellars, were at our service; 'the world was all before us;'* and we pitched our tent for the night in any spot we chose. This house I have already described as a large one; it stands in a conspicuous situation, and in a well-known part of London.* Many of my readers will have passed it, I doubt not, within a few hours of reading this. For myself, I never fail to visit it when business draws me to London; about ten o'clock, this very night, August 15, 1821, being my birth-day—I turned aside from my evening walk, down Oxford-street, purposely to take a glance at it: it is now occupied by a respectable family; and, by the lights in the front _house = reflection of himself_

drawing-room, I observed a domestic party, assembled perhaps at tea, and apparently cheerful and gay. Marvellous contrast in my eyes to the darkness—cold—silence—and desolation of that same house eighteen years ago, when its nightly occupants were one famishing scholar, and a neglected child.—Her, by the bye, in after years, I vainly endeavoured to trace. Apart from her situation, she was not what would be called an interesting child: she was neither pretty, nor quick in understanding, nor remarkably pleasing in manners. But, thank God! even in those years I needed not the embellishments of novel-accessaries to conciliate my affections; plain human nature, in its humblest and most homely apparel, was enough for me: and I loved the child because she was my partner in wretchedness. If she is now living, she is probably a mother, with children of her own; but, as I have said, I could never trace her.

This I regret, but another person there was at that time, whom I have since sought to trace with far deeper earnestness, and with far deeper sorrow at my failure. This person was a young woman, and one of that unhappy class who subsist upon the wages of prostitution. I feel no shame, nor have any reason to feel it, in avowing, that I was then on familiar and friendly terms with many women in that unfortunate condition. The reader needs neither smile at this avowal, nor frown. For, not to remind my classical readers of the old Latin proverb—'*Sine Cerere*,' &c.,* it may well be supposed that in the existing state of my purse, my connexion with such women could not have been an impure one.* But the truth is, that at no time of my life have I been a person to hold myself polluted by the touch or approach of any creature that wore a human shape: on the contrary, from my very earliest youth it has been my pride to converse familiarly, *more Socratico*,* with all human beings, man, woman, and child, that chance might fling in my way: a practice which is friendly to the knowledge of human nature, to good feelings, and to that frankness of address which becomes a man who would be thought a philosopher. For a philosopher should not see with the eyes of the poor limitary creature calling himself a man of the world, and filled with narrow and self-regarding prejudices of birth and education, but should look upon himself as a Catholic* creature, and as standing in an equal relation to high and low—to educated and uneducated, to the guilty and the innocent. Being myself at that time of necessity a peripatetic, or a walker of the streets, I naturally fell in more frequently with those female peripatetics who are technically called Street-walkers. Many of these women had occasionally taken my part against watchmen* who wished to drive me off the steps of houses where I was sitting. But one amongst them, the one on whose account I have at all introduced this subject—yet no! let me not class thee, Oh noble minded Ann ——, with that order of women; let me find, if it be possible, some gentler name to designate the condition of her to whose bounty and compassion, ministering to my necessities when all the world had forsaken me, I owe it that I am at this time alive.—For many weeks I had walked at nights with this poor friendless girl up and down Oxford Street, or had rested with her on steps and under the shelter of porticos. She could not be so old as myself: she told me, indeed, that she had not completed her sixteenth year. By such questions as my interest about her prompted, I had gradually drawn forth her simple history. Her's was a case of ordinary occurrence (as I have since had reason to think), and one in which, if London beneficence had better adapted its arrangements to meet it, the power of the law might oftener be interposed to protect, and to avenge. But the stream of London charity flows in a channel which, though deep and mighty, is yet noiseless and underground; not obvious or readily accessible to poor houseless wanderers: and it cannot be denied that the outside air and frame-work of London society is harsh, cruel, and repulsive. In any case, however, I saw that part of her injuries might easily have been redressed: and I urged her often and earnestly to lay her complaint before a magistrate: friendless as she was, I assured her that she would meet with immediate attention; and that English justice, which was no respecter of persons, would speedily and amply avenge her on the brutal ruffian who had plundered her little property. She promised me often that she would; but she delayed taking the steps I pointed out from time to time: for she was timid and dejected to a degree which showed how deeply sorrow had taken hold of her young heart: and perhaps she thought justly that the most upright judge, and the most righteous tribunals, could do nothing to repair her heaviest wrongs. Something, however, would perhaps have been done: for it had been settled between us at length, but unhappily on the very last time but one that I was ever to see her, that in a day or two we should go together before a magistrate, and that I should speak on her behalf. This little service it was destined, however, that I should never realise. Meantime, that which she rendered to me, and which was greater than I could ever have repaid her, was this:——One night, when we were pacing slowly along Oxford Street, and after a day when I had felt more than usually ill and faint, I requested her to turn off with me into Soho Square: thither we went; and we sate down on the steps of a house, which, to this hour, I never pass without a pang of grief, and an inner act of homage to the spirit of that unhappy girl, in memory of the noble action which she there performed. Suddenly, as we sate, I grew much worse: I had been leaning my head against her bosom; and all at once I sank from her arms and fell backwards on the steps. From the sensations I then had, I felt an inner conviction of the liveliest kind that without some powerful and reviving stimulus, I should either have died on the spot—or should at least have sunk to a point of exhaustion from which all reäscent under my friendless circumstances would soon have become hopeless. Then it was, at this crisis of my fate, that my poor orphan companion—who had herself met with little but injuries in this world—stretched out a saving hand to me. Uttering a cry of terror, but without a moment's delay, she ran off into Oxford Street, and in less time than could be imagined, returned to me with a glass of port wine and spices, that acted upon my empty stomach (which at that time would have rejected all solid food) with an instantaneous power of restoration: and for this glass the generous girl without a murmur paid out of her own humble purse at a time—be it remembered!— when she had scarcely wherewithal to purchase the bare necessaries of life, and when she could have no reason to expect that I should ever be able to reimburse her. ——— Oh! youthful benefactress! how often in succeeding years, standing in solitary places, and thinking of thee with grief of heart and perfect love, how often have I wished that, as in ancient times the curse of a father was believed to have a supernatural power,* and to pursue its object with a fatal necessity of self-fulfilment,—even so the benediction of a heart oppressed with gratitude, might have a like prerogative; might have power given to it from above to chace—to haunt—to way-lay*—to overtake—to pursue thee into the central darkness of a London brothel, or (if it were possible) into the darkness of the grave—there to awaken thee with an authentic message of peace and forgiveness, and of final reconciliation!

I do not often weep: for not only do my thoughts on subjects connected with the chief interests of man daily, nay hourly, descend a thousand fathoms 'too deep for tears;'* not only does the sternness of my habits of thought present an antagonism to the feelings which prompt tears—wanting of necessity to those who, being protected usually by their levity from any tendency to meditative sorrow, would by that same levity be made incapable of resisting it on any casual access of such feelings:—but also, I believe that all minds which have contemplated such objects as deeply as I have done, must, for their own protection from utter despondency, have early encouraged and cherished some tranquilizing belief as to the future balances and the hieroglyphic meanings of human sufferings. On these accounts, I am cheerful to this hour: and, as I have said, I do not often weep. Yet some feelings, though not deeper or more passionate, are more tender than others: and often, when I walk at this time in Oxford Street by dreamy lamp-light, and hear those airs played on a barrel-organ which years ago solaced me and my dear companion (as I must always call her) I shed tears, and muse with myself at the mysterious dispensation which so suddenly and so critically separated us for ever. How it happened, the reader will understand from what remains of this introductory narration.

Soon after the period of the last incident I have recorded, I met, in Albemarle Street, a gentleman of his late Majesty's household.* This gentleman had received hospitalities, on different occasions, from my family: and he challenged me upon the strength of my family likeness. I did not attempt any disguise: I answered his questions ingenuously,—and, on his pledging his word of honor that he would not betray me to my guardians, I gave him an address to my friend the Attorney's. The next day I received from him a 10*l.** Bank-note. The letter inclosing it was delivered with other letters of business to the Attorney: but, though his look and manner informed me that he suspected its contents, he gave it up to me honorably and without demur.

This present, from the particular service to which it was applied, leads me naturally to speak of the purpose which had allured me up to London, and which I had been (to use a forensic word) *soliciting** from the first day of my arrival in London, to that of my final departure.

In so mighty a world as London, it will surprise my readers that I should not have found some means of staving off the last extremities of penury: and it will strike them that two resources at least must have been open to me,—viz. either to seek assistance from the friends of my family, or to turn my youthful talents and attainments into some channel of pecuniary emolument. As to the first course, I may observe, generally, that what I dreaded beyond all other evils was the chance of being reclaimed by my guardians; not doubting that whatever power the law gave them would have been enforced against me to the utmost; that is, to the extremity of forcibly restoring me to the school which I had quitted: a restoration which as it would in my eyes have been a dishonor, even if submitted to voluntarily, could not fail, when extorted from me in contempt and defiance of my known wishes and efforts, to have been a humiliation worse to me than death, and which would indeed have terminated in death. I was, therefore, shy enough of applying for assistance even in those quarters where I was sure of receiving it—at the risk of furnishing my guardians with any clue for recovering me.* But, as to London in particular, though, doubtless, my father had in his life-time had many friends there, yet (as ten years had passed since his death) I remembered few of them even by name: and never having seen London before, except once for a few hours,* I knew not the address of even those few. To this mode of gaining help, therefore, in part the difficulty, but much more the paramount fear which I have mentioned, habitually indisposed me. In regard to the other mode, I now feel half inclined to join my reader in wondering that I should have overlooked it. As a corrector of Greek proofs (if in no other way), I might doubtless have gained enough for my slender wants. Such an office as this I could have discharged with an exemplary and punctual accuracy that would soon have gained me the confidence of my employers. But it must not be forgotten that, even for such an office as this, it was necessary that I should first of all have an introduction to some respectable publisher: and this I had no means of obtaining. To say the truth, however, it had never once occurred to me to think of literary labours as a source of profit. No mode sufficiently speedy of obtaining money had ever occurred to me, but that of borrowing it on the strength of my future claims and expectations. This mode I sought by every avenue to compass: and amongst other persons I applied to a Jew named D——.[1]

---

[1] To this same Jew,* by the way, some eighteen months afterwards, I applied again on the same business; and, dating at that time from a respectable college, I was fortunate enough to gain his serious attention to my proposals. My necessities had not arisen from any extravagance, or youthful levities (these my habits and the nature of my pleasures

To this Jew, and to other advertising money-lenders (some of whom were, I believe, also Jews), I had introduced myself with an account of my expectations; which account, on examining my father's will at Doctor's Commons,* they had ascertained to be correct. The person there mentioned as the second son of ————,* was found to have all the claims (or more than all) that I had stated: but one question still remained, which the faces of the Jews pretty significantly suggested,—was *I* that person? This doubt had never occurred to me as a possible one: I had rather feared, whenever my Jewish friends scrutinized me keenly, that I might be too well known to be that person—and that some scheme might be passing in their minds for entrapping me and selling me to my guardians. It was strange to me to find my own self, *materialiter* considered (so I expressed it, for I doated on logical accuracy of distinctions), accused, or at least suspected, of counterfeiting my own self, *formaliter** considered. However, to satisfy their scruples, I took the only course in my power. Whilst I was in Wales, I had received various letters from young friends: these I produced: for I carried them constantly in my pocket—being, indeed, by this time, almost the only relics of my personal incumbrances (excepting the clothes I wore) which I had not in one way or other disposed of. Most of these letters were from the Earl of ————,* who was at that time my chief (or rather only) confidential friend. These letters were dated from Eton.* I had also some from the Marquis of ————,* his father, who, though absorbed in

---

raised me far above), but simply from the vindictive malice of my guardian, who, when he found himself no longer able to prevent me from going to the university, had, as a parting token of his good nature, refused to sign an order for granting me a shilling beyond the allowance made to me at school—viz. 100*l.* per ann. Upon this sum it was, in my time, barely possible to have lived in college; and not possible to a man who, though above the paltry affectation of ostentatious disregard for money, and without any expensive tastes, confided nevertheless rather too much in servants, and did not delight in the petty details of minute economy. I soon, therefore, became embarrassed: and at length, after a most voluminous negotiation with the Jew, (some parts of which, if I had leisure to rehearse them, would greatly amuse my readers), I was put in possession of the sum I asked for—on the 'regular' terms of paying the Jew seventeen and a half per cent. by way of annuity on all the money furnished; Israel, on his part, graciously resuming no more than about ninety guineas of the said money, on account of an Attorney's bill, (for what services, to whom rendered, and when, whether at the siege of Jerusalem—at the building of the Second Temple*—or on some earlier occasion, I have not yet been able to discover). How many perches* this bill measured I really forget: but I still keep it in a cabinet of natural curiosities; and sometime or other I believe I shall present it to the British Museum.

agricultural pursuits, yet having been an Etonian himself, and as good a scholar as a nobleman needs to be—still retained an affection for classical studies, and for youthful scholars. He had, accordingly, from the time that I was fifteen, corresponded with me; sometimes upon the great improvements which he had made, or was meditating, in the counties of M—— and Sl——* since I had been there; sometimes upon the merits of a Latin poet; at other times, suggesting subjects to me on which he wished me to write verses.*

On reading the letters, one of my Jewish friends agreed to furnish two or three hundred pounds on my personal security—provided I could persuade the young Earl, who was, by the way, not older than myself, to guarantee the payment on our coming of age: the Jew's final object being, as I now suppose, not the trifling profit he could expect to make by me, but the prospect of establishing a connection with my noble friend, whose immense expectations were well known to him. In pursuance of this proposal on the part of the Jew, about eight or nine days after I had received the 10*l*., I prepared to go down to Eton. Nearly 3*l*. of the money I had given to my money-lending friend, on his alleging that the stamps must be bought, in order that the writings might be preparing whilst I was away from London. I thought in my heart that he was lying; but I did not wish to give him any excuse for charging his own delays upon me. A smaller sum I had given to my friend the attorney (who was connected with the money-lenders as their lawyer), to which, indeed, he was entitled for his unfurnished lodgings. About fifteen shillings I had employed in re-establishing (though in a very humble way) my dress. Of the remainder I gave one quarter to Ann, meaning on my return to have divided with her whatever might remain. These arrangements made,—soon after six o'clock, on a dark winter evening, I set off, accompanied by Ann, towards Piccadilly; for it was my intention to go down as far as Salt-hill on the Bath or Bristol Mail. Our course lay through a part of the town which has now all disappeared, so that I can no longer retrace its ancient boundaries: Swallow-street, I think it was called. Having time enough before us, however, we bore away to the left until we came into Golden-square: there, near the corner of Sherrard-street, we sat down; not wishing to part in the tumult and blaze of Piccadilly. I had told her of my plans some time before: and I now assured her again that she should share in my good fortune, if I met with any; and that I would never forsake her, as soon as

I had power to protect her. This I fully intended, as much from inclination as from a sense of duty: for, setting aside gratitude, which in any case must have made me her debtor for life, I loved her as affectionately as if she had been my sister: and at this moment, with sevenfold tenderness, from pity at witnessing her extreme dejection. I had, apparently, most reason for dejection, because I was leaving the saviour of my life: yet I, considering the shock my health had received, was cheerful and full of hope. She, on the contrary, who was parting with one who had had little means of serving her, except by kindness and brotherly treatment, was overcome by sorrow; so that, when I kissed her at our final farewell, she put her arms about my neck, and wept without speaking a word. I hoped to return in a week at farthest, and I agreed with her that on the fifth night from that, and every night afterwards, she should wait for me at six o'clock, near the bottom of Great Titchfield-street, which had been our customary haven, as it were, of rendezvous, to prevent our missing each other in the great Mediterranean of Oxford-street. This, and other measures of precaution I took: one only I forgot. She had either never told me, or (as a matter of no great interest) I had forgotten, her surname. It is a general practice, indeed, with girls of humble rank in her unhappy condition, not (as novel-reading women of higher pretensions) to style themselves—*Miss Douglass, Miss Montague*, &c. but simply by their Christian names, *Mary, Jane, Frances*, &c. Her surname, as the surest means of tracing her hereafter, I ought now to have inquired: but the truth is, having no reason to think that our meeting could, in consequence of a short interruption, be more difficult or uncertain than it had been for so many weeks, I had scarcely for a moment adverted to it as necessary, or placed it amongst my memoranda against this parting interview: and, my final anxieties being spent in comforting her with hopes, and in pressing upon her the necessity of getting some medicines for a violent cough and hoarseness with which she was troubled, I wholly forgot it until it was too late to recal her.

It was past eight o'clock when I reached the Gloucester Coffee-house:* and, the Bristol Mail being on the point of going off, I mounted on the outside. The fine fluent motion[1] of this Mail soon

---

[1] The Bristol Mail is the best appointed in the kingdom—owing to the double advantage of an unusually good road, and of an extra sum for expences subscribed by the Bristol merchants.

laid me asleep: it is somewhat remarkable, that the first easy or refreshing sleep which I had enjoyed for some months, was on the outside of a Mail-coach—a bed which, at this day, I find rather an uneasy one. Connected with this sleep was a little incident, which served, as hundreds of others did at that time, to convince me how easily a man who has never been in any great distress, may pass through life without knowing, in his own person at least, anything of the possible goodness of the human heart—or, as I must add with a sigh, of its possible vileness. So thick a curtain of *manners* is drawn over the features and expression of men's *natures*, that to the ordinary observer, the two extremities, and the infinite field of varieties which lie between them, are all confounded—the vast and multitudinous compass of their several harmonies reduced to the meagre outline of differences expressed in the gamut or alphabet of elementary sounds. The case was this: for the first four or five miles from London, I annoyed my fellow passenger on the roof by occasionally falling against him when the coach gave a lurch to his side; and indeed, if the road had been less smooth and level than it is, I should have fallen off from weakness. Of this annoyance he complained heavily, as perhaps, in the same circumstances most people would; he expressed his complaint, however, more morosely than the occasion seemed to warrant; and, if I had parted with him at that moment, I should have thought of him (if I had considered it worth while to think of him at all) as a surly and almost brutal fellow. However, I was conscious that I had given him some cause for complaint: and, therefore, I apologized to him, and assured him I would do what I could to avoid falling asleep for the future; and, at the same time, in as few words as possible, I explained to him that I was ill and in a weak state from long suffering; and that I could not afford at that time to take an inside place. The man's manner changed, upon hearing this explanation, in an instant: and when I next woke for a minute from the noise and lights of Hounslow (for in spite of my wishes and efforts I had fallen asleep again within two minutes from the time I had spoken to him) I found that he had put his arm round me to protect me from falling off: and for the rest of my journey he behaved to me with the gentleness of a woman, so that, at length, I almost lay in his arms: and this was the more kind, as he could not have known that I was not going the whole way to Bath or Bristol. Unfortunately, indeed, I *did* go rather farther than I intended: for so genial and refreshing was my sleep, that the next time, after leaving Hounslow that I fully awoke, was upon the sudden pulling up of the Mail (possibly at a Post-office); and, on inquiry, I found that we had reached Maidenhead—six or seven miles, I think, a-head of Salt-hill. Here I alighted: and for the half minute that the Mail stopped, I was entreated by my friendly companion (who, from the transient glimpse I had had of him in Piccadilly, seemed to me to be a gentleman's butler—or person of that rank) to go to bed without delay. This I promised, though with no intention of doing so: and in fact, I immediately set forward, or rather backward, on foot. It must then have been nearly midnight: but so slowly did I creep along, that I heard a clock in a cottage strike four before I turned down the lane from Slough to Eton. The air and the sleep had both refreshed me; but I was weary nevertheless. I remember a thought (obvious enough, and which has been prettily expressed by a Roman poet)* which gave me some consolation at that moment under my poverty. There had been some time before a murder committed on or near Hounslow-heath. I think I cannot be mistaken when I say that the name of the murdered person was *Steele*,* and that he was the owner of a lavender plantation in that neighbourhood.* Every step of my progress was bringing me nearer to the Heath: and it naturally occurred to me that I and the accursed murderer, if he were that night abroad, might at every instant be unconsciously approaching each other through the darkness: in which case, said I,—supposing I, instead of being (as indeed I am) little better than an outcast,—

Lord of my learning and no land beside,*

were, like my friend, Lord ————,* heir by general repute to 70,000*l.* per. ann., what a panic should I be under at this moment about my throat!—indeed, it was not likely that Lord ———— should ever be in my situation. But nevertheless, the spirit of the remark remains true—that vast power and possessions make a man shamefully afraid of dying: and I am convinced that many of the most intrepid adventurers, who, by fortunately being poor, enjoy the full use of their natural courage, would, if at the very instant of going into action news were brought to them that they had unexpectedly succeeded to an estate in England of 50,000*l.* a year, feel their dislike to bullets considerably sharpened[1]—and their efforts at

[1] It will be objected that many men, of the highest rank and wealth, have in our own day, as well as throughout our history, been amongst the foremost in courting danger

perfect equanimity and self-possession proportionably difficult. So true it is, in the language of a wise man whose own experience had made him acquainted with both fortunes, that riches are better fitted—

> To slacken virtue, and abate her edge,
> Than tempt her to do aught may merit praise.
> *Parad. Regained.**

I dally with my subject because, to myself, the remembrance of these times is profoundly interesting. But my reader shall not have any further cause to complain: for I now hasten to its close.—In the road between Slough and Eton, I fell asleep: and, just as the morning began to dawn, I was awakened by the voice of a man standing over me and surveying me. I know not what he was: he was an ill-looking fellow—but not therefore of necessity an ill-meaning fellow: or, if he were, I suppose he thought that no person sleeping out-of-doors in winter could be worth robbing. In which conclusion, however, as it regarded myself, I beg to assure him, if he should be among my readers, that he was mistaken. After a slight remark he passed on: and I was not sorry at his disturbance, as it enabled me to pass through Eton before people were generally up. The night had been heavy and lowering: but towards the morning it had changed to a slight frost: and the ground and the trees were now covered with rime. I slipped through Eton unobserved; washed myself, and, as far as possible, adjusted my dress at a little public-house in Windsor; and about eight o'clock went down towards Pote's.* On my road I met some junior boys of whom I made inquiries: an Etonian is always a gentleman; and, in spite of my shabby habiliments, they answered me civilly. My friend, Lord ————, was gone to the University of ————.* 'Ibi omnis effusus labor!'* I had, however, other friends at Eton: but it is not to all who wear that name in prosperity that a man is willing to present himself in distress. On recollecting myself, however, I asked for the Earl of D————,* to whom, (though my acquaintance with him was not so intimate as with some others) I should not have shrunk from presenting myself under any circumstances. He was still at Eton, though I believe on the wing for Cambridge. I called, was received kindly, and asked to breakfast.

---

in battle. True: but this is not the case supposed: long familiarity with power has to them deadened its effect and its attractions.

Here let me stop for a moment to check my reader from any erroneous conclusions: because I have had occasion incidentally to speak of various patrician friends, it must not be supposed that I have myself any pretensions to rank or high blood. I thank God that I have not:—I am the son of a plain English merchant, esteemed during his life for his great integrity, and strongly attached to literary pursuits (indeed, he was himself, anonymously, an author):* if he had lived, it was expected that he would have been very rich; but, dying prematurely, he left no more than about 30,000*l*. amongst seven different claimants. My mother I may mention with honour, as still more highly gifted. For, though unpretending to the name and honours of a *literary* woman, I shall presume to call her (what many literary women are not) an *intellectual* woman: and I believe that if ever her letters should be collected and published, they would be thought generally to exhibit as much strong and masculine sense, delivered in as pure 'mother English,'* racy and fresh with idiomatic graces, as any in our language—hardly excepting those of lady M. W. Montague.*—These are my honours of descent: I have no others: and I have thanked God sincerely that I have not, because, in my judgment, a station which raises a man too eminently above the level of his fellow-creatures is not the most favourable to moral, or to intellectual qualities.

Lord D—— placed before me a most magnificent breakfast. It was really so; but in my eyes it seemed trebly magnificent—from being the first regular meal, the first 'good man's table,'* that I had sate down to for months. Strange to say, however, I could scarcely eat any thing. On the day when I first received my 10*l*. Bank-note, I had gone to a baker's shop and bought a couple of rolls: this very shop I had two months or six weeks before surveyed with an eagerness of desire which it was almost humiliating to me to recollect. I remembered the story about Otway; and feared that there might be danger in eating too rapidly.* But I had no need for alarm, my appetite was quite sunk, and I became sick before I had eaten half of what I had bought. This effect from eating what approached to a meal, I continued to feel for weeks: or, when I did not experience any nausea, part of what I ate was rejected, sometimes with acidity, sometimes immediately, and without any acidity. On the present occasion, at lord D——'s table, I found myself not at all better than usual: and, in the midst of luxuries, I had no appetite. I had, however, unfortunately at all times a craving for wine: I explained my situation, therefore, to lord D———, and gave him a short account of my late sufferings, at which he expressed great compassion, and called for wine. This gave me a momentary relief and pleasure; and on all occasions when I had an opportunity, I never failed to drink wine—which I worshipped then as I have since worshipped opium. I am convinced, however, that this indulgence in wine contributed to strengthen my malady; for the tone of my stomach was apparently quite sunk; but by a better regimen it might sooner, and perhaps effectually, have been revived. I hope that it was not from this love of wine that I lingered in the neighbourhood of my Eton friends: I persuaded myself *then* that it was from reluctance to ask of Lord D———, on whom I was conscious I had not sufficient claims, the particular service in quest of which I had come down to Eton. I was, however, unwilling to lose my journey, and—I asked it. Lord D———, whose good nature was unbounded, and which, in regard to myself, had been measured rather by his compassion perhaps for my condition, and his knowledge of my intimacy with some of his relatives,* than by an over-rigorous inquiry into the extent of my own direct claims, faultered, nevertheless, at this request. He acknowledged that he did not like to have any dealings with money-lenders, and feared lest such a transaction might come to the ears of his connexions. Moreover, he doubted whether *his* signature, whose expectations were so much more bounded than those of ————, would avail with my unchristian friends. However, he did not wish, as it seemed, to mortify me by an absolute refusal: for after a little consideration, he promised, under certain conditions which he pointed out, to give his security. Lord D——— was at this time not eighteen years of age: but I have often doubted, on recollecting since the good sense and prudence which on this occasion he mingled with so much urbanity of manner (an urbanity which in him wore the grace of youthful sincerity), whether any statesman—the oldest and the most accomplished in diplomacy—could have acquitted himself better under the same circumstances. Most people, indeed, cannot be addressed on such a business, without surveying you with looks as austere and unpropitious as those of a Saracen's head.

Recomforted by this promise, which was not quite equal to the best, but far above the worst that I had pictured to myself as possible, I returned in a Windsor coach to London three days after I had quitted it. And now I come to the end of my story:—the Jews did not approve of Lord D——'s terms; whether they would in the end have acceded to them, and were only seeking time for making due inquiries, I know not; but many delays were made—time passed on—the small fragment of my bank note had just melted away; and before any conclusion could have been put to the business, I must have relapsed into my former state of wretchedness. Suddenly, however, at this crisis, an opening was made, almost by accident, for reconciliation with my friends. I quitted London, in haste, for a remote part of England: after some time, I proceeded to the university; and it was not until many months had passed away, that I had it in my power again to re-visit the ground which had become so interesting to me, and to this day remains so, as the chief scene of my youthful sufferings.

Meantime, what had become of poor Anne? For her I have reserved my concluding words: according to our agreement, I sought her daily, and waited for her every night, so long as I staid in London, at the corner of Titchfield-street. I inquired for her of every one who was likely to know her; and, during the last hours of my stay in London, I put into activity every means of tracing her that my knowledge of London suggested, and the limited extent of my power made possible. The street where she had lodged I knew, but not the house; and I remembered at last some account which she had given me of ill treatment from her landlord, which made it probable that she had quitted those lodgings before we parted. She had few acquaintance; most people, besides, thought that the earnestness of my inquiries arose from motives which moved their laughter, or their slight regard; and others, thinking I was in chase of a girl who had robbed me of some trifles, were naturally and excusably indisposed to give me any clue to her, if, indeed, they had any to give. Finally, as my despairing resource, on the day I left London I put into the hands of the only person who (I was sure) must know Anne by sight, from having been in company with us once or twice, an address to —————— in ——shire,* at that time the residence of my family. But, to this hour, I have never heard a syllable about her. This, amongst such troubles as most men meet with in this life, has been my heaviest affliction.—If she lived, doubtless we must have been sometimes in search of each other, at the very same moment, through the mighty labyrinths of London; perhaps, even within a few feet of each other—a barrier no wider in a London street, often amounting in the end to a separation for eternity! During some years, I hoped that she *did* live;·and I suppose that, in the literal and unrhetorical use of the word *myriad*, I may say that on my different visits to London, I have looked into many, many myriads of female faces, in the hope of meeting her. I should know her again amongst a thousand, if I saw her for a moment; for, though not handsome, she had a sweet expression of countenance, and a peculiar and graceful carriage of the head.—I sought her, I have said, in hope. So it was for years; but now I should fear to see her; and her cough, which grieved me when I parted with her, is now my consolation. I now wish to see her no longer; but think of her, more gladly, as one long since laid in the grave; in the grave, I would hope, of a Magdalen;* taken away, before injuries and cruelty had blotted out and transfigured her ingenuous nature, or the brutalities of ruffians had completed the ruin they had begun.

[*The remainder of this very interesting Article will be given in the next Number.* ED.*]

PART II

So then, Oxford-street, stony-hearted step-mother! thou that listenest to the sighs of orphans, and drinkest the tears of children, at length I was dismissed from thee: the time was come at last that I no more should pace in anguish thy never-ending terraces; no more should dream, and wake in captivity to the pangs of hunger. Successors, too many, to myself and Ann, have, doubtless, since then trodden in our footsteps—inheritors of our calamities: other orphans than Ann have sighed: tears have been shed by other children: and thou, Oxford-street, hast since, doubtless, echoed to the groans of innumerable hearts. For myself, however, the storm which I had outlived seemed to have been the pledge of a long fair-weather; the premature sufferings which I had paid down, to have been accepted as a ransom for many years to come, as a price of long immunity from sorrow: and if again I walked in London, a solitary and contemplative man (as oftentimes I did), I walked for the most part in serenity and peace of mind. And, although it is true that the calamities of my noviciate in London had struck root so deeply in my bodily constitution that afterwards they shot up and flourished afresh, and grew into a noxious umbrage that has overshadowed and darkened my latter years, yet these second assaults of suffering were met with a fortitude more confirmed, with the resources of a maturer intellect, and with alleviations from sympathising affection—how deep and tender!

Thus, however, with whatsoever alleviations, years that were far asunder were bound together by subtle links of suffering derived from a common root.* And herein I notice an instance of the shortsightedness of human desires, that oftentimes on moonlight nights, during my first mournful abode in London, my consolation was (if such it could be thought) to gaze from Oxford-street up every avenue in succession which pierces through the heart of Marylebone to the fields and the woods; for *that*, said I, travelling with my eyes up the long vistas which lay part in light and part in shade, '*that* is the road to the North, and therefore to ————,* and if I had the wings of a dove, *that* way I would fly for comfort.'* Thus I said, and thus I wished, in my blindness; yet, even in that very northern region it was, even in that very valley, nay, in that very house to which my erroneous wishes pointed, that this second birth of my sufferings began;* and that they again threatened to besiege the citadel of life and hope. There it was, that for years I was persecuted by visions as ugly, and as ghastly phantoms as ever haunted the couch of an Orestes:* and in this unhappier than he, that sleep, which comes to all as a respite and a restoration, and to him especially, as a blessed[1] balm for his wounded heart and his haunted brain, visited me as my bitterest scourge. Thus blind was I in my desires; yet, if a veil interposes between the dim-sightedness of man and his future calamities, the same veil hides from him their alleviations; and a grief which had not been feared is met by consolations which had not been hoped. I, therefore, who participated, as it were, in the troubles of Orestes (excepting only in his agitated conscience), participated no less in all his supports: my Eumenides,* like his, were at my bed-feet, and stared in upon me through the curtains: but, watching by my pillow, or defrauding herself of sleep to bear me company through the heavy watches of the night, sate my Electra: for thou, beloved M.,* dear companion of my later years, thou wast my Electra! and neither in nobility of mind nor in long-suffering affection, wouldst permit that a Grecian sister should excel an English wife. For thou thoughtst not

---

[1] φίλον ὕπνου θελγήτρον ἐπίκουρον νόσου.*

much to stoop to humble offices of kindness, and to servile[1] ministrations of tenderest affection;—to wipe away for years the unwholesome dews upon the forehead, or to refresh the lips when parched and baked with fever; nor, even when thy own peaceful slumbers had by long sympathy become infected with the spectacle of my dread contest with phantoms and shadowy enemies that oftentimes bade me 'sleep no more!'*—not even then, didst thou utter a complaint or any murmur, nor withdraw thy angelic smiles, nor shrink from thy service of love more than Electra did of old. For she too, though she was a Grecian woman, and the daughter of the king[2] of men, yet wept sometimes, and hid her face[3] in her robe.

But these troubles are past: and thou wilt read these records of a period so dolorous to us both as the legend of some hideous dream that can return no more. Meantime, I am again in London: and again I pace the terraces of Oxford-street by night: and oftentimes, when I am oppressed by anxieties that demand all my philosophy and the comfort of thy presence to support, and yet remember that I am separated from thee by three hundred miles, and the length of three dreary months,—I look up the streets that run northwards from Oxford-street, upon moonlight nights, and recollect my youthful ejaculation of anguish;—and remembering that thou art sitting alone in that same valley, and mistress of that very house* to which my heart turned in its blindness nineteen years ago, I think that, though blind indeed, and scattered to the winds of late, the promptings of my heart may yet have had reference to a remoter time, and may be justified if read in another meaning:—and, if I could allow myself to descend again to the impotent wishes of childhood, I should again say to myself, as I look to the north, 'Oh, that I had the wings of a dove—' and with how just a confidence in thy good and gracious nature might I add the other half of my early ejaculation—'And *that* way I would fly for comfort.'

[1] ἡδυ δουλευμα. *Eurip. Orest.**
[2] ἀναξάνδρων Ἀγαμεμνων.*
[3] ὀμμα θεισ' ἐισω πεπλων.* The scholar will know that throughout this passage I refer to the early scenes of the Orestes; one of the most beautiful exhibitions of the domestic affections which even the dramas of Euripides can furnish. To the English reader, it may be necessary to say, that the situation at the opening of the drama is that of a brother attended only by his sister during the demoniacal possession of a suffering conscience (or, in the mythology of the play, haunted by the furies), and in circumstances of immediate danger from enemies, and of desertion or cold regard from nominal friends.

THE PLEASURES OF OPIUM

It is so long since I first took opium, that if it had been a trifling incident in my life, I might have forgotten its date: but cardinal events are
not to be forgotten; and from circumstances connected with it,
I remember that it must be referred to the autumn of 1804. During
that season I was in London, having come thither for the first time
since my entrance at college.* And my introduction to opium arose in
the following way. From an early age I had been accustomed to wash
my head in cold water at least once a day: being suddenly seized with
tooth-ache, I attributed it to some relaxation caused by an accidental
intermission of that practice; jumped out of bed; plunged my head
into a bason of cold water; and with hair thus wetted went to sleep.
The next morning, as I need hardly say, I awoke with excruciating
rheumatic pains of the head and face, from which I had hardly any
respite for about twenty days. On the twenty-first day, I think it was,
and on a Sunday, that I went out into the streets; rather to run away,
if possible, from my torments, than with any distinct purpose. By
accident I met a college acquaintance who recommended opium.
Opium! dread agent of unimaginable pleasure and pain! I had heard
of it as I had of manna or of Ambrosia, but no further:* how unmean-
ing a sound was it at that time! what solemn chords does it now strike
upon my heart! what heart-quaking vibrations of sad and happy
remembrances! Reverting for a moment to these, I feel a mystic
importance attached to the minutest circumstances connected with
the place and the time, and the man (if man he was) that first laid open
to me the Paradise of Opium-eaters. It was a Sunday afternoon,
wet and cheerless: and a duller spectacle this earth of ours has not
to show* than a rainy Sunday in London. My road homewards
lay through Oxford-street; and near 'the *stately* Pantheon,'* (as
Mr Wordsworth has obligingly called it) I saw a druggist's shop. The
druggist—unconscious minister of celestial pleasures!—as if in
sympathy with the rainy Sunday, looked dull and stupid, just as any
mortal druggist might be expected to look on a Sunday: and, when
I asked for the tincture of opium, he gave it to me as any other man
might do: and furthermore, out of my shilling, returned me what
seemed to be real copper halfpence, taken out of a real wooden drawer.
Nevertheless, in spite of such indications of humanity, he has ever
since existed in my mind as the beatific vision of an immortal druggist,

sent down to earth on a special mission to myself. And it confirms me in this way of considering him, that, when I next came up to London, I sought him near the stately Pantheon, and found him not: and thus to me, who knew not his name (if indeed he had one) he seemed rather to have vanished from Oxford-street than to have removed in any bodily fashion. The reader may choose to think of him as, possibly, no more than a sublunary druggist: it may be so: but my faith is better: I believe him to have evanesced,[1] or evaporated. So unwillingly would I connect any mortal remembrances with that hour, and place, and creature, that first brought me acquainted with the celestial drug.

Arrived at my lodgings, it may be supposed that I lost not a moment in taking the quantity prescribed. I was necessarily ignorant of the whole art and mystery of opium-taking: and, what I took, I took under every disadvantage. But I took it:—and in an hour, oh! Heavens! what a revulsion!* what an upheaving, from its lowest depths, of the inner spirit!* what an apocalypse of the world within me!* That my pains had vanished, was now a trifle in my eyes:—this negative effect was swallowed up in the immensity of those positive effects which had opened before me—in the abyss of divine enjoyment thus suddenly revealed. Here was a panacea—a φαρμακον νήπενθες* for all human woes: here was the secret of happiness, about which philosophers had disputed for so many ages, at once discovered: happiness might now be bought for a penny, and carried in the waistcoat pocket: portable ecstacies might be had corked up in a pint bottle: and peace of mind could be sent down in gallons by the mail coach. But, if I talk in this way, the reader will think I am laughing: and I can assure him, that nobody will laugh long who deals much with opium: its pleasures even are of a grave and solemn complexion; and in his happiest state, the opium-eater cannot present himself in the character of *l'Allegro*: even then, he speaks and thinks as becomes *Il Penseroso*.* Nevertheless, I have a very reprehensible way of jesting

---

[1] *Evanesced*:—this way of going off the stage of life appears to have been well known in the 17th century, but at that time to have been considered a peculiar privilege of blood-royal, and by no means to be allowed to druggists. For about the year 1686, a poet of rather ominous name (and who, by the bye, did ample justice to his name), viz. Mr *Flat-man*, in speaking of the death of Charles II expresses his surprise that any prince should commit so absurd an act as dying; because, says he,

Kings should disdain to die, and only *disappear*.*

They should *abscond*, that is, into the other world.

at times in the midst of my own misery: and, unless when I am checked by some more powerful feelings, I am afraid I shall be guilty of this indecent practice even in these annals of suffering or enjoyment. The reader must allow a little to my infirm nature in this respect: and with a few indulgences of that sort, I shall endeavour to be as grave, if not drowsy, as fits a theme like opium, so anti-mercurial* as it really is, and so drowsy as it is falsely reputed.

And, first, one word with respect to its bodily effects: for upon all that has been hitherto written on the subject of opium, whether by travellers in Turkey* (who may plead their privilege of lying as an old immemorial right), or by professors of medicine, writing *ex cathedra*,*—I have but one emphatic criticism to pronounce—Lies! lies! lies! I remember once, in passing a book-stall, to have caught these words from a page of some satiric author:*—'By this time I became convinced that the London newspapers spoke truth at least twice a week, viz. on Tuesday and Saturday, and might safely be depended upon for—the list of bankrupts.'* In like manner, I do by no means deny that some truths have been delivered to the world in regard to opium: thus it has been repeatedly affirmed by the learned, that opium is a dusky brown in colour; and this, take notice, I grant: secondly, that it is rather dear; which also I grant:* for in my time, East-India opium has been three guineas a pound, and Turkey eight: and, thirdly, that if you eat a good deal of it, most probably you must——do what is particularly disagreeable to any man of regular habits, viz. die.[1] These weighty propositions are, all and singular, true: I cannot gainsay them: and truth ever was, and will be, commendable. But in these three theorems, I believe we have exhausted the stock of knowledge as yet accumulated by man on the subject of opium. And therefore, worthy doctors, as there seems to be room for further discoveries, stand aside, and allow me to come forward and lecture on this matter.

First, then, it is not so much affirmed as taken for granted, by all who ever mention opium, formally or incidentally, that it does, or

---

[1] Of this, however, the learned appear latterly to have doubted: for in a pirated edition of Buchan's *Domestic Medicine*,* which I once saw in the hands of a farmer's wife who was studying it for the benefit of her health, the Doctor was made to say—'Be particularly careful never to take above five-and-twenty *ounces* of laudanum at once:' the true reading being probably five and twenty *drops*, which are held equal to about one grain of crude opium.

can, produce intoxication. Now, reader, assure yourself, *meo peric-ulo*,* that no quantity of opium ever did, or could intoxicate. As to the tincture of opium (commonly called laudanum) *that* might certainly intoxicate if a man could bear to take enough of it; but why? because it contains so much proof spirit, and not because it contains so much opium.* But crude opium, I affirm peremptorily, is incapable of pro-ducing any state of body at all resembling that which is produced by alcohol; and not in *degree* only incapable, but even in *kind*: it is not in the quantity of its effects merely, but in the quality, that it differs altogether. The pleasure given by wine is always mounting, and tend-ing to a crisis, after which it declines: that from opium, when once generated, is stationary for eight or ten hours: the first, to borrow a technical distinction from medicine, is a case of acute—the second, of chronic pleasure: the one is a flame, the other a steady and equable glow. But the main distinction lies in this, that whereas wine dis-orders the mental faculties, opium, on the contrary (if taken in a proper manner), introduces amongst them the most exquisite order, legisla-tion, and harmony. Wine robs a man of his self-possession: opium greatly invigorates it. Wine unsettles and clouds the judgment, and gives a preternatural brightness, and a vivid exaltation to the con-tempts and the admirations, the loves and the hatreds, of the drinker: opium, on the contrary, communicates serenity and equipoise to all the faculties, active or passive: and with respect to the temper and moral feelings in general, it gives simply that sort of vital warmth which is approved by the judgment, and which would probably always accompany a bodily constitution of primeval or antedilu-vian health. Thus, for instance, opium, like wine, gives an expan-sion to the heart and the benevolent affections: but then, with this remarkable difference, that in the sudden developement of kind-heartedness which accompanies inebriation, there is always more or less of a maudlin character, which exposes it to the contempt of the by-stander. Men shake hands, swear eternal friendship, and shed tears—no mortal knows why: and the sensual creature is clearly uppermost. But the expansion of the benigner feelings, incident to opium, is no febrile access, but a healthy restoration to that state which the mind would naturally recover upon the removal of any deep-seated irritation of pain that had disturbed and quarrelled with the impulses of a heart originally just and good. True it is, that even wine, up to a certain point, and with certain men, rather tends to exalt and to steady the intellect: I myself, who have never been a great wine-drinker, used to find that half a dozen glasses of wine advantageously affected the faculties—brightened and intensified the consciousness—and gave to the mind a feeling of being 'ponderibus librata suis:'* and certainly it is most absurdly said, in popular language, of any man, that he is *disguised* in liquor: for, on the contrary, most men are disguised by sobriety; and it is when they are drinking (as some old gentleman says in Athenaeus), that men ἑαντούς ἐμφανίζουσιν οἵτινες εἰσίν—display themselves in their true complexion of character;* which surely is not disguising themselves. But still, wine constantly leads a man to the brink of absurdity and extravagance; and, beyond a certain point, it is sure to volatilize and to disperse the intellectual energies: whereas opium always seems to compose what had been agitated, and to concentrate what had been distracted. In short, to sum up all in one word, a man who is inebriated, or tending to inebriation, is, and feels that he is, in a condition which calls up into supremacy the merely human, too often the brutal, part of his nature: but the opium-eater (I speak of him who is not suffering from any disease, or other remote effects of opium) feels that the diviner part of his nature is paramount; that is, the moral affections are in a state of cloudless serenity; and over all is the great light of the majestic intellect.*

This is the doctrine of the true church on the subject of opium: of which church I acknowledge myself to be the only member—the alpha and the omega:* but then it is to be recollected, that I speak from the ground of a large and profound personal experience: whereas most of the unscientific[1] authors who have at all treated of opium, and

[1] Amongst the great herd of travellers, &c. who show sufficiently by their stupidity that they never held any intercourse with opium, I must caution my reader specially against the brilliant author of '*Anastasius.*'* This gentleman, whose wit would lead one to presume him an opium-eater, has made it impossible to consider him in that character from the grievous misrepresentation which he gives of its effects, at p. 215–17, of vol. I.—Upon consideration, it must appear such to the author himself: for, waiving the errors I have insisted on in the text, which (and others) are adopted in the fullest manner, he will himself admit, that an old gentleman 'with a snow-white beard,' who eats 'ample doses of opium,' and is yet able to deliver what is meant and received as very weighty counsel on the bad effects of that practice, is but an indifferent evidence that opium either kills people prematurely, or sends them into a madhouse. But, for my part, I see into this old gentleman and his motives: the fact is, he was enamoured of 'the little golden receptacle of the pernicious drug' which Anastasius carried about him; and no way of obtaining it so safe and so feasible occurred, as that of frightening its owner out of his wits (which, by the bye, are none of the strongest). This commentary throws a new light

even of those who have written expressly on the materia medica,* make it evident, from the horror they express of it, that their experimental knowledge of its action is none at all. I will, however, candidly acknowledge that I have met with one person* who bore evidence to its intoxicating power, such as staggered my own incredulity: for he was a surgeon, and had himself taken opium largely. I happened to say to him, that his enemies (as I had heard) charged him with talking nonsense on politics, and that his friends apologized for him, by suggesting that he was constantly in a state of intoxication from opium. Now the accusation, said I, is not *primâ facie*,* and of necessity, an absurd one: but the defence *is*. To my surprise, however, he insisted that both his enemies and his friends were in the right: 'I will maintain,' said he, 'that I *do* talk nonsense; and secondly, I will maintain that I do not talk nonsense upon principle, or with any view to profit, but solely and simply, said he, solely and simply,—solely and simply (repeating it three times over), because I am drunk with opium; and *that* daily.' I replied that, as to the allegation of his enemies, as it seemed to be established upon such respectable testimony, seeing that the three parties concerned all agreed in it, it did not become me to question it; but the defence set up I must demur to. He proceeded to discuss the matter, and to lay down his reasons: but it seemed to me so impolite to pursue an argument which must have presumed a man mistaken in a point belonging to his own profession, that I did not press him even when his course of argument seemed open to objection: not to mention that a man who talks nonsense, even though 'with no view to profit,' is not altogether the most agreeable partner in a dispute, whether as opponent or respondent. I confess, however, that the authority of a surgeon, and one who was reputed a good one, may seem a weighty one to my prejudice: but still I must plead my experience, which was greater than his greatest by 7000 drops a day; and, though it was not possible to suppose a medical man unacquainted with the characteristic symptoms of vinous intoxication, it yet struck me that he might proceed on a logical error of using the word intoxication with too great latitude, and extending it generically to all modes of nervous excitement, instead of restricting it as the expression for a specific sort of excitement, connected with

upon the case, and greatly improves it as a story: for the old gentleman's speech, considered as a lecture on pharmacy, is highly absurd: but, considered as a hoax on Anastasius, it reads excellently.

certain diagnostics. Some people have maintained, in my hearing, that they had been drunk upon green tea:* and a medical student in London, for whose knowledge in his profession I have reason to feel great respect, assured me, the other day, that a patient, in recovering from an illness, had got drunk on a beef-steak.

Having dwelt so much on this first and leading error, in respect to opium, I shall notice very briefly a second and a third; which are, that the elevation of spirits produced by opium is necessarily followed by a proportionate depression, and that the natural and even immediate consequence of opium is torpor and stagnation, animal and mental. The first of these errors I shall content myself with simply denying; assuring my reader, that for ten years, during which I took opium at intervals, the day succeeding to that on which I allowed myself this luxury was always a day of unusually good spirits.

With respect to the torpor supposed to follow, or rather (if we were to credit the numerous pictures of Turkish opium-eaters)* to accompany the practice of opium-eating, I deny that also. Certainly, opium is classed under the head of narcotics; and some such effect it may produce in the end: but the primary effects of opium are always, and in the highest degree, to excite and stimulate the system:* this first stage of its action always lasted with me, during my noviciate, for upwards of eight hours; so that it must be the fault of the opium-eater himself if he does not so time his exhibition of the dose (to speak medically)* as that the whole weight of its narcotic influence may descend upon his sleep. Turkish opium-eaters, it seems, are absurd enough to sit, like so many equestrian statues, on logs of wood as stupid as themselves. But that the reader may judge of the degree in which opium is likely to stupify the faculties of an Englishman, I shall (by way of treating the question illustratively, rather than argumentatively) describe the way in which I myself often passed an opium evening in London, during the period between 1804–1812. It will be seen, that at least opium did not move me to seek solitude, and much less to seek inactivity, or the torpid state of self-involution ascribed to the Turks. I give this account at the risk of being pronounced a crazy enthusiast or visionary: but I regard *that* little: I must desire my reader to bear in mind, that I was a hard student, and at severe studies for all the rest of my time: and certainly I had a right occasionally to relaxations as well as other people: these, however, I allowed myself but seldom.

The late Duke of ——— used to say, 'Next Friday, by the blessing of Heaven, I purpose to be drunk:'* and in like manner I used to
fix beforehand how often, within a given time, and when, I would
commit a debauch of opium. This was seldom more than once in
three weeks: for at that time I could not have ventured to call every
day (as I did afterwards) for '*a glass of laudanum negus, warm, and
without sugar.*'* No: as I have said, I seldom drank laudanum, at that
time, more than once in three weeks:* this was usually on a Tuesday
or a Saturday night; my reason for which was this. In those days
Grassini* sang at the Opera: and her voice was delightful to me
beyond all that I had ever heard. I know not what may be the state of
the Opera-house now, having never been within its walls for seven or
eight years, but at that time it was by much the most pleasant place of
public resort in London for passing an evening. Five shillings admitted one to the gallery, which was subject to far less annoyance than
the pit of the theatres: the orchestra was distinguished by its sweet
and melodious grandeur from all English orchestras, the composition
of which, I confess, is not acceptable to my ear, from the predomin-
ance of the clangorous instruments, and the absolute tyranny of the
violin.* The choruses were divine to hear: and when Grassini
appeared in some interlude, as she often did, and poured forth her
passionate soul as Andromache, at the tomb of Hector,* &c. I question whether any Turk, of all that ever entered the Paradise of opium-
eaters, can have had half the pleasure I had. But, indeed, I honour the
Barbarians too much by supposing them capable of any pleasures
approaching to the intellectual ones of an Englishman. For music is
an intellectual or a sensual pleasure, according to the temperament of
him who hears it. And, by the bye, with the exception of the fine
extravaganza on that subject in Twelfth Night,* I do not recollect
more than one thing said adequately on the subject of music in all
literature: it is a passage in the *Religio Medici*[1] of Sir T. Brown;* and,
though chiefly remarkable for its sublimity, has also a philosophic
value, inasmuch as it points to the true theory of musical effects. The
mistake of most people is to suppose that it is by the ear they communicate with music, and, therefore, that they are purely passive to
its effects. But this is not so: it is by the re-action of the mind upon

---

[1] I have not the book at this moment to consult: but I think the passage begins—'And
even that tavern music, which makes one man merry, another mad, in me strikes a deep
fit of devotion,' &c.

the notices of the ear, (the *matter* coming by the senses, the *form* from the mind) that the pleasure is constructed: and therefore it is that people of equally good ear differ so much in this point from one another. Now opium, by greatly increasing the activity of the mind generally, increases, of necessity, that particular mode of its activity by which we are able to construct out of the raw material of organic sound an elaborate intellectual pleasure. But, says a friend, a succession of musical sounds is to me like a collection of Arabic characters: I can attach no ideas to them. Ideas! my good sir? there is no occasion for them: all that class of ideas, which can be available in such a case, has a language of representative feelings. But this is a subject foreign to my present purposes: it is sufficient to say, that a chorus, &c. of elaborate harmony, displayed before me, as in a piece of arras work, the whole of my past life—not, as if recalled by an act of memory, but as if present and incarnated in the music: no longer painful to dwell upon: but the detail of its incidents removed, or blended in some hazy abstraction; and its passions exalted, spiritualized, and sublimed. All this was to be had for five shillings. And over and above the music of the stage and the orchestra, I had all around me, in the intervals of the performance, the music of the Italian language talked by Italian women: for the gallery was usually crowded with Italians: and I listened with a pleasure such as that with which Weld the traveller lay and listened, in Canada, to the sweet laughter of Indian women;* for the less you understand of a language, the more sensible you are to the melody or harshness of its sounds: for such a purpose, therefore, it was an advantage to me that I was a poor Italian scholar, reading it but little, and not speaking it at all, nor understanding a tenth part of what I heard spoken.

These were my Opera pleasures: but another pleasure I had which, as it could be had only on a Saturday night, occasionally struggled with my love of the Opera; for, at that time, Tuesday and Saturday were the regular Opera nights. On this subject I am afraid I shall be rather obscure, but, I can assure the reader, not at all more so than Marinus in his life of Proclus,* or many other biographers and auto-biographers of fair reputation. This pleasure, I have said, was to be had only on a Saturday night. What then was Saturday night to me more than any other night? I had no labours that I rested from;* no wages to receive: what needed I to care for Saturday night, more than as it was a summons to hear Grassini? True, most logical reader: what you say is unanswerable. And yet so it was and is, that, whereas different men throw their feelings into different channels, and most are apt to show their interest in the concerns of the poor, chiefly by sympathy, expressed in some shape or other, with their distresses and sorrows, I, at that time, was disposed to express my interest by sympathising with their pleasures. The pains of poverty I had lately seen too much of; more than I wished to remember: but the pleasures of the poor, their consolations of spirit, and their reposes from bodily toil, can never become oppressive to contemplate. Now Saturday night is the season for the chief, regular, and periodic return of rest to the poor: in this point the most hostile sects unite, and acknowledge a common link of brotherhood: almost all Christendom rests from its labours. It is a rest introductory to another rest: and divided by a whole day and two nights from the renewal of toil. On this account I feel always, on a Saturday night, as though I also were released from some yoke of labour, had some wages to receive, and some luxury of repose to enjoy. For the sake, therefore, of witnessing, upon as large a scale as possible, a spectacle with which my sympathy was so entire, I used often, on Saturday nights, after I had taken opium, to wander forth, without much regarding the direction or the distance, to all the markets, and other parts of London, to which the poor resort on a Saturday night,* for laying out their wages. Many a family party, consisting of a man, his wife, and sometimes one or two of his children, have I listened to, as they stood consulting on their ways and means, or the strength of their exchequer, or the price of household articles. Gradually I became familiar with their wishes, their difficulties, and their opinions. Sometimes there might be heard murmurs of discontent: but far oftener expressions on the countenance, or uttered in words, of patience, hope, and tranquillity. And taken generally, I must say, that, in this point at least, the poor are far more philosophic than the rich—that they show a more ready and cheerful submission to what they consider as irremediable evils, or irreparable losses. Whenever I saw occasion, or could do it without appearing to be intrusive, I joined their parties; and gave my opinion upon the matter in discussion, which, if not always judicious, was always received indulgently. If wages were a little higher, or expected to be so, or the quartern loaf* a little lower, or it was reported that onions and butter were expected to fall, I was glad: yet, if the contrary were true, I drew from opium some means of consoling myself. For opium (like the bee, that extracts its materials indiscriminately from roses and from the soot of chimneys)* can overrule all feelings into a compliance with the master key. Some of these rambles led me to great distances: for an opium-eater is too happy to observe the motion of time. And sometimes in my attempts to steer homewards, upon nautical principles, by fixing my eye on the pole-star, and seeking ambitiously for a north-west passage,* instead of circumnavigating all the capes and head-lands I had doubled in my outward voyage, I came suddenly upon such knotty problems of alleys, such enigmatical entries, and such sphynx's riddles of streets without thoroughfares, as must, I conceive, baffle the audacity of porters, and confound the intellects of hackney-coachmen. I could almost have believed, at times, that I must be the first discoverer of some of these *terrae incognitae*,* and doubted, whether they had yet been laid down in the modern charts of London. For all this, however, I paid a heavy price in distant years, when the human face tyrannized over my dreams, and the perplexities of my steps in London came back and haunted my sleep, with the feeling of perplexities moral or intellectual, that brought confusion to the reason, or anguish and remorse to the conscience.

Thus I have shown that opium does not, of necessity, produce inactivity or torpor; but that, on the contrary, it often led me into markets and theatres. Yet, in candour, I will admit that markets and theatres are not the appropriate haunts of the opium-eater, when in the divinest state incident to his enjoyment. In that state, crowds become an oppression to him; music even, too sensual and gross. He naturally seeks solitude and silence, as indispensable conditions of those trances, or profoundest reveries, which are the crown and consummation of what opium can do for human nature. I, whose disease it was to meditate too much, and to observe too little, and who, upon my first entrance at college, was nearly falling into a deep melancholy, from brooding too much on the sufferings which I had witnessed in London, was sufficiently aware of the tendencies of my own thoughts to do all I could to counteract them.—I was, indeed, like a person who, according to the old legend, had entered the cave of Trophonius:* and the remedies I sought were to force myself into society, and to keep my understanding in continual activity upon matters of science. But for these remedies, I should certainly have become hypochondriacally melancholy. In after years, however, when my cheerfulness was more fully re-established, I yielded to my natural inclination for a solitary life. And, at that time, I often fell into these reveries upon taking opium; and more than once it has happened to me, on a summer-night, when I have been at an open window, in a room from which I could overlook the sea at a mile below me, and could command a view of the great town of L————,* at about the same distance, that I have sate, from sun-set to sun-rise, motionless, and without wishing to move.

I shall be charged with mysticism, Behmenism, quietism,* &c. but *that* shall not alarm me. Sir H. Vane, the younger,* was one of our wisest men: and let my readers see if he, in his philosophical works, be half as unmystical as I am.—I say, then, that it has often struck me that the scene itself was somewhat typical of what took place in such a reverie. The town of L———— represented the earth, with its sorrows and its graves left behind,* yet not out of sight, nor wholly forgotten. The ocean, in everlasting but gentle agitation, and brooded over by a dove-like calm, might not unfitly typify the mind and the mood which then swayed it.* For it seemed to me as if then first I stood at a distance, and aloof from the uproar of life; as if the tumult, the fever, and the strife,* were suspended; a respite granted from the secret burthens of the heart; a sabbath of repose; a resting from human labours. Here were the hopes which blossom in the paths of life, reconciled with the peace which is in the grave; motions of the intellect as unwearied as the heavens, yet for all anxieties a halcyon calm: a tranquillity that seemed no product of inertia, but as if resulting from mighty and equal antagonisms; infinite activities, infinite repose.

Oh! just, subtle, and mighty opium!* that to the hearts of poor and rich alike, for the wounds that will never heal, and for 'the pangs that tempt the spirit to rebel,'* bringest an assuaging balm; eloquent opium! that with thy potent rhetoric stealest away the purposes of wrath; and to the guilty man, for one night givest back the hopes of his youth, and hands washed pure from blood; and to the proud man, a brief oblivion for

> Wrongs unredress'd, and insults unavenged;*

that summonest to the chancery of dreams, for the triumphs of suffering innocence, false witnesses; and confoundest perjury; and dost reverse the sentences of unrighteous judges:—thou buildest upon the bosom of darkness, out of the fantastic imagery of the brain, cities and temples, beyond the art of Phidias and Praxiteles*—beyond the splendour of Babylon and Hekatómpylos:* and 'from the anarchy of dreaming sleep,'* callest into sunny light the faces of long-buried beauties, and the blessed household countenances, cleansed from the 'dishonours of the grave.'* Thou only givest these gifts to man; and thou hast the keys of Paradise, oh, just, subtle, and mighty opium!

INTRODUCTION TO THE PAINS OF OPIUM

Courteous, and, I hope, indulgent reader (for all *my* readers must be indulgent ones, or else, I fear, I shall shock them too much to count on their courtesy), having accompanied me thus far, now let me request you to move onwards, for about eight years; that is to say, from 1804 (when I have said that my acquaintance with opium first began) to 1812. The years of academic life are now over and gone—almost forgotten:—the student's cap no longer presses my temples; if my cap exist at all, it presses those of some youthful scholar, I trust, as happy as myself, and as passionate a lover of knowledge. My gown is, by this time, I dare to say, in the same condition with many thousands of excellent books in the Bodleian,* viz. diligently perused by certain studious moths and worms: or departed, however (which is all that I know of its fate), to that great reservoir of *somewhere*, to which all the tea-cups, tea-caddies, tea-pots, tea-kettles, &c. have departed (not to speak of still frailer vessels, such as glasses, decanters, bed-makers,* &c.) which occasional resemblances in the present generation of tea-cups, &c. remind me of having once possessed, but of whose departure and final fate I, in common with most gownsmen of either university, could give, I suspect, but an obscure and conjectural history. The persecutions of the chapel-bell, sounding its unwelcome summons to six o'clock matins,* interrupts my slumbers no longer: the porter who rang it, upon whose beautiful nose (bronze, inlaid with copper) I wrote, in retaliation, so many Greek epigrams, whilst I was dressing, is dead, and has ceased to disturb any body: and I, and many others, who suffered much from his tintinnabulous* propensities, have now agreed to overlook his errors, and have forgiven him. Even with the bell I am now in charity: it rings, I suppose, as formerly, thrice a-day: and cruelly annoys, I doubt not, many worthy gentlemen, and disturbs their peace of mind: but as to me, in this year

1812, I regard its treacherous voice no longer (treacherous, I call it, for, by some refinement of malice, it spoke in as sweet and silvery tones as if it had been inviting one to a party): its tones have no longer, indeed, power to reach me, let the wind sit as favourable as the malice of the bell itself could wish: for I am 250 miles away from it, and buried in the depth of mountains. And what am I doing amongst the mountains? Taking opium. Yes, but what else? Why, reader, in 1812, the year we are now arrived at, as well as for some years previous, I have been chiefly studying German metaphysics, in the writings of Kant, Fichte, Schelling,* &c. And how, and in what manner, do I live? in short, what class or description of men do I belong to? I am at this period, viz. in 1812, living in a cottage;* and with a single female servant (honi soit qui mal y pense),* who, amongst my neighbours, passes by the name of my 'house-keeper.'* And, as a scholar and a man of learned education, and in that sense a gentleman, I may presume to class myself as an unworthy member of that indefinite body called *gentlemen*. Partly on the ground I have assigned, perhaps; partly because, from my having no visible calling or business, it is rightly judged that I must be living on my private fortune;* I am so classed by my neighbours: and, by the courtesy of modern England, I am usually addressed on letters, &c. *esquire*, though having, I fear, in the rigorous construction of heralds, but slender pretensions to that distinguished honour:* yes, in popular estimation, I am X. Y. Z.,* esquire, but not Justice of the Peace, nor Custos Rotulorum.* Am I married? Not yet. And I still take opium? On Saturday nights. And, perhaps, have taken it unblushingly ever since 'the rainy Sunday,' and 'the stately Pantheon,' and 'the beatific druggist' of 1804?—Even so. And how do I find my health after all this opium-eating? in short, how do I do? Why, pretty well, I thank you, reader: in the phrase of ladies in the straw,* 'as well as can be expected.' In fact, if I dared to say the real and simple truth, though, to satisfy the theories of medical men, I *ought* to be ill, I never was better in my life than in the spring of 1812; and I hope sincerely, that the quantity of claret, port, or 'particular Madeira,'* which, in all probability, you, good reader, have taken, and design to take, for every term of eight years, during your natural life, may as little disorder your health as mine was disordered by the opium I had taken for the eight years, between 1804 and 1812. Hence you may see again the danger of taking any medical advice from *Anastasius*;* in divinity, for aught I know, or law, he may be a safe

counsellor; but not in medicine. No: it is far better to consult
Dr Buchan; as I did: for I never forgot that worthy man's excellent
suggestion: and I was 'particularly careful not to take above five-and-
twenty ounces of laudanum.'* To this moderation and temperate use
of the article, I may ascribe it, I suppose, that as yet, at least, (*i.e.* in
1812,) I am ignorant and unsuspicious of the avenging terrors which
opium has in store for those who abuse its lenity. At the same time, it
must not be forgotten, that hitherto I have been only a dilettante eater
of opium: eight years' practice even, with the single precaution of
allowing sufficient intervals between every indulgence, has not been
sufficient to make opium necessary to me as an article of daily diet.
But now comes a different era. Move on, if you please, reader, to 1813.
In the summer of the year we have just quitted, I had suffered much
in bodily health from distress of mind connected with a very melancholy event.* This event, being no ways related to the subject now
before me, further than through the bodily illness which it produced,
I need not more particularly notice. Whether this illness of 1812
had any share in that of 1813, I know not: but so it was, that in the
latter year, I was attacked by a most appalling irritation of the stomach, in all respects the same as that which had caused me so much
suffering in youth, and accompanied by a revival of all the old dreams.
This is the point of my narrative on which, as respects my own self-
justification, the whole of what follows may be said to hinge. And here
I find myself in a perplexing dilemma:—Either, on the one hand,
I must exhaust the reader's patience, by such a detail of my malady,
and of my struggles with it, as might suffice to establish the fact of my
inability to wrestle any longer with irritation and constant suffering:
or, on the other hand, by passing lightly over this critical part of my
story, I must forego the benefit of a stronger impression left on the
mind of the reader, and must lay myself open to the misconstruction
of having slipped by the easy and gradual steps of self-indulging persons, from the first to the final stage of opium-eating (a misconstruction to which there will be a lurking predisposition in most readers,
from my previous acknowledgments.) This is the dilemma: the first
horn of which would be sufficient to toss and gore any column of
patient readers, though drawn up sixteen deep and constantly relieved
by fresh men: consequently *that* is not to be thought of. It remains
then, that I *postulate* so much as is necessary for my purpose. And let
me take as full credit for what I postulate as if I had demonstrated it,

good reader, at the expense of your patience and my own. Be not so ungenerous as to let me suffer in your good opinion through my own forbearance and regard for your comfort. No: believe all that I ask of you, viz. that I could resist no longer, believe it liberally, and as an act of grace: or else in mere prudence: for, if not, then in the next edition of my Opium Confessions revised and enlarged, I will make you believe and tremble: and *à force d'ennuyer,** by mere dint of pandiculation* I will terrify all readers of mine from ever again questioning any postulate that I shall think fit to make.

This then, let me repeat, I postulate—that, at the time I began to take opium daily, I could not have done otherwise. Whether, indeed, afterwards I might not have succeeded in breaking off the habit, even when it seemed to me that all efforts would be unavailing, and whether many of the innumerable efforts which I *did* make, might not have been carried much further, and my gradual reconquests of ground lost might not have been followed up much more energetically—these are questions which I must decline. Perhaps I might make out a case of palliation; but, shall I speak ingenuously? I confess it, as a besetting infirmity of mine, that I am too much of an Eudaemonist:* I hanker too much after a state of happiness, both for myself and others: I cannot face misery, whether my own or not, with an eye of sufficient firmness: and am little capable of encountering present pain for the sake of any reversionary benefit. On some other matters, I can agree with the gentlemen in the cotton-trade[1] at Manchester in affecting the Stoic philosophy:* but not in this. Here I take the liberty of an Eclectic philosopher,* and I look out for some courteous and considerate sect that will condescend more to the infirm condition of an opium-eater; that are 'sweet men,' as Chaucer says, 'to give absolution,'* and will show some conscience in the penances they inflict, and the efforts of abstinence they exact, from poor sinners like myself. An inhuman moralist I can no more endure in my nervous state than opium that has not been boiled.* At any rate, he, who summons me to send out a large freight of self-denial and mortification upon any cruising voyage of moral improvement, must make it clear to my understanding that the concern is a hopeful one. At my time of life

---

[1] A handsome news-room, of which I was very politely made free in passing through Manchester by several gentlemen of that place, is called, I think, *The Porch*: whence I, who am a stranger in Manchester, inferred that the subscribers meant to profess themselves followers of Zeno.* But I have been since assured that this is a mistake.

(six and thirty years of age) it cannot be supposed that I have much energy to spare: in fact, I find it all little enough for the intellectual labours I have on my hands: and, therefore, let no man expect to frighten me by a few hard words into embarking any part of it upon desperate adventures of morality.

Whether desperate or not, however, the issue of the struggle in 1813 was what I have mentioned; and from this date, the reader is to consider me as a regular and confirmed opium-eater, of whom to ask whether on any particular day he had or had not taken opium, would be to ask whether his lungs had performed respiration, or the heart fulfilled its functions.—You understand now, reader, what I am: and you are by this time aware, that no old gentleman, 'with a snow-white beard,' will have any chance of persuading me to surrender 'the little golden receptacle of the pernicious drug.'* No: I give notice to all, whether moralists or surgeons, that, whatever be their pretensions and skill in their respective lines of practice, they must not hope for any countenance from me, if they think to begin by any savage proposition for a Lent or Ramadan* of abstinence from opium. This then being all fully understood between us, we shall in future sail before the wind. Now then, reader, from 1813, where all this time we have been sitting down and loitering—rise up, if you please, and walk forward about three years more. Now draw up the curtain, and you shall see me in a new character.

If any man, poor or rich, were to say that he would tell us what had been the happiest day in his life, and the why, and the wherefore, I suppose that we should all cry out—Hear him! Hear him!—As to the happiest *day*, that must be very difficult for any wise man to name: because any event, that could occupy so distinguished a place in a man's retrospect of his life, or be entitled to have shed a special felicity on any one day, ought to be of such an enduring character, as that (accidents apart) it should have continued to shed the same felicity, or one not distinguishably less, on many years together. To the happiest *lustrum*,* however, or even to the happiest *year*, it may be allowed to any man to point without discountenance from wisdom. This year,* in my case, reader, was the one which we have now reached; though it stood, I confess, as a parenthesis between years of a gloomier character. It was a year of brilliant water (to speak after the manner of jewellers),* set as it were, and insulated, in the gloom and cloudy melancholy of opium. Strange as it may sound, I had a little before this time descended suddenly, and without any considerable effort, from 320 grains of opium (i.e. eight[1] thousand drops of laudanum) per day, to forty grains, or one eighth part. Instantaneously, and as if by magic, the cloud of profoundest melancholy which rested upon my brain, like some black vapours that I have seen roll away from the summits of mountains, drew off in one day (νυχθημερον);* passed off with its murky banners as simultaneously as a ship that has been stranded, and is floated off by a spring tide –

That moveth altogether, if it move at all.*

Now, then, I was again happy: I now took only 1000 drops of laudanum per day: and what was that? A latter spring had come to close up the season of youth: my brain performed its functions as healthily as ever before: I read Kant again; and again I understood him, or fancied that I did. Again my feelings of pleasure expanded themselves to all around me: and if any man from Oxford or Cambridge, or from neither had been announced to me in my unpretending cottage, I should have welcomed him with as sumptuous a reception as so poor a man could offer. Whatever else was wanting to a wise man's happiness,—of laudanum I would have given him as much as he wished, and in a golden cup. And, by the way, now that I speak of giving laudanum away, I remember, about this time, a little incident, which I mention, because, trifling as it was, the reader will soon meet it again in my dreams, which it influenced more fearfully than could be imagined. One day a Malay knocked at my door. What business a Malay could have to transact amongst English mountains, I cannot conjecture: but possibly he was on his road to a sea-port about forty miles distant.*

The servant who opened the door to him was a young girl born and bred amongst the mountains,* who had never seen an Asiatic dress of any sort: his turban, therefore, confounded her not a little: and, as it turned out, that his attainments in English were exactly of the same extent as hers in the Malay, there seemed to be an impassable gulph

---

[1] I here reckon twenty-five drops of laudanum as equivalent to one grain of opium,* which, I believe, is the common estimate. However, as both may be considered variable quantities (the crude opium varying much in strength, and the tincture still more), I suppose that no infinitesimal accuracy can be had in such a calculation. Tea-spoons vary as much in size as opium in strength. Small ones hold about 100 drops: so that 8000 drops are about eighty times a tea-spoonful. The reader sees how much I kept within Dr Buchan's indulgent allowance.

fixed* between all communication of ideas, if either party had happened to possess any. In this dilemma, the girl, recollecting the reputed learning of her master (and, doubtless, giving me credit for a knowledge of all the languages of the earth, besides, perhaps, a few of the lunar ones), came and gave me to understand that there was a sort of demon below, whom she clearly imagined that my art could exorcise from the house. I did not immediately go down: but, when I did, the group which presented itself, arranged as it was by accident, though not very elaborate, took hold of my fancy and my eye in a way that none of the statuesque attitudes exhibited in the ballets at the Opera House, though so ostentatiously complex, had ever done. In a cottage kitchen, but panelled on the wall with dark wood that from age and rubbing resembled oak, and looking more like a rustic hall of entrance than a kitchen, stood the Malay—his turban and loose trowsers of dingy white relieved upon the dark panelling: he had placed himself nearer to the girl than she seemed to relish; though her native spirit of mountain intrepidity contended with the feeling of simple awe which her countenance expressed as she gazed upon the tiger-cat before her. And a more striking picture there could not be imagined, than the beautiful English face of the girl, and its exquisite fairness, together with her erect and independent attitude, contrasted with the sallow and bilious skin of the Malay, enamelled or veneered with mahogany, by marine air, his small, fierce, restless eyes, thin lips, slavish gestures and adorations. Half-hidden by the ferocious looking Malay, was a little child from a neighbouring cottage who had crept in after him, and was now in the act of reverting its head, and gazing upwards at the turban and the fiery eyes beneath it, whilst with one hand he caught at the dress of the young woman for protection. My knowledge of the Oriental tongues is not remarkably extensive, being indeed confined to two words—the Arabic word for barley, and the Turkish for opium (madjoon), which I have learnt from Anastasius. And, as I had neither a Malay dictionary, nor even Adelung's *Mithridates*,* which might have helped me to a few words, I addressed him in some lines from the Iliad;* considering that, of such languages as I possessed, Greek, in point of longitude, came geographically nearest to an Oriental one. He worshipped me in a most devout manner, and replied in what I suppose was Malay. In this way I saved my reputation with my neighbours: for the Malay had no means of betraying the secret. He lay down upon the floor for about an hour, and then pursued his journey. On his departure, I presented him with a piece of opium. To him, as an Orientalist, I concluded that opium must be familiar: and the expression of his face convinced me that it was. Nevertheless, I was struck with some little consternation when I saw him suddenly raise his hand to his mouth, and (in the school-boy phrase) bolt the whole, divided into three pieces, at one mouthful. The quantity was enough to kill three dragoons and their horses: and I felt some alarm for the poor creature: but what could be done? I had given him the opium in compassion for his solitary life, on recollecting that if he had travelled on foot from London, it must be nearly three weeks since he could have exchanged a thought with any human being. I could not think of violating the laws of hospitality, by having him seized and drenched with an emetic, and thus frightening him into a notion that we were going to sacrifice him to some English idol. No: there was clearly no help for it:—he took his leave: and for some days I felt anxious: but as I never heard of any Malay being found dead, I became convinced that he was used[1] to opium: and that I must have done him the service I designed, by giving him one night of respite from the pains of wandering.

This incident I have digressed to mention, because this Malay (partly from the picturesque exhibition he assisted to frame, partly from the anxiety I connected with his image for some days) fastened afterwards upon my dreams, and brought other Malays with him worse than himself, that ran 'a-muck'[2] at me, and led me into a world of troubles.—But to quit this episode, and to return to my intercalary* year of happiness. I have said already, that on a subject so important to us all as happiness, we should listen with pleasure to any man's experience or experiments, even though he were but a plough-boy,

---

[1] This, however, is not a necessary conclusion: the varieties of effect produced by opium on different constitutions are infinite. A London Magistrate (Harriott's *Struggles through Life*, vol. iii. p. 391, Third Edition), has recorded that, on the first occasion of his trying laudanum for the gout, he took *forty* drops, the next night *sixty*, and on the fifth night *eighty*, without any effect whatever: and this at an advanced age.* I have an anecdote from a country surgeon,* however, which sinks Mr Harriott's case into a trifle; and in my projected medical treatise on opium,* which I will publish, provided the College of Surgeons will pay me for enlightening their benighted understandings upon this subject, I will relate it: but it is far too good a story to be published gratis.

[2] See the common accounts in any Eastern traveller or voyager* of the frantic excesses committed by Malays who have taken opium, or are reduced to desperation by ill luck at gambling.

who cannot be supposed to have ploughed very deep into such an intractable soil as that of human pains and pleasures, or to have conducted his researches upon any very enlightened principles. But I, who have taken happiness, both in a solid and a liquid shape,* both boiled and unboiled, both East India and Turkey*—who have conducted my experiments upon this interesting subject with a sort of galvanic battery—and have, for the general benefit of the world, inoculated myself, as it were, with the poison of 8000 drops of laudanum per day (just, for the same reason, as a French surgeon inoculated himself lately with cancer*—an English one, twenty years ago, with plague*—and a third, I know not of what nation, with hydrophobia*),—*I* (it will be admitted) must surely know what happiness is, if any body does. And, therefore, I will here lay down an analysis of happiness; and as the most interesting mode of communicating it, I will give it, not didactically, but wrapt up and involved in a picture of one evening, as I spent every evening during the intercalary year when laudanum, though taken daily, was to me no more than the elixir of pleasure. This done, I shall quit the subject of happiness altogether, and pass to a very different one—the *pains of opium*.

Let there be a cottage, standing in a valley, 18 miles from any town*—no spacious valley, but about two miles long, by three quarters of a mile in average width; the benefit of which provision is, that all the families resident within its circuit will compose, as it were, one larger household personally familiar to your eye, and more or less interesting to your affections. Let the mountains be real mountains, between 3 and 4000 feet high; and the cottage, a real cottage; not (as a witty author has it) 'a cottage with a double coach-house:'* let it be, in fact (for I must abide by the actual scene), a white cottage, embowered with flowering shrubs, so chosen as to unfold a succession of flowers upon the walls, and clustering round the windows through all the months of spring, summer, and autumn—beginning, in fact, with May roses, and ending with jasmine. Let it, however, *not* be spring, nor summer, nor autumn—but winter, in his sternest shape. This is a most important point in the science of happiness. And I am surprised to see people overlook it, and think it matter of congratulation that winter is going; or, if coming, is not likely to be a severe one. On the contrary, I put up a petition annually, for as much snow, hail, frost, or storm, of one kind or other, as the skies can possibly afford us. Surely every body is aware of the divine pleasures which attend a winter fire-side: candles at four o'clock, warm hearth-rugs, tea, a fair tea-maker, shutters closed, curtains flowing in ample draperies on the floor, whilst the wind and rain are raging audibly without,

> And at the doors and windows seem to call,
> As heav'n and earth they would together mell;
> Yet the least entrance find they none at all;
> Whence sweeter grows our rest secure in massy hall.
>   —*Castle of Indolence.**

All these are items in the description of a winter evening, which must surely be familiar to every body born in a high latitude. And it is evident, that most of these delicacies, like ice-cream, require a very low temperature of the atmosphere to produce them: they are fruits which cannot be ripened without weather stormy or inclement, in some way or other. I am not '*particular*,' as people say, whether it be snow, or black frost, or wind so strong, that (as Mr ————* says) 'you may lean your back against it like a post.' I can put up even with rain, provided it rains cats and dogs: but something of the sort I must have: and, if I have it not, I think myself in a manner ill-used: for why am I called on to pay so heavily for winter, in coals, and candles, and various privations that will occur even to gentlemen, if I am not to have the article good of its kind? No: a Canadian winter for my money: or a Russian one, where every man is but a co-proprietor with the north wind in the fee-simple* of his own ears. Indeed, so great an epicure am I in this matter, that I cannot relish a winter night fully if it be much past St Thomas's day,* and have degenerated into disgusting tendencies to vernal appearances: no: it must be divided by a thick wall of dark nights from all return of light and sunshine.—From the latter weeks of October to Christmas-eve, therefore, is the period during which happiness is in season, which, in my judgment, enters the room with the tea-tray: for tea, though ridiculed by those who are naturally of coarse nerves, or are become so from wine-drinking, and are not susceptible of influence from so refined a stimulant, will always be the favourite beverage of the intellectual: and, for my part, I would have joined Dr Johnson in a *bellum internecinum* against Jonas Hanway, or any other impious person, who should presume to disparage it.*—But here, to save myself the trouble of too much verbal description, I will introduce a painter; and give him directions for the rest of the picture. Painters do not like white cottages, unless a good deal weather-stained: but as the reader now understands that it is a winter night, his services will not be required, except for the inside of the house.

Paint me, then, a room seventeen feet by twelve, and not more than seven and a half feet high. This, reader, is somewhat ambitiously styled, in my family, the drawing-room: but, being contrived 'a double debt to pay,'* it is also, and more justly, termed the library; for it happens that books are the only article of property in which I am richer than my neighbours. Of these, I have about five thousand, collected gradually since my eighteenth year. Therefore, painter, put as many as you can into this room. Make it populous with books: and, furthermore, paint me a good fire; and furniture, plain and modest, befitting the unpretending cottage of a scholar. And, near the fire, paint me a tea-table; and (as it is clear that no creature can come to see one such* a stormy night,) place only two cups and saucers on the tea-tray: and, if you know how to paint such a thing symbolically, or otherwise, paint me an eternal tea-pot—eternal *à parte ante*, and *à parte post*;* for I usually drink tea from eight o'clock at night to four o'clock in the morning. And, as it is very unpleasant to make tea, or to pour it out for oneself, paint me a lovely young woman, sitting at the table. Paint her arms like Aurora's, and her smiles like Hebe's:*—But no, dear M., not even in jest let me insinuate that thy power to illuminate my cottage rests upon a tenure so perishable as mere personal beauty;* or that the witchcraft of angelic smiles lies within the empire of any earthly pencil. Pass, then, my good painter, to something more within its power: and the next article brought forward should naturally be myself—a picture of the Opium-eater, with his 'little golden receptacle of the pernicious drug,' lying beside him on the table. As to the opium, I have no objection to see a picture of *that*, though I would rather see the original: you may paint it, if you choose; but I apprize you, that no 'little' receptacle would, even in 1816, answer *my* purpose, who was at a distance from the 'stately Pantheon,' and all druggists (mortal or otherwise). No: you may as well paint the real receptacle, which was not of gold, but of glass, and as much like a wine-decanter as possible. Into this you may put a quart of ruby-coloured laudanum: that, and a book of German metaphysics placed by its side, will sufficiently attest my being in the neighbourhood; but, as to myself,—there I demur. I admit that, naturally, I ought to occupy the foreground of the picture; that being the hero of the piece, or (if you choose) the criminal at the bar, my body should be had into court. This seems reasonable: but why should I confess, on this point, to a painter? or why confess at all? If the public (into whose private ear I am confidentially whispering my confessions, and not into any painter's) should chance to have framed some agreeable picture for itself, of the Opium-eater's exterior,—should have ascribed to him, romantically, an elegant person, or a handsome face, why should I barbarously tear from it so pleasing a delusion—pleasing both to the public and to me?* No: paint me, if at all, according to your own fancy: and, as a painter's fancy should teem with beautiful creations, I cannot fail, in that way, to be a gainer. And now, reader, we have run through all the ten categories of my condition,* as it stood about 1816–17: up to the middle of which latter year I judge myself to have been a happy man: and the elements of that happiness I have endeavoured to place before you, in the above sketch of the interior of a scholar's library, in a cottage among the mountains, on a stormy winter evening.

But now farewell—a long farewell to happiness*—winter or summer! farewell to smiles and laughter! farewell to peace of mind! farewell to hope and to tranquil dreams, and to the blessed consolations of sleep! for more than three years and a half I am summoned away from these: I am now arrived at an Iliad of woes:* for I have now to record

THE PAINS OF OPIUM

> ———— as when some great painter dips
> His pencil in the gloom of earthquake and eclipse.*
> *Shelley's Revolt of Islam.*

Reader, who have thus far accompanied me, I must request your attention to a brief explanatory note on three points:

1. For several reasons, I have not been able to compose the notes for this part of my narrative into any regular and connected shape. I give the notes disjointed as I find them, or have now drawn them up from memory. Some of them point to their own date; some I have dated; and some are undated. Whenever it could answer my purpose to transplant them from the natural or chronological order, I have not scrupled to do so. Sometimes I speak in the present, sometimes in the past tense. Few of the notes, perhaps, were written exactly at the

period of time to which they relate; but this can little affect their accuracy; as the impressions were such that they can never fade from my mind. Much has been omitted. I could not, without effort, constrain myself to the task of either recalling, or constructing into a regular narrative, the whole burthen of horrors which lies upon my brain. This feeling partly I plead in excuse, and partly that I am now in London, and am a helpless sort of person, who cannot even arrange his own papers without assistance; and I am separated from the hands which are wont to perform for me the offices of an amanuensis.

2. You will think, perhaps, that I am too confidential and communicative of my own private history. It may be so. But my way of writing is rather to think aloud, and follow my own humours, than much to consider who is listening to me; and, if I stop to consider what is proper to be said to this or that person, I shall soon come to doubt whether any part at all is proper. The fact is, I place myself at a distance of fifteen or twenty years ahead of this time, and suppose myself writing to those who will be interested about me hereafter; and wishing to have some record of a time, the entire history of which no one can know but myself, I do it as fully as I am able with the efforts I am now capable of making, because I know not whether I can ever find time to do it again.

3. It will occur to you often to ask, why did I not release myself from the horrors of opium, by leaving it off, or diminishing it? To this I must answer briefly: it might be supposed that I yielded to the fascinations of opium too easily; it cannot be supposed that any man can be charmed by its terrors. The reader may be sure, therefore, that I made attempts innumerable to reduce the quantity. I add, that those who witnessed the agonies of those attempts, and not myself, were the first to beg me to desist. But could not I have reduced it a drop a day, or by adding water, have bisected or trisected a drop? A thousand drops bisected would thus have taken nearly six years to reduce; and that way would certainly not have answered. But this is a common mistake of those who know nothing of opium experimentally; I appeal to those who do, whether it is not always found that down to a certain point it can be reduced with ease and even pleasure, but that, after that point, further reduction causes intense suffering.* Yes, say many thoughtless persons, who know not what they are talking of, you will suffer a little low spirits and dejection for a few days. I answer, no; there is nothing like low spirits; on the contrary, the

mere animal spirits are uncommonly raised: the pulse is improved: the health is better. It is not there that the suffering lies. It has no resemblance to the sufferings caused by renouncing wine. It is a state of unutterable irritation of stomach (which surely is not much like dejection), accompanied by intense perspirations, and feelings such as I shall not attempt to describe without more space at my command.

I shall now enter '*in medias res*,'* and shall anticipate, from a time when my opium pains might be said to be at their *acmé*,* an account of their palsying effects on the intellectual faculties.

——

My studies have now been long interrupted. I cannot read to myself with any pleasure, hardly with a moment's endurance. Yet I read aloud sometimes for the pleasure of others; because, reading is an accomplishment of mine; and, in the slang use of the word *accomplishment* as a superficial and ornamental attainment, almost the only one I possess: and formerly, if I had any vanity at all connected with any endowment or attainment of mine, it was with this;* for I had observed that no accomplishment was so rare. Players are the worst readers of all: ——— reads vilely: and Mrs ———,* who is so celebrated, can read nothing well but dramatic compositions: Milton she cannot read sufferably. People in general either read poetry without any passion at all, or else overstep the modesty of nature,* and read not like scholars. Of late, if I have felt moved by any thing in books, it has been by the grand lamentations of Sampson Agonistes, or the great harmonies of the Satanic speeches in Paradise Regained,* when read aloud by myself. A young lady sometimes comes and drinks tea with us:* at her request and M.'s I now and then read W———'s* poems to them. (W. by the bye, is the only poet I ever met who could read his own verses: often indeed he reads admirably.)

For nearly two years I believe that I read no book but one: and I owe it to the author, in discharge of a great debt of gratitude, to mention what that was. The sublimer and more passionate poets I still read, as I have said, by snatches, and occasionally. But my proper vocation, as I well knew, was the exercise of the analytic understanding. Now, for the most part, analytic studies are continuous, and not to be pursued by fits and starts, or fragmentary efforts. Mathematics, for instance, intellectual philosophy, &c. were all become insupportable to me;* I shrunk from them with a sense of powerless and infantine feebleness that gave me an anguish the greater from remembering the time when I grappled with them to my own hourly delight; and for this further reason, because I had devoted the labour of my whole life, and had dedicated my intellect, blossoms and fruits, to the slow and elaborate toil of constructing one single work, to which I had presumed to give the title of an unfinished work of Spinosa's; viz. *De emendatione humani intellectûs*.* This was now lying locked up, as by frost, like any Spanish bridge or aqueduct, begun upon too great a scale for the resources of the architect; and, instead of surviving me as a monument of wishes at least, and aspirations, and a life of labour dedicated to the exaltation human nature in that way in which God had best fitted me to promote so great an object, it was likely to stand a memorial to my children of hopes defeated, of baffled efforts, of materials uselessly accumulated, of foundations laid that were never to support a superstructure,—of the grief and the ruin of the architect. In this state of imbecility, I had, for amusement, turned my attention to political economy; my understanding, which formerly had been as active and restless as a hyena, could not, I suppose (so long as I lived at all) sink into utter lethargy; and political economy offers this advantage to a person in my state, that though it is eminently an organic science (no part, that is to say, but what acts on the whole, as the whole again re-acts on each part), yet the several parts may be detached and contemplated singly. Great as was the prostration of my powers at this time, yet I could not forget my knowledge; and my understanding had been for too many years intimate with severe thinkers, with logic, and the great masters of knowledge, not to be aware of the utter feebleness of the main herd of modern economists. I had been led in 1811 to look into loads of books and pamphlets on many branches of economy; and, at my desire, M. sometimes read to me chapters from more recent works, or parts of parliamentary debates. I saw that these were generally the very dregs and rinsings of the human intellect; and that any man of sound head, and practised in wielding logic with a scholastic adroitness, might take up the whole academy of modern economists, and throttle them between heaven and earth with his finger and thumb, or bray their fungus heads to powder with a lady's fan. At length, in 1819, a friend in Edinburgh sent me down Mr Ricardo's book:* and recurring to my own prophetic anticipation of the advent of some legislator for this science, I said, before I had finished the first chapter,

'Thou art the man!'* Wonder and curiosity were emotions that had long been dead in me. Yet I wondered once more: I wondered at myself that I could once again be stimulated to the effort of reading: and much more I wondered at the book. Had this profound work been really written in England during the nineteenth century? Was it possible? I supposed thinking[1] had been extinct in England. Could it be that an Englishman, and he not in academic bowers, but oppressed by mercantile and senatorial cares,* had accomplished what all the universities of Europe, and a century of thought, had failed even to advance by one hair's breadth? All other writers had been crushed and overlaid by the enormous weight of facts and documents; Mr Ricardo had deduced, *à priori*,* from the understanding itself, laws which first gave a ray of light into the unwieldy chaos of materials, and had constructed what had been but a collection of tentative discussions into a science of regular proportions, now first standing on an eternal basis.

Thus did one single work of a profound understanding avail to give me a pleasure and an activity which I had not known for years:— it roused me even to write, or, at least, to dictate, what M. wrote for me. It seemed to me, that some important truths had escaped even 'the inevitable eye'* of Mr Ricardo: and, as these were, for the most part, of such a nature that I could express or illustrate them more briefly and elegantly by algebraic symbols than in the usual clumsy and loitering diction of economists, the whole would not have filled a pocket-book; and being so brief, with M. for my amanuensis, even at this time, incapable as I was of all general exertion, I drew up my *Prolegomena to all future Systems of Political Economy*.* I hope it will not be found redolent of opium; though, indeed, to most people, the subject itself is a sufficient opiate.

This exertion, however, was but a temporary flash; as the sequel showed—for I designed to publish my work: arrangements were made at a provincial press, about eighteen miles distant, for printing it. An additional compositor was retained, for some days, on this account. The work was even twice advertised: and I was, in a manner,

---

[1] The reader must remember what I here mean by *thinking*: because, else this would be a very presumptuous expression. England, of late, has been rich to excess in fine thinkers, in the departments of creative and combining thought; but there is a sad dearth of masculine thinkers in any analytic path. A Scotchman of eminent name has lately told us, that he is obliged to quit even mathematics, for want of encouragement.*

pledged to the fulfilment of my intention. But I had a preface to write; and a dedication, which I wished to make a splendid one, to Mr Ricardo. I found myself quite unable to accomplish all this. The arrangements were countermanded: the compositor dismissed: and my 'Prolegomena' rested peacefully by the side of its elder and more dignified brother.

I have thus described and illustrated my intellectual torpor, in terms that apply, more or less, to every part of the four years during which I was under the Circean* spells of opium. But for misery and suffering, I might, indeed, be said to have existed in a dormant state. I seldom could prevail on myself to write a letter; an answer of a few words, to any that I received, was the utmost that I could accomplish; and often *that* not until the letter had lain weeks, or even months, on my writing table. Without the aid of M. all records of bills paid, or *to be* paid, must have perished: and my whole domestic economy, whatever became of Political Economy, must have gone into irretrievable confusion.—I shall not afterwards allude to this part of the case: it is one, however, which the opium-eater will find, in the end, as oppressive and tormenting as any other, from the sense of incapacity and feebleness, from the direct embarrassments incident to the neglect or procrastination of each day's appropriate duties, and from the remorse which must often exasperate* the stings of these evils to a reflective and conscientious mind. The opium-eater loses none of his moral sensibilities, or aspirations: he wishes and longs, as earnestly as ever, to realize what he believes possible, and feels to be exacted by duty; but his intellectual apprehension of what is possible infinitely outruns his power, not of execution only, but even of power to attempt. He lies under the weight of incubus and night-mare: he lies in sight of all that he would fain perform, just as a man forcibly confined to his bed by the mortal languor of a relaxing disease, who is compelled to witness injury or outrage offered to some object of his tenderest love:—he curses the spells which chain him down from motion:—he would lay down his life if he might but get up and walk; but he is powerless as an infant, and cannot even attempt to rise.

I now pass to what is the main subject of these latter confessions, to the history and journal of what took place in my dreams; for these were the immediate and proximate cause of my acutest suffering.

The first notice I had of any important change going on in this part of my physical economy, was from the re-awakening of a state of eye generally incident to childhood, or exalted states of irritability. I know not whether my reader is aware that many children, perhaps most, have a power of painting, as it were, upon the darkness, all sorts of phantoms; in some, that power is simply a mechanic affection of the eye; others have a voluntary, or a semi-voluntary power to dismiss or to summon them; or, as a child once said to me when I questioned him on this matter, 'I can tell them to go, and they go; but sometimes they come, when I don't tell them to come.' Whereupon I told him that he had almost as unlimited a command over apparitions, as a Roman centurion over his soldiers.*—In the middle of 1817, I think it was, that this faculty became positively distressing to me: at night, when I lay awake in bed, vast processions passed along in mournful pomp; friezes of never-ending stories, that to my feelings were as sad and solemn as if they were stories drawn from times before Oedipus or Priam—before Tyre—before Memphis.* And, at the same time, a corresponding change took place in my dreams; a theatre seemed suddenly opened and lighted up within my brain, which presented nightly spectacles of more than earthly splendour. And the four following facts may be mentioned, as noticeable at this time:

1. That, as the creative state of the eye increased, a sympathy seemed to arise between the waking and the dreaming states of the brain in one point—that whatsoever I happened to call up and to trace by a voluntary act upon the darkness was very apt to transfer itself to my dreams; so that I feared to exercise this faculty; for, as Midas turned all things to gold,* that yet baffled his hopes and defrauded his human desires, so whatsoever things capable of being visually represented I did but think of in the darkness, immediately shaped themselves into phantoms of the eye; and, by a process apparently no less inevitable, when thus once traced in faint and visionary colours, like writings in sympathetic ink,* they were drawn out by the fierce chemistry of my dreams, into insufferable splendour that fretted my heart.

2. For this, and all other changes in my dreams, were accompanied by deep-seated anxiety and gloomy melancholy, such as are wholly incommunicable by words. I seemed every night to descend, not metaphorically, but literally to descend, into chasms and sunless abysses, depths below depths,* from which it seemed hopeless that I could ever re-ascend. Nor did I, by waking, feel that I *had* re-ascended. This I do not dwell upon; because the state of gloom which attended

these gorgeous spectacles, amounting at last to utter darkness, as of some suicidal despondency, cannot be approached by words.

3. The sense of space, and in the end, the sense of time, were both powerfully affected. Buildings, landscapes, &c. were exhibited in proportions so vast as the bodily eye is not fitted to receive. Space swelled, and was amplified to an extent of unutterable infinity. This, however, did not disturb me so much as the vast expansion of time; I sometimes seemed to have lived for 70 or 100 years in one night; nay, sometimes had feelings representative of a millenium passed in that time, or, however, of a duration far beyond the limits of any human experience.

4. The minutest incidents of childhood, or forgotten scenes of later years, were often revived: I could not be said to recollect them; for if I had been told of them when waking, I should not have been able to acknowledge them as parts of my past experience. But placed as they were before me, in dreams like intuitions, and clothed in all their evanescent circumstances and accompanying feelings, I *recognised* them instantaneously. I was once told by a near relative of mine,* that having in her childhood fallen into a river, and being on the very verge of death but for the critical assistance which reached her, she saw in a moment her whole life, in its minutest incidents, arrayed before her simultaneously as in a mirror; and she had a faculty developed as suddenly for comprehending the whole and every part. This, from some opium experiences of mine, I can believe; I have, indeed, seen the same thing asserted twice in modern books,* and accompanied by a remark which I am convinced is true; viz. that the dread book* of account, which the Scriptures speak of, is, in fact, the mind itself of each individual. Of this at least, I feel assured, that there is no such thing as *forgetting* possible to the mind;* a thousand accidents may, and will interpose a veil between our present consciousness and the secret inscriptions on the mind; accidents of the same sort will also rend away this veil; but alike, whether veiled or unveiled, the inscription remains for ever; just as the stars seem to withdraw before the common light of day,* whereas, in fact, we all know that it is the light which is drawn over them as a veil—and that they are waiting to be revealed when the obscuring daylight shall have withdrawn.

Having noticed these four facts as memorably distinguishing my dreams from those of health, I shall now cite a case illustrative of the first fact; and shall then cite any others that I remember, either in their chronological order, or any other that may give them more effect as pictures to the reader.

I had been in youth, and even since, for occasional amusement, a great reader of Livy,* whom, I confess, that I prefer, both for style and matter, to any other of the Roman historians: and I had often felt as most solemn and appalling sounds, and most emphatically representative of the majesty of the Roman people, the two words so often occurring in Livy—*Consul Romanus*;* especially when the consul is introduced in his military character. I mean to say, that the words king—sultan—regent, &c. or any other titles of those who embody in their own persons the collective majesty of a great people, had less power over my reverential feelings. I had also, though no great reader of history, made myself minutely and critically familiar with one period of English history, viz. the period of the Parliamentary War,* having been attracted by the moral grandeur of some who figured in that day, and by the many interesting memoirs which survive those unquiet times.* Both these parts of my lighter reading, having furnished me often with matter of reflection, now furnished me with matter for my dreams. Often I used to see, after painting upon the blank darkness a sort of rehearsal whilst waking, a crowd of ladies, and perhaps a festival, and dances. And I heard it said, or I said to myself, 'these are English ladies from the unhappy times of Charles I.* These are the wives and the daughters of those who met in peace, and sate at the same tables, and were allied by marriage or by blood; and yet, after a certain day in August, 1642,* never smiled upon each other again, nor met but in the field of battle; and at Marston Moor, at Newbury, or at Naseby,* cut asunder all ties of love by the cruel sabre, and washed away in blood the memory of ancient friendship.'—The ladies danced, and looked as lovely as the court of George IV.* Yet I knew, even in my dream, that they had been in the grave for nearly two centuries.—This pageant would suddenly dissolve: and, at a clapping of hands, would be heard the heart-quaking sound of *Consul Romanus*: and immediately came 'sweeping by,'* in gorgeous paludaments,* Paulus or Marius,* girt round by a company of centurions, with the crimson tunic hoisted on a spear,* and followed by the *alalagmos** of the Roman legions.

Many years ago, when I was looking over Piranesi's Antiquities of Rome, Mr Coleridge, who was standing by, described to me a set of plates by that artist, called his *Dreams*,* and which record the scenery of his own visions during the delirium of a fever. Some of them (I describe only from memory of Mr Coleridge's account) represented vast Gothic halls: on the floor of which stood all sorts of engines and machinery, wheels, cables, pulleys, levers, catapults, &c. &c. expressive of enormous power put forth, and resistance overcome. Creeping along the sides of the walls, you perceived a staircase; and upon it, groping his way upwards, was Piranesi himself: follow the stairs a little further, and you perceive it come to a sudden abrupt termination, without any balustrade, and allowing no step onwards to him who had reached the extremity, except into the depths below. Whatever is to become of poor Piranesi, you suppose, at least, that his labours must in some way terminate here. But raise your eyes, and behold a second flight of stairs still higher: on which again Piranesi is perceived, but this time standing on the very brink of the abyss. Again elevate your eye, and a still more aerial flight of stairs is beheld: and again is poor Piranesi busy on his aspiring labours: and so on, until the unfinished stairs and Piranesi both are lost in the upper gloom of the hall.—With the same power of endless growth and self-reproduction did my architecture proceed in dreams. In the early stage of my malady, the splendours of my dreams were indeed chiefly architectural: and I beheld such pomp of cities and palaces as was never yet beheld by the waking eye, unless in the clouds. From a great modern poet I cite part of a passage which describes, as an appearance actually beheld in the clouds, what in many of its circumstances I saw frequently in sleep:

> The appearance, instantaneously disclosed,
> Was of a mighty city—boldly say
> A wilderness of building, sinking far
> And self-withdrawn into a wondrous depth,
> Far sinking into splendor—without end!
> Fabric it seem'd of diamond, and of gold,
> With alabaster domes, and silver spires,
> And blazing terrace upon terrace, high
> Uplifted; here, serene pavilions bright
> In avenues disposed; there towers begirt
> With battlements that on their restless fronts
> Bore stars—illumination of all gems!
> By earthly nature had the effect been wrought
> Upon the dark materials of the storm

> Now pacified; on them, and on the coves,
> And mountain-steeps and summits, whereunto
> The vapours had receded,—taking there
> Their station under a cerulean sky. &c. &c.*

The sublime circumstance—'battlements that on their *restless* fronts bore stars,'—might have been copied from my architectural dreams, for it often occurred.—We hear it reported of Dryden,* and of Fuseli* in modern times, that they thought proper to eat raw meat for the sake of obtaining splendid dreams: how much better for such a purpose to have eaten opium, which yet I do not remember that any poet is recorded to have done, except the dramatist Shadwell:* and in ancient days, Homer* is, I think, rightly reputed to have known the virtues of opium.

To my architecture succeeded dreams of lakes—and silvery expanses of water:—these haunted me so much, that I feared (though possibly it will appear ludicrous to a medical man) that some dropsical state or tendency of the brain might thus be making itself (to use a metaphysical word) *objective*;* and the sentient organ *project* itself as its own object.—For two months I suffered greatly in my head,—a part of my bodily structure which had hitherto been so clear from all touch or taint of weakness (physically, I mean), that I used to say of it, as the last Lord Orford said of his stomach, that it seemed likely to survive the rest of my person.*—Till now I had never felt a head-ach even, or any the slightest pain, except rheumatic pains caused by my own folly. However, I got over this attack, though it must have been verging on something very dangerous.

The waters now changed their character,—from translucent lakes, shining like mirrors, they now became seas and oceans. And now came a tremendous change, which, unfolding itself slowly like a scroll, through many months, promised an abiding torment; and, in fact, it never left me until the winding up of my case. Hitherto the human face had mixed often in my dreams, but not despotically, nor with any special power of tormenting. But now that which I have called the tyranny of the human face began to unfold itself. Perhaps some part of my London life* might be answerable for this. Be that as it may, now it was that upon the rocking waters of the ocean the human face began to appear: the sea appeared paved with innumerable faces, upturned to the heavens: faces, imploring, wrathful, despairing, surged upwards by thousands, by myriads, by generations, by centuries:—my agitation was infinite,—my mind tossed—and surged with the ocean.

———

May, 1818.

The Malay has been a fearful enemy for months. I have been every night, through his means, transported into Asiatic scenes. I know not whether others share in my feelings on this point; but I have often thought that if I were compelled to forego England, and to live in China, and among Chinese manners and modes of life and scenery, I should go mad. The causes of my horror lie deep; and some of them must be common to others. Southern Asia, in general, is the seat of awful images and associations. As the cradle of the human race, it would alone have a dim and reverential feeling connected with it. But there are other reasons. No man can pretend that the wild, barbarous, and capricious superstitions of Africa, or of savage tribes elsewhere, affect him in the way that he is affected by the ancient, monumental, cruel, and elaborate religions of Indostan, &c. The mere antiquity of Asiatic things, of their institutions, histories, modes of faith, &c. is so impressive, that to me the vast age of the race and name overpowers the sense of youth in the individual. A young Chinese seems to me an antediluvian man renewed. Even Englishmen, though not bred in any knowledge of such institutions, cannot but shudder at the mystic sublimity of *castes* that have flowed apart, and refused to mix, through such immemorial tracts of time; nor can any man fail to be awed by the names of the Ganges, or the Euphrates.* It contributes much to these feelings, that southern Asia is, and has been for thousands of years, the part of the earth most swarming with human life; the great *officina gentium.** Man is a weed in those regions. The vast empires also, into which the enormous population of Asia has always been cast, give a further sublimity to the feelings associated with all oriental names or images. In China, over and above what it has in common with the rest of southern Asia, I am terrified by the modes of life, by the manners, and the barrier of utter abhorrence, and want of sympathy, placed between us by feelings deeper than I can analyze. I could sooner live with lunatics, or brute animals. All this, and much more than I can say, or have time to say, the reader must enter into before he can comprehend the unimaginable horror which these dreams of oriental imagery, and mythological tortures, impressed upon me. Under the connecting feeling of tropical heat and vertical sun-lights,

I brought together all creatures, birds, beasts, reptiles, all trees and plants, usages and appearances, that are found in all tropical regions, and assembled them together in China or Indostan. From kindred feelings, I soon brought Egypt and all her gods under the same law. I was stared at, hooted at, grinned at, chattered at, by monkeys, by paroquets, by cockatoos. I ran into pagodas: and was fixed, for centuries, at the summit, or in secret rooms; I was the idol; I was the priest; I was worshipped; I was sacrificed. I fled from the wrath of Brama through all the forests of Asia: Vishnu hated me: Seeva* laid wait for me. I came suddenly upon Isis and Osiris:* I had done a deed, they said, which the ibis* and the crocodile trembled at. I was buried, for a thousand years, in stone coffins, with mummies and sphynxes, in narrow chambers at the heart of eternal pyramids. I was kissed, with cancerous kisses, by crocodiles; and laid, confounded with all unutterable slimy things, amongst reeds and Nilotic mud.

I thus give the reader some slight abstraction of my oriental dreams, which always filled me with such amazement at the monstrous scenery, that horror seemed absorbed, for a while, in sheer astonishment. Sooner or later, came a reflux of feeling that swallowed up the astonishment, and left me, not so much in terror, as in hatred and abomination of what I saw. Over every form, and threat, and punishment, and dim sightless incarceration, brooded a sense of eternity and infinity that drove me into an oppression as of madness. Into these dreams only, it was, with one or two slight exceptions, that any circumstances of physical horror entered. All before had been moral and spiritual terrors. But here the main agents were ugly birds, or snakes, or crocodiles; especially the last. The cursed crocodile became to me the object of more horror than almost all the rest. I was compelled to live with him; and (as was always the case almost in my dreams) for centuries. I escaped sometimes, and found myself in Chinese houses, with cane tables, &c. All the feet of the tables, sophas, &c. soon became instinct with life: the abominable head of the crocodile, and his leering eyes, looked out at me, multiplied into a thousand repetitions: and I stood loathing and fascinated. And so often did this hideous reptile haunt my dreams, that many times the very same dream was broken up in the very same way: I heard gentle voices speaking to me (I hear every thing when I am sleeping); and instantly I awoke: it was broad noon; and my children were standing, hand in hand, at my bed-side;* come to show me their coloured shoes, or new frocks, or to let me see them dressed for going out. I protest that so awful was the transition from the damned crocodile, and the other unutterable monsters and abortions of my dreams, to the sight of innocent *human* natures and of infancy, that, in the mighty and sudden revulsion of mind, I wept, and could not forbear it, as I kissed their faces.

————

June, 1819.

I have had occasion to remark, at various periods of my life, that the deaths of those whom we love, and indeed the contemplation of death generally, is (*caeteris paribus*)* more affecting in summer than in any other season of the year. And the reasons are these three, I think: first, that the visible heavens in summer appear far higher, more distant, and (if such a solecism may be excused) more infinite; the clouds, by which chiefly the eye expounds the distance of the blue pavilion stretched over our heads, are in summer more voluminous, massed, and accumulated in far grander and more towering piles: secondly, the light and the appearances of the declining and the setting sun are much more fitted to be types and characters of the Infinite: and, thirdly, (which is the main reason) the exuberant and riotous prodigality of life naturally forces the mind more powerfully upon the antagonist thought of death, and the wintry sterility of the grave. For it may be observed, generally, that wherever two thoughts stand related to each other by a law of antagonism, and exist, as it were, by mutual repulsion, they are apt to suggest each other. On these accounts it is that I find it impossible to banish the thought of death when I am walking alone in the endless days of summer; and any particular death, if not more affecting, at least haunts my mind more obstinately and besiegingly in that season. Perhaps this cause, and a slight incident which I omit, might have been the immediate occasions of the following dream; to which, however, a predisposition must always have existed in my mind; but having been once roused, it never left me, and split into a thousand fantastic varieties, which often suddenly reunited, and composed again the original dream.

I thought that it was a Sunday morning in May, that it was Easter Sunday,* and as yet very early in the morning. I was standing, as it seemed to me, at the door of my own cottage. Right before me lay the very scene which could really be commanded from that situation, but exalted, as was usual, and solemnized by the power of dreams.

There were the same mountains, and the same lovely valley at their feet; but the mountains were raised to more than Alpine height, and there was interspace far larger between them of meadows and forest lawns; the hedges were rich with white roses; and no living creature was to be seen, excepting that in the green church-yard there were cattle tranquilly reposing upon the verdant graves, and particularly round about the grave of a child* whom I had tenderly loved, just as I had really beheld them, a little before sun-rise in the same summer, when that child died. I gazed upon the well-known scene, and I said aloud (as I thought) to myself, 'it yet wants much of sun-rise; and it is Easter Sunday; and that is the day on which they celebrate the first fruits of resurrection.* I will walk abroad; old griefs shall be forgotten to-day; for the air is cool and still, and the hills are high, and stretch away to Heaven; and the forest-glades are as quiet as the church-yard; and, with the dew, I can wash the fever from my forehead, and then I shall be unhappy no longer.' And I turned, as if to open my garden gate; and immediately I saw upon the left a scene far different; but which yet the power of dreams had reconciled into harmony with the other. The scene was an oriental one; and there also it was Easter Sunday, and very early in the morning. And at a vast distance were visible, as a stain upon the horizon, the domes and cupolas of a great city—an image or faint abstraction, caught perhaps in childhood from some picture of Jerusalem. And not a bow-shot from me, upon a stone, and shaded by Judean palms, there sat a woman; and I looked; and it was—Ann! She fixed her eyes upon me earnestly; and I said to her at length: 'So then I have found you at last.' I waited: but she answered me not a word. Her face was the same as when I saw it last, and yet again how different! Seventeen years ago, when the lamp-light fell upon her face, as for the last time I kissed her lips (lips, Ann, that to me were not polluted), her eyes were streaming with tears: the tears were now wiped away; she seemed more beautiful than she was at that time, but in all other points the same, and not older. Her looks were tranquil, but with unusual solemnity of expression; and I now gazed upon her with some awe, but suddenly her countenance grew dim, and, turning to the mountains, I perceived vapours rolling between us; in a moment, all had vanished; thick darkness came on; and, in the twinkling of an eye,* I was far away from mountains, and by lamp-light in Oxford-street, walking again with Ann—just as we walked seventeen years before, when we were both children.

As a final specimen, I cite one of a different character, from 1820.

The dream commenced with a music which now I often heard in dreams—a music of preparation and of awakening suspense; a music like the opening of the Coronation Anthem,* and which, like *that*, gave the feeling of a vast march—of infinite cavalcades filing off—and the tread of innumerable armies. The morning was come of a mighty day—a day of crisis and of final hope for human nature, then suffering some mysterious eclipse, and labouring in some dread extremity. Somewhere, I knew not where—somehow, I knew not how—by some beings, I knew not whom—a battle, a strife, an agony, was conducting,—was evolving like a great drama, or piece of music; with which my sympathy was the more insupportable from my confusion as to its place, its cause, its nature, and its possible issue. I, as is usual in dreams (where, of necessity, we make ourselves central to every movement), had the power, and yet had not the power, to decide it. I had the power, if I could raise myself, to will it; and yet again had not the power, for the weight of twenty Atlantics was upon me, or the oppression of inexpiable guilt. 'Deeper than ever plummet sounded,'* I lay inactive. Then, like a chorus, the passion deepened. Some greater interest was at stake; some mightier cause than ever yet the sword had pleaded, or trumpet had proclaimed. Then came sudden alarms: hurryings to and fro: trepidations of innumerable fugitives, I knew not whether from the good cause or the bad: darkness and lights: tempest and human faces; and at last, with the sense that all was lost, female forms, and the features that were worth all the world to me, and but a moment allowed,—and clasped hands, and heart-breaking partings, and then—everlasting farewells! and with a sigh, such as the caves of hell sighed when the incestuous mother uttered the abhorred name of death,* the sound was reverberated—everlasting farewells! and again, and yet again reverberated—everlasting farewells!

And I awoke in struggles, and cried aloud—'I will sleep no more!'*

But I am now called upon to wind up a narrative which has already extended to an unreasonable length. Within more spacious limits, the materials which I have used might have been better unfolded; and much which I have not used might have been added with effect. Perhaps, however, enough has been given. It now remains that I should say something of the way in which this conflict of horrors was finally brought to its crisis. The reader is already aware (from a passage near the beginning of the introduction to the first part) that the opium-eater has, in some way or other, 'unwound, almost to its final links, the accursed chain which bound him.' By what means? To have narrated this, according to the original intention, would have far exceeded the space which can now be allowed. It is fortunate, as such a cogent reason exists for abridging it, that I should, on a maturer view of the case, have been exceedingly unwilling to injure, by any such unaffecting details, the impression of the history itself, as an appeal to the prudence and the conscience of the yet unconfirmed opium-eater—or even (though a very inferior consideration) to injure its effect as a composition. The interest of the judicious reader will not attach itself chiefly to the subject of the fascinating spells, but to the fascinating power. Not the opium-eater, but the opium, is the true hero of the tale; and the legitimate centre on which the interest revolves. The object was to display the marvellous agency of opium, whether for pleasure or for pain: if that is done, the action of the piece has closed.

However, as some people, in spite of all laws to the contrary, will persist in asking what became of the opium-eater, and in what state he now is, I answer for him thus: The reader is aware that opium had long ceased to found its empire on spells of pleasure; it was solely by the tortures connected with the attempt to abjure it, that it kept its hold. Yet, as other tortures, no less it may be thought, attended the non-abjuration of such a tyrant, a choice only of evils was left; and *that* might as well have been adopted, which, however terrific in itself, held out a prospect of final restoration to happiness. This appears true; but good logic gave the author no strength to act upon it. However, a crisis arrived for the author's life, and a crisis for other objects still dearer to him—and which will always be far dearer to him than his life, even now that it is again a happy one.—I saw that I must die if I continued the opium: I determined, therefore, if that should be required, to die in throwing it off. How much I was at that time taking I cannot say; for the opium which I used had been purchased for me by a friend who afterwards refused to let me pay him; so that I could not ascertain even what quantity I had used within the year. I apprehend, however, that I took it very irregularly: and that I varied from about fifty or sixty grains, to 150 a-day. My first task was to reduce it to forty, to thirty, and, as fast as I could, to twelve grains.

I triumphed: but think not, reader, that therefore my sufferings were ended; nor think of me as of one sitting in a *dejected* state. Think of me as of one, even when four months had passed, still agitated, writhing, throbbing, palpitating, shattered; and much, perhaps, in the situation of him who has been racked, as I collect the torments of that state from the affecting account of them left by a most innocent sufferer[1] (of the times of James I).* Meantime, I derived no benefit from any medicine, except one prescribed to me by an Edinburgh surgeon of great eminence, viz. ammoniated tincture of Valerian.* Medical account, therefore, of my emancipation I have not much to give: and even that little, as managed by a man so ignorant of medicine as myself, would probably tend only to mislead. At all events, it would be misplaced in this situation. The moral of the narrative is addressed to the opium-eater; and therefore, of necessity, limited in its application. If he is taught to fear and tremble, enough has been effected. But he may say, that the issue of my case is at least a proof that opium, after a seventeen years' use, and an eight years' abuse of its powers, may still be renounced: and that *he* may chance to bring to the task greater energy than I did, or that with a stronger constitution than mine he may obtain the same results with less. This may be true: I would not presume to measure the efforts of other men by my own: I heartily wish him more energy: I wish him the same success. Nevertheless, I had motives external to myself which he may unfortunately want: and these supplied me with conscientious supports which mere personal interests might fail to supply to a mind debilitated by opium.

Jeremy Taylor conjectures that it may be as painful to be born as to die:* I think it probable: and, during the whole period of diminishing the opium, I had the torments of a man passing out of one mode of existence into another. The issue was not death, but a sort of physical regeneration: and I may add, that ever since, at intervals, I have had a restoration of more than youthful spirits, though under the pressure of difficulties, which, in a less happy state of mind, I should have called misfortunes.

One memorial of my former condition still remains: my dreams are not yet perfectly calm: the dread swell and agitation of the storm have

[1] William Lithgow: his book (Travels, &c.) is ill and pedantically written: but the account of his own sufferings on the rack at Malaga is overpoweringly affecting.*

not wholly subsided: the legions that encamped in them are drawing off, but not all departed: my sleep is still tumultuous, and, like the gates of Paradise to our first parents when looking back from afar, it is still (in the tremendous line of Milton)—

> With dreadful faces throng'd and fiery arms.*

SUSPIRIA DE PROFUNDIS:*

BEING A SEQUEL TO THE CONFESSIONS OF
AN ENGLISH OPIUM-EATER

INTRODUCTORY NOTICE

In 1821, as a contribution to a periodical work—in 1822, as a separate volume—appeared the 'Confessions of an English Opium-Eater.' The object of that work was to reveal something of the grandeur which belongs *potentially* to human dreams.* Whatever may be the number of those in whom this faculty of dreaming splendidly can be supposed to lurk, there are not perhaps very many in whom it is developed. He whose talk is of oxen, will probably dream of oxen:* and the condition of human life, which yokes so vast a majority to a daily experience incompatible with much elevation of thought, oftentimes neutralizes the tone of grandeur in the reproductive faculty of dreaming, even for those whose minds are populous with solemn imagery. Habitually to dream magnificently, a man must have a constitutional determination to reverie. This in the first place; and even this, where it exists strongly, is too much liable to disturbance from the gathering agitation of our present English life. Already, in this year 1845, what by the procession through fifty years of mighty revolutions amongst the kingdoms of the earth, what by the continual development of vast physical agencies—steam in all its applications, light getting under harness as a slave for man,[1] powers from heaven descending upon education and accelerations of the press, powers from hell (as it might seem, but these also celestial) coming round upon artillery and the forces of destruction—the eye of the calmest observer is troubled; the brain is haunted as if by some jealousy of ghostly beings moving amongst us; and it becomes too evident that, unless this colossal pace of advance can be retarded, (a thing not to be expected,) or, which is happily more probable, can be met by counter-forces of corresponding magnitude, forces in the direction of religion or profound philosophy, that shall radiate centrifugally against this storm of life so perilously centripetal towards the vortex of the merely

[1] Daguerreotype, &c.*

human, left to itself the natural tendency of so chaotic a tumult must be to evil; for some minds to lunacy, for others to a reagency of fleshly torpor.* How much this fierce condition of eternal hurry,* upon an arena too exclusively human in its interests, is likely to defeat the grandeur which is latent in all men, may be seen in the ordinary effect from living too constantly in varied company. The word *dissipation*, in one of its uses, expresses that effect; the action of thought and feeling is too much dissipated and squandered. To reconcentrate them into meditative habits, a necessity is felt by all observing persons for some-times retiring from crowds. No man ever will unfold the capacities of his own intellect who does not at least chequer his life with solitude. How much solitude, so much power.* Or, if not true in that rigour of expression, to this formula undoubtedly it is that the wise rule of life must approximate.

Among the powers in man which suffer by this too intense life of the *social* instincts, none suffers more than the power of dreaming. Let no man think this a trifle. The machinery for dreaming planted in the human brain was not planted for nothing. That faculty, in alliance with the mystery of darkness, is the one great tube through which man communicates with the shadowy. And the dreaming organ, in connexion with the heart, the eye, and the ear, compose the magnificent apparatus which forces the infinite into the chambers of a human brain, and throws dark reflections from eternities below all life upon the mirrors of the sleeping mind.

But if this faculty suffers from the decay of solitude, which is becom-ing a visionary idea in England, on the other hand, it is certain that some merely physical agencies can and do assist the faculty of dreaming almost preternaturally. Amongst these is intense exercise; to some extent at least, and for some persons: but beyond all others is opium, which indeed seems to possess a *specific* power in that direction; not merely for exalting the colours of dream-scenery, but for deepening its shadows; and, above all, for strengthening the sense of its fearful *realities*.

The *Opium Confessions* were written with some slight secondary purpose of exposing this specific power of opium upon the faculty of dreaming, but much more with the purpose of displaying the faculty itself; and the outline of the work travelled in this course. Supposing a reader acquainted with the true object of the Confessions as here stated, viz. the revelation of dreaming, to have put this question:—

'But how came you to dream more splendidly than others?'

The answer would have been:—'Because (*praemissis praemittendis*)* I took excessive quantities of opium.'

Secondly, suppose him to say, 'But how came you to take opium in this excess?'

The answer to *that* would be, 'Because some early events in my life had left a weakness in one organ which required (or seemed to require) that stimulant.'

Then, because the opium dreams could not always have been understood without a knowledge of these events, it became necessary to relate them. Now, these two questions and answers exhibit the *law* of the work, *i.e.* the principle which determined its form, but precisely in the inverse or regressive order. The work itself opened with the narration of my early adventures. These, in the natural order of succession, led to the opium as a resource for healing their consequences; and the opium as naturally led to the dreams. But in the synthetic order* of presenting the facts, what stood last in the succession of development, stood first in the order of my purposes.

At the close of this little work, the reader was instructed to believe— and *truly* instructed—that I had mastered the tyranny of opium. The fact is, that *twice* I mastered it, and by efforts even more prodigious, in the second of these cases, than in the first. But one error I committed in both. I did not connect with the abstinence from opium—so trying to the fortitude under *any* circumstances—that enormity of exercise which (as I have since learned) is the one sole resource for making it endurable. I overlooked, in those days, the one *sine quâ non** for making the triumph permanent. Twice I sank, twice I rose again. A third time I sank; partly from the cause mentioned, (the oversight as to exercise,) partly from other causes, on which it avails not now to trouble the reader. I could moralize if I chose; and perhaps *he* will moralize whether I choose it or not. But, in the mean time, neither of us is acquainted properly with the circumstances of the case; I, from natural bias of judgment, not altogether acquainted; and he (with his permission) not at all.

During this third prostration before the dark idol, and after some years, new and monstrous phenomena began slowly to arise. For a time, these were neglected as accidents, or palliated by such remedies as I knew of. But when I could no longer conceal from myself that these dreadful symptoms were moving forward for ever, by a pace steadily, solemnly, and equably increasing, I endeavoured, with some feeling of panic, for a third time to retrace my steps. But I had not reversed my motions for many weeks, before I became profoundly aware that this was impossible. Or, in the imagery of my dreams, which translated every thing into their own language, I saw through vast avenues of gloom those towering gates of ingress which hitherto had always seemed to stand open, now at last barred against my retreat, and hung with funeral crape.

As applicable to this tremendous situation, (the situation of one escaping by some refluent current from the maelstrom roaring for him in the distance, who finds suddenly that this current is but an eddy, wheeling round upon the same maelstrom,) I have since remembered a striking incident in a modern novel.* A lady abbess of a convent, herself suspected of Protestant leanings, and in that way already disarmed of all effectual power, finds one of her own nuns (whom she knows to be innocent) accused of an offence leading to the most terrific of punishments. The nun will be immured alive if she is found guilty; and there is no chance that she will not—for the evidence against her is strong—unless something were made known that cannot be made known; and the judges are hostile. All follows in the order of the reader's fears. The witnesses depose; the evidence is without effectual contradiction; the conviction is declared; the judgment is delivered; nothing remains but to see execution done. At this crisis the abbess, alarmed too late for effectual interposition, considers with herself that, according to the regular forms, there will be one single night open during which the prisoner cannot be withdrawn from her own separate jurisdiction. This one night, therefore, she will use, at any hazard to herself, for the salvation of her friend. At midnight, when all is hushed in the convent, the lady traverses the passages which lead to the cells of prisoners. She bears a master-key under her professional habit. As this will open every door in every corridor,—already, by anticipation, she feels the luxury of holding her emancipated friend within her arms. Suddenly she has reached the door; she descries a dusky object; she raises her lamp; and, ranged within the recess of the entrance, she beholds the funeral banner of the Holy Office,* and the black robes of its inexorable officials.

I apprehend that, in a situation such as this, supposing it a real one, the lady abbess would not start, would not show any marks externally of consternation or horror. The case was beyond *that*. The sentiment which attends the sudden revelation that *all is lost!* silently is gathered up into the heart; it is too deep for gestures or for words; and no part of it passes to the outside. Were the ruin conditional, or were it in any point doubtful, it would be natural to utter ejaculations, and to seek sympathy. But where the ruin is understood to be absolute, where sympathy cannot be consolation, and counsel cannot be hope, this is otherwise. The voice perishes; the gestures are frozen; and the spirit of man flies back upon its own centre. I, at least, upon seeing those awful gates closed and hung with draperies of woe, as for a death already past, spoke not, nor started, nor groaned. One profound sigh ascended from my heart, and I was silent for days.

It is the record of this third, or final stage of opium, as one differing in something more than degree from the others, that I am now undertaking. But a scruple arises as to the true interpretation of these final symptoms. I have elsewhere explained, that it was no particular purpose of mine, and *why* it was no particular purpose, to warn other opium-eaters.* Still, as some few persons may use the record in that way, it becomes a matter of interest to ascertain how far it is likely, that, even with the same excesses, other opium-eaters could fall into the same condition. I do not mean to lay a stress upon any supposed idiosyncrasy in myself. Possibly every man has an idiosyncrasy. In some things, undoubtedly, he has. For no man ever yet resembled another man so far, as not to differ from him in features innumerable of his inner nature. But what I point to are not peculiarities of temperament or of organization, so much as peculiar circumstances and incidents through which my own separate experience had revolved. Some of these were of a nature to alter the whole economy of my mind. Great convulsions, from whatever cause, from conscience, from fear, from grief, from struggles of the will, sometimes, in passing away themselves, do not carry off the changes which they have worked. *All* the agitations of this magnitude which a man may have threaded in his life, he neither ought to report, nor *could* report. But one which affected my childhood is a privileged exception. It is privileged as a proper communication for a stranger's ear; because, though relating to a man's proper self, it is a self so far removed from his present self as to wound no feelings of delicacy or just reserve. It is privileged also as a proper subject for the sympathy of the narrator. An adult sympathizes with himself in childhood because he *is* the same, and because (being the same) yet he is *not* the same.* He acknowledges the deep, mysterious identity between himself, as adult and as infant, for the ground of his sympathy; and yet, with this general agreement, and necessity of agreement, he feels the differences between his two selves as the main quickeners of his sympathy. He pities the infirmities, as they arise to light in his young forerunner, which now perhaps he does not share; he looks indulgently upon errors of the understanding, or limitations of view which now he has long survived; and sometimes, also, he honours in the infant that rectitude of will which, under *some* temptations, he may since have felt it so difficult to maintain.

The particular case to which I refer in my own childhood, was one of intolerable grief; a trial, in fact, more severe than many people at *any* age are called upon to stand. The relation in which the case stands to my latter opium experiences, is this:—Those vast clouds of gloomy grandeur which overhung my dreams at all stages of opium, but which grew into the darkest of miseries in the last, and that haunting of the human face, which latterly towered into a curse—were they not partly derived from this childish experience? It is certain that, from the essential solitude in which my childhood was passed; from the depth of my sensibility; from the exaltation of this by the resistance of an intellect too prematurely developed, it resulted that the terrific grief which I passed through, drove a shaft for me into the worlds of death and darkness which never again closed, and through which it might be said that I ascended and descended at will, according to the temper of my spirits. Some of the phenomena developed in my dream-scenery, undoubtedly, do but repeat the experiences of childhood; and others seem likely to have been growths and fructifications from seeds at that time sown.

The reasons, therefore, for prefixing some account of a 'passage' in childhood, to this record of a dreadful visitation from opium excess, are—1st, That, in colouring, it harmonizes with that record, and, therefore, is related to it at least in point of feeling; 2dly, That possibly it was in part the origin of some features in that record, and so far is related to it in logic; 3dly, That, the final assault of opium being of a nature to challenge the attention of medical men, it is important to clear away all doubts and scruples which can gather about the roots of such a malady. Was it opium, or was it opium in combination with something else, that raised these storms?

Some cynical reader will object—that for this last purpose it would have been sufficient to state the fact, without rehearsing *in extenso** the particulars of that case in childhood. But the reader of more kindness (for a surly reader is always a bad critic) will also have more discernment; and he will perceive that it is not for the mere facts that the case is reported, but because these facts move through a wilderness of natural thoughts or feelings; some in the child who suffers; some in the man who reports; but all so far interesting as they relate to solemn objects. Meantime, the objection of the sullen critic reminds me of a scene sometimes beheld at the English lakes. Figure to yourself an energetic tourist, who protests every where that he comes only to see the lakes. He has no business whatever; he is not searching for any recreant indorser of a bill,* but simply in search of the picturesque.* Yet this man adjures every landlord, 'by the virtue of his oath,'* to tell him, and as he hopes for peace in this world to tell him truly, which is the *nearest* road to Keswick. Next, he applies to the postilions—the Westmoreland* postilions always fly down hills at full stretch without locking*—but nevertheless, in the full career of their fiery race,* our picturesque man lets down the glasses,* pulls up four horses and two postilions, at the risk of six necks and twenty legs, adjuring them to reveal whether they are taking the *shortest* road. Finally, he descries my unworthy self upon the road; and, instantly stopping his flying equipage, he demands of me (as one whom he believes to be a scholar and a man of honour) whether there is not, in the possibility of things, a *shorter* cut to Keswick. Now, the answer which rises to the lips of landlord, two postilions, and myself, is this—'Most excellent stranger, as you come to the lakes simply to see their loveliness, might it not be as well to ask after the most beautiful road, rather than the shortest? Because, if abstract shortness, if τὸ brevity* is your object, then the shortest of all possible tours would seem, with submission—never to have left London.' On the same principle, I tell my critic that the whole course of this narrative resembles, and was meant to resemble, a *caduceus** wreathed about with meandering ornaments, or the shaft of a tree's stem hung round and surmounted with some vagrant parasitical plant. The mere medical subject of the opium answers to the dry withered pole, which shoots all the rings of the flowering plants, and seems to do so by some dexterity of its own; whereas, in fact, the plant and its tendrils have curled round the sullen cylinder by mere luxuriance of *theirs*. Just as in Cheapside,* if you look right and left, the streets so narrow, that lead off at right angles, seem quarried and blasted out of some Babylonian brick kiln; bored, not raised artificially by the builder's hand. But, if you enquire of the worthy men who live in that neighbourhood, you will find it unanimously deposed—that not the streets were quarried out of the bricks, but, on the contrary, (most ridiculous as it seems,) that the bricks have supervened upon the streets.

The streets did not intrude amongst the bricks, but those cursed bricks came to imprison the streets. So, also, the ugly pole—hop pole, vine pole, espalier, no matter what—is there only for support. Not the flowers are for the pole, but the pole is for the flowers. Upon the same analogy view me, as one (in the words of a true and most impassioned poet[1]) '*viridantem floribus hastas*'—making verdant, and gay with the life of flowers, murderous spears and halberts*— things that express death in their origin, (being made from dead substances that once had lived in forests,) things that express ruin in their use. The true object in my 'Opium Confessions' is not the naked physiological theme—on the contrary, *that* is the ugly pole, the murderous spear, the halbert—but those wandering musical variations upon the theme—those parasitical thoughts, feelings, digressions, which climb up with bells and blossoms round about the arid stock; ramble away from it at times with perhaps too rank a luxuriance; but at the same time, by the eternal interest attached to the *subjects* of these digressions, no matter what were the execution, spread a glory over incidents that for themselves would be—less than nothing.

PART I

THE AFFLICTION OF CHILDHOOD

It is so painful to a lover of open-hearted sincerity, that any indirect traits of vanity should even *seem* to creep into records of profound passion; and yet, on the other hand, it is so impossible, without an unnatural restraint upon the freedom of the narrative, to prevent oblique gleams reaching the reader from such circumstances of luxury or elegance as did really surround my childhood, that on all accounts I think it better to tell him from the first, with the simplicity of truth, in what order of society my family moved at the time from

---

[1] Valerius Flaccus.

which this preliminary narrative is dated. Otherwise it would happen that, merely by moving truly and faithfully through the circumstances of this early experience, I could hardly prevent the reader from receiving an impression as of some higher rank than did really belong to my family. My father was a merchant;* not in the sense of Scotland, where it means a man who sells groceries in a cellar, but in the English sense, a sense severely exclusive—viz. he was a man engaged in *foreign* commerce, and no other; therefore, in *wholesale* commerce, and no other,—which last circumstance it is important to mention, because it brings him within the benefit of Cicero's condescending distinction[1]—as one to be despised, certainly, but not too intensely to be despised even by a Roman senator. He, this imperfectly despicable man, died at an early age, and very soon after the incidents here recorded, leaving to his family, then consisting of a wife and six children, an unburthened estate producing exactly £1600 a-year. Naturally, therefore, at the date of my narrative, if narrative it can be called, he had an income still larger, from the addition of current commercial profits. Now, to any man who is acquainted with commercial life, but above all, with such life in England, it will readily occur that in an opulent English family of that class—opulent, though not rich in a mercantile estimate—the domestic economy is likely to be upon a scale of liberality altogether unknown amongst the corresponding orders in foreign nations. Whether as to the establishment of servants, or as to the provision made for the comfort of all its members, such a household not uncommonly eclipses the scale of living even amongst the poorer classes of our nobility, though the most splendid in Europe—a fact which, since the period of my infancy, I have had many personal opportunities for verifying both in England and in Ireland. From this peculiar anomaly affecting the domestic economy of merchants, there arises a disturbance upon the general scale of outward signs by which we measure the relations of rank. The equation, so to speak, between one order of society and another, which usually travels in the natural line of their comparative expenditure, is here interrupted and defeated, so that one rank would be collected from the name of the occupation, and another rank, much higher, from the splendour of the domestic *ménage*.* I warn the reader,

---

[1] Cicero, in a well-known passage of his *Ethics*, speaks of trade as irredeemably base, if petty; but as not so absolutely felonious if wholesale.* He gives a *real* merchant (one who is such in the English sense) leave to think himself a shade above small-beer.*

therefore, (or rather, my explanation has already warned him,) that he is not to infer from any casual gleam of luxury or elegance a corresponding elevation of rank.

We, the children of the house, stood in fact upon the very happiest tier in the scaffolding of society for all good influences. The prayer of Agar—'Give me neither poverty nor riches'*—was realized for us. That blessing had we, being neither too high nor too low; high enough we were to see models of good manners; obscure enough to be left in the sweetest of solitudes. Amply furnished with the nobler benefits of wealth, *extra* means of health, of intellectual culture, and of elegant enjoyment, on the other hand, we knew nothing of its social distinctions. Not depressed by the consciousness of privations too sordid, not tempted into restlessness by the consciousness of privileges too aspiring, we had no motives for shame, we had none for pride. Grateful also to this hour I am, that, amidst luxuries in all things else, we were trained to a Spartan simplicity of diet—that we fared, in fact, very much less sumptuously than the servants. And if (after the model of the emperor Marcus Aurelius)* I should return thanks to Providence for all the separate blessings of my early situation, these four I would single out as chiefly worthy to be commemorated—that I lived in the country; that I lived in solitude; that my infant feelings were moulded by the gentlest of sisters, not by horrid pugilistic brothers;* finally, that I and they were dutiful children of a pure, holy, and magnificent church.

————

The earliest incidents in my life which affected me so deeply as to be rememberable at this day, were two, and both before I could have completed my second year, viz. a remarkable dream of terrific grandeur about a favourite nurse, which is interesting for a reason to be noticed hereafter; and secondly, the fact of having connected a profound sense of pathos with the re-appearance, very early in spring, of some crocuses. This I mention as inexplicable, for such annual resurrections of plants and flowers affect us only as memorials, or suggestions of a higher change, and therefore in connexion with the idea of death; but of death I could, at that time, have had no experience whatever.

This, however, I was speedily to acquire. My two eldest sisters—eldest of three *then* living, and also elder than myself—were summoned to an early death. The first who died was Jane*—about a

year older than myself. She was three and a half, I two and a half,*
plus or *minus* some trifle that I do not recollect. But death was then
scarcely intelligible to me, and I could not so properly be said to suffer sorrow as a sad perplexity.* There was another death in the house
about the same time, viz. of a maternal grandmother;* but as she had
in a manner come to us for the express purpose of dying in her daughter's society, and from illness had lived perfectly secluded, our nursery party knew her but little, and were certainly more affected by the
death (which I witnessed) of a favourite bird, viz. a kingfisher who
had been injured by an accident. With my sister Jane's death (though
otherwise, as I have said, less sorrowful than unintelligible) there
was, however, connected an incident which made a most fearful
impression upon myself, deepening my tendencies to thoughtfulness
and abstraction beyond what would seem credible for my years. If
there was one thing in this world from which, more than from any
other, nature had forced me to revolt, it was brutality and violence.*
Now a whisper arose in the family, that a woman-servant, who by
accident was drawn off from her proper duties to attend my sister
Jane for a day or two, had on one occasion treated her harshly, if not
brutally; and as this ill treatment happened within two days of her
death—so that the occasion of it must have been some fretfulness in
the poor child caused by her sufferings—naturally there was a sense
of awe diffused through the family. I believe the story never reached
my mother, and possibly it was exaggerated; but upon me the effect
was terrific. I did not often see the person charged with this cruelty;
but, when I did, my eyes sought the ground; nor could I have borne
to look her in the face—not through anger; and as to vindictive
thoughts, how could these lodge in a powerless infant? The feeling
which fell upon me was a shuddering awe, as upon a first glimpse of
the truth that I was in a world of evil and strife. Though born in a
large town, I had passed the whole of my childhood, except for the
few earliest weeks, in a rural seclusion.* With three innocent little
sisters for playmates,* sleeping always amongst them, and shut up
for ever in a silent garden from all knowledge of poverty, or oppression, or outrage, I had not suspected until this moment the true
complexion of the world in which myself and my sisters were living.
Henceforward the character of my thoughts must have changed
greatly; for so *representative* are some acts, that one single case of the
class is sufficient to throw open before you the whole theatre of

possibilities in that direction. I never heard that the woman, accused of this cruelty, took it at all to heart, even after the event, which so immediately succeeded, had reflected upon it a more painful emphasis. On the other hand, I knew of a case, and will pause to mention it, where a mere semblance and shadow of such cruelty, under similar circumstances, inflicted the grief of self-reproach through the remainder of life. A boy, interesting in his appearance, as also from his remarkable docility, was attacked, on a cold day of spring, by a complaint of the trachea—not precisely croup, but like it. He was three years old, and had been ill perhaps for four days; but at intervals had been in high spirits, and capable of playing. This sunshine, gleaming through dark clouds, had continued even on the fourth day; and from nine to eleven o'clock at night, he had showed more animated pleasure than ever. An old servant, hearing of his illness, had called to see him; and her mode of talking with him had excited all the joyousness of his nature. About midnight his mother, fancying that his feet felt cold, was muffling them up in flannels; and, as he seemed to resist her a little, she struck lightly on the sole of one foot as a mode of admonishing him to be quiet. He did not repeat his motion; and in less than a minute his mother had him in her arms with his face looking upwards. 'What is the meaning,' she exclaimed, in sudden affright, 'of this strange repose settling upon his features?' She called loudly to a servant in another room; but before the servant could reach her, the child had drawn two inspirations—deep, yet gentle—and had died in his mother's arms. Upon this the poor afflicted lady made the discovery that those struggles, which she had supposed to be expressions of resistance to herself, were the struggles of departing life. It followed, or seemed to follow, that with these final struggles had blended an expression, on *her* part, of displeasure. Doubtless the child had not distinctly perceived it; but the mother could never look back to the incident without self-reproach. And seven years after, when her own death happened, no progress had been made in reconciling her thoughts to that which only the depth of love could have viewed as any offence.*

So passed away from earth one out of those sisters that made up my nursery playmates; and so did my acquaintance (if such it could be called) commence with mortality. Yet, in fact, I knew little more of mortality than that Jane had disappeared. She had gone away; but, perhaps, she would come back. Happy interval of heaven-born

ignorance! Gracious immunity of infancy from sorrow dispropor-
tioned to its strength! I was sad for Jane's absence. But still in my
heart I trusted that she would come again. Summer and winter came
again—crocuses and roses; why not little Jane?

Thus easily was healed, then, the first wound in my infant heart.
Not so the second. For thou, dear, noble Elizabeth, around whose
ample brow, as often as thy sweet countenance rises upon the darkness, I fancy a tiara of light or a gleaming *aureola* in token of thy
premature intellectual grandeur—thou whose head, for its superb
developments, was the astonishment of science[1]—thou next, but
after an interval of happy years, thou also wert summoned away from
our nursery; and the night which, for me, gathered upon that event,
ran after my steps far into life; and perhaps at this day I resemble little for good or for ill that which else I should have been. Pillar of fire,*
that didst go before me to guide and to quicken—pillar of darkness,
when thy countenance was turned away to God, that didst too truly
shed the shadow of death* over my young heart—in what scales
should I weigh thee? Was the blessing greater from thy heavenly
presence, or the blight which followed thy departure? Can a man
weigh off and value the glories of dawn against the darkness of hurricane? Or, if he could, how is it that, when a memorable love has
been followed by a memorable bereavement, even suppose that God
would replace the sufferer in a point of time anterior to the entire
experience, and offer to cancel the woe, but so that the sweet face
which had caused the woe should also be obliterated—vehemently
would every man shrink from the exchange! In the *Paradise Lost*, this

[1] '*The astonishment of science.*'—Her medical attendants were Dr Percival,* a well-
known literary physician, who had been a correspondent of Condorcet, D'Alembert,*
&c., and Mr Charles White, a very distinguished surgeon. It was he who pronounced her
head to be the finest in its structure and development of any that he had ever seen—an
assertion which, to my own knowledge, he repeated in after years, and with enthusiasm.
That he had some acquaintance with the subject may be presumed from this, that he
wrote and published a work on the human skull, supported by many measurements
which he had made of heads selected from all varieties of the human species.* Meantime,
as I would be loth that any trait of what might seem vanity should creep into this record,
I will candidly admit that she died of hydrocephalus;* and it has been often supposed
that the premature expansion of the intellect in cases of that class, is altogether morbid—forced on, in fact, by the mere stimulation of the disease. I would, however,
suggest, as a possibility, the very inverse order of relation between the disease and the
intellectual manifestations. Not the disease may always have caused the preternatural
growth of the intellect, but, on the contrary, this growth coming on spontaneously, and
outrunning the capacities of the physical structure, may have caused the disease.

strong instinct of man—to prefer the heavenly, mixed and polluted with the earthly, to a level experience offering neither one nor the other—is divinely commemorated. What worlds of pathos are in that speech of Adam's—'If God should make another Eve,'* &c.—that is, if God should replace him in his primitive state, and should condescend to bring again a second Eve, one that would listen to no temptation—still that original partner of his earliest solitude—

> 'Creature in whom excell'd
> Whatever can to sight or thought be form'd,
> Holy, divine, good, amiable, or sweet'—*

even now, when she appeared in league with an eternity of woe, and ministering to his ruin, could not be displaced for him by any better or happier Eve. 'Loss of thee!'* he exclaims in this anguish of trial—

> 'Loss of thee
> Would never from my heart; no, no, I feel
> The link of nature draw me; flesh of flesh,
> Bone of my bone thou art; and from thy state
> Mine never shall be parted, bliss or woe.'[1]

But what was it that drew my heart, by gravitation so strong, to my sister? Could a child, little above six years of age, place any special value upon her intellectual forwardness? Serene and capacious as her mind appeared to me upon after review, was *that* a charm for stealing away the heart of an infant? Oh, no! I think of it *now* with interest, because it lends, in a stranger's ear, some justification to the excess of my fondness. But then it was lost upon me; or, if not lost, was but dimly perceived. Hadst thou been an idiot, my sister, not the less I must have loved thee—having that capacious heart overflowing, even as mine overflowed, with tenderness, and stung, even as mine was

---

[1] Amongst the oversights in the *Paradise Lost*, some of which have not yet been perceived, it is certainly *one*—that, by placing in such overpowering light of pathos the sublime sacrifice of Adam to his love for his frail companion, he has too much lowered the guilt of his disobedience to God. All that Milton can say afterwards, does not, and cannot, obscure the beauty of that action: reviewing it calmly, we condemn—but taking the impassioned station of Adam at the moment of temptation, we approve in our hearts. This was certainly an oversight; but it was one very difficult to redress. I remember, amongst the many exquisite thoughts of John Paul, (Richter,) one which strikes me as peculiarly touching upon this subject. He suggests—not as any grave theological comment, but as the wandering fancy of a poetic heart—that, had Adam conquered the anguish of separation as a pure sacrifice of obedience to God, his reward would have been the pardon and reconciliation of Eve, together with her restoration to innocence.*

stung, by the necessity of being loved. This it was which crowned thee with beauty—

'Love, the holy sense,
Best gift of God, in thee was most intense.'*

That lamp lighted in Paradise was kindled for me which shone so steadily in thee; and never but to thee only, never again since thy departure, *durst* I utter the feelings which possessed me. For I was the shiest of children; and a natural sense of personal dignity held me back at all stages of life, from exposing the least ray of feelings which I was not encouraged *wholly* to reveal.

It would be painful, and it is needless, to pursue the course of that sickness which carried off my leader and companion. She (according to my recollection at this moment) was just as much above eight years as I above six.* And perhaps this natural precedency in authority of judgment, and the tender humility with which she declined to assert it, had been amongst the fascinations of her presence. It was upon a Sunday evening, or so people fancied, that the spark of fatal fire fell upon that train of predispositions to a brain-complaint which had hitherto slumbered within her. She had been permitted to drink tea at the house of a labouring man, the father of an old female servant. The sun had set when she returned in the company of this servant through meadows reeking with exhalations after a fervent day. From that time she sickened. Happily a child in such circumstances feels no anxieties. Looking upon medical men as people whose natural commission it is to heal diseases, since it is their natural function to profess it, knowing them only as *ex-officio** privileged to make war upon pain and sickness—I never had a misgiving about the result. I grieved indeed that my sister should lie in bed: I grieved still more sometimes to hear her moan. But all this appeared to me no more than a night of trouble on which the dawn would soon arise. Oh! moment of darkness and delirium, when a nurse awakened me from that delusion, and launched God's thunderbolt at my heart in the assurance that my sister *must* die. Rightly it is said of utter, utter misery, that it 'cannot be *remembered*.'[1] Itself, as a remembrable thing, is swallowed up in its own chaos. Mere anarchy and confusion of mind

---

[1] 'I stood in unimaginable trance
And agony, which cannot be remember'd.'
—*Speech of Alhadra in Coleridge's Remorse.**

fell upon me. Deaf and blind I was, as I reeled under the revelation. I wish not to recal the circumstances of that time, when *my* agony was at its height, and hers in another sense was approaching. Enough to say—that all was soon over; and the morning of that day had at last arrived which looked down upon her innocent face, sleeping the sleep from which there is no awaking,* and upon me sorrowing the sorrow for which there is no consolation.

On the day after my sister's death, whilst the sweet temple of her brain was yet unviolated by human scrutiny, I formed my own scheme for seeing her once more. Not for the world would I have made this known, nor have suffered a witness to accompany me. I had never heard of feelings that take the name of 'sentimental,' nor dreamed of such a possibility. But grief even in a child hates the light, and shrinks from human eyes. The house was large; there were two staircases; and by one of these I knew that about noon, when all would be quiet, I could steal up into her chamber. I imagine that it was exactly high noon when I reached the chamber door; it was locked; but the key was not taken away. Entering, I closed the door so softly, that, although it opened upon a hall which ascended through all the stories, no echo ran along the silent walls. Then turning round, I sought my sister's face. But the bed had been moved; and the back was now turned. Nothing met my eyes but one large window wide open, through which the sun of midsummer at noonday was showering down torrents of splendour. The weather was dry, the sky was cloudless, the blue depths seemed the express types of infinity; and it was not possible for eye to behold or for heart to conceive any symbols more pathetic of life and the glory of life.

Let me pause for one instant in approaching a remembrance so affecting and revolutionary for my own mind, and one which (if any earthly remembrance) will survive for me in the hour of death,—to remind some readers, and to inform others, that in the original *Opium Confessions* I endeavoured to explain the reason[1] why death, *caeteris paribus*,* is more profoundly affecting in summer than in other parts of the year;* so far at least as it is liable to any modification at all from accidents of scenery or season. The reason, as I there suggested, lies in the antagonism between the tropical redundancy of life in summer

---

[1] Some readers will question the *fact*, and seek no reason. But did they ever suffer grief at *any* season of the year?

and the dark sterilities of the grave. The summer we see, the grave we haunt with our thoughts; the glory is around us, the darkness is within us. And, the two coming into collision, each exalts the other into stronger relief. But in my case there was even a subtler reason why the summer had this intense power of vivifying the spectacle or the thoughts of death. And, recollecting it, often I have been struck with the important truth—that far more of our deepest thoughts and feelings pass to us through perplexed combinations of *concrete* objects, pass to us as *involutes* (if I may coin that word) in compound experiences incapable of being disentangled, than ever reach us *directly*, and in their own abstract shapes.* It had happened that amongst our nursery collection of books was the Bible illustrated with many pictures. And in long dark evenings, as my three sisters with myself sate by the firelight round the *guard** of our nursery, no book was so much in request amongst us. It ruled us and swayed us as mysteriously as music. One young nurse, whom we all loved, before any candle was lighted, would often strain her eyes to read it for us; and sometimes, according to her simple powers, would endeavour to explain what we found obscure. We, the children, were all constitutionally touched with pensiveness; the fitful gloom and sudden lambencies of the room by fire-light, suited our evening state of feelings; and they suited also the divine revelations of power and mysterious beauty which awed us. Above all, the story of a just man,—man and yet *not* man, real above all things and yet shadowy above all things, who had suffered the passion of death in Palestine, slept upon our minds like early dawn upon the waters. The nurse knew and explained to us the chief differences in Oriental climates; and all these differences (as it happens) express themselves in the great varieties of summer. The cloudless sunlights of Syria—those seemed to argue everlasting summer; the disciples plucking the ears of corn*—that *must* be summer; but, above all, the very name of Palm Sunday, (a festival in the English church,) troubled me like an anthem. 'Sunday!' what was *that*? That was the day of peace which masqued another peace deeper than the heart of man can comprehend. 'Palms!'—what were they? *That* was an equivocal word: palms, in the sense of trophies, expressed the pomps of life: palms, as a product of nature, expressed the pomps of summer. Yet still even this explanation does not suffice: it was not merely by the peace and by the summer, by the deep sound of rest below all rest, and of ascending glory,—that I had been haunted.

It was also because Jerusalem stood near to those deep images both in time and in place. The great event of Jerusalem was at hand when Palm Sunday came; and the scene of that Sunday was near in place to Jerusalem.* Yet what then was Jerusalem? Did I fancy it to be the *omphalos* (navel) of the earth? That pretension had once been made for Jerusalem, and once for Delphi;* and both pretensions had become ridiculous, as the figure of the planet became known. Yes; but if not of the earth, for earth's tenant Jerusalem was the *omphalos* of mortality. Yet how? there on the contrary it was, as we infants understood, that mortality had been trampled under foot. True; but for that very reason there it was that mortality had opened its very gloomiest crater. There it was indeed that the human had risen on wings from the grave; but for that reason there also it was that the divine had been swallowed up by the abyss: the lesser star could not rise, before the greater would submit to eclipse. Summer, therefore, had connected itself with death not merely as a mode of antagonism, but also through intricate relations to Scriptural scenery and events.

Out of this digression, which was almost necessary for the purpose of showing how inextricably my feelings and images of death were entangled with those of summer, I return to the bedchamber of my sister. From the gorgeous sunlight I turned round to the corpse. There lay the sweet childish figure, there the angel face: and, as people usually fancy, it was said in the house that no features had suffered any change. Had they not? The forehead indeed, the serene and noble forehead, *that* might be the same; but the frozen eyelids, the darkness that seemed to steal from beneath them, the marble lips, the stiffening hands, laid palm to palm, as if repeating the supplications of closing anguish, could these be mistaken for life? Had it been so, wherefore did I not spring to those heavenly lips with tears and never-ending kisses? But so it was *not*. I stood checked for a moment; awe, not fear, fell upon me; and, whilst I stood, a solemn wind began to blow—the most mournful that ear ever heard. Mournful! that is saying nothing. It was a wind that had swept the fields of mortality for a hundred centuries. Many times since, upon a summer day, when the sun is about the hottest, I have remarked the same wind arising and uttering the same hollow, solemn, Memnonian,* but saintly swell: it is in this world the one sole *audible* symbol of eternity. And three times in my life I have happened to hear the same sound in the same circumstances, viz. when standing between an open window and a dead body on a summer day.

Instantly, when my ear caught this vast Aeolian intonation,* when my eye filled with the golden fulness of life, the pomps and glory of the heavens outside, and turning when it settled upon the frost which overspread my sister's face, instantly a trance fell upon me. A vault seemed to open in the zenith of the far blue sky, a shaft which ran up for ever. I in spirit rose as if on billows that also ran up the shaft for ever; and the billows seemed to pursue the throne of God; but *that* also ran before us and fled away continually. The flight and the pursuit seemed to go on for ever and ever. Frost, gathering frost, some Sarsar wind of death,* seemed to repel me; I slept—for how long I cannot say; slowly I recovered my self-possession, and found myself standing, as before, close to my sister's bed.

Oh[1] flight of the solitary child to the solitary God—flight from the ruined corpse to the throne that could not be ruined!—how rich wert thou in truth for after years. Rapture of grief, that, being too mighty for a child to sustain, foundest a happy oblivion in a heaven-born sleep, and within that sleep didst conceal a dream, whose meanings in after years, when slowly I deciphered, suddenly there flashed upon me new light; and even by the grief of a child, as I will show you reader hereafter, were confounded the falsehoods of philosophers.[2]

In the *Opium Confessions* I touched a little upon the extraordinary power connected with opium (after long use) of amplifying the dimensions of time. Space also it amplifies by degrees that are sometimes terrific. But time it is upon which the exalting and multiplying power of opium chiefly spends its operation. Time becomes infinitely elastic, stretching out to such immeasurable and vanishing termini, that it seems ridiculous to compute the sense of it on waking by expressions commensurate to human life. As in starry fields one computes by diameters of the earth's orbit, or of Jupiter's, so in valuing the *virtual* time lived during some dreams, the measurement by generations is ridiculous—by millennia is ridiculous: by aeons, I should say, if aeons were more determinate, would be also ridiculous. On this single occasion, however, in my life, the very inverse phenomenon occurred. But why speak of it in connexion with opium? Could a

---

[1] Φυγὴ μονου προς μονον.*—PLOTINUS.

[2] The thoughts referred to will be given in final notes; as at this point they seemed too much to interrupt the course of the narrative.*

child of six years old have been under that influence? No, but simply because it so exactly reversed the operation of opium. Instead of a short interval expanding into a vast one, upon this occasion a long one had contracted into a minute. I have reason to believe that a *very* long one had elapsed during this wandering or suspension of my perfect mind. When I returned to myself, there was a foot (or I fancied so) on the stairs. I was alarmed. For I believed that, if any body should detect me, means would be taken to prevent my coming again. Hastily, therefore, I kissed the lips that I should kiss no more, and slunk like a guilty thing* with stealthy steps from the room. Thus perished the vision, loveliest amongst all the shows which earth has revealed to me; thus mutilated was the parting which should have lasted for ever; thus tainted with fear was the farewell sacred to love and grief, to perfect love and perfect grief.

Oh, Ahasuerus, everlasting Jew![1] fable or not a fable, thou when first starting on thy endless pilgrimage of woe, thou when first flying through the gates of Jerusalem, and vainly yearning to leave the pursuing curse behind thee, couldst not more certainly have read thy doom of sorrow in the misgivings of thy troubled brain than I when passing for ever from my sister's room. The worm was at my heart: and, confining myself to that stage of life, I may say—the worm that could not die. For if, when standing upon the threshold of manhood, I had ceased to feel its perpetual gnawings, *that* was because a vast expansion of intellect, it was because new hopes, new necessities, and the frenzy of youthful blood, had translated me into a new creature. Man is doubtless *one* by some subtle *nexus* that we cannot perceive, extending from the newborn infant to the superannuated dotard: but as regards many affections and passions incident to his nature at different stages, he is *not* one; the unity of man in this respect is coextensive only with the particular stage to which the passion belongs. Some passions, as that of sexual love, are celestial by one half of their origin, animal and earthly by the other half. These will not survive their own appropriate stage. But love, which is *altogether* holy, like that between two children, will revisit undoubtedly by glimpses the silence and the darkness of old age: and I repeat my belief—that, unless bodily torment should forbid it, that final experience in my

---

[1] 'Everlasting Jew!'—*der ewige Jude*—which is the common German expression for *The Wandering Jew*, and sublimer even than our own.*

sister's bedroom, or some other in which her innocence was concerned, will rise again for me to illuminate the hour of death.*

On the day following this which I have recorded, came a body of
medical men to examine the brain, and the particular nature of the
complaint, for in some of its symptoms it had shown perplexing
anomalies. Such is the sanctity of death, and especially of death
alighting on an innocent child, that even gossiping people do not gos-
sip on such a subject. Consequently, I knew nothing of the purpose
which drew together these surgeons, nor suspected any thing of the
cruel changes which might have been wrought in my sister's head.
Long after this I saw a similar case; I surveyed the corpse (it was that
of a beautiful boy, eighteen years old, who had died of the same complaint)* one hour *after* the surgeons had laid the skull in ruins; but the
dishonours of this scrutiny were hidden by bandages, and had not
disturbed the repose of the countenance. So it might have been here;
but, if it were *not* so, then I was happy in being spared the shock,
from having that marble image of peace, icy and rigid as it was, unset-
tled by disfiguring images. Some hours after the strangers had withdrawn, I crept again to the room, but the door was now locked—the
key was taken away—and I was shut out for ever.

Then came the funeral. I, as a point of decorum, was carried
thither. I was put into a carriage with some gentlemen whom I did
not know. They were kind to me; but naturally they talked of things
disconnected with the occasion, and their conversation was a torment. At the church,* I was told to hold a white handkerchief to my
eyes. Empty hypocrisy! What need had *he* of masques or mockeries,
whose heart died within him at every word that was uttered? During
that part of the service which passed within the church, I made an
effort to attend, but I sank back continually into my own solitary
darkness, and I heard little consciously, except some fugitive strains
from the sublime chapter of St Paul, which in England is always
read at burials.* And here I notice a profound error of our present
illustrious Laureate.* When I heard those dreadful words—for dreadful they were to me—'It is sown in corruption, it is raised in incor-
ruption; it is sown in dishonour, it is raised in glory;' such was the
recoil of my feelings, that I could even have shrieked out a protest-
ing—'Oh, no, no!' if I had not been restrained by the publicity of the
occasion. In after years, reflecting upon this revolt of my feelings,
which, being the voice of nature in a child, must be as true as any

mere *opinion* of a child might probably be false, I saw at once the unsoundness of a passage in *The Excursion*. The book is not here, but the substance I remember perfectly. Mr Wordsworth argues, that if it were not for the unsteady faith which people fix upon the beatific condition after death of those whom they deplore, nobody could be found so selfish, as even secretly to wish for the restoration to earth of a beloved object.* A mother, for instance, could never dream of yearning for her child, and secretly calling it back by her silent aspirations from the arms of God, if she were but reconciled to the belief that really it *was* in those arms. But this I utterly deny. To take my own case, when I heard those dreadful words of St Paul applied to my sister—viz. that she should be raised a spiritual body—nobody can suppose that selfishness, or any other feeling than that of agonizing love, caused the rebellion of my heart against them. I knew already that she was to come again in beauty and power. I did not now learn this for the first time. And that thought, doubtless, made my sorrow sublimer; but also it made it deeper. For here lay the sting of it, viz. in the fatal words—'We shall be *changed*.'* How was the unity of my interest in her to be preserved, if she were to be altered, and no longer to reflect in her sweet countenance the traces that were sculptured on my heart? Let a magician ask any woman whether she will permit him to improve her child, to raise it even from deformity to perfect beauty, if that must be done at the cost of its identity, and there is no loving mother but would reject his proposal with horror. Or, to take a case that has actually happened, if a mother were robbed of her child at two years old by gipsies, and the same child were restored to her at twenty, a fine young man, but divided by a sleep as it were of death from all remembrances that could restore the broken links of their once-tender connexion, would she not feel her grief unhealed, and her heart defrauded? Undoubtedly she would. All of us ask not of God for a better thing than that we have lost; we ask for the same, even with its faults and its frailties. It is true that the sorrowing person will also be changed eventually, but that must be by death. And a prospect so remote as that, and so alien from our present nature, cannot console us in an affliction which is not remote but present— which is not spiritual but human.

Lastly came the magnificent service which the English church performs at the side of the grave. There is exposed once again, and for the last time, the coffin. All eyes survey the record of name, of sex, of age, and the day of departure from earth—records how useless! and dropped into darkness as if messages addressed to worms. Almost at the very last comes the symbolic ritual, tearing and shattering the heart with volleying discharges, peal after peal, from the final artillery of woe. The coffin is lowered into its home; it has disappeared from the eye. The sacristan stands ready with his shovel of earth and stones. The priest's voice is heard once more—*earth to earth*, and the dread rattle ascends from the lid of the coffin; *ashes to ashes*, and again the killing sound is heard; *dust to dust*,* and the farewell volley announces that the grave—the coffin—the face are sealed up for ever and ever.

Oh, grief! thou art classed amongst the depressing passions. And true it is, that thou humblest to the dust, but also thou exaltest to the clouds. Thou shakest as with ague, but also thou steadiest like frost. Thou sickenest the heart, but also thou healest its infirmities. Among the very foremost of mine was morbid sensibility to shame. And ten years afterwards, I used to reproach myself with this infirmity, by supposing the case, that, if it were thrown upon me to seek aid for a perishing fellow-creature, and that I could obtain that aid only by facing a vast company of critical or sneering faces, I might perhaps shrink basely from the duty. It is true, that no such case had ever actually occurred, so that it was a mere romance of casuistry to tax myself with cowardice so shocking. But to feel a doubt, was to feel condemnation; and the crime which *might* have been, was in my eyes the crime which *had* been. Now, however, all was changed; and for any thing which regarded my sister's memory, in one hour I received a new heart. Once in Westmoreland I saw a case resembling it. I saw a ewe suddenly put off and abjure her own nature, in a service of love—yes, slough it as completely, as ever serpent sloughed his skin. Her lamb had fallen into a deep trench, from which all escape was hopeless without the aid of man. And to a man she advanced boldly, bleating clamorously, until he followed her and rescued her beloved. Not less was the change in myself. Fifty thousand sneering faces would not have troubled me in any office of tenderness to my sister's memory. Ten legions would not have repelled me from seeking her, if there was a chance that she could be found. Mockery! it was lost upon me. Laugh at me, as one or two people did! I valued not their laughter. And when I was told insultingly to cease 'my girlish tears,' that word '*girlish*' had no sting for me, except as a verbal echo to the one eternal thought of my heart—that a girl was the sweetest thing I, in my short life, had known—that a girl it was who had crowned the earth with beauty, and had opened to my thirst fountains of pure celestial love, from which, in this world, I was to drink no more.

Interesting it is to observe how certainly all deep feelings agree in this, that they seek for solitude, and are nursed by solitude. Deep grief, deep love, how naturally do these ally themselves with religious feeling; and all three, love, grief, religion, are haunters of solitary places. Love, grief, the passion of reverie, or the mystery of devotion—what were these without solitude? All day long, when it was not impossible for me to do so, I sought the most silent and sequestered nooks in the grounds about the house, or in the neighbouring fields. The awful stillness occasionally of summer noons, when no winds were abroad, the appealing silence of grey or misty afternoons—these were fascinations as of witchcraft. Into the woods or the desert air I gazed as if some comfort lay hid in *them*. I wearied the heavens with my inquest of beseeching looks. I tormented the blue depths with obstinate scrutiny, sweeping them with my eyes and searching them for ever after one angelic face that might perhaps have permission to reveal itself for a moment. The faculty of shaping images in the distance out of slight elements, and grouping them after the yearnings of the heart, aided by a slight defect in my eyes,* grew upon me at this time. And I recal at the present moment one instance of that sort, which may show how merely shadows, or a gleam of brightness, or nothing at all, could furnish a sufficient basis for this creative faculty. On Sunday mornings I was always taken to church: it was a church on the old and natural model of England, having aisles, galleries, organ, all things ancient and venerable, and the proportions majestic. Here, whilst the congregation knelt through the long Litany, as often as we came to that passage, so beautiful amongst many that are so, where God is supplicated on behalf of 'all sick persons and young children,' and that he would 'show his pity upon all prisoners and captives'—I wept in secret, and raising my streaming eyes to the windows of the galleries, saw, on days when the sun was shining, a spectacle as affecting as ever prophet can have beheld. The sides of the windows were rich with storied glass; through the deep purples and crimsons streamed the golden light; emblazonries of heavenly illumination mingling with the earthly emblazonries of what is grandest in man. There were the apostles that had trampled upon earth, and the glories of earth, out of celestial love to man. There were the martyrs that had borne witness to the truth through flames, through torments, and through armies of fierce insulting faces. There were the saints who, under intolerable pangs, had glorified God by meek submission to his will. And all the time, whilst this tumult of sublime memorials held on as the deep chords from an accompaniment in the bass, I saw through the wide central field of the window, where the glass was uncoloured, white fleecy clouds sailing over the azure depths of the sky; were it but a fragment or a hint of such a cloud, immediately under the flash of my sorrow-haunted eye, it grew and shaped itself into a vision of beds with white lawny curtains; and in the beds lay sick children, dying children, that were tossing in anguish, and weeping clamorously for death. God, for some mysterious reason, could not suddenly release them from their pain; but he suffered the beds, as it seemed, to rise slowly through the clouds; slowly the beds ascended into the chambers of the air; slowly, also, his arms descended from the heavens, that he and his young children whom in Judea, once and for ever, he had blessed, though they *must* pass slowly through the dreadful chasm of separation, might yet meet the sooner.* These visions were self-sustained. These visions needed not that any sound should speak to me, or music mould my feelings. The hint from the Litany, the fragment from the clouds, those and the storied windows were sufficient. But not the less the blare of the tumultuous organ wrought its own separate creations. And oftentimes in anthems, when the mighty instrument threw its vast columns of sound, fierce yet melodious, over the voices of the choir—when it rose high in arches, as might seem, surmounting and overriding the strife of the vocal parts, and gathering by strong coercion the total storm into unity—sometimes I seemed to walk triumphantly upon those clouds which so recently I had looked up to as mementos of prostrate sorrow, and even as ministers of sorrow in its creations; yes, sometimes under the transfigurations of music I felt[1]

---

[1] '*I felt.*'—The reader must not forget, in reading this and other passages, that, though a child's feelings are spoken of, it is not the child who speaks. *I* decipher what the child only felt in cipher. And so far is this distinction or this explanation from pointing to any thing metaphysical or doubtful, that a man must be grossly unobservant who is not aware of what I am here noticing, not as a peculiarity of this child or that, but as a necessity of all children. Whatsoever in a man's mind blossoms and expands to his own consciousness in mature life, must have pre-existed in germ during his infancy.* I, for

of grief itself as a fiery chariot for mounting victoriously above the causes of grief.

I point so often to the feelings, the ideas, or the ceremonies of religion, because there never yet was profound grief nor profound philosophy which did not inosculate* at many points with profound religion. But I request the reader to understand, that of all things I was not, and could not have been, a child trained to *talk* of religion, least of all to talk of it controversially or polemically. Dreadful is the picture, which in books we sometimes find, of children discussing the doctrines of Christianity, and even teaching their seniors the boundaries and distinctions between doctrine and doctrine. And it has often struck me with amazement, that the two things which God made most beautiful among his works, viz. infancy and pure religion, should, by the folly of man, (in yoking them together on erroneous principles,) neutralize each other's beauty, or even form a combination positively hateful. The religion becomes nonsense, and the child becomes a hypocrite. The religion is transfigured into cant, and the innocent child into a dissembling lair.[1]

God, be assured, takes care for the religion of children wheresoever his Christianity exists. Wheresoever there is a national church established, to which a child sees his friends resorting; wheresoever he beholds all whom he honours periodically prostrate before those illimitable heavens which fill to overflowing his young adoring heart; wheresoever he sees the sleep of death falling at intervals upon men and women whom he knows, depth as confounding to the plummet of his mind as those heavens ascend beyond his power to pursue—*there* take you no thought for the religion of a child, any more

---

instance, did not, as a child, *consciously* read in my own deep feelings these ideas. No, not at all; nor was it possible for a child to do so. I the child had the feelings, I the man deciphered them. In the child lay the handwriting mysterious to *him*; in me the interpretation and the comment.

[1] I except, however, one case—the case of a child dying of an organic disorder, so therefore as to die slowly, and aware of its own condition. Because such a child is solemnized, and sometimes, in a partial sense, inspired—inspired by the depths of its sufferings, and by the awfulness of its prospect. Such a child having put off the earthly mind in many things, may naturally have put off the childish mind in all things. I therefore, speaking for myself only, acknowledge to have read with emotion a record of a little girl, who, knowing herself for months to be amongst the elect of death, became anxious even to sickness of heart for what she called the *conversion* of her father. Her filial duty and reverence had been swallowed up in filial love.

than for the lilies how they shall be arrayed, or for the ravens how they shall feed their young.*

God speaks to children also in dreams, and by the oracles that lurk in darkness. But in solitude, above all things, when made vocal by the truths and services of a national church, God holds 'communion undisturbed'* with children. Solitude, though silent as light, is, like light, the mightiest of agencies; for solitude is essential to man. All men come into this world *alone*—all leave it *alone*. Even a little child has a dread, whispering consciousness, that if he should be summoned to travel into God's presence, no gentle nurse will be allowed to lead him by the hand, nor mother to carry him in her arms, nor little sister to share his trepidations. King and priest, warrior and maiden, philosopher and child, all must walk those mighty galleries alone. The solitude, therefore, which in this world appals or fascinates a child's heart, is but the echo of a far deeper solitude through which already he has passed, and of another solitude deeper still, through which he *has* to pass: reflex of one solitude—prefiguration of another.

Oh, burthen of solitude, that cleavest to man through every stage of his being—in his birth, which *has* been—in his life, which *is*—in his death, which *shall* be—mighty and essential solitude! that wast, and art, and art to be;—thou broodest, like the spirit of God moving upon the surface of the deeps, over every heart that sleeps in the nurseries of Christendom. Like the vast laboratory of the air, which, seeming to be nothing, or less than the shadow of a shade, hides within itself the principles of all things, solitude for a child is the Agrippa's mirror* of the unseen universe. Deep is the solitude in life of millions upon millions who, with hearts welling forth love, have none to love them. Deep is the solitude of those who, with secret griefs, have none to pity them. Deep is the solitude of those who, fighting with doubts or darkness, have none to counsel them. But deeper than the deepest of these solitudes is that which broods over childhood, bringing before it at intervals the final solitude which watches for it, and is waiting for it within the gates of death. Reader, I tell you a truth, and hereafter I will convince you of this truth,* that for a Grecian child solitude was nothing, but for a Christian child it has become the power of God and the mystery of God. Oh, mighty and essential solitude, that wast, and art, and art to be—thou, kindling under the torch of Christian revelations, art now transfigured for ever, and hast passed from a blank negation into a secret hieroglyphic from God, shadowing in the hearts of infancy the very dimmest of his truths!*

'*But you forgot her*,' says the Cynic; '*you happened one day to forget this sister of yours?*'—Why not? To cite the beautiful words of Wallenstein,

> 'What pang
> Is permanent with man? From the highest
> As from the vilest thing of every day
> He learns to wean himself. For the strong hours
> Conquer him.'[1]

Yes, *there* lies the fountain of human oblivions. It is time, the great conqueror, it is the 'strong hours' whose batteries storm every passion of men. For, in the fine expression of Schiller, '*Was verschmerzte nicht der mensch?*'* What sorrow is it in man that will not finally fret itself to sleep? Conquering, at last, gates of brass, or pyramids of granite, why should it be a marvel to us, or a triumph to TIME, that he is able to conquer a frail human heart?

However, for this once my Cynic must submit to be told—that he is wrong. Doubtless, it is presumption in me to suggest that his sneers can ever go awry, any more than the shafts of Apollo.* But still, however impossible such a thing is, in this one case it happens that they *have*. And when it happens that they do not, I will tell you, reader, why in my opinion it is; and you will see that it warrants no exultation in the Cynic. Repeatedly I have heard a mother reproaching herself, when the birthday revolved of the little daughter whom so suddenly she had lost, with her own insensibility that could so soon need a remembrancer of the day. But, besides, that the majority of people in this world (as being people called to labour) have no time left for cherishing grief by solitude and meditation, always it is proper to ask whether the memory of the lost person were chiefly dependent upon a visual image. No death is usually half so affecting as the death of a young child from two to five years old.

But yet for the same reason which makes the grief more exquisite, generally for such a loss it is likely to be more perishable. Wherever the image, visually or audibly, of the lost person is more essential to the life of the grief, there the grief will be more transitory.

---

[1] *Death of Wallenstein*, Act v. Scene 1, (Coleridge's Translation,) relating to his remembrances of the younger Piccolomini.*

Faces begin soon (in Shakespeare's fine expression) to 'dislimn:'* features fluctuate: combinations of feature unsettle. Even the expression becomes a mere idea that you can describe to another, but not an image that you can reproduce for yourself. Therefore it is that the faces of infants, though they are divine as flowers in a savanna of Texas, or as the carolling of birds in a forest, are, like flowers in Texas, and the carolling of birds in a forest, soon overtaken by the pursuing darkness that swallows up all things human. All glories of flesh vanish; and this, the glory of infantine beauty seen in the mirror of the memory, soonest of all. But when the departed person worked upon yourself by powers that were intellectual and moral—powers *in* the flesh, though not *of* the flesh—the memorials in your own heart become more steadfast, if less affecting at the first. Now, in my sister were combined for me both graces—the graces of childhood, and the graces of expanding thought. Besides that, as regards merely the *personal* image, always the smooth rotundity of baby features must vanish sooner, as being less individual than the features in a child of eight, touched with a pensive tenderness,* and exalted into a characteristic expression by a premature intellect.

Rarely do things perish from my memory that are worth remembering. Rubbish dies instantly. Hence it happens that passages in Latin or English poets which I never could have read but once, (and *that* thirty years ago,) often begin to blossom anew when I am lying awake, unable to sleep. I become a distinguished compositor in the darkness; and, with my aërial composing-stick,* sometimes I 'set up' half a page of verses, that would be found tolerably correct if collated with the volume that I never had in my hand but once. I mention this in no spirit of boasting. Far from it; for, on the contrary, amongst my mortifications have been compliments to my memory, when, in fact, any compliment that I had merited was due to the higher faculty of an electric aptitude for seizing analogies, and by means of those aërial pontoons passing over like lightning from one topic to another. Still it is a fact, that this pertinacious life of memory for things that simply touch the ear without touching the consciousness, does in fact beset me. Said but once, said but softly, not marked at all, words revive before me in darkness and solitude; and they arrange themselves gradually into sentences, but through an effort sometimes of a distressing kind, to which I am in a manner forced to become a party. This being so, it was no great instance of that

power—that three separate passages in the funeral service, all of
which but one had escaped my notice at the time, and even that one
as to the part I am going to mention, but all of which must have
struck on my ear, restored themselves perfectly when I was lying
awake in bed; and though struck by their beauty, I was also incensed
by what seemed to me the harsh sentiment expressed in two of these
passages. I will cite all the three in an abbreviated form, both for my
immediate purpose, and for the indirect purpose of giving to those
unacquainted with the English funeral service some specimen of its
beauty.

The first passage was this, 'Forasmuch as it hath pleased Almighty
God, of his great mercy, to take unto himself the soul of our dear
sister here departed, we therefore commit her body to the ground,
earth to earth, ashes to ashes, dust to dust, in sure and certain hope of
the resurrection to eternal life.' * * * *

I pause to remark that a sublime effect arises at this point through
a sudden rapturous interpolation from the Apocalypse, which,
according to the rubric, 'shall be said or sung;' but always let it be
sung, and by the full choir:—

'I heard a voice from heaven saying unto me, Write, from henceforth blessed are the dead which die in the Lord; even so saith the
Spirit; for they rest from their labours.'

The second passage, almost immediately succeeding to this awful
burst of heavenly trumpets, and the one which more particularly
offended me, though otherwise even then, in my seventh year, I could
not but be touched by its beauty, was this:—'Almighty God, with
whom do live the spirits of them that depart hence in the Lord, and
with whom the souls of the faithful, after they are delivered from the
burden of the flesh, are in joy and felicity; WE give thee hearty thanks
that it hath pleased thee to deliver this our sister out of the miseries
of this sinful world; beseeching thee, that it may please thee of thy
gracious goodness shortly to accomplish the number of thine elect,
and to hasten thy kingdom.' * * *

In what world was I living when a man (calling himself a man of
God) could stand up publicly and give God 'hearty thanks' that he
had taken away my sister? But, young child, understand—taken her
away from the miseries of this sinful world. Oh yes! I hear what you
say; I understand *that*; but that makes no difference at all. She being
gone, this world doubtless (as you say) is a world of unhappiness.

But for me *ubi Caesar, ibi Roma**—where my sister was, there was paradise; no matter whether in heaven above, or on the earth beneath. And he had taken her away, cruel priest! of his *'great* mercy?' I did not presume, child though I was, to think rebelliously against *that*. The reason was not any hypocritical or canting submission where my heart yielded none, but because already my deep musing intellect had perceived a mystery and a labyrinth in the economies of this world. God, I saw, moved not as *we* moved—walked not as *we* walked— thought not as *we* think. Still I saw no mercy to myself, a poor frail dependent creature—torn away so suddenly from the prop on which altogether it depended. Oh yes! perhaps there was; and many years after I came to suspect it. Nevertheless it was a benignity that pointed far a-head; such as by a child could not have been perceived, because then the great arch had not come round; could not have been recognized if it *had* come round; could not have been valued if it had even been dimly recognized.

Finally, as the closing prayer in the whole service stood, this— which I acknowledged then, and now acknowledge, as equally beautiful and consolatory; for in this was no harsh peremptory challenge to the infirmities of human grief as to a thing not meriting notice in a religious rite. On the contrary, there was a gracious condescension from the great apostle to grief, as to a passion that he might perhaps himself have participated.

'Oh, merciful God! the father of our Lord Jesus Christ, who is the resurrection and the life, in whom whosoever believeth shall live, though he die; who also taught us by his holy apostle St Paul not to be sorry, as men without hope, for them that sleep in *him*; WE meekly beseech thee, O Father! to raise us from the death of sin unto the life of righteousness; that, when we shall depart this life, we may rest in *him* as our hope is—that this our sister doth.'

Ah, *that* was beautiful; that was heavenly! We might be sorry, we had leave to be sorry; only not without hope. And we were by hope to rest in *Him*, as this our sister doth. And howsoever a man may think that he is without hope, I, that have read the writing upon these great abysses of grief, and viewed their shadows under the correction of mightier shadows from deeper abysses since then, abysses of aboriginal fear and eldest darkness, in which yet I believe that all hope had not absolutely died, know that he is in a natural error. If, for a moment, I and so many others, wallowing in the dust of affliction, could yet rise up suddenly like the dry corpse[1] which stood upright in the glory of life when touched by the bones of the prophet; if in those vast choral anthems, heard by my childish ear, the voice of God wrapt itself as in a cloud of music, saying—'Child, that sorrowest, I command thee to rise up and ascend for a season into my heaven of heavens'—then it was plain that despair, that the anguish of darkness, was not *essential* to such sorrow, but might come and go even as light comes and goes upon our troubled earth.

Yes! the light may come and go; grief may wax and wane; grief may sink; and grief again may rise, as in impassioned minds oftentimes it does, even to the heaven of heavens; but there is a necessity—that, if too much left to itself in solitude, finally it will descend into a depth from which there is no re-ascent; into a disease which seems no disease; into a languishing which, from its very sweetness, perplexes the mind and is fancied to be very health. Witchcraft has seized upon you, nympholepsy* has struck you. Now you rave no more. You acquiesce; nay, you are passionately delighted in your condition. Sweet becomes the grave, because you also hope immediately to travel thither: luxurious is the separation, because only perhaps for a few weeks shall it exist for you; and it will then prove but the brief summer night that had retarded a little, by a refinement of rapture, the heavenly dawn of reunion. Inevitable sometimes it is in solitude—that this should happen with minds morbidly meditative; that, when we stretch out our arms in darkness, vainly striving to draw back the sweet faces that have vanished, slowly arises a new stratagem of grief, and we say—'Be it that they no more come back to us, yet what hinders but we should go to *them?*'

Perilous is that crisis for the young. In its effect perfectly the same as the ignoble witchcraft of the poor African *Obeah*,[2] this sublimer

---

[1] '*Like the dry corpse which stood upright.*'—See the *Second* Book of Kings, chap. xiii. v. 20 and 21. Thirty years ago this impressive incident was made the subject of a large altar-piece by Mr Alston,* an interesting American artist, then resident in London.

[2] '*African Obeah.*'*—Thirty years ago it would not have been necessary to say one word of the Obi or Obeah magic; because at that time several distinguished writers (Miss Edgeworth, for instance, in her Belinda)* had made use of this superstition in fictions, and because the remarkable history of Three-finger'd Jack,* a story brought upon the stage, had made the superstition notorious as a fact. Now, however, so long after the case has probably passed out of the public mind, it may be proper to mention—that when an Obeah man, *i.e.*, a professor of this dark collusion with human fears and human credulity, had once woven his dreadful net of ghostly terrors, and had thrown it over his selected victim, vainly did that victim flutter, struggle, languish in the meshes; unless the

witchcraft of grief will, if left to follow its own natural course, terminate in the same catastrophe of death. Poetry, which neglects no phenomena that are interesting to the heart of man, has sometimes touched a little

'On the sublime attractions of the grave.'*

But you think that these attractions, existing at times for the adult, could not exist for the child. Understand that you are wrong. Understand that these attractions *do* exist for the child; and perhaps as much more strongly than they *can* exist for the adult, by the whole difference between the concentration of a childish love, and the inevitable distraction upon multiplied objects of any love that can affect an adult. There is a German superstition (well-known by a popular translation) of the Erl-king's Daughter,* who fixes her love upon some child, and seeks to wile him away into her own shadowy kingdom in forests.

'Who is it that rides through the forest so fast?'

It is a knight, who carries his child before him on the saddle. The Erl-king's Daughter rides on his right hand, and still whispers temptations to the infant audible only to *him*.

'If thou wilt, dear baby, with me go away,
We will see a fine show, we will play a fine play.'

The consent of the baby is essential to her success. And finally she *does* succeed. Other charms, other temptations, would have been requisite for me. My intellect was too advanced for those fascinations. But could the Erl-king's Daughter have revealed herself to me, and promised to lead me where my sister was, she might have wiled me by the hand into the dimmest forests upon earth. Languishing was my condition at that time. Still I languished for things 'which' (a voice from heaven seemed to answer through my own heart) '*can*not be granted;' and which, when again I languished, again the voice repeated, '*cannot* be granted.'

———

Well it was for me that, at this crisis, I was summoned to put on the harness of life, by commencing my classical studies under one of my

spells were reversed, he generally perished; and without a wound except from his own too domineering fancy.

guardians, a clergyman of the English Church, and (so far as regarded Latin) a most accomplished scholar.*

At the very commencement of my new studies, there happened an incident which afflicted me much for a short time, and left behind a gloomy impression, that suffering and wretchedness were diffused amongst all creatures that breathe. A person had given me a kitten. There are three animals which seem, beyond all others, to reflect the beauty of human infancy in two of its elements—viz. joy, and guileless innocence, though less in its third element of simplicity, because *that* requires language for its full expression: these three animals are the kitten, the lamb, and the fawn. Other creatures may be as happy, but they do not show it so much. Great was the love which poor silly I had for this little kitten; but, as I left home at ten in the morning, and did not return till near five in the afternoon, I was obliged, with some anxiety, to throw it for those seven hours upon its own discretion, as infirm a basis for reasonable hope as could be imagined. I did not wish the kitten, indeed, at all less foolish than it was, except just when I was leaving home, and then its exceeding folly gave me a pang. Just about that time, it happened that we had received, as a present from Leicestershire,* a fine young Newfoundland dog, who was under a cloud of disgrace for crimes of his youthful blood committed in that county. One day he had taken too great a liberty with a pretty little cousin of mine, Emma H——,* about four years old. He had, in fact, bitten off her cheek, which, remaining attached by a shred, was, through the energy of a governess, replaced, and subsequently healed without a scar. His name being *Turk*, he was immediately pronounced by the best Greek scholar of that neighbourhood, ἐπώνυμος* (*i. e.* named significantly, or reporting his nature in his name). But as Miss Emma confessed to having been engaged in taking away a bone from him, on which subject no dog can be taught to understand a joke, it did not strike our own authorities that he was to be considered in a state of reprobation; and as our gardens (near to a great town) were, on account chiefly of melons, constantly robbed, it was held that a moderate degree of fierceness was rather a favourable trait in his character. My poor kitten, it was supposed, had been engaged in the same playful trespass upon Turk's property as my Leicestershire cousin, and Turk laid her dead on the spot. It is impossible to describe my grief when the case was made known to me at five o'clock in the evening, by a man's holding out the little creature dead:

she that I had left so full of glorious life—life which even in a kitten is infinite—was now stretched in motionless repose. I remember that there was a large coal stack in the yard. I dropped my Latin books, sat down upon a huge block of coal, and burst into a passion of tears. The man, struck with my tumultuous grief, hurried into the house; and from the lower regions deployed instantly the women of the laundry and the kitchen. No one subject is so absolutely sacred, and enjoys so *classical* a sanctity among servant girls, as 1. Grief; and 2. Love which is unfortunate. All the young women took me up in their arms and kissed me; and last of all, an elderly woman, who was the cook, not only kissed me, but wept so audibly, from some suggestion doubtless of grief personal to herself, that I threw my arms about her neck and kissed *her* also. It is probable, as I now suppose, that some account of my grief for my sister had reached them. Else I was never allowed to visit *their* region of the house. But, however *that* might be, afterwards it struck me, that if I had met with so much sympathy, or with any sympathy at all, from the servant chiefly connected with myself in the desolating grief I had suffered, possibly I should not have been so profoundly shaken.

But did I in the mean time feel anger towards Turk? Not the least. And the reason was this:—My guardian, who taught me Latin, was in the habit of coming over and dining at my mother's table whenever he pleased. On these occasions he, who like myself pitied *dependant* animals, went invariably into the yard of the offices, taking me with him, and unchained the dogs. There were two—*Grim*, a mastiff, and *Turk*, our young friend. My guardian was a bold athletic man, and delighted in dogs. He told me, which also my own heart told me, that these poor dogs languished out their lives under this confinement. The moment that I and my guardian (*ego et rex meus*)* appeared in sight of the two kennels, it is impossible to express the joy of the dogs. Turk was usually restless; Grim slept away his life in surliness. But at the sight of us—of my little insignificant self and my six-foot guardian—both dogs yelled with delight. We unfastened their chains with our own hands, they licking our hands; and as to myself, licking my miserable little face; and at one bound they re-entered upon their natural heritage of joy. Always we took them through the fields, where they molested nothing, and closed with giving them a cold bath in the brook which bounded my father's property. What despair must have possessed our dogs when they were taken back to their hateful prisons! and I, for my part, not enduring to see their misery, slunk away when the rechaining commenced. It was in vain to tell me that all people, who had property out of doors to protect, chained up dogs in the same way; *this* only proved the extent of the oppression; for a monstrous oppression it *did* seem, that creatures, boiling with life and the desires of life, should be thus detained in captivity until they were set free by death. That liberation visited poor *Grim* and *Turk* sooner than any of us expected, for they were both poisoned within the year that followed by a party of burglars. At the end of that year I was reading the Aeneid; and it struck me, who remembered the howling recusancy of *Turk*, as a peculiarly fine circumstance, introduced amongst the horrors of Tartarus, that sudden gleam of powerful animals, full of life and conscious rights, rebelling against chains:—

'Iraeque leonum
Vincla recusantum.'[1]

Virgil had doubtless picked up that gem in his visits at feeding-time to the *caveae*** of the Roman amphitheatre. But the rights of brute creatures to a merciful forbearance on the part of man, could not enter into the feeblest conceptions of one belonging to a nation that, (although too noble to be *wantonly* cruel,) yet in the same amphitheatre manifested so little regard even to human rights. Under Christianity, the condition of the brute has improved, and will improve much more. There is ample room. For I am sorry to say, that the commonest vice of Christian children, too often surveyed with careless eyes by mothers, that in their *human* relations are full of kindness, is cruelty to the inferior creatures thrown upon their mercy. For my own part, what had formed the groundwork of my happiness, (since joyous was my nature, though overspread with a cloud of sadness,) had been from the first a heart overflowing with love. And I had drunk in too profoundly the spirit of Christianity from our many nursery readings, not to read also in its divine words the justification of my own tendencies. That which I desired, was the thing which I ought to desire; the mercy that I loved was the mercy that God had blessed. From the sermon on the Mount resounded

---

[1] What follows, I think, (for book I have none of any kind where this paper is proceeding,)* viz. *et serâ sub nocte rudentum,** is probably a mistake of Virgil's; the lions did not roar because night was approaching, but because night brought with it their principal meal, and consequently the impatience of hunger.

for ever in my ears—'Blessed are the merciful!' I needed not to add—
'For they shall obtain mercy.'* By lips so holy, and when standing in
the atmosphere of truths so divine, simply to have been blessed—
that was a sufficient ratification; every truth so revealed, and so hal-
lowed by position, starts into sudden life, and becomes to itself its
own authentication, needing no proof to convince, needing no promise to allure.

It may well be supposed, therefore, that, having so early awakened
within me what may be philosophically called the *transcendental* justice of Christianity, I blamed not *Turk* for yielding to the coercion of
his nature. He had killed the object of my love. But, besides that he
was under the constraint of a primary appetite—Turk was himself
the victim of a killing oppression. He was doomed to a fretful existence so long as he should exist at all. Nothing could reconcile this to
my benignity, which at that time rested upon two pillars—upon the
deep, deep heart which God had given to me at my birth, and upon
exquisite health. Up to the age of two, and almost through that entire
space of twenty-four months, I had suffered from ague;* but when
that left me, all germs and traces of ill health fled away for ever—except
only such (and those how curable!) as I inherited from my schoolboy
distresses in London, or had created by means of opium. Even the
long ague was not without ministrations of favour to my prevailing
temper; and on the whole, no subject for pity; since naturally it won
for me the sweet caresses of female tenderness, both young and old.
I was a little petted; but you see by this time, reader, that I must have
been too much of a philosopher, even in the year one *ab urbe condita**
of my frail earthly tenement, to abuse such indulgence. It also won
for me a ride on horseback whenever the weather permitted. I was
placed on a pillow, in front of a cankered old man, upon a large white
horse, not so young as *I* was, but still showing traces of blood. And
even the old man, who was both the oldest and the worst of the three,
talked with gentleness to myself, reserving his surliness—for all the
rest of the world.

These things pressed with a gracious power of incubation upon my
predispositions; and in my overflowing love I did things fitted to
make the reader laugh, and sometimes fitted to bring myself into
perplexity. One instance from a thousand may illustrate the combination of both effects. At four years old, I had repeatedly seen the house-
maid raising her long broom and pursuing (generally destroying)

a vagrant spider. The holiness of all life, in my eyes, forced me to devise plots for saving the poor doomed wretch; and thinking inter-cession likely to prove useless, my policy was—to draw off the house-maid on pretence of showing her a picture, until the spider, already *en route*, should have had time to escape. Very soon, however, the shrewd housemaid, marking the coincidence of these picture exhibi-tions with the agonies of fugitive spiders, detected my stratagem; so that, if the reader will pardon an expression borrowed from the street, henceforwards the picture was 'no go.' However, as she approved of my motive, she told me of the many murders that the spider had committed, and next (which was worse) of the many that he certainly *would* commit if reprieved. This staggered me. I could have gladly forgiven the past; but it *did* seem a false mercy to spare one spider in order to scatter death amongst fifty flies. I thought timidly for a moment, of suggesting that people sometimes repented, and that *he* might repent; but I checked myself, on considering that I had never read any account, and that she might laugh at the idea, of a penitent spider. To desist was a necessity in these circumstances. But the dif-ficulty which the housemaid had suggested, did not depart; it troubled my musing mind to perceive, that the welfare of one creature might stand upon the ruin of another: and the case of the spider remained thenceforwards even more perplexing to my understanding than it was painful to my heart.

The reader is likely to differ from me upon the question, moved by recurring to such experiences of childhood, whether much value attaches to the perceptions and intellectual glimpses of a child. Children, like men, range through a gamut that is infinite, of tem-peraments and characters, ascending from the very dust below our feet to highest heaven. I have seen children that were sensual, brutal, devilish. But, thanks be to the *vis medicatrix** of human nature, and to the goodness of God, these are as rare exhibitions as all other monsters. People thought, when seeing such odious travesties and burlesques upon lovely human infancy, that perhaps the little wretches might be *kilcrops*.[1] Yet, possibly, (it has since occurred to me,) even these children of the fiend, as they seemed, might have one chord in their horrible natures that answered to the call of some

---

[1] '*Kilcrops*.'*—See, amongst Southey's early poems, one upon this superstition. Southey argues *contra*; but for my part, I should have been more disposed to hold a brief on the other side.

sublime purpose. There is a mimic instance of this kind, often found amongst ourselves in natures that are not really 'horrible,' but which *seem* such to persons viewing them from a station not sufficiently central:—Always there are mischievous boys in a neighbourhood, boys who tie canisters to the tails of cats belonging to ladies—a thing which *greatly* I disapprove; and who rob orchards—a thing which *slightly* I disapprove; and behold! the next day, on meeting the injured ladies, they say to me, 'Oh, my dear friend, never pretend to argue for him! This boy, we shall all see, will come to be hanged.' Well, *that* seems a disagreeable prospect for all parties; so I change the subject; and lo! five years later, there is an English frigate fighting with a frigate of heavier metal, (no matter of what nation). The noble captain has manoeuvred, as only *his* countrymen can manoeuvre; he has delivered his broadsides, as only the proud islanders can deliver them. Suddenly he sees the opening for a *coup-de-main*;* through his speaking-trumpet he shouts—'*Where are my boarders?*' And instantly rise upon the deck, with the gaiety of boyhood, in white shirt sleeves bound with black ribands, fifty men, the *élite* of the crew; and behold! at the very head of them, cutlass in hand, is our friend the tyer of canisters to the tails of ladies' cats—a thing which *greatly* I disapprove, and also the robber of orchards—a thing which *slightly* I disapprove. But here is a man that will not suffer you either greatly or slightly to disapprove him. Fire celestial burns in his eye; his nation, his glorious nation, is in his mind; himself he regards no more than the life of a cat, or the ruin of a canister. On the deck of the enemy he throws himself with rapture; and if *he* is amongst the killed, if he for an object so gloriously unselfish lays down with joy his life and glittering youth, mark this—that, perhaps, he will not be the least in heaven.*

But coming back to the case of childhood, I maintain steadfastly—that, into all the *elementary* feelings of man, children look with more searching gaze than adults. My opinion is, that where circumstances favour, where the heart is deep, where humility and tenderness exist in strength, where the situation is favourable as to solitude and as to genial feelings, children have a specific power of contemplating the truth, which departs as they enter the world. It is clear to me, that children, upon elementary paths which require no knowledge of the world to unravel, tread more firmly than men; have a more pathetic sense of the beauty which lies in justice; and, according to the immortal ode of our great laureate, (ode 'On the Intimations of Immortality in Childhood,')* a far closer communion with God. I, if you observe, do not much intermeddle with religion, properly so called. My path lies on the interspace between religion and philosophy, that connects them both. Yet here for once I shall trespass on grounds not properly mine, and desire you to observe in St Matthew, chap. xxi., and v. 15, *who* were those that, crying in the temple, made the first public recognition of Christianity. Then, if you say, 'Oh, but children echo what they hear, and are no independent authorities!' I must request you to extend your reading into v. 16,* where you will find that the testimony of these children, as bearing an *original* value, was ratified by the highest testimony; and the recognition of these children did itself receive a heavenly recognition. And this could *not* have been, unless there were children in Jerusalem who saw into truth with a far sharper eye than Sanhedrims* and Rabbis.

It is impossible, with respect to any memorable grief, that it can be adequately exhibited so as to indicate the enormity of the convulsion which really it caused, without viewing it under a variety of aspects— a thing which is here almost necessary for the effect of proportion to what follows: 1st, for instance, in its immediate pressure, so stunning and confounding; 2dly, in its oscillations, as in its earlier agitations, frantic with tumults, that borrow the wings of the winds; or in its diseased impulses of sick languishing desire, through which sorrow transforms itself to a sunny angel, that beckons us to a sweet repose. These phases of revolving affection I have already sketched. And I shall also sketch a third, *i. e.* where the affliction, seemingly hushing itself to sleep, suddenly soars upwards again upon combining with *another* mode of sorrow; viz. anxiety without definite limits, and the trouble of a reproaching conscience. As sometimes,[1] upon the English lakes, waterfowl that have careered in the air until the eye is wearied with the eternal wheelings of their inimitable flight— Grecian simplicities of motion, amidst a labyrinthine infinity of curves that would baffle the geometry of Apollonius*—seek the water at last, as if with some settled purpose (you imagine) of reposing.

---

[1] In this place I derive my feeling partly from a lovely sketch of the appearance, in verse, by Mr Wordsworth;* partly from my own experience of the case; and, not having the poems here, I know not how to proportion my acknowledgments.

Ah, how little have you understood the omnipotence of that life which they inherit! *They* want no rest; they laugh at resting; all is 'make believe,' as when an infant hides its laughing face behind its mother's shawl. For a moment it is still. Is it meaning to rest? Will its impatient heart endure to lurk there for long? Ask rather if a cataract will stop from fatigue. Will a sunbeam sleep on its travels? Or the Atlantic rest from its labours? As little can the infant, as little can the waterfowl of the lakes, suspend their play, except as a variety of play, or rest unless when nature compels them. Suddenly starts off the infant, suddenly ascend the birds, to new evolutions as incalculable as the caprices of a kaleidoscope;* and the glory of their motions, from the mixed immortalities of beauty and inexhaustible variety, becomes at least* pathetic to survey. So also, and with such life of variation, do the *primary* convulsions of nature—such, perhaps, as only *primary*[1] formations in the human system can experience—come round again and again by reverberating shocks.

The new intercourse with my guardian, and the changes of scene which naturally it led to, were of use in weaning my mind from the mere disease which threatened it in case I had been left any longer to my total solitude. But out of these changes grew an incident which restored my grief, though in a more troubled shape, and now for the first time associated with something like remorse and deadly anxiety. I can safely say that this was my earliest trespass, and perhaps a venial one—all things considered. Nobody ever discovered it; and but for my own frankness it would not be known to this day. But *that* I could not know; and for years, that is from seven or earlier up to ten, such was my simplicity, that I lived in constant terror. This, though it revived my grief, did me probably great service; because it was no longer a state of languishing desire tending to torpor, but of feverish irritation and gnawing care that kept alive the activity of

---

[1] 'And so, then,' the Cynic objects, 'you rank your own mind (and you tell us so frankly) amongst the primary formations?' As I love to annoy him, it would give me pleasure to reply—'Perhaps I do.' But as I never answer more questions than are necessary, I confine myself to saying, that this is not a necessary construction of the words. Some minds stand nearer to the type of the original nature in man, are truer than others to the great magnet in our dark planet. Minds that are impassioned on a more colossal scale than ordinary, deeper in their vibrations, and more extensive in the scale of their vibrations—whether, in other parts of their intellectual system, they had or had not a corresponding compass—will tremble to greater depths from a fearful convulsion, and will come round by a longer curve of undulations.

my understanding. The case was this:—It happened that I had now, and commencing with my first introduction to Latin studies, a large weekly allowance of pocket-money, too large for my age, but safely entrusted to myself, who never spent or desired to spend one fraction of it upon any thing but books. But all proved too little for my colossal schemes. Had the Vatican, the Bodleian, and the *Bibliothéque du Roi** been all emptied into one collection for my private gratification, little progress would have been made towards content in this particular craving. Very soon I had run ahead of my allowance, and was about three guineas deep in debt. There I paused; for deep anxiety now began to oppress me as to the course in which this mysterious (and indeed guilty) current of debt would finally flow. For the present it was frozen up; but I had some reason for thinking that Christmas thawed all debts whatsoever, and set them in motion towards innumerable pockets. Now *my* debt would be thawed with all the rest; and in what direction would it flow? There was no river that would carry it off to sea; to somebody's pocket it would beyond a doubt make its way; and who *was* that somebody? This question haunted me for ever. Christmas had come, Christmas had gone, and I heard nothing of the three guineas. But I was not easier for *that*. Far rather I *would* have heard of it; for this indefinite approach of a loitering catastrophe gnawed and fretted my feelings. No Grecian audience ever waited with more shuddering horror for the anagnorisis[1] of the Oedipus, than I for the explosion of my debt. Had I been less ignorant, I should have proposed to mortgage my weekly allowance for the debt, or to form a sinking fund for redeeming it; for the *weekly* sum was nearly five per cent on the entire debt. But I had a mysterious awe of ever alluding to it. This arose from my want of some confidential friend; whilst my grief pointed continually to the remembrance—that *so* it had not always been. But was not the bookseller to blame in suffering a child scarcely seven years old to contract such a debt? Not in the least. He was both a rich man, who could not possibly care for my trifling custom, and notoriously an honourable man. Indeed the money which I myself spent every week in books, would reasonably have caused him to presume that so small a sum as three guineas

---

[1] *i. e.* (As on account of English readers is added,) the recognition of his true identity, which in one moment, and by a horrid flash of revelation, connects him with acts incestuous, murderous, parricidal, in the past, and with a mysterious fatality of woe lurking in the future.*

might well be authorized by my family. He stood, however, on plainer ground. For my guardian, who was very indolent, (as people chose to call it,) that is, like his little melancholy ward, spent all his time in reading, often enough would send me to the bookseller's with a written order for books. This was to prevent my forgetting. But when he found that such a thing as 'forgetting' in the case of a book, was wholly out of the question for me, the trouble of writing was dismissed. And thus I had become factor-general on the part of my guardian, both for *his* books, and for such as were wanted on my own account in the natural course of my education. My private 'little account' had therefore in fact flowed homewards at Christmas, not (as I anticipated) in the shape of an independent current, but as a little tributary rill that was lost in the waters of some more important river. This I now know, but could not then have known with any certainty. So far, however, the affair would gradually have sunk out of my anxieties as time wore on. But there was another item in the case, which, from the excess of my ignorance, preyed upon my spirits far more keenly; and this, keeping itself alive, kept also the other incident alive. With respect to the debt, I was not so ignorant as to think it of much danger by the mere amount: my own allowance furnished a scale for preventing *that* mistake: it was the principle, the having presumed to contract debts on my own account, that I feared to have exposed. But this other case was a ground for anxiety even as regarded the amount; not really; but under the jesting representation made to me, which I (as ever before and after) swallowed in perfect faith. Amongst the books which I had bought, all English, was a history of Great Britain, commencing of course with Brutus and a thousand years of impossibilities;* these fables being generously thrown in as a little gratuitous *extra* to the mass of truths which were to follow. This was to be completed in sixty or eighty parts, I believe. But there was another work left more indefinite as to its ultimate extent, and which from its nature seemed to imply a far wider range. It was a general history of navigation, supported by a vast body of voyages. Now, when I considered with myself what a huge thing the sea was, and that so many thousands of captains, commodores, admirals, were eternally running up and down it, and scoring lines upon its face so rankly, that in some of the main 'streets' and 'squares' (as one might call them) their tracks would blend into one undistinguishable blot,—I began to fear that such a work tended to infinity. What was

little England to the universal sea?* And yet *that* went perhaps to
fourscore parts. Not enduring the uncertainty that now besieged my
tranquillity, I resolved to know the worst; and on a day ever memorable to me I went down to the bookseller's. He was a mild elderly man,
and to myself had always shown a kind indulgent manner. Partly perhaps he had been struck by my extreme gravity; and partly, during
the many conversations I had with him, on occasion of my guardian's
orders for books, with my laughable simplicity. But there was another
reason which had early won for me his paternal regard. For the first
three or four months I had found Latin something of a drudgery;
and the incident which for ever knocked away the 'shores,'* at that
time preventing my launch upon the general bosom of Latin literature, was this:—One day the bookseller took down a Beza's *Latin
Testament*;* and, opening it, asked me to translate for him the chapter
which he pointed to. I was struck by perceiving that it was the great
chapter of St Paul* on the grave and resurrection. I had never seen a
Latin version: yet from the simplicity of the scriptural style in *any*
translation, (though Beza's is far from good,) I could not well have
failed in construing. But as it happened to be this particular chapter,
which in English I had read again and again with so passionate a
sense of its grandeur, I read it off with a fluency and effect like some
great opera-singer uttering a rapturous *bravura*.* My kind old friend
expressed himself gratified, making me a present of the book as a
mark of his approbation. And it is remarkable, that from this moment,
when the deep memory of the English words had forced me into seeing the precise correspondence of the two concurrent streams—
Latin and English—never again did any difficulty arise to check the
velocity of my progress in this particular language. At less than eleven
years of age, when as yet I was a very indifferent Grecian, I had
become a brilliant master of Latinity, as my Alcaics and Choriambics*
remain to testify: and the whole occasion of a change so memorable
to a boy, was this casual summons to translate a composition with
which my heart was filled. Ever after this he showed me a caressing
kindness, and so condescendingly, that generally he would leave any
people for a moment with whom he was engaged, to come and speak
to me. On this fatal day, however, for such it proved to me, he could
not do this. He saw me, indeed, and nodded, but could not leave a
party of elderly strangers. This accident threw me unavoidably upon
one of his young people. Now this was a market-day; and there was a

press of country people present, whom I did not wish to hear my question. Never did human creature, with his heart palpitating at Delphi* for the solution of some killing mystery, stand before the priestess of the oracle, with lips that moved more sadly than mine, when now advancing to a smiling young man at a desk. His answer was to decide, though I could not exactly know *that*, whether for the next two years I was to have an hour of peace. He was a handsome, good-natured young man, but full of fun and frolic; and I dare say was amused with what must have seemed to *him* the absurd anxiety of my features. I described the work to him, and he understood me at once: how many volumes did he think it would extend to? There was a whimsical expression perhaps of drollery about his eyes, but which unhappily, under my preconceptions, I translated into scorn, as he replied,—'How many volumes? Oh! really I can't say, maybe a matter of 15,000, be the same more or less.' '*More?*' I said in horror, altogether neglecting the contingency of 'less.' 'Why,' he said, 'we can't settle these things to a nicety. But, considering the subject,' (ay, *that* was the very thing which I myself considered,) 'I should say, there might be some trifle over, as suppose 400 or 500 volumes, be the same more or less.' What, then, here there might be supplements to supplements—the work might positively *never* end. On one pretence or another, if an author or publisher might add 500 volumes, he might add another round 15,000. Indeed it strikes one even now, that by the time all the one-legged commodores and yellow admirals* of that generation had exhausted their long yarns, another generation would have grown another crop of the same gallant spinners. I asked no more, but slunk out of the shop, and never again entered it with cheerfulness, or propounded any frank questions as heretofore. For I was now seriously afraid of pointing attention to myself as one that, by having purchased some numbers, and obtained others on credit, had silently contracted an engagement to take all the rest, though they should stretch to the crack of doom.* Certainly I had never heard of a work that extended to 15,000 volumes; but still there was no natural impossibility that it should; and, if in any case, in none so reasonably as one upon the inexhaustible sea. Besides, any slight mistake as to the letter of the number, could not affect the horror of the final prospect. I saw by the imprint, and I heard, that this work emanated from London, a vast centre of mystery to me, and the more so, as a thing unseen at any time by my eyes, and nearly

200 miles distant. I felt the fatal truth, that here was a ghostly cobweb radiating into all the provinces from the mighty metropolis. I secretly had trodden upon the outer circumference, had damaged or deranged the fine threads and links,—concealment or reparation there could be none. Slowly perhaps, but surely, the vibration would travel back to London. The ancient spider that sat there at the centre, would rush along the network through all longitudes and latitudes, until he found the responsible caitiff,* author of so much mischief. Even, with less ignorance than mine, there *was* something to appal a child's imagination in the vast systematic machinery by which any elaborate work could disperse itself, could levy money, could put questions and get answers—all in profound silence, nay, even in darkness—searching every nook of every town, and of every hamlet in so populous a kingdom. I had some dim terrors, also, connected with the Stationers' Company.* I had often observed them in popular works threatening unknown men with unknown chastisements, for offences equally unknown; nay, to myself, absolutely inconceivable. Could *I* be the mysterious criminal so long pointed out, as it were, in prophecy? I figured the stationers, doubtless all powerful men, pulling at one rope, and my unhappy self hanging at the other end. But an image, which seems now even more ludicrous than the rest, at that time was the one most connected with the revival of my grief. It occurred to my subtlety, that the Stationers' Company, or any other company, could not possibly demand the money until they had delivered the volumes. And, as no man could say that I had ever positively refused to receive them, they would have no pretence for not accomplishing this delivery in a civil manner. Unless I should turn out to be no customer at all, at present it was clear that I had a right to be considered a most excellent customer; one, in fact, who had given an order for fifteen thousand volumes. Then rose up before me this great opera-house 'scena'* of the delivery. There would be a ring at the front door. A waggoner in the front, with a bland voice, would ask for 'a young gentleman who had given an order to *their* house.' Looking out, I should perceive a procession of carts and waggons, all advancing in measured movements; each in turn would present its rear, deliver its cargo of volumes, by shooting them, like a load of coals, on the lawn, and wheel off to the rear, by way of clearing the road for its successors. Then the impossibility of even asking the servants to cover with sheets, or counterpanes,* or table-cloths, such

a mountainous, such a 'star-y-pointing'* record of my past offences
lying in so conspicuous a situation! Men would not know my guilt
merely, they would see it. But the reason why this form of the consequences, so much more than any other, stuck by my imagination was,
that it connected itself with one of the Arabian nights which had
particularly interested myself and my sister. It was that tale, where a
young porter, having his ropes about his person, had stumbled into
the special 'preserve' of some old magician.* He finds a beautiful lady
imprisoned, to whom (and not without prospects of success) he rec-
ommends himself as a suitor, more in harmony with her own years
than a withered magician. At this crisis the magician returns. The
young man bolts, and for that day successfully; but unluckily he
leaves his ropes behind. Next morning he hears the magician, too
honest by half, enquiring at the front door, with much expression of
condolence, for the unfortunate young man who had lost his ropes
in his own zenana.* Upon this story I used to amuse my sister, by
ventriloquizing to the magician from the lips of the trembling young
man—'Oh, Mr Magician, these ropes cannot be mine! They are far
too good; and one wouldn't like, you know, to rob some other poor
young man. If you please, Mr Magician, I never had money enough
to buy so beautiful a set of ropes.' But argument is thrown away upon
a magician, and off he sets on his travels with the young porter—not
forgetting to take the ropes along with him.

Here now was the case, that had once seemed so impressive to me
in a mere fiction from a far-distant age and land, literally reproduced
in myself. For what did it matter whether a magician dunned one
with old ropes for his engines of torture, or Stationers' Hall with
15,000 volumes, (in the rear of which there might also be ropes?)
Should *I* have ventriloquized, would my sister have laughed, had
either of us but guessed the possibility that I myself, and within one
twelve months, and, alas! standing alone in the world as regarded
confidential counsel, should repeat within my own inner experience
the shadowy panic of the young Bagdat intruder upon the privacy
of magicians? It appeared, then, that I had been reading a legend
concerning myself in the *Arabian Nights*. I had been contemplated
in types a thousand years before on the banks of the Tigris.* It was
horror and grief that prompted that thought.

Oh, heavens! that the misery of a child should by possibility
become the laughter of adults!—that even I, the sufferer, should be

capable of amusing myself, as if it had been a jest, with what for three years had constituted the secret affliction of my life, and its eternal trepidation—like the ticking of a death-watch* to patients lying awake in the plague. I durst ask no counsel; there was no one to ask. Possibly my sister could have given me none in a case which neither of us should have understood, and where to seek for information from others, would have been at once to betray the whole reason for seeking it. But, if no advice, she would have given me her pity, and the expression of her endless love; and, with the relief of sympathy, that heals for a season all distresses, she would have given me that exquisite luxury—the knowledge that, having parted with my secret, yet also I had *not* parted with it, since it was in the power only of one that could much less betray me than I could betray myself. At this time, that is about the year when I suffered most, I was reading Caesar.* Oh, laurelled scholar—sunbright intellect—'foremost man of all this world'*—how often did I make out of thy immortal volume a pillow to support my wearied brow, as at evening, on my homeward road, I used to turn into some silent field, where I might give way unobserved to the reveries which besieged me!* I wondered, and found no end of wondering, at the revolution that one short year had made in my happiness. I wondered that such billows *could* overtake me! At the beginning of that year how radiantly happy! At the end how insupportably alone!

> 'Into what depth thou see'st,
> From what height fallen.'*

For ever I searched the abysses with some wandering thoughts unintelligible to myself. For ever I dallied with some obscure notion, how my sister's love might be made in some dim way available for delivering me from misery; or else how the misery I had suffered and was suffering might be made, in some way equally dim, the ransom for winning back her love.

———

Here pause, reader! Imagine yourself seated in some cloud-scaling swing, oscillating under the impulse of lunatic hands; for the strength of lunacy may belong to human dreams, the fearful caprice of lunacy, and the malice of lunacy, whilst the *victim* of those dreams may be all the more certainly removed from lunacy; even as a bridge gathers cohesion and strength from the increasing resistance into which it is forced by increasing pressure. Seated in such a swing, fast as you reach the lowest point of depression, may you rely on racing up to a starry altitude of corresponding ascent. Ups and downs you will see, heights and depths, in our fiery course together, such as will some-times tempt you to look shyly and suspiciously at me, your guide, and the ruler of the oscillations. Here, at the point where I have called a halt, the reader has reached the lowest depth in my nursery afflic-tions. From that point, according to the principles of *art* which govern the movement of these Confessions, I had meant to launch him upwards through the whole arch of ascending visions which seemed requisite to balance the sweep downwards, so recently described in his course. But accidents of the press have made it impossible to accomplish this purpose in the present month's journal. There is rea-son to regret that the advantages of position, which were essential to the full effect of passages planned for equipoise and mutual resist-ance, have thus been lost.* Meantime, upon the principle of the mariner who rigs a *jury*-mast* in default of his regular spars, I find my resource in a sort of 'jury' peroration—not sufficient in the way of a balance by its *proportions*, but sufficient to indicate the *quality* of the balance which I had contemplated. He who has *really* read the preceding parts of these present Confessions, will be aware that a stricter scrutiny of the past, such as was natural after the whole econ-omy of the dreaming faculty had been convulsed beyond all prece-dents on record, led me to the conviction that not one agency, but two agencies, had co-operated to the tremendous result. The nursery experience had been the ally and the natural co-efficient of the opium. For that reason it was that the nursery experience has been narrated. Logically, it bears the very same relation to the convulsions of the dreaming faculty as the opium. The idealizing tendency existed in the dream-theatre of my childhood; but the preternatural strength of its action and colouring was first developed after the confluence of the *two* causes. The reader must suppose me at Oxford: twelve years and a half are gone by; I am in the glory of youthful happiness; but I have now first tampered with opium; and now first the agitations of my childhood reopened in strength, now first they swept in upon the brain with power and the grandeur of recovered life, under the separ-ate and the concurring inspirations of opium.

Once again, after twelve years' interval, the nursery of my child-hood expanded before me—my sister was moaning in bed—I was beginning to be restless with fears not intelligible to myself. Once again the nurse, but now dilated to colossal proportions, stood as upon some Grecian stage with her uplifted hand, and like the superb Medea standing alone with her children in the nursery at Corinth,[1] smote me senseless to the ground. Again, I was in the chamber with my sister's corpse—again the pomps of life rose up in silence, the glory of summer, the frost of death.* Dream formed itself mysteriously within dream; within these Oxford dreams remoulded itself continually the trance in my sister's chamber,—the blue heavens, the everlasting vault, the soaring billows, the throne steeped in the thought (but not the sight) of 'Him that sate thereon;'* the flight, the pursuit, the irrecoverable steps of my return to earth. Once more the funeral procession gathered; the priest in his white surplice stood waiting with a book in his hand by the side of an open grave, the sacristan with his shovel; the coffin sank; the *dust to dust* descended. Again I was in the church on a heavenly Sunday morning. The golden sunlight of God slept amongst the heads of his apostles, his martyrs, his saints; the fragment from the litany—the fragment from the clouds—awoke again the lawny beds that went up to scale the heavens—awoke again the shadowy arms that moved downwards to meet them. Once again, arose the swell of the anthem—the burst of the Hallelujah chorus—the storm—the trampling movement of the choral passion—the agitation of my own trembling sympathy—the tumult of the choir—the wrath of the organ. Once more I, that wallowed, became he that rose up to the clouds. And now in Oxford, all was bound up into unity; the first state and the last were melted into each other as in some sunny glorifying haze. For high above my own station, hovered a gleaming host of heavenly beings, surrounding the pillows of the dying children. And such beings sympathize equally with sorrow that grovels and with sorrow that soars. Such beings pity alike the children that are languishing in death, and the children that live only to languish in tears.*

THE PALIMPSEST

You know perhaps, masculine reader, better than I can tell you, what is a *Palimpsest*. Possibly you have one in your own library. But yet, for

---

[1] Euripides.*

the sake of others who may *not* know, or may have forgotten, suffer me to explain it here: lest any female reader,* who honours these papers with her notice, should tax me with explaining it once too seldom; which would be worse to bear than a simultaneous complaint from twelve proud men, that I had explained it three times too often. You therefore, fair reader, understand that for *your* accommodation exclusively, I explain the meaning of this word. It is Greek; and our sex enjoys the office and privilege of standing counsel to yours, in all questions of Greek. We are, under favour, perpetual and hereditary dragomans* to you. So that if, by accident, you know the meaning of a Greek word, yet by courtesy to us, your counsel learned in that matter, you will always seem *not* to know it.

A palimpsest, then, is a membrane or roll cleansed of its manuscript by reiterated successions.

What was the reason that the Greeks and the Romans had not the advantage of printed books? The answer will be, from ninety-nine persons in a hundred—Because the mystery of printing was not then discovered. But this is altogether a mistake. The secret of printing must have been discovered many thousands of times before it was used, or *could* be used. The inventive powers of man are divine; and also his stupidity is divine—as Cowper so playfully illustrates in the slow development of the *sofa* through successive generations of immortal dulness. It took centuries of blockheads to raise a joint stool into a chair; and it required something like a miracle of genius, in the estimate of elder generations, to reveal the possibility of lengthening a chair into a *chaise-longue*, or a sofa.* Yes, these were inventions that cost mighty throes of intellectual power. But still, as respects printing, and admirable as is the stupidity of man, it was really not quite equal to the task of evading an object which stared him in the face with so broad a gaze. It did not require an Athenian intellect to read the main secret of printing in many scores of processes which the ordinary uses of life were *daily* repeating. To say nothing of analogous artifices amongst various mechanic artisans, all that is essential in printing must have been known to every nation that struck coins and medals. Not, therefore, any want of a printing art—that is, of an art for multiplying impressions—but the want of a cheap material for *receiving* such impressions, was the obstacle to an introduction of printed books even as early as Pisistratus.* The ancients *did* apply printing to records of silver and gold; to marble and many other substances cheaper than gold and silver, they did *not*, since each monument required a *separate* effort of inscription. Simply this defect it was of a cheap material for receiving impresses, which froze in its very fountains the early resources of printing.

Some twenty years ago, this view of the case was luminously expounded by Dr Whately, the present archbishop of Dublin,* and with the merit, I believe, of having first suggested it. Since then, this theory has received indirect confirmation. Now, out of that original scarcity affecting all materials proper for durable books, which continued up to times comparatively modern, grew the opening for palimpsests. Naturally, when once a roll of parchment or of vellum had done its office, by propagating through a series of generations what once had possessed an interest for *them*, but which, under changes of opinion or of taste, had faded to their feelings or had become obsolete for their understandings, the whole *membrana* or vellum skin, the twofold product of human skill, costly material, and costly freight of thought, which it carried, drooped in value concurrently—supposing that each were inalienably associated to the other. Once it had been the impress of a human mind which stamped its value upon the vellum; the vellum, though costly, had contributed but a secondary element of value to the total result. At length, however, this relation between the vehicle and its freight has gradually been undermined. The vellum, from having been the setting of the jewel, has risen at length to be the jewel itself; and the burden of thought, from having given the chief value to the vellum, has now become the chief obstacle to its value; nay, has totally extinguished its value, unless it can be dissociated from the connexion. Yet, if this unlinking *can* be effected, then—fast as the inscription upon the membrane is sinking into rubbish—the membrane itself is reviving in its separate importance; and, from bearing a ministerial value, the vellum has come at last to absorb the whole value.

Hence the importance for our ancestors that the separation *should* be effected. Hence it arose in the middle ages, as a considerable object for chemistry, to discharge the writing from the roll, and thus to make it available for a new succession of thoughts. The soil, if cleansed from what once had been hot-house plants, but now were held to be weeds, would be ready to receive a fresh and more appropriate crop. In that object the monkish chemists succeeded; but after a fashion which seems almost incredible; incredible not as regards the extent of their success, but as regards the delicacy of restraints under which it moved; so equally adjusted was their success to the immediate interests of that period, and to the reversionary interests of our own. They did the thing; but not so radically as to prevent us, their posterity, from *un*doing it. They expelled the writing sufficiently to leave a field for the new manuscript, and yet not sufficiently to make the traces of the elder manuscript irrecoverable for us. Could magic, could Hermes Trismegistus,* have done more? What would you think, fair reader, of a problem such as this—to write a book which should be sense for your own generation, nonsense for the next, should revive into sense for the next after that, but again became nonsense for the fourth; and so on by alternate successions, sinking into night or blazing into day, like the Sicilian river Arethusa, and the English river Mole*—or like the undulating motions of a flattened stone which children cause to skim the breast of a river, now diving below the water, now grazing its surface, sinking heavily into darkness, rising buoyantly into light, through a long vista of alternations? Such a problem, you say, is impossible. But really it is a problem not harder apparently than—to bid a generation kill, but so that a subsequent generation may call back into life; bury, but so that posterity may command to rise again. Yet *that* was what the rude chemistry of past ages effected when coming into combination with the reaction from the more refined chemistry of our own. Had *they* been better chemists, had *we* been worse—the mixed result, viz. that, dying for *them*, the flower should revive for *us*, could not have been effected: They did the thing proposed to them: they did it effectually; for they founded upon it all that was wanted: and yet ineffectually, since we unravelled their work; effacing all above which they had superscribed; restoring all below which they had effaced.

Here, for instance, is a parchment which contained some Grecian tragedy, the Agamemnon of Aeschylus, or the Phoenissae of Euripides.* This had possessed a value almost inappreciable in the eyes of accomplished scholars, continually growing rarer through generations. But four centuries are gone by since the destruction of the Western Empire.* Christianity, with towering grandeurs of another class, has founded a different empire; and some bigoted yet perhaps holy monk has washed away (as he persuades himself) the heathen's tragedy, replacing it with a monastic legend; which legend is disfigured with fables in its incidents, and yet, in a higher sense, is

true, because interwoven with Christian morals and with the sub-
limest of Christian revelations. Three, four, five, centuries more find
man still devout as ever; but the language has become obsolete, and
even for Christian devotion a new era has arisen, throwing it into the
channel of crusading zeal or of chivalrous enthusiasm. The *membrana*
is wanted now for a knightly romance—for 'my Cid,' or Coeur de
Lion; for Sir Tristrem, or Lybaeus Disconus.* In this way, by means
of the imperfect chemistry known to the mediaeval period, the same
roll has served as a conservatory for three separate generations of
flowers and fruits, all perfectly different, and yet all specially adapted
to the wants of the successive possessors. The Greek tragedy, the
monkish legend, the knightly romance, each has ruled its own period.
One harvest after another has been gathered into the garners of man
through ages far apart. And the same hydraulic machinery has distributed, through the same marble fountains, water, milk, or wine,
according to the habits and training of the generations that came to
quench their thirst.

Such were the achievements of rude monastic chemistry. But the
more elaborate chemistry of our own days* has reversed all these
motions of our simple ancestors, with results in every stage that to
them would have realized the most fantastic amongst the promises of
thaumaturgy.* Insolent vaunt of Paracelsus, that he would restore
the original rose or violet out of the ashes settling from its combustion*—*that* is now rivalled in this modern achievement. The traces
of each successive handwriting, regularly effaced, as had been
imagined, have, in the inverse order, been regularly called back: the
footsteps of the game pursued, wolf or stag, in each several chase,
have been unlinked, and hunted back through all their doubles;* and,
as the chorus of the Athenian stage unwove through the antistrophe
every step that had been mystically woven through the strophe, so,
by our modern conjurations of science, secrets of ages remote from
each other have been exorcised[1] from the accumulated shadows of
centuries. Chemistry, a witch as potent as the Erictho of Lucan,
(*Pharsalia*, lib. vi. or vii.,)* has extorted by her torments, from the
dust and ashes of forgotten centuries, the secrets of a life extinct for

---

[1] Some readers may be apt to suppose, from all English experience, that the word
exorcise means properly banishment to the shades. Not so. Citation *from* the shades, or
sometimes the torturing coercion of mystic adjurations, is more truly the primary
sense.

the general eye, but still glowing in the embers. Even the fable of the Phoenix*—that secular bird, who propagated his solitary existence, and his solitary births, along the line of centuries, through eternal relays of funeral mists—is but a type of what we have done with Palimpsests. We have backed upon each Phoenix in the long *regressus*,* and forced him to expose his ancestral Phoenix, sleeping in the ashes below his own ashes. Our good old forefathers would have been aghast at our sorceries; and, if they speculated on the propriety of burning Dr Faustus,* *us* they would have burned by acclamation. Trial there would have been none; and they could no otherwise have satisfied their horror of the brazen profligacy marking our modern magic, than by ploughing up the houses of all who had been parties to it, and sowing the ground with salt.

Fancy not, reader, that this tumult of images, illustrative or allusive, moves under any impulse or purpose of mirth. It is but the coruscation of a restless understanding, often made ten times more so by irritation of the nerves, such as you will first learn to comprehend (its *how* and its *why*) some stage or two ahead. The image, the memorial, the record, which for me is derived from a palimpsest, as to one great fact in our human being, and which immediately I will show you, is but too repellent of laughter; or, even if laughter *had* been possible, it would have been such laughter as oftentimes is thrown off from the fields of ocean[1]—laughter that hides, or that seems to evade mustering tumult; foam-bells that weave garlands of phosphoric radiance for one moment round the eddies of gleaming abysses; mimicries of earth-born flowers that for the eye raise phantoms of gaiety, as oftentimes for the ear they raise echoes of fugitive laughter, mixing with the ravings and choir-voices of an angry sea.

What else than a natural and mighty palimpsest is the human brain? Such a palimpsest is my brain; such a palimpsest, O reader! is yours. Everlasting layers of ideas, images, feelings, have fallen upon your brain softly as light. Each succession has seemed to bury all that went before. And yet in reality not one has been extinguished. And if,

---

[1] '*Laughter from the fields of ocean.*'—Many readers will recall, though at the moment of writing my own thoughts did *not* recall, the well-known passage in the Prometheus*—

$$-\pi o\nu\tau\iota\omega\nu \ \tau\epsilon \ \kappa\upsilon\mu\alpha\tau\omega\nu$$
$$'A\nu\eta\rho\iota\theta\mu o\nu \ \gamma\epsilon\lambda\alpha\sigma\mu\alpha.$$

'Oh multitudinous laughter of the ocean billows!' It is not clear whether Aeschylus contemplated the laughter as addressing the ear or the eye.

in the vellum palimpsest, lying amongst the other *diplomata** of
human archives or libraries, there is any thing fantastic or which
moves to laughter, as oftentimes there is in the grotesque collisions
of those successive themes, having no natural connexion, which by
pure accident have consecutively occupied the roll, yet, in our own
heaven-created palimpsest, the deep memorial palimpsest of the
brain, there are not and cannot be such incoherencies. The fleeting
accidents of a man's life, and its external shows, may indeed be irre-
late and incongruous; but the organizing principles which fuse into
harmony, and gather about fixed predetermined centres, whatever
heterogeneous elements life may have accumulated from without,
will not permit the grandeur of human unity greatly to be violated, or
its ultimate repose to be troubled in the retrospect from dying
moments, or from other great convulsions.

Such a convulsion is the struggle of gradual suffocation, as in
drowning; and, in the original Opium Confessions, I mentioned a
case of that nature communicated to me by a lady from her own childish experience. The lady is still living, though now of unusually great
age;* and I may mention—that amongst her faults never was numbered any levity of principle, or carelessness of the most scrupulous
veracity; but, on the contrary, such faults as arise from austerity, too
harsh perhaps, and gloomy—indulgent neither to others nor herself.
And, at the time of relating this incident, when already very old, she
had become religious to asceticism.* According to my present belief,
she had completed her ninth year, when playing by the side of a solitary brook, she fell into one of its deepest pools. Eventually, but after
what lapse of time nobody ever knew, she was saved from death by a
farmer, who, riding in some distant lane, had seen her rise to the
surface; but not until she had descended within the abyss of death,
and looked into its secrets, as far, perhaps, as ever human eye *can*
have looked that had permission to return. At a certain stage of this
descent, a blow seemed to strike her—phosphoric radiance sprang
forth from her eyeballs; and immediately a mighty theatre expanded
within her brain. In a moment, in the twinkling of an eye,* every
act—every design of her past life lived again—arraying themselves
not as a succession, but as parts of a coexistence. Such a light fell
upon the whole path of her life backwards into the shades of infancy,
as the light perhaps which wrapt the destined apostle on his road to
Damascus.* Yet that light blinded for a season; but hers poured

celestial vision upon the brain, so that her consciousness became omnipresent at one moment to every feature in the infinite review.

This anecdote was treated sceptically at the time by some critics. But besides that it has since been confirmed by other experiences essentially the same, reported by other parties in the same circumstances who had never heard of each other; the true point for astonishment is not the *simultaneity* of arrangement under which the past events of life—though in fact successive—had formed their dread line of revelation. This was but a secondary phenomenon; the deeper lay in the resurrection itself, and the possibility of resurrection, for what had so long slept in the dust. A pall, deep as oblivion, had been thrown by life over every trace of these experiences; and yet suddenly, at a silent command, at the signal of a blazing rocket sent up from the brain, the pall draws up, and the whole depths of the theatre are exposed. Here was the greater mystery: now this mystery is liable to no doubt; for it is repeated, and ten thousand times repeated by opium, for those who are its martyrs.

Yes, reader, countless are the mysterious handwritings of grief or joy which have inscribed themselves successively upon the palimpsest of your brain; and, like the annual leaves of aboriginal forests, or the undissolving snows on the Himalaya, or light falling upon light, the endless strata have covered up each other in forgetfulness. But by the hour of death, but by fever, but by the searchings of opium, all these can revive in strength. They are not dead, but sleeping. In the illustration imagined by myself, from the case of some individual palimpsest, the Grecian tragedy had seemed to be displaced, but was *not* displaced, by the monkish legend; and the monkish legend had seemed to be displaced, but was *not* displaced, by the knightly romance. In some potent convulsion of the system, all wheels back into its earliest elementary stage. The bewildering romance, light tarnished with darkness, the semi-fabulous legend, truth celestial mixed with human falsehoods, these fade even of themselves as life advances. The romance has perished that the young man adored. The legend has gone that deluded the boy. But the deep deep tragedies of infancy, as when the child's hands were unlinked for ever from his mother's neck, or his lips for ever from his sister's kisses, these remain lurking below all, and these lurk to the last. Alchemy there is none of passion or disease that can scorch away these immortal impresses. And the dream which closed the preceding section, together with the succeeding dreams of this, (which may be viewed as in the nature of choruses winding up the overture contained in Part I,) are but illustrations of this truth, such as every man probably will meet experimentally who passes through similar convulsions of dreaming or delirium from any similar or equal disturbance in his nature.[1]

LEVANA AND OUR LADIES OF SORROW

Oftentimes at Oxford I saw Levana* in my dreams. I knew her by her Roman symbols. Who is Levana? Reader, that do not pretend to have leisure for very much scholarship, you will not be angry with me for telling you. Levana was the Roman goddess that performed for the new-born infant the earliest office of ennobling kindness—typical, by its mode, of that grandeur which belongs to man every where, and of that benignity in powers invisible, which even in Pagan worlds sometimes descends to sustain it. At the very moment of birth, just as the infant tasted for the first time the atmosphere of our troubled planet, it was laid on the ground. *That* might bear different interpretations. But immediately, lest so grand a creature should grovel there for more than one instant, either the paternal hand, as proxy for the goddess Levana, or some near kinsman, as proxy for the father, raised it upright, bade it look erect as the king of all this world, and presented its forehead to the stars, saying, perhaps, in his heart—'Behold what is greater than yourselves!' This symbolic act represented the function of Levana. And that mysterious lady, who never revealed her face, (except to me in dreams,) but always acted by delegation, had her name from the Latin verb (as still it is the Italian verb) *levare*, to raise aloft.

This is the explanation of Levana. And hence it has arisen that some people have understood by Levana the tutelary power that controls the education of the nursery. She, that would not suffer at his birth even a prefigurative or mimic degradation for her awful ward,

---

[1] This, it may be said, requires a corresponding duration of experience; but, as an argument for this mysterious power lurking in our nature, I may remind the reader of one phenomenon open to the notice of every body, viz. the tendency of very aged persons to throw back and concentrate the light of their memory upon scenes of early childhood, as to which they recall many traces that had faded even to *themselves* in middle life, whilst they often forget altogether the whole intermediate stages of their experience. This shows that naturally, and without violent agencies, the human brain is by tendency a palimpsest.

far less could be supposed to suffer the real degradation attaching to the non-development of his powers. She therefore watches over human education. Now, the word *edŭco*, with the penultimate short, was derived (by a process often exemplified in the crystallization of languages) from the word *edūco*, with the penultimate long. Whatsoever *educes* or developes—*educates.* By the education of Levana, therefore, is meant—not the poor machinery that moves by spelling-books and grammars, but that mighty system of central forces hidden in the deep bosom of human life, which by passion, by strife, by temptation, by the energies of resistance, works for ever upon children—resting not day or night, any more than the mighty wheel of day and night themselves, whose moments, like restless spokes, are glimmering[1] for ever as they revolve.

If, then, *these* are the ministries by which Levana works, how profoundly must she reverence the agencies of grief! But you, reader! think—that children generally are not liable to grief such as mine. There are two senses in the word *generally*—the sense of Euclid where it means *universally* (or in the whole extent of the *genus*,)* and a foolish sense of this world* where it means *usually*. Now I am far from saying that children universally are capable of grief like mine. But there are more than you ever heard of, who die of grief in this island of ours. I will tell you a common case. The rules of Eton require that a boy on the *foundation** should be there twelve years: he is superannuated at eighteen, consequently he must come at six. Children torn away from mothers and sisters at that age not unfrequently die. I speak of what I know.* The complaint is not entered by the registrar as grief; but *that* it is. Grief of that sort, and at that age, has killed more than ever have been counted amongst its martyrs.

Therefore it is that Levana often communes with the powers that shake man's heart: therefore it is that she doats upon grief.

---

[1] *'Glimmering.'*—As I have never allowed myself to covet any man's ox nor his ass,* nor any thing that is his, still less would it become a philosopher to covet other people's images, or metaphors. Here, therefore, I restore to Mr Wordsworth this fine image of the revolving wheel, and the glimmering spokes, as applied by him to the flying successions of day and night.* I borrowed it for one moment in order to point my own sentence; which being done, the reader is witness that I now pay it back instantly by a note made for that sole purpose. On the same principle I often borrow their seals from young ladies—when closing my letters. Because there is sure to be some tender sentiment upon them about 'memory,' or 'hope,' or 'roses,' or 'reunion:' and my correspondent must be a sad brute who is not touched by the eloquence of the seal, even if his taste is so bad that he remains deaf to mine.

'These ladies,' said I softly to myself, on seeing the ministers with whom Levana was conversing, 'these are the Sorrows; and they are three in number, as the *Graces* are three,* who dress man's life with beauty; the *Parcae* are three,* who weave the dark arras of man's life in their mysterious loom always with colours sad in part, sometimes angry with tragic crimson and black; the *Furies* are three,* who visit with retributions called from the other side of the grave offences that walk upon this; and once even the *Muses* were but three,* who fit the harp, the trumpet, or the lute, to the great burdens of man's impassioned creations. These are the Sorrows, all three of whom I know.' The last words I say *now*; but in Oxford I said—'one of whom I know, and the others too surely I *shall* know.' For already, in my fervent youth, I saw (dimly relieved upon the dark background of my dreams) the imperfect lineaments of the awful sisters. These sisters—by what name shall we call them?

If I say simply—'The Sorrows,' there will be a chance of mistaking the term; it might be understood of individual sorrow—separate cases of sorrow,—whereas I want a term expressing the mighty abstractions that incarnate themselves in all individual sufferings of man's heart; and I wish to have these abstractions presented as impersonations, that is, as clothed with human attributes of life, and with functions pointing to flesh. Let us call them, therefore, *Our Ladies of Sorrow*. I know them thoroughly, and have walked in all their kingdoms. Three sisters they are, of one mysterious household; and their paths are wide apart; but of their dominion there is no end. Them I saw often conversing with Levana, and sometimes about myself. Do they talk, then? Oh, no! Mighty phantoms like these disdain the infirmities of language. They may utter voices through the organs of man when they dwell in human hearts, but amongst themselves is no voice nor sound—eternal silence reigns in *their* kingdoms. *They* spoke not as they talked with Levana. *They* whispered not. *They* sang not. Though oftentimes methought they *might* have sung; for I upon earth had heard their mysteries oftentimes deciphered by harp and timbrel, by dulcimer and organ.* Like God, whose servants they are, they utter their pleasure, not by sounds that perish, or by words that go astray, but by signs in heaven—by changes on earth—by pulses in secret rivers—heraldries painted on darkness—and hieroglyphics written on the tablets of the brain. *They* wheeled in mazes; *I* spelled the steps. *They* telegraphed* from afar; *I* read the signals. *They* conspired together; and on the mirrors of darkness *my* eye traced the plots. *Theirs* were the symbols,—*mine* are the words.

What is it the sisters are? What is it that they do? Let me describe their form, and their presence; if form it were that still fluctuated in its outline; or presence it were that for ever advanced to the front, or for ever receded amongst shades.

The eldest of the three is named *Mater Lachrymarum*, Our Lady of Tears. She it is that night and day raves and moans, calling for vanished faces. She stood in Rama, when a voice was heard of lamentation—Rachel weeping for her children, and refusing to be comforted. She it was that stood in Bethlehem on the night when Herod's sword swept its nurseries of Innocents, and the little feet were stiffened for ever, which, heard at times as they tottered along floors overhead, woke pulses of love in household hearts that were not unmarked in heaven.*

Her eyes are sweet and subtle, wild and sleepy by turns; oftentimes rising to the clouds; oftentimes challenging the heavens. She wears a diadem round her head. And I knew by childish memories that she could go abroad upon the winds, when she heard the sobbing of litanies or the thundering of organs, and when she beheld the mustering of summer clouds. This sister, the elder, it is that carries keys more than Papal at her girdle, which open every cottage and every palace. She, to my knowledge, sate all last summer by the bedside of the blind beggar, him that so often and so gladly I talked with, whose pious daughter, eight years old, with the sunny countenance, resisted the temptations of play and village mirth to travel all day long on dusty roads with her afflicted father. For this did God send her a great reward. In the spring-time of the year, and whilst yet her own spring was budding, he recalled her to himself. But her blind father mourns for ever over *her*; still he dreams at midnight that the little guiding hand is locked within his own; and still he wakens to a darkness that is *now* within a second and a deeper darkness. This *Mater Lachrymarum* also has been sitting all this winter of 1844–5 within the bedchamber of the Czar,* bringing before his eyes a daughter (not less pious) that vanished to God not less suddenly, and left behind her a darkness not less profound. By the power of her keys it is that Our Lady of Tears glides a ghostly intruder into the chambers of sleepless men, sleepless women, sleepless children, from Ganges to the Nile, from Nile to Mississippi.* And her, because she is the first-born of her house, and has the widest empire, let us honour with the title of 'Madonna.'

The second sister is called *Mater Suspiriorum*, Our Lady of Sighs. She never scales the clouds, nor walks abroad upon the winds. She wears no diadem. And her eyes, if they were ever seen, would be neither sweet nor subtle; no man could read their story; they would be found filled with perishing dreams, and with wrecks of forgotten delirium. But she raises not her eyes; her head, on which sits a dilapidated turban, droops for ever; for ever fastens on the dust. She weeps not. She groans not. But she sighs inaudibly at intervals. Her sister, Madonna, is oftentimes stormy and frantic; raging in the highest against heaven; and demanding back her darlings. But Our Lady of Sighs never clamours, never defies, dreams not of rebellious aspirations. She is humble to abjectness. Hers is the meekness that belongs to the hopeless. Murmur she may, but it is in her sleep. Whisper she may, but it is to herself in the twilight. Mutter she does at times, but it is in solitary places that are desolate as she is desolate, in ruined cities, and when the sun has gone down to his rest. This sister is the visitor of the Pariah,* of the Jew, of the bondsman to the oar in Mediterranean galleys, of the English criminal in Norfolk island,* blotted out from the books of remembrance in sweet far-off England, of the baffled penitent reverting his eye for ever upon a solitary grave, which to him seems the altar overthrown of some past and bloody sacrifice, on which altar no oblations can now be availing, whether towards pardon that he might implore, or towards reparation that he might attempt. Every slave that at noonday looks up to the tropical sun with timid reproach, as he points with one hand to the earth, our general mother, but for *him* a stepmother, as he points with the other hand to the Bible, our general teacher, but against *him* sealed and sequestered;[1]—every woman sitting in darkness, without love to shelter her head, or hope to illumine her solitude, because the heaven-born instincts kindling in her nature germs of holy affections, which God implanted in her womanly bosom, having been stifled by social necessities, now burn sullenly to waste, like sepulchral lamps amongst the ancients;—every nun defrauded of her unreturning

---

[1] This, the reader will be aware, applies chiefly to the cotton and tobacco States of North America; but not to them only: on which account I have not scrupled to figure the sun, which looks down upon slavery, as *tropical*—no matter if strictly within the tropics, or simply so near to them as to produce a similar climate.

May-time by wicked kinsmen, whom God will judge;—every captive in every dungeon;—all that are betrayed, and all that are rejected; outcasts by traditionary law, and children of *hereditary* disgrace—all these walk with 'Our Lady of Sighs.' She also carries a key; but she needs it little. For her kingdom is chiefly amongst the tents of Shem,* and the houseless vagrant of every clime. Yet in the very highest ranks of man she finds chapels of her own; and even in glorious England there are some that, to the world, carry their heads as proudly as the reindeer, who yet secretly have received her mark upon their foreheads.

But the third sister, who is also the youngest———! Hush! whisper, whilst we talk of *her*! Her kingdom is not large, or else no flesh should live; but within that kingdom all power is hers. Her head, turreted like that of Cybèle,* rises almost beyond the reach of sight. She droops not; and her eyes rising so high, *might* be hidden by distance. But, being what they are, they cannot be hidden; through the treble veil of crape which she wears, the fierce light of a blazing misery, that rests not for matins or for vespers—for noon of day or noon of night—for ebbing or for flowing tide—may be read from the very ground. She is the defier of God. She also is the mother of lunacies, and the suggestress of suicides. Deep lie the roots of her power; but narrow is the nation that she rules. For she can approach only those in whom a profound nature has been upheaved by central convulsions; in whom the heart trembles and the brain rocks under conspiracies of tempest from without and tempest from within. Madonna moves with uncertain steps, fast or slow, but still with tragic grace. Our Lady of Sighs creeps timidly and stealthily. But this youngest sister moves with incalculable motions, bounding, and with a tiger's leaps. She carries no key; for, though coming rarely amongst men, she storms all doors at which she is permitted to enter at all. And *her* name is *Mater Tenebrarum*—Our Lady of Darkness.

These were the *Semnai Theai*, or Sublime Goddesses[1]—these were the *Eumenides*,* or Gracious Ladies, (so called by antiquity in shuddering propitiation)—of my Oxford dreams. MADONNA spoke. She spoke by her mysterious hand. Touching my head, she beckoned

---

[1] '*Sublime Goddesses.*'—The word σεμνος is usually rendered *venerable* in dictionaries; not a very flattering epithet for females. But by weighing a number of passages in which the word is used pointedly, I am disposed to think that it comes nearest to our idea of the *sublime*; as near as a Greek word *could* come.*

to Our Lady of Sighs; and *what* she spoke, translated out of the signs which (except in dreams) no man reads, was this:—

'Lo! here is he, whom in childhood I dedicated to my altars. This is he that once I made my darling. Him I led astray, him I beguiled, and from heaven I stole away his young heart to mine. Through me did he become idolatrous; and through me it was, by languishing desires, that he worshipped the worm, and prayed to the wormy grave. Holy was the grave to him; lovely was its darkness; saintly its corruption. Him, this young idolater, I have seasoned for thee, dear gentle Sister of Sighs! Do thou take him now to *thy* heart, and season him for our dreadful sister. And thou'—turning to the *Mater Tenebrarum*, she said—'wicked sister, that temptest and hatest, do thou take him from *her*. See that thy sceptre lie heavy on his head. Suffer not woman and her tenderness to sit near him in his darkness. Banish the frailties of hope—wither the relentings of love—scorch the fountains of tears: curse him as only thou canst curse. So shall he be accomplished in the furnace—so shall he see the things that ought *not* to be seen—sights that are abominable, and secrets that are unutterable. So shall he read elder truths, sad truths, grand truths, fearful truths. So shall he rise again *before* he dies. And so shall our commission be accomplished which from God we had—to plague his heart until we had unfolded the capacities of his spirit.'[1]

THE APPARITION OF THE BROCKEN*

Ascend with me on this dazzling Whitsunday* the Brocken of North Germany.* The dawn opened in cloudless beauty; it is a dawn of bridal June; but, as the hours advance, her youngest sister April, that sometimes cares little for racing across both frontiers of May, frets the bridal lady's sunny temper with sallies of wheeling and careering

---

[1] The reader, who wishes at all to understand the course of these Confessions, ought not to pass over this dream-legend. There is no great wonder that a vision, which occupied my waking thoughts in those years, should re-appear in my dreams. It was in fact a legend recurring in sleep, most of which I had myself silently written or sculptured in my daylight reveries. But its importance to the present Confessions is this—that it rehearses or prefigures their course.* This FIRST part belongs to Madonna. The THIRD belongs to the 'Mater Suspiriorum,' and will be entitled *The Pariah Worlds*. The FOURTH, which terminates the work, belongs to the 'Mater Tenebrarum,' and will be entitled *The Kingdom of Darkness*. As to the SECOND, it is an interpolation requisite to the effect of the others; and will be explained in its proper place.

showers—flying and pursuing, opening and closing, hiding and restoring. On such a morning, and reaching the summits of the forest-mountain about sunrise, we shall have one chance the more for seeing the famous Spectre of the Brocken.[1] Who and what is he? He is a solitary apparition, in the sense of loving solitude; else he is not always solitary in his personal manifestations, but on proper occasions has been known to unmask a strength quite sufficient to alarm those who had been insulting him.

Now, in order to test the nature of this mysterious apparition, we will try two or three experiments upon him. What we fear, and with some reason, is, that as he lived so many ages with foul Pagan sorcerers, and witnessed so many centuries of dark idolatries, his heart may have been corrupted; and that even now his faith may be wavering or impure. We will try.

---

[1] *'Spectre of the Brocken.'*—This very striking phenomenon has been continually described by writers, both German and English, for the last fifty years. Many readers, however, will not have met with these descriptions: and on *their* account I add a few words in explanation; referring them for the best scientific comment on the case to Sir David Brewster's 'Natural Magic.'* The spectre takes the shape of a human figure, or, if the visitors are more than one, then the spectres multiply; they arrange themselves on the blue ground of the sky, or the dark ground of any clouds that may be in the right quarter, or perhaps they are strongly relieved against a curtain of rock, at a distance of some miles, and always exhibiting gigantic proportions. At first, from the distance and the colossal size, every spectator supposes the appearance to be quite independent of himself. But very soon he is surprised to observe his own motions and gestures mimicked; and wakens to the conviction that the phantom is but a dilated reflection of himself. This Titan amongst the apparitions of earth is exceedingly capricious, vanishing abruptly for reasons best known to himself, and more coy in coming forward than the Lady Echo of Ovid.* One reason why he is seen so seldom must be ascribed to the concurrence of conditions under which only the phenomenon can be manifested: the sun must be near to the horizon, (which of itself implies a time of day inconvenient to a person starting from a station as distant as Elbingerode;) the spectator must have his back to the sun; and the air must contain some vapour—but *partially* disturbed. Coleridge ascended the Brocken on the Whitsunday of 1799, with a party of English students from Goettingen, but failed to see the phantom;* afterwards in England (and under the same three conditions) he saw a much rarer phenomenon, which he described in the following eight lines. I give them from a corrected copy: (the apostrophe in the beginning must be understood as addressed to an ideal conception):—

> 'And art thou nothing? Such thou art as when
> The woodman winding westward up the glen
> At wintry dawn, when o'er the sheep-track's maze
> The viewless snow-mist weaves a glist'ning haze,
> Sees full before him, gliding without tread,
> An image with a glory round its head:
> This shade he worships for its golden hues,
> And *makes* (not knowing) that which he pursues.'*

Make the sign of the cross, and observe whether he repeats it, (as, on Whitsunday,[1] he surely ought to do). Look! he *does* repeat it; but the driving showers perplex the images, and *that*, perhaps, it is which gives him the air of one who acts reluctantly or evasively. Now, again, the sun shines more brightly, and the showers have swept off like squadrons of cavalry to the rear. We will try him again.

Pluck an anemone, one of these many anemones which once was called the sorcerer's flower,[2] and bore a part perhaps in his horrid ritual of fear; carry it to that stone which mimics the outline of a heathen altar, and once was called the sorcerer's altar;[2] then, bending your knee, and raising your right hand to God, say,—'Father, which art in heaven—this lovely anemone, that once glorified the worship of fear, has travelled back into thy fold; this altar, which once reeked with bloody rites to Cortho, has long been rebaptized into thy holy service. The darkness is gone—the cruelty is gone which the darkness bred; the moans have passed away which the victims uttered; the cloud has vanished which once sate continually upon their graves—cloud of protestation that ascended for ever to thy throne from the tears of the defenceless, and the anger of the just. And lo! I thy servant, with this dark phantom, whom, for one hour on this thy festival of Pentecost, I make *my* servant, render thee united worship in this thy recovered temple.'

Look, now! the apparition plucks an anemone, and places it on an altar; he also bends his knee, he also raises his right hand to God. Dumb he is; but sometimes the dumb serve God acceptably. Yet still it occurs to you, that perhaps on this high festival of the Christian Church, he may be overruled by supernatural influence into confession of his homage, having so often been made to bow and bend his knee at murderous rites. In a service of religion he may be timid. Let us try him, therefore, with an earthly passion, where he will have no bias either from favour or from fear.

If, then, once in childhood you suffered an affliction that was

---

[1] '*On Whitsunday.*'—It is singular, and perhaps owing to the temperature and weather likely to prevail in that early part of summer, that more appearances of the spectre have been witnessed on Whitsunday than on any other day.

[2] '*The sorcerer's flower,*' and '*the sorcerer's altar.*'—These are names still clinging to the anemone of the Brocken, and to an altar-shaped fragment of granite near one of the summits; and it is not doubted that they both connect themselves through links of ancient tradition with the gloomy realities of Paganism, when the whole Hartz and the Brocken formed for a very long time the last asylum to a ferocious but perishing idolatry.

ineffable; If once, when powerless to face such an enemy, you were
summoned to fight with the tiger that couches within the separations
of the grave; in that case, after the example of Judaea (on the Roman
coins)*—sitting under her palm-tree to weep, but sitting with her
head veiled—do you also veil your head. Many years are passed away
since then; and you were a little ignorant thing at that time, hardly
above six years old; or perhaps (if you durst tell all the truth) not
quite so much. But your heart was deeper than the Danube;* and, as
was your love, so was your grief. Many years are gone since that darkness settled on your head; many summers, many winters; yet still its
shadows wheel round upon you at intervals, like these April showers
upon this glory of bridal June. Therefore now, on this dovelike morning of Pentecost, do you veil your head like Judaea in memory of that
transcendant woe, and in testimony that, indeed, it surpassed all
utterance of words. Immediately you see that the apparition of the
Brocken veils *his* head, after the model of Judaea weeping under her
palm-tree, as if he also had a human heart, and that *he* also, in childhood, having suffered an affliction which was ineffable, wished by
these mute symbols to breathe a sigh towards heaven in memory of
that affliction, and by way of record, though many a year after, that it
was indeed unutterable by words.

This trial is decisive. You are now satisfied that the apparition is
but a reflex of yourself; and, in uttering your secret feelings to *him*,
you make this phantom the dark symbolic mirror for reflecting to the
daylight what else must be hidden for ever.

Such a relation does the Dark Interpreter, whom immediately the
reader will learn to know as an intruder into my dreams, bear to my
own mind. He is originally a mere reflex of my inner nature. But as
the apparition of the Brocken sometimes is disturbed by storms or by
driving showers, so as to dissemble his real origin, in like manner the
Interpreter sometimes swerves out of my orbit, and mixes a little with
alien natures. I do not always know him in these cases as my own
parhelion.* What he says, generally is but that which *I* have said in
daylight, and in meditation deep enough to sculpture itself on my
heart. But sometimes, as his face alters, his words alter; and they do
not always seem such as I have used, or *could* use. No man can account
for all things that occur in dreams. Generally I believe this—that he
is a faithful representative of myself; but he also is at times subject to
the action of the god *Phantasus*,* who rules in dreams.

Hailstone choruses[1] besides, and storms, enter my dreams. Hailstones and fire that run along the ground, sleet and blinding hurricanes, revelations of glory insufferable pursued by volleying darkness—these are powers able to disturb any features that originally were but shadow, and to send drifting the anchors of any vessel that rides upon deeps so treacherous as those of dreams. Understand, however, the Interpreter to bear generally the office of a tragic chorus at Athens. The Greek chorus is perhaps not quite understood by critics,* any more than the Dark Interpreter by myself. But the leading function of both must be supposed this—not to tell you any thing absolutely new, *that* was done by the actors in the drama; but to recall you to your own lurking thoughts—hidden for the moment or imperfectly developed, and to place before you, in immediate connexion with groups vanishing too quickly for any effort of meditation on your own part, such commentaries, prophetic or looking back, pointing the moral or deciphering the mystery, justifying Providence, or mitigating the fierceness of anguish, as would or might have occurred to your own meditative heart—had only time been allowed for its motions.

The Interpreter is anchored and stationary in my dreams; but great storms and driving mists cause him to fluctuate uncertainly, or even to retire altogether, like his gloomy counterpart the shy Phantom of the Brocken—and to assume new features or strange features, as in dreams always there is a power not contented with reproduction, but which absolutely creates or transforms. This dark being the reader will see again in a further stage of my opium experience; and I warn him that he will not always be found sitting inside my dreams, but at times outside, and in open daylight.

FINALE TO PART I — SAVANNAH-LA-MAR

God smote Savannah-la-Mar,* and in one night, by earthquake, removed her, with all her towers standing and population sleeping, from the steadfast foundations of the shore to the coral floors of ocean. And God said—'Pompeii* did I bury and conceal from men through seventeen centuries: this city I will bury, but not conceal. She shall be a monument to men of my mysterious anger; set in azure

---

[1] '*Hailstone choruses.*'—I need not tell any lover of Handel that his oratorio of 'Israel in Egypt' contains a chorus familiarly known by this name. The words are—'And he gave them hailstones for rain; fire, mingled with the hail, ran along upon the ground.'*

light through generations to come: for I will enshrine her in a crystal dome of my tropic seas.' This city, therefore, like a mighty galleon with all her apparel mounted, streamers flying, and tackling perfect, seems floating along the noiseless depths of ocean: and oftentimes in glassy calms, through the translucid atmosphere of water that now stretches like an air-woven awning above the silent encampment, mariners from every clime look down into her courts and terraces, count her gates, and number the spires of her churches. She is one ample cemetery, and *has* been for many a year; but in the mighty calms that brood for weeks over tropic latitudes, she fascinates the eye with a *Fata-Morgana** revelation, as of human life still subsisting in submarine asylums sacred from the storms that torment our upper air.

Thither, lured by the loveliness of cerulean depths, by the peace of human dwellings privileged from molestation, by the gleam of marble altars sleeping in everlasting sanctity, oftentimes in dreams did I and the dark Interpreter cleave the watery veil that divided us from her streets. We looked into the belfries, where the pendulous bells were waiting in vain for the summons which should awaken their marriage peals; together we touched the mighty organ keys, that sang no *jubilates** for the ear of Heaven—that sang no requiems for the ear of human sorrow; together we searched the silent nurseries, where the children were all asleep, and *had* been asleep through five generations. 'They are waiting for the heavenly dawn,' whispered the Interpreter to himself; 'and, when *that* comes, the bells and the organs will utter a *jubilate* repeated by the echoes of Paradise.' Then, turning to me, he said—'This is sad: this is piteous: but less would not have sufficed for the purposes of God. Look here: put into a Roman clepsydra* one hundred drops of water; let these run out as the sands in an hourglass; every drop measuring the hundredth part of a second, so that each shall represent but the three-hundred-and-sixty-thousandth part of an hour. Now, count the drops as they race along; and, when the fiftieth of the hundred is passing, behold! forty-nine are not, because already they have perished; and fifty are not, because they are yet to come. You see, therefore, how narrow, how incalculably narrow, is the true and actual present. Of that time which we call the present, hardly a hundredth part but belongs either to a past which has fled, or to a future which is still on the wing. It has perished, or it is not born. It was, or it is not. Yet even this approximation to the truth is *infinitely* false. For again subdivide that solitary drop, which only was found to represent the present, into a lower series of similar fractions, and the actual present which you arrest measures now but the thirty-sixth millionth of an hour; and so by infinite declensions the true and very present, in which only we live and enjoy, will vanish into a mote of a mote, distinguishable only by a heavenly vision. Therefore the present, which only man possesses, offers less capacity for his footing than the slenderest film that ever spider twisted from her womb. Therefore, also, even this incalculable shadow from the narrowest pencil of moonlight, is more transitory than geometry can measure, or thought of angel can overtake. The time which *is*, contracts into a mathematic point; and even that point perishes a thousand times before we can utter its birth. All is finite in the present; and even that finite is infinite in its velocity of flight towards death. But in God there is nothing finite; but in God there is nothing transitory; but in God there *can* be nothing that tends to death. Therefore, it follows—that for God there can be no present. The future is the present of God; and to the future it is that he sacrifices the human present. Therefore it is that he works by earthquake. Therefore it is that he works by grief. Oh, deep is the ploughing of earthquake! Oh, deep,' (and his voice swelled like a *sanctus** rising from the choir of a cathedral,)—'oh, deep is the ploughing of grief! But oftentimes less would not suffice for the agriculture of God. Upon a night of earthquake he builds a thousand years of pleasant habitations for man. Upon the sorrow of an infant, he raises oftentimes from human intellects glorious vintages that could not else have been. Less than these fierce ploughshares would not have stirred the stubborn soil. The one is needed for earth, our planet—for earth itself as the dwelling-place of man. But the other is needed yet oftener for God's mightiest instrument; yes,' (and he looked solemnly at myself,) 'is needed for the mysterious children of the earth!'

END OF PART I*

PART II

The Oxford visions, of which some have been given, were but anticipations necessary to illustrate the glimpse opened of childhood, (as being its reaction). In this SECOND part, returning from that anticipation,

I retrace an abstract of my boyish and youthful days so far as they furnished or exposed the germs of later experiences in worlds more shadowy.

Upon me, as upon others scattered thinly by tens and twenties over every thousand years, fell too powerfully and too early the vision of life. The horror of life mixed itself already in earliest youth with the heavenly sweetness of life; that grief, which one in a hundred has sensibility enough to gather from the sad retrospect of life in its closing stage, for me shed its dews as a prelibation upon the fountains of life whilst yet sparkling to the morning sun. I saw from afar and from before what I was to see from behind. Is this the description of an early youth passed in the shades of gloom? No, but of a youth passed in the divinest happiness. And if the reader has (which so few have) the passion, without which there is no reading of the legend and superscription upon man's brow, if he is not (as most are) deafer than the grave to every *deep* note that sighs upwards from the Delphic caves of human life, he will know that the rapture of life (or any thing which by approach can merit that name) does not arise, unless as perfect music arises—music of Mozart or Beethoven*—by the confluence of the mighty and terrific discords with the subtle concords. Not by contrast, or as reciprocal foils do these elements act, which is the feeble conception of many, but by union. They are the sexual forces in music: 'male and female created he them;'* and these mighty antagonists do not put forth their hostilities by repulsion, but by deepest attraction.

As 'in to-day already walks to-morrow,'* so in the past experience of a youthful life may be seen dimly the future. The collisions with alien interests or hostile views, of a child, boy, or very young man, so insulated as each of these is sure to be,—those aspects of opposition which such a person *can* occupy, are limited by the exceedingly few and trivial lines of connexion along which he is able to radiate any essential influence whatever upon the fortunes or happiness of others. Circumstances may magnify his importance for the moment; but, after all, any cable which he carries out upon other vessels is easily slipped upon a feud arising. Far otherwise is the state of relations connecting an adult or responsible man with the circles around him as life advances. The network of these relations is a thousand times more intricate, the jarring of these intricate relations a thousand times more frequent, and the vibrations a thousand times harsher which these jarrings diffuse. This truth is felt beforehand misgivingly and in troubled vision, by a young man who stands upon the threshold of manhood. One earliest instinct of fear and horror would darken his spirit if it could be revealed to itself and self-questioned at the moment of birth: a second instinct of the same nature would again pollute that tremulous mirror, if the moment were as punctually marked as physical birth is marked, which dismisses him finally upon the tides of absolute self-controul. A dark ocean would seem the total expanse of life from the first: but far darker and more appalling would seem that interior and second chamber of the ocean which called him away for ever from the direct accountability of others. Dreadful would be the morning which should say—'Be thou a human child incarnate;' but more dreadful the morning which should say—'Bear thou henceforth the sceptre of thy self-dominion through life, and the passion of life!' Yes, dreadful would be both: but without a basis of the dreadful there is no perfect rapture. It is a part* through the sorrow of life, growing out of its events, that this basis of awe and solemn darkness slowly accumulates. *That* I have illustrated. But, as life expands, it is more through the *strife* which besets us, strife from conflicting opinions, positions, passions, interests, that the funereal ground settles and deposits itself, which sends upward the dark lustrous brilliancy through the jewel of life—else revealing a pale and superficial glitter. Either the human being must suffer and struggle as the price of a more searching vision, or his gaze must be shallow and without intellectual revelation.

Through accident it was in part, and, where through no accident but my own nature, not through features of it at all painful to recollect, that constantly in early life (that is, from boyish days until eighteen, when by going to Oxford, practically I became my own master) I was engaged in duels of fierce continual struggle, with some person or body of persons, that sought, like the Roman *retiarius*,* to throw a net of deadly coercion or constraint over the undoubted rights of my natural freedom. The steady rebellion upon my part in one-half, was a mere human reaction of justifiable indignation; but in the other half it was the struggle of a conscientious nature—disdaining to feel it as any mere right or discretional privilege—no, feeling it as the noblest of duties to resist, though it should be mortally, those that would have enslaved me, and to retort scorn upon those that would have put my head below their feet. Too much, even in later life, I have perceived in men that pass for good men, a disposition to degrade (and if possible to degrade through self-degradation) those in whom unwillingly they feel any weight of oppression to themselves, by commanding qualities of intellect or character. They respect you: they are compelled to do so: and they hate to do so. Next, therefore, they seek to throw off the sense of this oppression, and to take vengeance for it, by co-operating with any unhappy accidents in your life, to inflict a sense of humiliation upon you, and (if possible) to force you into becoming a consenting party to that humiliation. Oh, wherefore is it that those who presume to call themselves the 'friends' of this man or that woman, are so often those above all others, whom in the hour of death that man or woman is most likely to salute with the valediction—Would God I had never seen your face?

In citing one or two cases of these early struggles, I have chiefly in view the effect of these upon my subsequent visions under the reign of opium. And this indulgent reflection should accompany the mature reader through all such records of boyish inexperience. A good-tempered man, who is also acquainted with the world, will easily evade, without needing any artifice of servile obsequiousness, those quarrels which an upright simplicity, jealous of its own rights, and unpractised in the science of worldly address, cannot always evade without some loss of self-respect. Suavity in this manner may, it is true, be reconciled with firmness in the matter; but not easily by a young person who wants all the appropriate resources of knowledge, of adroit and guarded language, for making his good temper available. Men are protected from insult and wrong, not merely by their own skill, but also in the absence of any skill at all, by the general spirit of forbearance to which society has trained all those whom they are likely to meet. But boys meeting with no such forbearance or training in other boys, must sometimes be thrown upon feuds in the ratio of their own firmness, much more than in the ratio of any natural proneness to quarrel. Such a subject, however, will be best illustrated by a sketch or two of my own principal feuds.

The first, but merely transient and playful, nor worth noticing at all, but for its subsequent resurrection under other and awful colouring in my dreams, grew out of an imaginary slight, as I viewed it, put upon me by one of my guardians. I had four guardians: and the one of these who had the most knowledge and talent of the whole, a banker, living about a hundred miles from my home, had invited me when eleven years old to his house.* His eldest daughter, perhaps a year younger than myself, wore at that time upon her very lovely face the most angelic expression of character and temper that I have almost ever seen. Naturally, I fell in love with her. It seems absurd to say so; and the more so, because two children more absolutely innocent than we were cannot be imagined, neither of us having ever been at any school;—but the simple truth is, that in the most chivalrous sense I was in love with her. And the proof that I was so showed itself in three separate modes: I kissed her glove on any rare occasion when I found it lying on a table; secondly, I looked out for some excuse to be jealous of her; and, thirdly, I did my very best to get up a quarrel. What I wanted the quarrel for was the luxury of a reconciliation; a hill cannot be had, you know, without going to the expense of a valley. And though I hated the very thought of a moment's difference with so truly gentle a girl, yet how, but through such a purgatory, could one win the paradise of her returning smiles? All this, however, came to nothing; and simply because she positively would *not* quarrel. And the jealousy fell through, because there was no decent subject for such a passion, unless it had settled upon an old music-master whom lunacy itself could not adopt as a rival. The quarrel meantime, which never prospered with the daughter, silently kindled on my part towards the father. His offence was this. At dinner, I naturally placed myself by the side of M., and it gave me great pleasure to touch her hand at intervals. As M. was my cousin, though twice or even three times removed, I did not feel taking too great a liberty in this little act of tenderness. No matter if three thousand times removed, I said, my cousin is my cousin: nor had I very much designed to conceal the act; or if so, rather on her account than my own. One evening, however, papa observed my manoeuvre. Did he seem displeased? Not at all: he even condescended to smile. But the next day he placed M. on the side opposite to myself. In one respect this was really an improvement; because it gave me a better view of my cousin's sweet countenance. But then there was the loss of the hand to be considered, and secondly there was the affront. It was clear that vengeance must be had. Now there was but one thing in this world that I could do even decently: but *that* I could do admirably. This was writing Latin hexameters. Juvenal, though it was not very much of him that I had then read, seemed to me a divine model. The inspiration of wrath spoke through him as through a Hebrew prophet. The same inspiration

spoke now in me. *Facit indignatio versum,** said Juvenal. And it must
be owned that Indignation has never made such good verses since as
she did in that day. But still, even to me this agile passion proved a
Muse of genial inspiration for a couple of paragraphs: and one line
I will mention as worthy to have taken its place in Juvenal himself.
I say this without scruple, having not a shadow of vanity, nor on the
other hand a shadow of false modesty connected with such boyish
accomplishments. The poem opened thus—

> 'Te nimis austerum, sacrae qui foedera mensae
> Diruis, insector Satyrae reboante flagello.'*

But the line, which I insist upon as of Roman strength, was the closing one of the next sentence. The general effect of the sentiment
was—that my clamorous wrath should make its way even into ears
that were past hearing:

> '———mea saeva querela
> Auribus insidet ceratis, auribus etsi
> Non audituris hybernâ nocte procellam.'*

The power, however, which inflated my verse, soon collapsed; having
been soothed from the very first by finding—that except in this one
instance at the dinner-table, which probably had been viewed as an
indecorum, no further restraint of any kind whatever was meditated
upon my intercourse with M. Besides, it was too painful to lock up
good verses in one's own solitary breast. Yet how could I shock the
sweet filial heart of my cousin by a fierce lampoon or *stylites** against
her father, had Latin even figured amongst her accomplishments?
Then it occurred to me that the verses might be shown to the father.
But was there not something treacherous in gaining a man's approbation under a mask to a satire upon himself? Or would he have always
understood me? For one person a year after took the *sacrae mensae* (by
which I had meant the sanctities of hospitality) to mean the sacramental table. And on consideration I began to suspect, that many
people would pronounce myself the party who had violated the holy
ties of hospitality, which are equally binding on guest as on host.
Indolence, which sometimes comes in aid of good impulses as well as
bad, favoured these relenting thoughts; the society of M. did still
more to wean me from further efforts of satire: and, finally, my Latin
poem remained a *torso*. But upon the whole my guardian had a narrow

escape of descending to posterity in a disadvantageous light, had he rolled down to it through my hexameters.

Here was a case of merely playful feud. But the same talent of Latin verses soon after connected me with a real feud that harassed my mind more than would be supposed, and precisely by this agency, viz. that it arrayed one set of feelings against another. It divided my mind as by domestic feud against itself. About a year after, returning from the visit to my guardian's, and when I must have been nearly completing my twelfth year, I was sent to a great public school.* Every man has reason to rejoice who enjoys so great an advantage. I condemned and *do* condemn the practice of sometimes sending out into such stormy exposures those who are as yet too young, too dependent on female gentleness, and endowed with sensibilities too exquisite. But at nine or ten the masculine energies of the character are beginning to be developed: or, if not, no discipline will better aid in their development than the bracing intercourse of a great English classical school.* Even the selfish are forced into accommodating themselves to a public standard of generosity, and the effeminate into conforming to a rule of manliness. I was myself at two public schools; and I think with gratitude of the benefit which I reaped from both; as also I think with gratitude of the upright guardian in whose quiet household I learned Latin so effectually. But the small private schools which I witnessed for brief periods, containing thirty to forty boys, were models of ignoble manners as respected some part of the juniors, and of favouritism amongst the masters.* Nowhere is the sublimity of public justice so broadly exemplified as in an English school. There is not in the universe such an areopagus* for fair play and abhorrence of all crooked ways, as an English mob, or one of the English time-honoured public schools. But my own first introduction to such an establishment was under peculiar and contradictory circumstances. When my 'rating,' or graduation* in the school, was to be settled, naturally my altitude (to speak astronomically) was taken by the proficiency in Greek. But I could then barely construe books so easy as the Greek Testament and the Iliad. This was considered quite well enough for my age; but still it caused me to be placed three steps below the highest rank in the school. Within one week, however, my talent for Latin verses, which had by this time gathered strength and expansion, became known. I was honoured as never was man or boy since Mordecai the Jew.* Not properly belonging to the flock of the head master, but to the leading section of the second, I was now weekly paraded for distinction at the supreme tribunal of the school; out of which at first grew nothing but a sunshine of approbation delightful to my heart, still brooding upon solitude. Within six weeks this had changed. The approbation indeed continued, and the public testimony of it. Neither would there, in the ordinary course, have been any painful reaction from jealousy or fretful resistance to the soundness of my pretensions; since it was sufficiently known to some of my schoolfellows, that I, who had no male relatives but military men, and those in India,* could not have benefited by any clandestine aid. But, unhappily, the head master was at that time dissatisfied with some points in the progress of his head form; and, as it soon appeared, was continually throwing in their teeth the brilliancy of my verses at twelve, by comparison with theirs at seventeen, eighteen, and nineteen. I had observed him sometimes pointing to myself; and was perplexed at seeing this gesture followed by gloomy looks, and what French reporters call 'sensation,' in these young men, whom naturally I viewed with awe as my leaders, boys that were called young men, men that were reading Sophocles*—(a name that carried with it the sound of something seraphic to my ears)—and who never had vouchsafed to waste a word on such a child as myself. The day was come, however, when all that would be changed. One of these leaders strode up to me in the public playgrounds, and delivering a blow on my shoulder, which was not intended to hurt me, but as a mere formula of introduction, asked me, 'What the d——l I meant by bolting out of the course, and annoying other people in that manner? Were other people to have no rest for me and my verses, which, after all, were horribly bad?' There might have been some difficulty in returning an answer to this address, but none was required. I was briefly admonished to see that I wrote worse for the future, or else——— At this *aposiopesis** I looked enquiringly at the speaker, and he filled up the chasm by saying, that he would 'annihilate' me. Could any person fail to be aghast at such a demand? I was to write worse than my own standard, which, by his account of my verses, must be difficult; and I was to write worse than himself, which might be impossible. My feelings revolted, it may be supposed, against so arrogant a demand, unless it had been far otherwise expressed; and on the next occasion for sending up verses, so far from attending to the orders issued, I double-shotted my guns; double applause descended on myself; but I remarked with some awe, though not repenting of what I had done, that double confusion seemed to agitate the ranks of my enemies. Amongst them loomed out in the distance my 'annihilating' friend, who shook his huge fist at me, but with something like a grim smile about his eyes. He took an early opportunity of paying his respects to me—saying, 'You little devil, do you call this writing your worst?' 'No,' I replied; 'I call it writing my best.' The annihilator, as it turned out, was really a good-natured young man; but he soon went off to Cambridge; and with the rest, or some of them, I continued to wage war for nearly a year. And yet, for a word spoken with kindness, I would have resigned the peacock's feather in my cap as the merest of baubles. Undoubtedly, praise sounded sweet in my ears also. But *that* was nothing by comparison with what stood on the other side. I detested distinctions that were connected with mortification to others. And, even if I could have got over *that*, the eternal feud fretted and tormented my nature. Love, that once in childhood had been so mere a necessity to me, *that* had long been a mere reflected ray from a departed sunset. But peace, and freedom from strife, if love were no longer possible, (as so rarely it is in this world,) was the absolute necessity of my heart. To contend with somebody was still my fate; how to escape the contention I could not see; and yet for itself, and the deadly passions into which it forced me, I hated and loathed it more than death. It added to the distraction and internal feud of my own mind—that I could not *altogether* condemn the upper boys. I was made a handle of humiliation to them. And in the mean time, if I had an advantage in one accomplishment, which is all a matter of accident, or peculiar taste and feeling, they, on the other hand, had a great advantage over me in the more elaborate difficulties of Greek, and of choral Greek poetry. I could not altogether wonder at their hatred of myself. Yet still, as they had chosen to adopt this mode of conflict with me, I did not feel that I had any choice but to resist. The contest was terminated for me by my removal from the school, in consequence of a very threatening illness affecting my head;* but it lasted nearly a year; and it did not close before several amongst my public enemies had become my private friends. They were much older, but they invited me to the houses of their friends, and showed me a respect which deeply affected me—this respect having more reference, apparently, to the firmness I had exhibited than to the splendour of my verses. And, indeed, these had rather drooped from a natural accident; several persons of my own class had formed the practice of asking me to write verses for *them*. I could not refuse. But, as the subjects given out were the same for all of us, it was not possible to take so many crops off the ground without starving the quality of all.

Two years and a half from this time, I was again at a public school of ancient foundation.* Now I was myself one of the three who formed the highest class. Now I myself was familiar with Sophocles, who once had been so shadowy a name in my ear. But, strange to say, now in my sixteenth year, I cared nothing at all for the glory of Latin verse. All the business of school was slight and trivial in my eyes. Costing me not an effort, it could not engage any part of my attention; that was now swallowed up altogether by the literature of my native land.* I still reverenced the Grecian drama, as always I must. But else I cared little then for classical pursuits. A deeper spell had mastered me; and I lived only in those bowers where deeper passions spoke.

Here, however, it was that began another and more important struggle. I was drawing near to seventeen, and, in a year after *that*, would arrive the usual time for going to Oxford. To Oxford my guardians made no objection; and they readily agreed to make the allowance then universally regarded as the *minimum* for an Oxford student, viz. £200 per annum.* But they insisted, as a previous condition, that I should make a positive and definitive choice of a profession. Now I was well aware that, if I *did* make such a choice, no law existed, nor could any obligation be created through deeds or signature, by which I could finally be compelled into keeping my engagement. But this evasion did not suit me. Here, again, I felt indignantly that the principle of the attempt was unjust. The object was certainly to do me service by saving money, since, if I selected the bar as my profession, it was contended by some persons, (misinformed, however,) that not Oxford, but a special pleader's office, would be my proper destination; but I cared not for arguments of that sort. Oxford I was determined to make my home; and also to bear my future course utterly untrammeled by promises that I might repent. Soon came the catastrophe of this struggle. A little before my seventeenth birthday, I walked off one lovely summer morning to North Wales—rambled there for months—and, finally, under some obscure hopes of raising money on my personal security, I went up to London. Now I was in my eighteenth year; and, during this period it was that I passed through that trial of severe distress, of which I gave some account in my former Confessions. Having a motive, however, for glancing backwards briefly at that period in the present series, I will do so at this point.

I saw in one journal an insinuation that the incidents in the *preliminary* narrative were possibly without foundation. To such an expression of mere gratuitous malignity, as it happened to be supported by no one argument except a remark, apparently absurd, but certainly false, I did not condescend to answer.* In reality, the possibility had never occurred to me that any person of judgment would seriously suspect me of taking liberties with that part of the work, since, though no one of the parties concerned but myself stood in so central a position to the circumstances as to be acquainted with *all* of them, many were acquainted with each separate section of the memoir. Relays of witnesses might have been summoned to mount guard, as it were, upon the accuracy of each particular in the whole succession of incidents; and some of these people had an interest, more or less strong, in exposing any deviation from the strictest *letter* of the truth, had it been in their power to do so. It is now twenty-two years since I saw the objection here alluded to; and, in saying that I did not condescend to notice it,* the reader must not find any reason for taxing me with a blamable haughtiness. But every man is entitled to be haughty when his veracity is impeached; and, still more, when it is impeached by a dishonest objection, or, if not *that*, by an objection which argues a carelessness of attention almost amounting to dishonesty, in a case where it was meant to sustain an imputation of falsehood. Let a man read carelessly if he will, but not where he is meaning to use his reading for a purpose of wounding another man's honour. Having thus, by twenty-two years' silence, sufficiently expressed my contempt for the slander,[1] I now feel myself at liberty to draw it into notice, for the sake, *inter alia*,* of showing in how rash a spirit malignity often works. In the preliminary account of certain

---

[1] Being constantly almost an absentee from London, and very often from other great cities, so as to command oftentimes no favourable opportunities for overlooking the great mass of public journals, it is possible enough that other slanders of the same tenor may have existed. I speak of what met my own eye, or was accidentally reported to me—but in fact all of us are exposed to this evil of calumnies lurking unseen—for no degree of energy, and no excess of disposable time, would enable any one man to exercise this sort of vigilant police over *all* journals. Better, therefore, tranquilly to leave all such malice to confound itself.

boyish adventures which had exposed me to suffering of a kind not commonly incident to persons in my station of life, and leaving behind a temptation to the use of opium under certain arrears of weakness, I had occasion to notice a disreputable attorney in London,* who showed me some attentions, partly on my own account as a boy of some expectations, but much more with the purpose of fastening his professional grappling-hooks upon the young Earl of A———t,* my former companion, and my present correspondent. This man's house was slightly described, and, with more minuteness, I had exposed some interesting traits in his household economy. A question, therefore, naturally arose in several people's curiosity—Where was this house situated? and the more so because I had pointed a renewed attention to it by saying, that on that very evening, (viz. the evening on which that particular page of the Confessions was written,) I had visited the street, looked up at the windows, and, instead of the gloomy desolation reigning there when myself and a little girl were the sole nightly tenants, sleeping in fact (poor freezing creatures that we both were) on the floor of the attorney's law-chamber, and making a pillow out of his infernal parchments, I had seen with pleasure the evidences of comfort, respectability, and domestic animation, in the lights and stir prevailing through different stories of the house. Upon this the upright critic told his readers that I had described the house as standing in Oxford Street, and then appealed to their own knowledge of that street whether such a house could be *so* situated.* Why not—he neglected to tell us. The houses at the east end of Oxford Street are certainly of too small an order to meet my account of the attorney's house; but why should it be at the east end? Oxford Street is a mile and a quarter long, and being built continuously on both sides, finds room for houses of *many* classes. Meantime it happens that, although the true house was most obscurely indicated, *any* house whatever in Oxford Street was most luminously excluded. In all the immensity of London there was but one single street that could be challenged by an attentive reader of the Confessions as peremptorily *not* the street of the attorney's house—and *that* one was Oxford Street; for, in speaking of my own renewed acquaintance with the outside of this house, I used some expression implying that, in order to make such a visit of reconnoissance, I had turned *aside* from Oxford Street. The matter is a perfect trifle in itself, but it is no trifle in a question affecting a writer's accuracy. If in a thing so absolutely impossible to be forgotten as the true situation of a house painfully memorable to a man's feelings, from being the scene of boyish distresses the most exquisite—nights passed in the misery of cold, and hunger preying upon him both night and day, in a degree which very many would not have survived,—he, when retracing his schoolboy annals, could have shown indecision even, far more dreaded inaccuracy, in identifying the house, not one syllable after *that*, which he could have said on any other subject, would have won any confidence, or deserved any, from a judicious reader. I may now mention—the Herod being dead* whose persecutions I had reason to fear—that the house in question stands in Greek Street on the west, and is the house on that side nearest to Soho-Square, but without looking into the Square. This it was hardly safe to mention at the date of the published Confessions. It was my private opinion, indeed, that there were probably twenty-five chances to one in favour of my friend the attorney having been by that time hanged. But then this argued inversely; one chance to twenty-five that my friend might be *un*hanged, and knocking about the streets of London; in which case it would have been a perfect god-send to him that here lay an opening (of *my* contrivance, not *his*) for requesting the opinion of a jury on the amount of *solatium** due to his wounded feelings in an action on the passage in the Confessions. To have indicated even the street would have been enough. Because there could surely be but one such Grecian in Greek Street, or but one that realized the other conditions of the unknown quantity. There was also a separate danger not absolutely so laughable as it sounds. Me there was little chance that the attorney should meet; but my book he might easily have met (supposing always that the warrant of *Sus. per coll.** had not yet on *his* account travelled down to Newgate).* For he was literary; admired literature; and, as a lawyer, he wrote on some subjects fluently; Might he not publish *his* Confessions? Or, which would be worse, a supplement to mine—printed so as exactly to match? In which case I should have had the same affliction that Gibbon the historian dreaded so much;* viz. that of seeing a refutation of himself, and his own answer to the refutation, all bound up in one and the same self-combating volume. Besides, he would have cross-examined me before the public in Old Bailey* style; no story, the most straightforward that ever was told, could be sure to stand *that*. And my readers might be left in a state of painful doubt whether *he* might not, after all, have been a model of suffering innocence—I (to say the kindest thing possible) plagued with the natural treacheries of a schoolboy's memory. In taking leave of this case and the remembrances connected with it, let me say that, although really believing in the probability of the attorney's having at least found his way to Australia,* I had no satisfaction in thinking of that result. I knew my friend to be the very perfection of a scamp. And in the running account between us, (I mean, in the ordinary sense, as to money,) the balance could not be in *his* favour; since I, on receiving a sum of money, (considerable in the eyes of us both,) had transferred pretty nearly the whole of it to *him*, for the purpose ostensibly held out to me (but of course a hoax) of purchasing certain law 'stamps;' for he was then pursuing a diplomatic correspondence with various Jews who lent money to young heirs, in some trifling proportion on my own insignificant account, but much more truly on the account of Lord A———t, my young friend. On the other side, he had given to me simply the reliques of his breakfast-table, which itself was hardly more than a relique. But in this he was not to blame. He could not give to me what he had not for himself, nor sometimes for the poor starving child whom I now suppose to have been his illegitimate daughter. So desperate was the running fight, yard-arm to yard-arm,* which he maintained with creditors fierce as famine and hungry as the grave;* so deep also was his horror (I know not for which of the various reasons supposable) against falling into a prison, that he seldom ventured to sleep twice successively in the same house. That expense of itself must have pressed heavily in London, where you pay half-a-crown at least for a bed that would cost only a shilling* in the provinces. In the midst of his knaveries, and what were even more shocking to my remembrance, his confidential discoveries in his rambling conversations of knavish *designs*, (not always pecuniary,) there was a light of wandering misery in his eye at times, which affected me afterwards at intervals when I recalled it in the radiant happiness of nineteen, and amidst the solemn tranquillities of Oxford. That of itself was interesting; the man was worse by far than he had been meant to be; he had not the mind that reconciles itself to evil. Besides, he respected scholarship, which appeared by the deference he generally showed to myself, then about seventeen; he had an interest in literature; *that* argues something good; and was pleased at any time, or even cheerful, when I turned the conversation upon books; nay, he seemed touched with emotion, when I quoted some sentiment noble and impassioned from one of the great poets, and would ask me to repeat it. He would have been a man of memorable energy, and for good purposes, had it not been for his agony of conflict with pecuniary embarrassments. These probably had commenced in some fatal compliance with temptation arising out of funds confided to him by a client. Perhaps he had gained fifty guineas for a moment of necessity, and had sacrificed for that trifle *only* the serenity and the comfort of a life. Feelings of relenting kindness, it was not in my nature to refuse in such a case; and I wished to * * * *

But I never succeeded in tracing his steps through the wilderness of London until some years back, when I ascertained that he was dead. Generally speaking, the few people whom I have disliked in this world were flourishing people of good repute. Whereas the knaves whom I have known, one and all, and by no means few, I think of with pleasure and kindness.

Heavens! when I look back to the sufferings which I have witnessed or heard of even from this one brief London experience, I say if life could throw open its long suits of chambers to our eyes from some station *beforehand*, if from some secret stand we could look *by anticipation* along its vast corridors, and aside into the recesses opening upon them from either hand, halls of tragedy or chambers of retribution, simply in that small wing and no more of the great caravanserai* which we ourselves shall haunt, simply in that narrow tract of time and no more where we ourselves shall range, and confining our gaze to those and no others for whom personally we shall be interested, what a recoil we should suffer of horror in our estimate of life! What if those sudden catastrophes, or those inexpiable afflictions, which *have* already descended upon the people within my own knowledge, and almost below my own eyes, all of them now gone past, and some long past, had been thrown open before me as a secret exhibition when first I and they stood within the vestibule of morning hopes; when the calamities themselves had hardly begun to gather in their elements of possibility, and when some of the parties to them were as yet no more than infants! The past viewed not *as* the past, but by a spectator who steps back ten years deeper into the rear, in order that he may regard it as a future; the calamity of 1840 contemplated from the station of 1830—the doom that rang the knell of happiness viewed from a point of time when as yet it was neither feared nor would even have been intelligible—the name that killed in 1843, which in 1835

would have struck no vibration upon the heart—the portrait that on
the day of her Majesty's coronation* would have been admired by
you with a pure disinterested admiration, but which if seen to-day
would draw forth an involuntary groan—cases such as these are
strangely moving for all who add deep thoughtfulness to deep sensibility. As the hastiest of improvisations, accept—fair reader, (for you
it is that will chiefly feel such an invocation of the past)—three or
four illustrations from my own experience.

Who is this distinguished-looking young woman with her eyes
drooping, and the shadow of a dreadful shock yet fresh upon every
feature? Who is the elderly lady with her eyes flashing fire? Who is
the downcast child of sixteen? What is that torn paper lying at their
feet? Who is the writer? Whom does the paper concern? Ah! if she, if
the central figure in the group—twenty-two at the moment when she
is revealed to us—could, on her happy birth-day at sweet seventeen,
have seen the image of herself five years onwards, just as *we* see it
now, would she have prayed for life as for an absolute blessing? or
would she not have prayed to be taken from the evil to come—to be
taken away one evening at least before this day's sun arose? It is true,
she still wears a look of gentle pride, and a relic of that noble smile
which belongs to *her* that suffers an injury which many times over she
would have died sooner than inflict. Womanly pride refuses itself
before witnesses to the total prostration of the blow; but, for all *that*,
you may see that she longs to be left alone, and that her tears will flow
without restraint when she is so. This room is her pretty boudoir, in
which, till to-night—poor thing!—she has been glad and happy.
There stands her miniature conservatory, and there expands her
miniature library; as we circumnavigators of literature are apt (you
know) to regard all female libraries in the light of miniatures. None of
these will ever rekindle a smile on *her* face; and there, beyond, is her
music, which only of all that she possesses, will now become dearer to
her than ever; but not, as once, to feed a self-mocked pensiveness, or
to cheat a half-visionary sadness. She will be sad indeed. But she is
one of those that will suffer in silence. Nobody will ever detect *her*
failing in any point of duty, or querulously seeking the support in
others which she can find for herself in this solitary room. Droop
she will not in the sight of men; and, for all beyond, nobody has any
concern with *that* except God. You shall hear what becomes of
her, before we take our departure; but now let me tell you what

has happened. In the main outline I am sure you guess already without aid of mine, for we leaden-eyed men, in such cases, see nothing by comparison with you our quick-witted sisters. That haughty-looking lady with the Roman cast of features, who must once have been strikingly handsome—an Agrippina,* even yet, in a favourable presentation—is the younger lady's aunt. She, it is rumoured, once sustained, in her younger days, some injury of that same cruel nature which has this day assailed her niece, and ever since she has worn an air of disdain, not altogether unsupported by real dignity, towards men. This aunt it was that tore the letter which lies upon the floor. It deserved to be torn; and yet she that had the best right to do so would *not* have torn it. That letter was an elaborate attempt on the part of an accomplished young man to release himself from sacred engagements. What need was there to argue the case of *such* engagements? Could it have been requisite with pure female dignity to plead any thing, or do more than *look* an indisposition to fulfil them? The aunt is now moving towards the door, which I am glad to see; and she is followed by that pale timid girl of sixteen, a cousin, who feels the case profoundly, but is too young and shy to offer an intellectual sympathy.

One only person in this world there is, who *could* to-night have been a supporting friend to our young sufferer, and *that* is her dear loving twin-sister, that for eighteen years read and wrote, thought and sang, slept and breathed, with the dividing-door open for ever between their bedrooms, and never once a separation between their hearts; but she is in a far distant land. Who else is there at her call? Except God, nobody. Her aunt had somewhat sternly admonished her, though still with a relenting in her eye as she glanced aside at the expression in her niece's face, that she must 'call pride to her assistance.' Ay, true; but pride, though a strong ally in public, is apt in private to turn as treacherous as the worst of those against whom she is invoked. How could it be dreamed by a person of sense, that a brilliant young man of merits, various and eminent, in spite of his baseness, to whom, for nearly two years, this young woman had given her whole confiding love, might be dismissed from a heart like hers on the earliest summons of pride, simply because she herself had been dismissed from *his*, or seemed to have been dismissed, on a summons of mercenary calculation? Look! now that she is relieved from the weight of an unconfidential presence, she has sat for two hours with her head buried in her hands. At last she rises to look for something. A thought has struck her; and, taking a little golden key which hangs by a chain within her bosom, she searches for something locked up amongst her few jewels. What is it? It is a Bible exquisitely illumin- ated, with a letter attached, by some pretty silken artifice, to the blank leaves at the end. This letter is a beautiful record, wisely and pathetically composed, of maternal anxiety still burning strong in death, and yearning, when all objects beside were fast fading from *her* eyes, after one parting act of communion with the twin darlings of her heart. Both were thirteen years old, within a week or two, as on the night before her death they sat weeping by the bedside of their mother, and hanging on her lips, now for farewell whispers, and now for farewell kisses. They both knew that, as her strength had permit- ted during the latter month of her life, she had thrown the last anguish of love in her beseeching heart into a letter of counsel to themselves. Through this, of which each sister had a copy, she trusted long to converse with her orphans. And the last promise which she had entreated on this evening from both, was—that in either of two con- tingencies they would review her counsels, and the passages to which she pointed their attention in the Scriptures; namely, first, in the event of any calamity, that, for one sister or for both, should over- spread their paths with total darkness; and secondly, in the event of life flowing in too profound a stream of prosperity, so as to threaten them with an alienation of interest from all spiritual objects. She had not concealed that, of these two extreme cases, she would prefer for her own children the first. And now had that case arrived indeed, which she in spirit had desired to meet. Nine years ago, just as the silvery voice of a dial in the dying lady's bedroom was striking nine upon a summer evening, had the last visual ray streamed from her seeking eyes upon her orphan twins, after which, throughout the night, she had slept away into heaven. Now again had come a summer evening memorable for unhappiness; now again the daughter thought of those dying lights of love which streamed at sunset from the clos- ing eyes of her mother; again, and just as she went back in thought to this image, the same silvery voice of the dial sounded nine o'clock. Again she remembered her mother's dying request; again her own tear-hallowed promise—and with her heart in her mother's grave she now rose to fulfil it. Here, then, when this solemn recurrence to a testamentary counsel has ceased to be a mere office of duty towards the departed, having taken the shape of a consolation for herself, let us pause.

. . . .

Now, fair companion in this exploring voyage of inquest into hidden scenes, or forgotten scenes of human life—perhaps it might be instructive to direct our glasses upon the false perfidious lover. It might. But do not let us do so. We might like him better, or pity him more, than either of us would desire. His name and memory have long since dropped out of every body's thoughts. Of prosperity, and (what is more important) of internal peace, he is reputed to have had no gleam from the moment when he betrayed his faith, and in one day threw away the jewel of good conscience, and 'a pearl richer than all his tribe.'* But, however that may be, it is certain that, finally, he became a wreck; and of any *hopeless* wreck it is painful to talk—much more so, when through him others also became wrecks.

Shall we, then, after an interval of nearly two years has passed over the young lady in the boudoir, look in again upon *her*? You hesitate, fair friend: and I myself hesitate. For in fact she also has become a wreck; and it would grieve us both to see her altered. At the end of twenty-one months she retains hardly a vestige of resemblance to the fine young woman we saw on that unhappy evening with her aunt and cousin. On consideration, therefore, let us do this. We will direct our glasses to her room, at a point of time about six weeks further on. Suppose this time gone; suppose her now dressed for her grave, and placed in her coffin. The advantage of that is—that, though no change can restore the ravages of the past, yet (as often is found to happen with young persons) the expression has revived from her girlish years. The child-like aspect has revolved, and settled back upon her features. The wasting away of the flesh is less apparent in the face; and one might imagine that, in this sweet marble countenance, was seen the very same upon which, eleven years ago, her mother's dark-ening eyes had lingered to the last, until clouds had swallowed up the vision of her beloved *twins*. Yet, if that were in part a fancy, this at least is no fancy—that not only much of a child-like truth and sim-plicity has reinstated itself in the temple of her now reposing features, but also that tranquillity and perfect peace, such as are appropriate to eternity; but which from the *living* countenance had taken their flight for ever, on that memorable evening when we looked in upon the impassioned group—upon the towering and denouncing aunt, the sympathizing but silent cousin, the poor blighted niece, and the wicked letter lying in fragments at their feet.

Cloud, that hast revealed to us this young creature and her blighted hopes, close up again. And now, a few years later, not more than four or five, give back to us the latest arrears of the changes which thou concealest within thy draperies. Once more, 'open sesame!'* and show us a third generation. Behold a lawn islanded with thickets. How perfect is the verdure—how rich the blossoming shrubberies that screen with verdurous walls from the possibility of intrusion, whilst by their own wandering line of distribution they shape and umbrageously embay, what one might call lawny saloons and vestibules—sylvan galleries and closets. Some of these recesses, which unlink themselves as fluently as snakes, and unexpectedly as the shyest nooks, watery cells, and crypts, amongst the shores of a forest-lake, being formed by the mere caprices and ramblings of the luxuriant shrubs, are so small and so quiet, that one might fancy them meant for *boudoirs*. Here is one that, in a less fickle climate, would make the loveliest of studies for a writer of breathings from some solitary heart, or of *suspiria* from some impassioned memory! And opening from one angle of this embowered study, issues a little narrow corridor, that, after almost wheeling back upon itself, in its playful mazes, finally widens into a little circular chamber; out of which there is no exit, (except back again by the entrance,) small or great; so that, adjacent to his study, the writer would command how sweet a bed-room, permitting him to lie the summer through, gazing all night long at the burning host of heaven. How silent *that* would be at the noon of summer nights, how grave-like in its quiet! And yet, need there be asked a stillness or a silence more profound than is felt at this present noon of day? One reason for such peculiar repose, over and above the tranquil character of the day, and the distance of the place from high-roads, is the outer zone of woods, which almost on every quarter invests the shrubberies—swathing them, (as one may express it,) belting them, and overlooking them, from a varying distance of two and three furlongs, so as oftentimes to keep the winds at a distance. But, however caused and supported, the silence of these fanciful lawns and lawny chambers is oftentimes oppressive in the depth of summer to people unfamiliar with solitudes, either mountainous or sylvan; and many would be apt to suppose that the villa, to which these pretty shrubberies form the chief dependencies, must be untenanted. But that is not the case. The house is inhabited, and by its own legal mistress—the proprietress of the whole domain; and not at all a silent mistress, but as noisy as most little ladies of five years old, for that is her age. Now, and just as we are speaking, you may hear her little joyous clamour as she issues from the house. This way she comes, bounding like a fawn; and soon she rushes into the little recess which I pointed out as a proper study for any man who should be weaving the deep harmonies of memorial *suspiria*. But I fancy that she will soon dispossess it of that character, for her *suspiria* are not many at this stage of her life. Now she comes dancing into sight; and you see that, if she keeps the promise of her infancy, she will be an interesting creature to the eye in after life. In other respects, also, she is an engaging child—loving, natural, and wild as any one of her neighbours for some miles round; viz. leverets, squirrels, and ring-doves. But what will surprise you most is—that, although a child of pure English blood, she speaks very little English; but more Bengalee than perhaps you will find it convenient to construe. That is her Ayah,* who comes up from behind at a pace so different from her youthful mistress's. But, if their paces are different, in other things they agree most cordially; and dearly they love each other. In reality, the child has passed her whole life in the arms of this ayah. She remembers nothing elder than *her*; eldest of things is the ayah in her eyes; and, if the ayah should insist on her worshipping herself as the goddess Railroadina or Steamboatina, that made England and the sea and Bengal, it is certain that the little thing would do so, asking no question but this—whether kissing would do for worshipping.

Every evening at nine o'clock, as the ayah sits by the little creature lying awake in bed, the silvery tongue of a dial tolls the hour. Reader, you know who she is. She is the grand-daughter of her that faded away about sunset in gazing at her twin orphans. Her name is Grace. And she is the niece of that elder and once happy Grace, who spent so much of her happiness in this very room, but whom, in her utter desolation, we saw in the boudoir with the torn letter at her feet. She is the daughter of that other sister, wife to a military officer, who died abroad. Little Grace never saw her grandmamma, nor her lovely aunt that was her namesake, nor consciously her mamma. She was born six months after the death of the elder Grace; and her mother saw her only through the mists of mortal suffering, which carried her off three weeks after the birth of her daughter.

This view was taken several years ago; and since then the younger Grace in her turn is under a cloud of affliction. But she is still under eighteen; and of her there may be hopes. Seeing such things in so short a space of years, for the grandmother died at thirty-two, we say—Death we can face: but knowing, as some of us do, what is human life, which of us is it that without shuddering could (if consciously we were summoned) face the hour of birth?

THE ENGLISH MAIL-COACH,
OR THE GLORY OF MOTION

SOME twenty or more years before I matriculated at Oxford, Mr Palmer, M.P. for Bath,* had accomplished two things, very hard to do on our little planet, the Earth, however cheap they may happen to be held by the eccentric people in comets: he had invented mail-coaches, and he had married the daughter[1] of a duke. He was, therefore, just twice as great a man as Galileo, who certainly invented (or *discovered*) the satellites of Jupiter,* those very next things extant to mail-coaches in the two capital points of speed and keeping time, but who did *not* marry the daughter of a duke.

These mail-coaches, as organised by Mr Palmer, are entitled to a circumstantial notice from myself—having had so large a share in developing the anarchies of my subsequent dreams, an agency which they accomplished, first, through velocity, at that time unprecedented; they first revealed the glory of motion: suggesting, at the same time, an under-sense, not unpleasurable, of possible though indefinite danger; secondly, through grand effects for the eye between lamp-light and the darkness upon solitary roads; thirdly, through animal beauty and power so often displayed in the class of horses selected for this mail service; fourthly, through the conscious presence of a central intellect, that, in the midst of vast distances,[2] of storms, of darkness, of night, overruled all obstacles into one steady co-operation in a national result. To my own feeling, this Post-office service recalled some mighty orchestra, where a thousand instruments, all disregarding each other, and so far in danger of discord, yet all obedient as slaves to the supreme *baton* of some great leader, terminate in a perfection of harmony like that of heart, veins, and arteries, in a healthy animal organisation. But, finally, that particular element in this whole combination which most impressed myself,

---

[1] Lady Madeline Gordon.*

[2] '*Vast distances.*'—One case was familiar to mail-coach travellers, where two mails in opposite directions, north and south, starting at the same minute from points six hundred miles apart, met almost constantly at a particular bridge which exactly bisected the total distance.

and through which it is that to this hour Mr Palmer's mail-coach system tyrannises by terror and terrific beauty over my dreams, lay in the awful political mission which at that time it fulfilled. The mail-coaches it was that distributed over the face of the land, like the opening of apocalyptic vials, the heart-shaking news of Trafalgar, of Salamanca, of Vittoria, of Waterloo.* These were the harvests that, in the grandeur of their reaping, redeemed the tears and blood in which they had been sown. Neither was the meanest peasant so much below the grandeur and the sorrow of the times as to confound these battles, which were gradually moulding the destinies of Christendom, with the vulgar conflicts of ordinary warfare, which are oftentimes but gladiatorial trials of national prowess. The victories of England in this stupendous contest rose of themselves as natural *Te Deums** to heaven; and it was felt by the thoughtful that such victories, at such a crisis of general prostration, were not more beneficial to ourselves than finally to France, and to the nations of western and central Europe, through whose pusillanimity it was that the French domination had prospered.

The mail-coach, as the national organ for publishing these mighty events, became itself a spiritualised and glorified object to an impassioned heart; and naturally, in the Oxford of that day, all hearts were awakened. There were, perhaps, of us gownsmen, two thousand *resident*[1] in Oxford, and dispersed through five-and-twenty colleges. In some of these the custom permitted the student to keep what are called 'short terms;' that is, the four terms of Michaelmas, Lent, Easter, and Act,* were kept severally by a residence, in the aggregate, of ninety-one days, or thirteen weeks. Under this interrupted residence, accordingly, it was possible that a student might have a reason for going down* to his home four times in the year. This made eight journeys to and fro. And as these homes lay dispersed through all the shires of the island, and most of us disdained all coaches except his majesty's mail, no city out of London could pretend to so extensive a connexion with Mr Palmer's establishment as Oxford. Naturally, therefore, it became a point of some interest with us, whose journeys revolved every six weeks on an average, to look a little into the executive details of the system. With some of these Mr Palmer had no

---

[1] '*Resident*.'—The number on the books was far greater, many of whom kept up an intermitting communication with Oxford. But I speak of those only who were steadily pursuing their academic studies, and of those who resided constantly as *fellows*.*

concern; they rested upon bye-laws not unreasonable, enacted by posting-houses for their own benefit, and upon others equally stern, enacted by the inside passengers for the illustration of their own exclusiveness. These last were of a nature to rouse our scorn, from which the transition was not *very long* to mutiny. Up to this time, it had been the fixed assumption of the four inside people, (as an old tradition of all public carriages from the reign of Charles II,)* that they, the illustrious quaternion, constituted a porcelain variety of the human race, whose dignity would have been compromised by exchanging one word of civility with the three miserable delf ware* outsides. Even to have kicked an outsider might have been held to attaint* the foot concerned in that operation; so that, perhaps, it would have required an act of parliament to restore its purity of blood. What words, then, could express the horror, and the sense of treason, in that case, which *had* happened, where all three outsides, the trinity of Pariahs, made a vain attempt to sit down at the same breakfast-table or dinner-table with the consecrated four? I myself witnessed such an attempt; and on that occasion a benevolent old gentleman endeavoured to soothe his three holy associates, by suggesting that, if the outsides were indicted for this criminal attempt at the next assizes,* the court would regard it as a case of lunacy (or *delirium tremens*)* rather than of treason. England owes much of her grandeur to the depth of the aristocratic element in her social composition. I am not the man to laugh at it. But sometimes it expressed itself in extravagant shapes. The course taken with the infatuated outsiders, in the particular attempt which I have noticed, was, that the waiter, beckoning them away from the privileged *salle-à-manger*,* sang out, 'This way, my good men;' and then enticed them away off to the kitchen. But that plan had not always answered. Sometimes, though very rarely, cases occurred where the intruders, being stronger than usual, or more vicious than usual, resolutely refused to move, and so far carried their point, as to have a separate table arranged for themselves in a corner of the room. Yet, if an Indian screen could be found ample enough to plant them out from the very eyes of the high table, or *dais*, it then became possible to assume as a fiction of law—that the three delf fellows, after all, were not present. They could be ignored by the porcelain men, under the maxim, that objects not appearing, and not existing, are governed by the same logical construction.*

Such now being, at that time, the usages of mail-coaches, what was to be done by us of young Oxford? We, the most aristocratic of people, who were addicted to the practice of looking down superciliously even upon the insides themselves as often very suspicious characters, were we voluntarily to court indignities? If our dress and bearing sheltered us, generally, from the suspicion of being 'raff,'* (the name at that period for 'snobs,')[1] we really *were* such constructively, by the place we assumed. If we did not submit to the deep shadow of eclipse, we entered at least the skirts of its penumbra. And the analogy of theatres was urged against us, where no man can complain of the annoyances incident to the pit or gallery, having his instant remedy in paying the higher price of the boxes. But the soundness of this analogy we disputed. In the case of the theatre, it cannot be pretended that the inferior situations have any separate attractions, unless the pit suits the purpose of the dramatic reporter. But the reporter or critic is a rarity. For most people, the sole benefit is in the price. Whereas, on the contrary, the outside of the mail had its own incommunicable advantages. These we could not forego. The higher price we should willingly have paid, but *that* was connected with the condition of riding inside, which was insufferable. The air, the freedom of prospect, the proximity to the horses, the elevation of seat—these were what we desired; but, above all, the certain anticipation of purchasing occasional opportunities of driving.

Under coercion of this great practical difficulty, we instituted a searching inquiry into the true quality and valuation of the different apartments about the mail. We conducted this inquiry on metaphysical principles; and it was ascertained satisfactorily, that the roof of the coach, which some had affected to call the attics, and some the garrets, was really the drawing-room, and the box was the chief ottoman or sofa in that drawing-room; whilst it appeared that the inside, which had been traditionally regarded as the only room tenantable by gentlemen, was, in fact, the coal-cellar in disguise.

Great wits jump.* The very same idea had not long before struck the celestial intellect of China.* Amongst the presents carried out by our first embassy to that country was a state-coach. It had been

---

[1] 'Snobs,' and its antithesis, 'nobs,'* arose among the internal factions of shoemakers perhaps ten years later. Possibly enough, the terms may have existed much earlier; but they were then first made known, picturesquely and effectively, by a trial at some assizes which happened to fix the public attention.

specially selected as a personal gift by George III; but the exact mode of using it was a mystery to Pekin. The ambassador, indeed, (Lord Macartney,)* had made some dim and imperfect explanations upon the point; but as his excellency communicated these in a diplomatic whisper, at the very moment of his departure, the celestial mind was very feebly illuminated; and it became necessary to call a cabinet council on the grand state question—'Where was the emperor* to sit?' The hammer-cloth* happened to be unusually gorgeous; and partly on that consideration, but partly also because the box offered the most elevated seat, and undeniably went foremost, it was resolved by acclamation that the box was the imperial place, and, *for the scoundrel who drove, he might sit where he could find a perch.* The horses, therefore, being harnessed, under a flourish of music and a salute of guns, solemnly his imperial majesty ascended his new English throne, having the first lord of the treasury* on his right hand, and the chief jester on his left. Pekin gloried in the spectacle; and in the whole flowery people,* constructively present by representation, there was but one discontented person, which was the coachman. This mutinous individual, looking as blackhearted as he really was, audaciously shouted—'Where am *I* to sit?' But the privy council, incensed by his disloyalty, unanimously opened the door, and kicked him into the inside. He had all the inside places to himself; but such is the rapacity of ambition, that he was still dissatisfied. 'I say,' he cried out in an extempore petition, addressed to the emperor through a window, 'how am I to catch hold of the reins?'—'Any how,' was the answer; 'don't trouble *me*, man, in my glory; through the windows, through the key-holes—how you please.' Finally, this contumacious coachman lengthened the checkstrings into a sort of jury-reins,* communicating with the horses; with these he drove as steadily as may be supposed. The emperor returned after the briefest of circuits: he descended in great pomp from his throne, with the severest resolution never to remount it. A public thanksgiving was ordered for his majesty's prosperous escape from the disease of a broken neck; and the state-coach was dedicated for ever as a votive offering to the God Fo, Fo—whom the learned more accurately call Fi, Fi.*

A revolution of this same Chinese character did young Oxford of that era effect in the constitution of mail-coach society. It was a perfect French revolution; and we had good reason to say, *Ca ira*.* In fact, it soon became *too* popular. The 'public,' a well-known character, particularly disagreeable, though slightly respectable, and notorious for affecting the chief seats in synagogues,* had at first loudly opposed this revolution; but when all opposition showed itself to be ineffectual, our disagreeable friend went into it with headlong zeal. At first it was a sort of race between us; and, as the public is usually above 30, (say generally from 30 to 50 years old,) naturally we of young Oxford, that averaged about 20, had the advantage. Then the public took to bribing, giving fees to horse-keepers, &c., who hired out their persons as warming-pans on the box-seat. *That*, you know, was shocking to our moral sensibilities. Come to bribery, we observed, and there is an end to all morality, Aristotle's, Cicero's,* or anybody's. And, besides, of what use was it? For *we* bribed also. And as our bribes to those of the public being demonstrated out of Euclid to be as five shillings to sixpence,* here again young Oxford had the advantage. But the contest was ruinous to the principles of the stable-establishment about the mails. The whole corporation was constantly bribed, rebribed, and often sur-rebribed; so that a horse-keeper, ostler, or helper, was held by the philosophical at that time to be the most corrupt character in the nation.

There was an impression upon the public mind, natural enough from the continually augmenting velocity of the mail, but quite erroneous, that an outside seat on this class of carriages was a post of danger. On the contrary, I maintained that, if a man had become nervous from some gipsy prediction in his childhood, allocating to a particular moon now approaching some unknown danger, and he should inquire earnestly,—'Whither can I go for shelter? Is a prison the safest retreat? Or a lunatic hospital? Or the British Museum?' I should have replied—'Oh, no; I'll tell you what to do. Take lodgings for the next forty days on the box of his majesty's mail. Nobody can touch you there. If it is by bills at ninety days after date that you are made unhappy—if noters and protesters* are the sort of wretches whose astrological shadows darken the house of life—then note you what I vehemently protest, viz., that no matter though the sheriff in every county should be running after you with his *posse*,* touch a hair of your head he cannot whilst you keep house, and have your legal domicile, on the box of the mail. It's felony to stop the mail; even the sheriff cannot do that. And an *extra* (no great matter if it grazes the sheriff) touch of the whip to the leaders at any time guarantees your safety.' In fact, a bed-room in a quiet house seems a safe enough retreat; yet it is liable to its own notorious nuisances, to robbers by night, to rats, to fire. But the mail laughs at these terrors. To robbers, the answer is packed up and ready for delivery in the barrel of the guard's blunderbuss. Rats again! there *are* none about mail-coaches, any more than snakes in Von Troil's Iceland;* except, indeed, now and then a parliamentary rat,* who always hides his shame in the 'coal-cellar.' And, as to fire, I never knew but one in a mail-coach, which was in the Exeter mail, and caused by an obstinate sailor bound to Devonport.* Jack,* making light of the law and the lawgiver that had set their faces against his offence, insisted on taking up a forbidden seat* in the rear of the roof, from which he could exchange his own yarns with those of the guard. No greater offence was then known to mail-coaches; it was treason, it was *laesa majestas,** it was by tendency arson; and the ashes of Jack's pipe, falling amongst the straw of the hinder boot,* containing the mail-bags, raised a flame which (aided by the wind of our motion) threatened a revolution in the republic of letters. But even this left the sanctity of the box unviolated. In dignified repose, the coachman and myself sat on, resting with benign composure upon our knowledge—that the fire would have to burn its way through four inside passengers before it could reach ourselves. With a quotation rather too trite, I remarked to the coachman,—

———'Jam proximus ardet
Ucalegon.'*

But, recollecting that the Virgilian part of his education might have been neglected, I interpreted so far as to say, that perhaps at that moment the flames were catching hold of our worthy brother and next-door neighbour Ucalegon. The coachman said nothing, but by his faint sceptical smile he seemed to be thinking that he knew better; for that in fact, Ucalegon, as it happened, was not in the way-bill.*

No dignity is perfect which does not at some point ally itself with the indeterminate and mysterious. The connexion of the mail with the state and the executive government—a connexion obvious, but yet not strictly defined—gave to the whole mail establishment a grandeur and an official authority which did us service on the roads, and invested us with seasonable terrors. But perhaps these terrors were not the less impressive, because their exact legal limits were imperfectly ascertained. Look at those turnpike gates; with what deferential hurry, with what an obedient start, they fly open at our

approach! Look at that long line of carts and carters ahead, audaciously usurping the very crest of the road: ah! traitors, they do not
hear us as yet, but as soon as the dreadful blast of our horn reaches
them with the proclamation of our approach, see with what frenzy
of trepidation they fly to their horses' heads, and deprecate our wrath
by the precipitation of their crane-neck quarterings.* Treason they
feel to be their crime; each individual carter feels himself under the
ban of confiscation and attainder:* his blood is attainted through six
generations, and nothing is wanting but the headsman and his axe,
the block and the sawdust, to close up the vista of his horrors. What!
shall it be within benefit of clergy,* to delay the king's message on
the highroad?—to interrupt the great respirations, ebb or flood, of
the national intercourse—to endanger the safety of tidings running
day and night between all nations and languages? Or can it be fancied,
amongst the weakest of men, that the bodies of the criminals will be
given up to their widows for Christian burial? Now, the doubts which
were raised as to our powers did more to wrap them in terror, by wrap-
ping them in uncertainty, than could have been effected by the sharp-
est definitions of the law from the Quarter Sessions.* We, on our parts,
(we, the collective mail, I mean,) did our utmost to exalt the idea of
our privileges by the insolence with which we wielded them. Whether
this insolence rested upon law that gave it a sanction, or upon conscious power, haughtily dispensing with that sanction, equally it spoke
from a potential station; and the agent in each particular insolence of
the moment, was viewed reverentially, as one having authority.*

Sometimes after breakfast his majesty's mail would become frisky;
and in its difficult wheelings amongst the intricacies of early markets,
it would upset an apple-cart, a cart loaded with eggs, &c. Huge was
the affliction and dismay, awful was the smash, though, after all,
I believe the damage might be levied upon the hundred.* I, as far as
was possible, endeavoured in such a case to represent the conscience
and moral sensibilities of the mail; and, when wildernesses of eggs
were lying poached* under our horses' hoofs, then would I stretch
forth my hands in sorrow, saying (in words too celebrated in those
days from the false[1] echoes of Marengo)—'Ah! wherefore have we

---

[1] 'False echoes'—yes, false! for the words ascribed to Napoleon, as breathed to the
memory of Desaix, never were uttered at all.* They stand in the same category of theatrical inventions as the cry of the foundering *Vengeur*, as the vaunt of General Cambronne
at Waterloo, '*La Garde meurt, mais ne se rend pas*,'* as the repartees of Talleyrand.*

not time to weep over you?' which was quite impossible, for in fact we had not even time to laugh over them. Tied to post-office time, with an allowance in some cases of fifty minutes for eleven miles, could the royal mail pretend to undertake the offices of sympathy and condolence? Could it be expected to provide tears for the accidents of the road? If even it seemed to trample on humanity, it did so, I contended, in discharge of its own more peremptory duties.

Upholding the morality of the mail, *à fortiori** I upheld its rights, I stretched to the uttermost its privilege of imperial precedency, and astonished weak minds by the feudal powers which I hinted to be lurking constructively in the charters of this proud establishment. Once I remember being on the box of the Holyhead mail, between Shrewsbury and Oswestry,* when a tawdry thing from Birmingham, some *Tallyho* or *Highflier*,* all flaunting with green and gold, came up alongside of us. What a contrast to our royal simplicity of form and colour is this plebeian wretch! The single ornament on our dark ground of chocolate colour was the mighty shield of the imperial arms, but emblazoned in proportions as modest as a signet-ring bears to a seal of office. Even this was displayed only on a single panel, whispering, rather than proclaiming, our relations to the state; whilst the beast from Birmingham had as much writing and painting on its sprawling flanks as would have puzzled a decipherer from the tombs of Luxor.* For some time this Birmingham machine ran along by our side,—a piece of familiarity that seemed to us sufficiently jacobinical.* But all at once a movement of the horses announced a desperate intention of leaving us behind. 'Do you see *that*?' I said to the coachman. 'I see,' was his short answer. He was awake, yet he waited longer than seemed prudent; for the horses of our audacious opponent had a disagreeable air of freshness and power. But his motive was loyal; his wish was that the Birmingham conceit should be full-blown before he froze it. When *that* seemed ripe, he unloosed, or, to speak by a stronger image, he sprang his known resources, he slipped our royal horses like cheetas, or hunting leopards after the affrighted game. How they could retain such a reserve of fiery power after the work they had accomplished, seemed hard to explain. But on our side, besides the physical superiority, was a tower of strength, namely, the king's name, 'which they upon the adverse faction wanted.'* Passing them without an effort, as it seemed, we threw them into the rear with so lengthening an interval between us, as proved in itself the bitterest mockery of their presumption; whilst our guard blew back a shattering blast of triumph, that was really too painfully full of derision.

I mention this little incident for its connexion with what followed. A Welshman, sitting behind me, asked if I had not felt my heart burn within me during the continuance of the race? I said—No; because we were not racing with a mail, so that no glory could be gained. In fact, it was sufficiently mortifying that such a Birmingham thing should dare to challenge us. The Welshman replied, that he didn't see *that*; for that a cat might look at a king,* and a Brummagem* coach might lawfully race the Holyhead mail. '*Race* us perhaps,' I replied, 'though even *that* has an air of sedition, but not *beat* us. This would have been treason; and for its own sake I am glad that the Tallyho was disappointed.' So dissatisfied did the Welshman seem with this opinion, that at last I was obliged to tell him a very fine story from one of our elder dramatists,* viz.—that once, in some Oriental region, when the prince of all the land, with his splendid court, were flying their falcons, a hawk suddenly flew at a majestic eagle; and in defiance of the eagle's prodigious advantages, in sight also of all the astonished field-sportsmen, spectators, and followers, killed him on the spot. The prince was struck with amazement at the unequal contest, and with burning admiration for its unparalleled result. He commanded that the hawk should be brought before him; caressed the bird with enthusiasm, and ordered that, for the commemoration of his matchless courage, a crown of gold should be solemnly placed on the hawk's head; but then that, immediately after this coronation, the bird should be led off to execution, as the most valiant indeed of traitors, but not the less a traitor that had dared to rise in rebellion against his liege lord the eagle. 'Now,' said I to the Welshman, 'how painful it would have been to you and me as men of refined feelings, that this poor brute, the Tallyho, in the impossible case of a victory over us, should have been crowned with jewellery, gold, with Birmingham ware, or paste diamonds, and then led off to instant execution.' The Welshman doubted if that could be warranted by law. And when I hinted at the 10th of Edward III chap. 15,* for regulating the precedency of coaches, as being probably the statute relied on for the capital punishment of such offences, he replied drily—That if the attempt to pass a mail was really treasonable, it was a pity that the Tallyho appeared to have so imperfect an acquaintance with law.

These were among the gaieties of my earliest and boyish acquaintance with mails. But alike the gayest and the most terrific of my experiences rose again after years of slumber, armed with preternatural
power to shake my dreaming sensibilities; sometimes, as in the slight
case of Miss Fanny on the Bath road, (which I will immediately
mention,) through some casual or capricious association with images
originally gay, yet opening at some stage of evolution into sudden
capacities of horror; sometimes through the more natural and fixed
alliances with the sense of power so various lodged in the mail system.

The modern modes of travelling cannot compare with the mail-
coach system in grandeur and power. They boast of more velocity,
but not however as a consciousness, but as a fact of our lifeless knowledge, resting upon *alien* evidence; as, for instance, because somebody
says that we have gone fifty miles in the hour, or upon the evidence of
a result, as that actually we find ourselves in York four hours after
leaving London.* Apart from such an assertion, or such a result, I am
little aware of the pace. But, seated on the old mail-coach, we needed
no evidence out of ourselves to indicate the velocity. On this system
the word was—*Non magna loquimur*, as upon railways, but *magna
vivimus*.* The vital experience of the glad animal sensibilities made
doubts impossible on the question of our speed; we heard our speed,
we saw it, we felt it as a thrilling; and this speed was not the product
of blind insensate agencies, that had no sympathy to give, but was
incarnated in the fiery eyeballs of an animal, in his dilated nostril,
spasmodic muscles, and echoing hoofs. This speed was incarnated in
the *visible* contagion amongst brutes of some impulse, that, radiating
into *their* natures, had yet its centre and beginning in man. The sensibility of the horse uttering itself in the maniac light of his eye, might
be the last vibration in such a movement; the glory of Salamanca
might be the first—but the intervening link that connected them,
that spread the earthquake of the battle into the eyeball of the horse,
was the heart of man—kindling in the rapture of the fiery strife, and
then propagating its own tumults by motions and gestures to the
sympathies, more or less dim, in his servant the horse.

But now, on the new system of travelling, iron tubes and boilers
have disconnected man's heart from the ministers of his locomotion.
Nile nor Trafalgar* has power any more to raise an extra bubble in a
steam-kettle. The galvanic cycle is broken up for ever; man's imperial
nature no longer sends itself forward through the electric sensibility

of the horse; the inter-agencies are gone in the mode of communication between the horse and his master, out of which grew so many aspects of sublimity under accidents of mists that hid, or sudden blazes that revealed, of mobs that agitated, or midnight solitudes that awed. Tidings, fitted to convulse all nations, must henceforwards travel by culinary process; and the trumpet that once announced from afar the laurelled mail, heart-shaking, when heard screaming on the wind, and advancing through the darkness to every village or solitary house on its route, has now given way for ever to the potwallopings of the boiler.

Thus have perished multiform openings for sublime effects, for interesting personal communications, for revelations of impressive faces that could not have offered themselves amongst the hurried and fluctuating groups of a railway station. The gatherings of gazers about a mail-coach had one centre, and acknowledged only one interest. But the crowds attending at a railway station have as little unity as running water, and own as many centres as there are separate carriages in the train.

How else, for example, than as a constant watcher for the dawn, and for the London mail that in summer months entered about dawn into the lawny thickets of Marlborough Forest,* couldst thou, sweet Fanny of the Bath road, have become known to myself? Yet Fanny, as the loveliest young woman for face and person that perhaps in my whole life I have beheld, merited the station which even *her* I could not willingly have spared; yet (thirty-five years later) she holds in my dreams; and though, by an accident of fanciful caprice, she brought along with her into those dreams a troop of dreadful creatures, fabulous and not fabulous, that were more abominable to a human heart than Fanny and the dawn were delightful.

Miss Fanny of the Bath road, strictly speaking, lived at a mile's distance from that road, but came so continually to meet the mail, that I on my frequent transits rarely missed her, and naturally connected her name with the great thoroughfare where I saw her; I do not exactly know, but I believe with some burthen of commissions to be executed in Bath, her own residence being probably the centre to which these commissions gathered. The mail coachman, who wore the royal livery, being one amongst the privileged few,[1] happened to

---

[1] 'Privileged few.' The general impression was that this splendid costume belonged of right to the mail coachmen as their professional dress. But that was an error. To the

be Fanny's grandfather. A good man he was, that loved his beautiful granddaughter; and, loving her wisely, was vigilant over her
deportment in any case where young Oxford might happen to be
concerned. Was I then vain enough to imagine that I myself individually could fall within the line of his terrors? Certainly not, as regarded
any physical pretensions that I could plead; for Fanny (as a chance
passenger from her own neighbourhood once told me) counted in
her train a hundred and ninety-nine professed admirers, if not
open aspirants to her favour; and probably not one of the whole brigade but excelled myself in personal advantages.* Ulysses even, with
the unfair advantage of his accursed bow, could hardly have undertaken that amount of suitors.* So the danger might have seemed
slight—only that woman is universally aristocratic: it is amongst her
nobilities of heart that she *is* so. Now, the aristocratic distinctions in
my favour might easily with Miss Fanny have compensated my physical deficiencies. Did I then make love to Fanny? Why, yes; *mais oui
donc*;* as much love as one *can* make whilst the mail is changing
horses, a process which ten years later did not occupy above eighty
seconds; but *then*, viz. about Waterloo, it occupied five times eighty.
Now, four hundred seconds offer a field quite ample enough for
whispering into a young woman's ear a great deal of truth; and (by
way of parenthesis) some trifle of falsehood. Grandpapa did right,
therefore, to watch me. And yet, as happens too often to the grand-
papas of earth, in a contest with the admirers of granddaughters, how
vainly would he have watched me had I meditated any evil whispers
to Fanny! She, it is my belief, would have protected herself against
any man's evil suggestions. But he, as the result showed, could not
have intercepted the opportunities for such suggestions. Yet he was
still active; he was still blooming. Blooming he was as Fanny herself.

> 'Say, all our praises why should lords—'

No, that's not the line:

> 'Say, all our roses why should girls engross?'*

The coachman showed rosy blossoms on his face deeper even than his

---

guard it *did* belong as a matter of course, and was essential as an official warrant, and a
means of instant identification for his person, in the discharge of his important public
duties. But the coachman, and especially if his place in the series did not connect him
immediately with London and the General Post Office, obtained the scarlet coat only as
an honorary distinction after long or special service.

granddaughter's,—*his* being drawn from the ale-cask, Fanny's from youth and innocence, and from the fountains of the dawn. But, in spite of his blooming face, some infirmities he had; and one particularly, (I am very sure, no *more* than one,) in which he too much resembled a crocodile. This lay in a monstrous inaptitude for turning round. The crocodile, I presume, owes that inaptitude to the absurd *length* of his back; but in our grandpapa it arose rather from the absurd *breadth* of his back, combined, probably, with some growing stiffness in his legs. Now upon this crocodile infirmity of his I planted an easy opportunity for tendering my homage to Miss Fanny. In defiance of all his honourable vigilance, no sooner had he presented to us his mighty Jovian* back, (what a field for displaying to mankind his royal scarlet!) whilst inspecting professionally the buckles, the straps, and the silver turrets* of his harness, than I raised Miss Fanny's hand to my lips, and, by the mixed tenderness and respectfulness of my manner, caused her easily to understand how happy it would have made me to rank upon her list as No. 10 or 12, in which case a few casualties amongst her lovers (and observe—they *hanged* liberally in those days) might have promoted me speedily to the top of the tree; as, on the other hand, with how much loyalty of submission I acquiesced in her allotment, supposing that she had seen reason to plant me in the very rearward of her favour, as No. 199+1. It must not be supposed that I allowed any trace of jest, or even of playfulness, to mingle with these expressions of my admiration; that would have been insulting to her, and would have been false as regarded my own feelings. In fact, the utter shadowyness of our relations to each other, even after our meetings through seven or eight years had been very numerous, but of necessity had been very brief, being entirely on mail-coach allowance—timed, in reality, by the General Post-Office—and watched by a crocodile belonging to the antepenultimate generation, left it easy for me to do a thing which few people ever *can* have done—viz., to make love for seven years, at the same time to be as sincere as ever creature was, and yet never to compromise myself by overtures that might have been foolish as regarded my own interests, or misleading as regarded hers. Most truly I loved this beautiful and ingenuous girl; and had it not been for the Bath and Bristol mail, heaven only knows what might have come of it. People talk of being over head and ears in love—now, the mail was the cause that I sank only over ears in love, which, you know, still left a trifle of brain to overlook the whole conduct of the affair. I have mentioned the case at all for the sake of a dreadful result from it in after years of dreaming. But it seems, *ex abundanti*,* to yield this moral—viz. that as, in England, the idiot and the half-wit are held to be under the guardianship of Chancery,* so the man making love, who is often but a variety of the same imbecile class, ought to be made a ward of the General Post-Office, whose severe course of *timing* and periodical interruption might intercept many a foolish declaration, such as lays a solid foundation for fifty years' repentance.

Ah, reader! when I look back upon those days, it seems to me that all things change or perish. Even thunder and lightning, it pains me to say, are not the thunder and lightning which I seem to remember about the time of Waterloo. Roses, I fear, are degenerating, and, without a Red revolution, must come to the dust. The Fannies of our island—though this I say with reluctance—are not improving; and the Bath road is notoriously superannuated. Mr Waterton* tells me that the crocodile does *not* change—that a cayman,* in fact, or an alligator, is just as good for riding upon as he was in the time of the Pharaohs. *That* may be; but the reason is, that the crocodile does not live fast—he is a slow coach. I believe it is generally understood amongst naturalists, that the crocodile is a blockhead. It is my own impression that the Pharaohs were also blockheads. Now, as the Pharaohs and the crocodile domineered over Egyptian society, this accounts for a singular mistake that prevailed on the Nile. The crocodile made the ridiculous blunder of supposing man to be meant chiefly for his own eating. Man, taking a different view of the subject, naturally met that mistake by another; he viewed the crocodile as a thing sometimes to worship, but always to run away from. And this continued until Mr Waterton changed the relations between the animals. The mode of escaping from the reptile he showed to be, not by running away, but by leaping on its back, booted and spurred. The two animals had misunderstood each other. The use of the crocodile has now been cleared up—it is to be ridden;* and the use of man is, that he may improve the health of the crocodile by riding him a fox-hunting before breakfast. And it is pretty certain that any crocodile, who has been regularly hunted through the season, and is master of the weight he carries, will take a six-barred gate now as well as ever he would have done in the infancy of the Pyramids.

Perhaps, therefore, the crocodile does *not* change, but all things else *do*: even the shadow of the Pyramids grows less. And often the restoration in vision of Fanny and the Bath road, makes me too pathetically sensible of that truth. Out of the darkness, if I happen to call up the image of Fanny from thirty-five years back, arises suddenly a rose in June;* or, if I think for an instant of the rose in June, up rises the heavenly face of Fanny. One after the other, like the antiphonies in a choral service, rises Fanny and the rose in June, then back again the rose in June and Fanny. Then come both together, as in a chorus; roses and Fannies, Fannies and roses, without end—thick as blossoms in paradise. Then comes a venerable crocodile, in a royal livery of scarlet and gold, or in a coat with sixteen capes; and the crocodile is driving four-in-hand* from the box of the Bath mail. And suddenly we upon the mail are pulled up by a mighty dial, sculptured with the hours, and with the dreadful legend of TOO LATE. Then all at once we are arrived in Marlborough forest, amongst the lovely households[1] of the roe-deer: these retire into the dewy thickets; the thickets are rich with roses; the roses call up (as ever) the sweet countenance of Fanny, who, being the granddaughter of a crocodile, awakens a dreadful host of wild semi-legendary animals—griffins, dragons, basilisks, sphinxes—till at length the whole vision of fighting images crowds into one towering armorial shield, a vast emblazonry of human charities and human loveliness that have perished, but quartered heraldically with unutterable horrors of monstrous and demoniac natures; whilst over all rises, as a surmounting crest, one fair female hand, with the fore-finger pointing, in sweet, sorrowful admonition, upwards to heaven,* and having power (which, without experience, I never could have believed) to awaken the pathos that kills in the very bosom of the horrors that madden the grief that gnaws at the heart, together with the monstrous creations of darkness that shock the belief, and make dizzy the reason of man. This is the peculiarity that I wish the reader to notice, as having first been made known to me for a possibility by this early vision of Fanny on the Bath road. The peculiarity consisted in the confluence of two different keys, though apparently repelling each other, into the music

---

[1] '*Households*.'—Roe-deer do not congregate in herds like the fallow or the red deer, but by separate families, parents, and children; which feature of approximation to the sanctity of human hearths, added to their comparatively miniature and graceful proportions, conciliate to them an interest of a peculiarly tender character, if less dignified by the grandeurs of savage and forest life.

and governing principles of the same dream; horror, such as possesses the maniac, and yet, by momentary transitions, grief, such as may be supposed to possess the dying mother when leaving her infant children to the mercies of the cruel. Usually, and perhaps always, in an unshaken nervous system, these two modes of misery exclude each other—here first they met in horrid reconciliation. There was also a separate peculiarity in the quality of the horror. This was afterwards developed into far more revolting complexities of misery and incomprehensible darkness; and perhaps I am wrong in ascribing any value as a *causative* agency to this particular case on the Bath road—possibly it furnished merely an *occasion* that accidentally introduced a mode of horrors certain, at any rate, to have grown up, with or without the Bath road, from more advanced stages of the nervous derangement. Yet, as the cubs of tigers or leopards, when domesticated, have been observed to suffer a sudden development of their latent ferocity under too eager an appeal to their playfulness—the gaieties of sport in *them* being too closely connected with the fiery brightness of their murderous instincts—so I have remarked that the caprices, the gay arabesques, and the lovely floral luxuriations of dreams, betray a shocking tendency to pass into finer maniacal splendours. That gaiety, for instance, (for such at first it was,) in the dreaming faculty, by which one principal point of resemblance to a crocodile in the mail-coachman was soon made to clothe him with the form of a crocodile, and yet was blended with accessory circumstances derived from his *human* functions, passed rapidly into a further development, no longer gay or playful, but terrific, the most terrific that besieges dreams, viz.—the horrid inoculation upon each other of incompatible natures. This horror has always been secretly felt by man; it was felt even under pagan forms of religion, which offered a very feeble, and also a very limited gamut for giving expression to the human capacities of sublimity or of horror. We read it in the fearful composition of the sphinx. The dragon, again, is the snake inoculated upon the scorpion. The basilisk unites the mysterious malice of the evil eye, unintentional on the part of the unhappy agent, with the intentional venom of some other malignant natures. But these horrid complexities of evil agency are but *objectively* horrid; they inflict the horror suitable to their compound nature; but there is no insinuation that they *feel* that horror. Heraldry is so full of these fantastic creatures, that, in some zoologies, we find a separate chapter or a supplement dedicated to what is denominated heraldic zoology. And why not? For these hideous creatures, however visionary,[1] have a real traditionary ground in medieval belief—sincere and partly reasonable, though adulterating with mendacity, blundering, credulity, and intense superstition. But the dream-horror which I speak of is far more frightful. The dreamer finds housed within himself—occupying, as it were, some separate chamber in his brain—holding, perhaps, from that station a secret and detestable commerce with his own heart—some horrid alien nature. What if it were his own nature repeated,—still, if the duality were distinctly perceptible, even *that*—even this mere numerical double of his own consciousness—might be a curse too mighty to be sustained. But how, if the alien nature contradicts his own, fights with it, perplexes, and confounds it? How, again, if not one alien nature, but two, but three, but four, but five, are introduced within what once he thought the inviolable sanctuary of himself? These, however, are horrors from the kingdoms of anarchy and darkness, which, by their very intensity, challenge the sanctity of concealment, and gloomily retire from exposition. Yet it was necessary to mention them, because the first introduction to such appearances (whether causal, or merely casual) lay in the heraldic monsters, which monsters were themselves introduced (though playfully) by the transfigured coachman of the Bath mail.

---

[1] '*However visionary*.'—But *are* they always visionary? The unicorn, the kraken,* the sea-serpent, are all, perhaps, zoological facts. The unicorn, for instance, so far from being a lie, is rather *too* true; for, simply as a *monokeras*,* he is found in the Himalaya, in Africa, and elsewhere, rather too often for the peace of what in Scotland would be called the *intending* traveller. That which really *is* a lie in the account of the unicorn—viz., his legendary rivalship with the lion—which lie may God preserve, in preserving the mighty imperial shield that embalms it*—cannot be more destructive to the zoological pretensions of the unicorn, than are to the same pretensions in the lion our many popular crazes about his goodness and magnanimity, or the old fancy (adopted by Spenser, and noticed by so many among our elder poets)* of his graciousness to maiden innocence. The wretch is the basest and most cowardly among the forest tribes; nor has the sublime courage of the English bull-dog ever been so memorably exhibited as in his hopeless fight at Warwick with the cowardly and cruel lion called Wallace.* Another of the traditional creatures, still doubtful, is the mermaid, upon which Southey* once remarked to me, that, if it had been differently named, (as, suppose, a mer-ape,) nobody would have questioned its existence any more than that of sea-cows, sea-lions, &c. The mermaid has been discredited by her human name and her legendary human habits. If she would not coquette so much with melancholy sailors, and brush her hair so assiduously upon solitary rocks, she would be carried on our books for as honest a reality, as decent a female, as many that are assessed to the poor-rates.*

GOING DOWN WITH VICTORY

But the grandest chapter of our experience, within the whole mail-coach service, was on those occasions when we went down from London with the news of victory. A period of about ten years stretched from Trafalgar to Waterloo: the second and third years of which period (1806 and 1807) were comparatively sterile; but the rest, from 1805 to 1815 inclusively, furnished a long succession of victories; the least of which, in a contest of that portentous nature, had an inappreciable value of position—partly for its absolute interference with the plans of our enemy, but still more from its keeping alive in central Europe the sense of a deep-seated vulnerability in France. Even to tease the coasts of our enemy, to mortify them by continual blockades, to insult them by capturing if it were but a baubling schooner* under the eyes of their arrogant armies, repeated from time to time a sullen proclamation of power lodged in a quarter to which the hopes of Christendom turned in secret. How much more loudly must this proclamation have spoken in the audacity[1] of having bearded the *élite* of their troops, and having beaten them in pitched battles! Five years of life it was worth paying down for the privilege of an outside place on a mail-coach, when carrying down the first tidings of any such event. And it is to be noted that, from our insular situation, and the multitude of our frigates disposable for the rapid transmission of intelligence, rarely did any unauthorised rumour steal away a pre-libation from the aroma of the regular despatches. The government official news was generally the first news.

From eight P.M. to fifteen or twenty minutes later, imagine the mails assembled on parade in Lombard Street, where, at that time, was seated the General Post-Office.* In what exact strength we mustered I do not remember; but, from the length of each separate *attelage*,* we filled the street, though a long one, and though we were

---

[1] *'Audacity!'* Such the French accounted it; and it has struck me that Soult would not have been so popular in London, at the period of her present Majesty's coronation, or in Manchester,* on occasion of his visit to that town, if they had been aware of the insolence with which he spoke of us in notes written at intervals from the field of Waterloo. As though it had been mere felony in our army to look a French one in the face, he said more than once—'Here are the English—we have them: they are caught *en flagrant delit*.'* Yet no man should have known us better; no man had drunk deeper from the cup of humiliation than Soult had in the north of Portugal, during his flight from an English army, and subsequently at Albuera, in the bloodiest of recorded battles.*

drawn up in double file. On *any* night the spectacle was beautiful. The absolute perfection of all the appointments about the carriages and the harness, and the magnificence of the horses, were what might first have fixed the attention. Every carriage, on every morning in the year, was taken down to an inspector for examination—wheels, axles, linchpins, pole, glasses, &c., were all critically probed and tested. Every part of every carriage had been cleaned, every horse had been groomed, with as much rigour as if they belonged to a private gentleman; and that part of the spectacle offered itself always. But the night before us is a night of victory; and behold! to the ordinary display, what a heart-shaking addition!—horses, men, carriages—all are dressed in laurels and flowers, oak leaves and ribbons. The guards, who are his Majesty's servants, and the coachmen, who are within the privilege of the Post-Office, wear the royal liveries of course; and as it is summer (for all the *land* victories were won in summer,) they wear, on this fine evening, these liveries exposed to view, without any covering of upper coats. Such a costume, and the elaborate arrangement of the laurels in their hats, dilated their hearts, by giving to them openly an *official* connection with the great news, in which already they have the general interest of patriotism. That great national sentiment surmounts and quells all sense of ordinary distinctions. Those passengers who happen to be gentlemen are now hardly to be distinguished as such except by dress. The usual reserve of their manner in speaking to the attendants has on this night melted away. One heart, one pride, one glory, connects every man by the transcendant bond of his English blood.* The spectators, who are numerous beyond precedent, express their sympathy with these fervent feelings by continual hurrahs. Every moment are shouted aloud by the Post-Office servants the great ancestral names of cities known to history through a thousand years,—Lincoln, Winchester, Portsmouth, Gloucester, Oxford, Bristol, Manchester, York, Newcastle, Edinburgh, Perth, Glasgow—expressing the grandeur of the empire by the antiquity of its towns, and the grandeur of the mail establishment by the diffusive radiation of its separate missions. Every moment you hear the thunder of lids locked down upon the mail-bags. That sound to each individual mail is the signal for drawing off, which process is the finest part of the entire spectacle. Then come the horses into play;—horses! can these be horses that (unless powerfully reined in) would bound off with the action and

gestures of leopards? What stir!—what sea-like ferment!—what a
thundering of wheels, what a trampling of horses!—what farewell
cheers—what redoubling peals of brotherly congratulation, connecting the name of the particular mail—'Liverpool for ever!'—with the
name of the particular victory—'Badajoz for ever!' or 'Salamanca*
for ever!' The half-slumbering consciousness that, all night long and
all the next day—perhaps for even a longer period—many of these
mails, like fire racing along a train of gunpowder, will be kindling
at every instant new successions of burning joy, has an obscure effect
of multiplying the victory itself, by multiplying to the imagination into infinity the stages of its progressive diffusion. A fiery
arrow seems to be let loose, which from that moment is destined to
travel, almost without intermission, westwards for three hundred[1]
miles—northwards for six hundred; and the sympathy of our
Lombard Street friends at parting is exalted a hundredfold by a sort
of visionary sympathy with the approaching sympathies, yet unborn,
which we were going to evoke.

Liberated from the embarrassments of the city, and issuing into
the broad uncrowded avenues of the northern suburbs, we begin to

[1] '*Three hundred.*' Of necessity this scale of measurement, to an American, if he happens to be a thoughtless man, must sound ludicrous. Accordingly, I remember a case in
which an American writer* indulges himself in the luxury of a little lying, by ascribing to
an Englishman a pompous account of the Thames, constructed entirely upon American
ideas of grandeur, and concluding in something like these terms:—'And, sir, arriving at
London, this mighty father of rivers attains a breadth of at least two furlongs, having, in
its winding course, traversed the astonishing distance of 170 miles.' And this the candid
American thinks it fair to contrast with the scale of the Mississippi. Now, it is hardly
worth while to answer a pure falsehood gravely, else one might say that no Englishman
out of Bedlam ever thought of looking in an island for the rivers of a continent; nor,
consequently, could have thought of looking for the peculiar grandeur of the Thames in
the length of its course, or in the extent of soil which it drains: yet, if he *had* been so
absurd, the American might have recollected that a river, not to be compared with the
Thames even as to volume of water—viz. the Tiber*—has contrived to make itself heard
of in this world for twenty-five centuries to an extent not reached, nor likely to be reached
very soon, by any river, however corpulent, of his own land. The glory of the Thames is
measured by the density of the population to which it ministers, by the commerce which
it supports, by the grandeur of the empire in which, though far from the largest, it is the
most influential stream. Upon some such scale, and not by a transfer of Columbian
standards, is the course of our English mails to be valued. The American may fancy the
effect of his own valuations to our English ears, by supposing the case of a Siberian
glorifying his country in these terms:—'Those rascals, sir, in France and England, cannot march half a mile in any direction without finding a house where food can be had and
lodging: whereas, such is the noble desolation of our magnificent country, that in many
a direction for a thousand miles, I will engage a dog shall not find shelter from a snow-
storm, nor a wren find an apology for breakfast.'

enter upon our natural pace of ten miles an hour. In the broad light of the summer evening, the sun perhaps only just at the point of setting, we are seen from every storey of every house. Heads of every age crowd to the windows—young and old understand the language of our victorious symbols—and rolling volleys of sympathising cheers run along behind and before our course. The beggar, rearing himself against the wall, forgets his lameness—real or assumed—thinks not of his whining trade, but stands erect, with bold exulting smiles, as we pass him. The victory has healed him, and says—Be thou whole! Women and children, from garrets alike and cellars, look down or look up with loving eyes upon our gay ribbons and our martial laurels—sometimes kiss their hands, sometimes hang out, as signals of affection, pocket handkerchiefs, aprons, dusters, anything that lies ready to their hands. On the London side of Barnet,* to which we draw near within a few minutes after nine, observe that private carriage which is approaching us. The weather being so warm, the glasses* are all down; and one may read, as on the stage of a theatre, everything that goes on within the carriage. It contains three ladies, one likely to be 'mama,' and two of seventeen or eighteen, who are probably her daughters. What lovely animation, what beautiful unpremeditated pantomime, explaining to us every syllable that passes, in these ingenuous girls! By the sudden start and raising of the hands, on first discovering our laurelled equipage—by the sudden movement and appeal to the elder lady from both of them—and by the heightened colour on their animated countenances, we can almost hear them saying—'See, see! Look at their laurels. Oh, mama! there has been a great battle in Spain; and it has been a great victory.' In a moment we are on the point of passing them. We passengers—I on the box, and the two on the roof behind me—raise our hats, the coachman makes his professional salute with the whip; the guard even, though punctilious on the matter of his dignity as an officer under the crown, touches his hat. The ladies move to us, in return, with a winning graciousness of gesture: all smile on each side in a way that nobody could misunderstand, and that nothing short of a grand national sympathy could so instantaneously prompt. Will these ladies say that we are nothing to *them*? Oh, no; they will not say *that*. They cannot deny—they do not deny—that for this night they are our sisters: gentle or simple, scholar or illiterate servant, for twelve hours to come—we on the outside have the honour to be their brothers.

Those poor women again, who stop to gaze upon us with delight at the entrance of Barnet, and seem by their air of weariness to be returning from labour—do you mean to say that they are washer-women and charwomen? Oh, my poor friend, you are quite mistaken; they are nothing of the kind. I assure you, they stand in a higher rank: for this one night they feel themselves by birthright to be daughters of England, and answer to no humbler title.

Every joy, however, even rapturous joy—such is the sad law of earth—may carry with it grief, or fear of grief, to some.* Three miles beyond Barnet, we see approaching us another private carriage, nearly repeating the circumstances of the former case. Here also the glasses are all down—here also is an elderly lady seated; but the two amiable daughters are missing; for the single young person, sitting by the lady's side, seems to be an attendant—so I judge from her dress, and her air of respectful reserve. The lady is in mourning; and her coun-tenance expresses sorrow. At first she does not look up; so that I believe she is not aware of our approach, until she hears the meas-ured beating of our horses' hoofs. Then she raises her eyes to settle them painfully on our triumphal equipage. Our decorations explain the case to her at once; but she beholds them with apparent anxiety, or even with terror. Some time before this, I, finding it difficult to hit a flying mark, when embarrassed by the coachman's person and reins intervening, had given to the guard a *Courier* evening paper, containing the gazette,* for the next carriage that might pass. Accordingly he tossed it in so folded that the huge capitals express-ing some such legend as—GLORIOUS VICTORY, might catch the eye at once. To see the paper, however, at all, interpreted as it was by our ensigns of triumph, explained everything; and, if the guard were right in thinking the lady to have received it with a gesture of horror, it could not be doubtful that she had suffered some deep personal affliction in connexion with this Spanish war.

Here now was the case of one who, having formerly suffered, might, erroneously perhaps, be distressing herself with anticipa-tions of another similar suffering. That same night, and hardly three hours later, occurred the reverse case. A poor woman, who too prob-ably would find herself, in a day or two, to have suffered the heavi-est of afflictions by the battle, blindly allowed herself to express an exultation so unmeasured in the news, and its details, as gave to her the appearance which amongst Celtic Highlanders is called *fey*.*

This was at some little town, I forget what, where we happened to change horses near midnight. Some fair or wake had kept the people up out of their beds. We saw many lights moving about as we drew near; and perhaps the most impressive scene on our route was our reception at this place. The flashing of torches and the beautiful radiance of blue lights (technically Bengal lights)* upon the heads of our horses; the fine effect of such a showery and ghostly illumination falling upon flowers and glittering laurels, whilst all around the massy darkness seemed to invest us with walls of impenetrable blackness, together with the prodigious enthusiasm of the people, composed a picture at once scenical and affecting. As we staid for three or four minutes, I alighted. And immediately from a dismantled stall in the street, where perhaps she had been presiding at some part of the evening, advanced eagerly a middle-aged woman. The sight of my newspaper it was that had drawn her attention upon myself. The victory which we were carrying down to the provinces on *this* occasion was the imperfect one of Talavera.* I told her the main outline of the battle. But her agitation, though not the agitation of fear, but of exultation rather, and enthusiasm, had been so conspicuous when listening, and when first applying for information, that I could not but ask her if she had not some relation in the Peninsular army. Oh! yes: her only son was there. In what regiment? He was a trooper in the 23d Dragoons. My heart sank within me as she made that answer. This sublime regiment, which an Englishman should never mention without raising his hat to their memory, had made the most memorable and effective charge recorded in military annals. They leaped their horses—*over* a trench, where they could *into* it, and with the result of death or mutilation when they could *not*. What proportion cleared the trench is nowhere stated. Those who *did*, closed up and went down upon the enemy with such divinity of fervour—(I use the word *divinity* by design: the inspiration of God must have prompted this movement to those whom even then he was calling to his presence)—that two results followed. As regarded the enemy, this 23d Dragoons, not, I believe, originally 350 strong, paralysed a French column, 6000 strong, then ascending the hill, and fixed the gaze of the whole French army. As regarded themselves, the 23d were supposed at first to have been all but annihilated; but eventually, I believe, not so many as one in four survived.* And this, then, was the regiment—a regiment already for some hours known to myself and all

London as stretched, by a large majority, upon one bloody aceldama*—in which the young trooper served whose mother was now talking with myself in a spirit of such hopeful enthusiasm. Did I tell her the truth? Had I the heart to break up her dream? No. I said to myself, To-morrow, or the next day, she will hear the worst. For this night, wherefore should she not sleep in peace? After to-morrow, the chances are too many that peace will forsake her pillow. This brief respite, let her owe this to *my* gift and *my* forbearance. But, if I told her not of the bloody price that had been paid, there was no reason for suppressing the contributions from her son's regiment to the service and glory of the day. For the very few words that I had time for speaking, I governed myself accordingly. I showed her not the funeral banners under which the noble regiment was sleeping. I lifted not the overshadowing laurels from the bloody trench in which horse and rider lay mangled together. But I told her how these dear children of England, privates and officers, had leaped their horses over all obstacles as gaily as hunters to the morning's chase. I told her how they rode their horses into the mists of death, (saying to myself, but not saying to *her*,) and laid down their young lives for thee, O mother England! as willingly—poured out their noble blood as cheerfully—as ever, after a long day's sport, when infants, they had rested their wearied heads upon their mothers' knees, or had sunk to sleep in her arms. It is singular that she seemed to have no fears, even after this knowledge that the 23d Dragoons had been conspicuously engaged, for her son's safety: but so much was she enraptured by the knowledge that *his* regiment, and therefore *he*, had rendered eminent service in the trying conflict—a service which had actually made them the foremost topic of conversation in London—that in the mere simplicity of her fervent nature, she threw her arms round my neck, and, poor woman, kissed me.*

THE VISION OF SUDDEN DEATH

(The reader is to understand this present paper, in its two sections of *The Vision*, &c., and *The Dream-Fugue*, as connected with a previous paper on *The English Mail-Coach*, published in the Magazine for October. The ultimate object was the Dream-Fugue,* as an attempt to wrestle with the utmost efforts of music in dealing with a colossal form of impassioned horror. The Vision of Sudden Death contains the mail-coach incident, which did really occur, and did really suggest the variations of the Dream, here taken up by the Fugue, as well as other variations not now recorded. Confluent with these impressions, from the terrific experience on the Manchester and Glasgow mail, were other and more general impressions, derived from long familiarity with the English mail, as developed in the former paper; impressions, for instance, of animal beauty and power, of rapid motion, at that time unprecedented, of connexion with the government and public business of a great nation, but, above all, of connexion with the national victories at an unexampled crisis,—the mail being the privileged organ for publishing and dispersing all news of that kind. From this function of the mail, arises naturally the introduction of Waterloo into the fourth variation of the Fugue; for the mail itself having been carried into the dreams by the incident in the Vision, naturally all the accessory circumstances of pomp and grandeur investing this national carriage followed in the train of the principal image.)

WHAT is to be thought of sudden death? It is remarkable that, in different conditions of society, it has been variously regarded, as the consummation of an earthly career most fervently to be desired, and, on the other hand, as that consummation which is most of all to be deprecated. Caesar the Dictator, at his last dinner party, (*caena*,) and the very evening before his assassination, being questioned as to the mode of death which, in *his* opinion, might seem the most eligible, replied—'That which should be most sudden.'* On the other hand, the divine Litany of our English Church, when breathing forth supplications, as if in some representative character for the whole human race prostrate before God, places such a death in the very van of horrors. 'From lightning and tempest; from plague, pestilence, and famine; from battle and murder, and from sudden death,—*Good Lord, deliver us.*'* Sudden death is here made to crown the climax in a grand ascent of calamities; it is the last of curses; and yet, by the noblest of Romans, it was treated as the first of blessings. In that difference, most readers will see little more than the difference between Christianity and Paganism. But there I hesitate. The Christian church may be right in its estimate of sudden death; and it is a natural feeling, though after all it may also be an infirm one, to wish for a quiet dismissal from life—as that which *seems* most reconcilable with meditation, with penitential retrospects, and with the humilities of farewell prayer. There does not, however, occur to me any direct scriptural warrant for this earnest petition of the English Litany. It seems rather a petition indulged to human infirmity, than exacted from human piety. And, however *that* may be, two remarks suggest themselves as prudent restraints upon a doctrine, which else *may* wander, and *has* wandered, into an uncharitable superstition. The first is this: that many people are likely to exaggerate the horror of a sudden death, (I mean the *objective* horror to him who contemplates such a death, not the *subjective* horror to him who suffers it) from the false disposition to lay a stress upon words or acts, simply because by an accident they have become words or acts.* If a man dies, for instance, by some sudden death when he happens to be intoxicated, such a death is falsely regarded with peculiar horror; as though the intoxication were suddenly exalted into a blasphemy. But *that* is unphilosophic. The man was, or he was not, *habitually* a drunkard. If not, if his intoxication were a solitary accident, there can be no reason at all for allowing special emphasis to this act, simply because through misfortune it became his final act. Nor, on the other hand, if it were no accident, but one of his *habitual* transgressions, will it be the more habitual or the more a transgression, because some sudden calamity, surprising him, has caused this habitual transgression to be also a final one? Could the man have had any reason even dimly to foresee his own sudden death, there would have been a new feature in his act of intemperance—a feature of presumption and irreverence, as in one that by possibility felt himself drawing near to the presence of God. But this is no part of the case supposed. And the only new element in the man's act is not any element of extra immorality, but simply of extra misfortune.*

The other remark has reference to the meaning of the word *sudden*. And it is a strong illustration of the duty which for ever calls us to the stern valuation of words—that very possibly Caesar and the Christian church do not differ in the way supposed; that is, do not differ by any difference of doctrine as between Pagan and Christian views of the moral temper appropriate to death, but that they are contemplating different cases. Both contemplate a violent death; a Βιαθανατος—death that is Βιαιος:* but the difference is—that the Roman by the word 'sudden' means an *unlingering* death: whereas the Christian litany by 'sudden' means a death *without warning*, consequently without any available summons to religious preparation. The poor mutineer, who kneels down to gather into his heart the bullets from twelve firelocks of his pitying comrades, dies by a most sudden death in Caesar's sense: one shock, one mighty spasm, one (possibly *not* one) groan, and all is over. But, in the sense of the Litany, his death is far from sudden; his offence originally, his imprisonment, his trial, the interval between his sentence and its execution, having all furnished him with separate warnings of his fate—having all summoned him to meet it with solemn preparation.

Meantime, whatever may be thought of a sudden death as a mere variety in the modes of dying, where death in some shape is inevitable—a question which, equally in the Roman and the Christian sense, will be variously answered according to each man's variety of temperament—certainly, upon one aspect of sudden death there can be no opening for doubt, that of all agonies incident to man it is the most frightful, that of all martyrdoms it is the most freezing to human sensibilities—namely, where it surprises a man under circumstances which offer (or which seem to offer) some hurried and inappreciable chance of evading it. Any effort, by which such an evasion can be accomplished, must be as sudden as the danger which it affronts. Even *that*, even the sickening necessity for hurrying in extremity where all hurry seems destined to be vain, self-baffled, and where the dreadful knell of *too late* is already sounding in the ears by anticipation—even that anguish is liable to a hideous exasperation in one particular case, namely, where the agonising appeal is made not exclusively to the instinct of self-preservation, but to the conscience, on behalf of another life besides your own, accidentally cast upon *your* protection. To fail, to collapse in a service merely your own, might seem comparatively venial; though, in fact, it is far from venial. But to fail in a case where Providence has suddenly thrown into your hands the final interests of another—of a fellow-creature shuddering between the gates of life and death; this, to a man of apprehensive conscience, would mingle the misery of an atrocious criminality with the misery of a bloody calamity. The man is called upon, too probably, to die; but to die at the very moment when, by any momentary collapse, he is self-denounced as a murderer. He had but the twinkling of an eye* for his effort, and that effort might, at the best, have been unavailing; but from this shadow of a chance, small or great, how if he has recoiled by a treasonable *lâcheté*?* The effort *might* have been without hope; but to have risen to the level of that effort—would have rescued him, though not from dying, yet from dying as a traitor to his duties.

The situation here contemplated exposes a dreadful ulcer, lurking far down in the depths of human nature. It is not that men generally are summoned to face such awful trials. But potentially, and in shadowy outline, such a trial is moving subterraneously in perhaps all men's natures—muttering under ground in one world, to be realised perhaps in some other. Upon the secret mirror of our dreams such a trial is darkly projected at intervals, perhaps, to every one of us. That dream, so familiar to childhood, of meeting a lion, and, from languishing prostration in hope and vital energy, that constant sequel of lying down before him,* publishes the secret frailty of human nature—reveals its deep-seated Pariah falsehood to itself—records its abysmal treachery. Perhaps not one of us escapes that dream; perhaps, as by some sorrowful doom of man, that dream repeats for every one of us, through every generation, the original temptation in Eden. Every one of us, in this dream, has a bait offered to the infirm places of his own individual will; once again a snare is made ready for leading him into captivity to a luxury of ruin; again, as in aboriginal Paradise, the man falls from innocence; once again, by infinite iteration, the ancient Earth groans to God, through her secret caves, over the weakness of her child; 'Nature from her seat, sighing through all her works,' again 'gives signs of woe that all is lost;'* and again the counter sigh is repeated to the sorrowing heavens of the endless rebellion against God. Many people think that one man, the patriarch of our race, could not in his single person execute this rebellion for all his race. Perhaps they are wrong. But, even if not, perhaps in the world of dreams every one of us ratifies for himself the original act. Our English rite of 'Confirmation,' by which, in years of awakened reason, we take upon us the engagements contracted for us in our slumbering infancy,—how sublime a rite is that! The little postern gate, through which the baby in its cradle had been silently placed for a time within the glory of God's countenance, suddenly rises to the clouds as a triumphal arch, through which, with banners displayed and martial pomps, we make our second entry as crusading soldiers militant for God, by personal choice and by sacramental oath. Each man says in effect—'Lo! I rebaptise myself; and that which once was sworn on my behalf, now I swear for myself.' Even so in dreams, perhaps, under some secret conflict of the midnight sleeper, lighted up to the consciousness at the time, but darkened to the memory as soon as all is finished, each several child of our mysterious race completes for himself the aboriginal fall.

As I drew near to the Manchester post-office, I found that it was considerably past midnight;* but to my great relief, as it was important for me to be in Westmorland* by the morning, I saw by the huge saucer eyes of the mail, blazing through the gloom of overhanging houses, that my chance was not yet lost. Past the time it was; but by some luck, very unusual in my experience, the mail was not even yet ready to start.* I ascended to my seat on the box, where my cloak was still lying as it had lain at the Bridgewater Arms. I had left it there in imitation of a nautical discoverer, who leaves a bit of bunting on the shore of his discovery, by way of warning off the ground the whole human race, and signalising to the Christian and the heathen worlds, with his best compliments, that he has planted his throne for ever upon that virgin soil; henceforward claiming the *jus dominii* to the top of the atmosphere above it, and also the right of driving shafts to the centre of the earth below it; so that all people found after this warning, either aloft in the atmosphere, or in the shafts, or squatting on the soil, will be treated as trespassers—that is, decapitated by their very faithful and obedient servant, the owner of the said bunting. Possibly my cloak might not have been respected, and the *jus gentium** might have been cruelly violated in my person—for, in the dark, people commit deeds of darkness, gas being a great ally of morality*—but it so happened that, on this night, there was no other outside passenger; and the crime, which else was but too probable, missed fire for want of a criminal. By the way, I may as well mention at this point, since a circumstantial accuracy is essential to the effect of my narrative, that there was no other person of any description whatever about the mail—the guard, the coachman, and myself being allowed for—except only one—a horrid creature of the class known to the world as insiders, but whom young Oxford called sometimes 'Trojans,' in opposition to our Grecian selves, and sometimes 'vermin.' A Turkish Effendi,* who piques himself on good-breeding, will never mention by name a pig. Yet it is but too often that he has reason to mention this animal; since constantly, in the streets of Stamboul,* he has his trousers deranged or polluted by this vile creature running between his legs. But under any excess of hurry he is always careful, out of respect to the company he is dining with, to suppress the odious name, and to call the wretch 'that other creature,' as though all animal life beside formed one group, and this odious beast (to whom, as Chrysippus observed, salt serves as an apology for a soul)* formed another and alien group on the outside of creation. Now I, who am an English Effendi, that think myself to understand good-breeding as well as any son of Othman,* beg my reader's pardon for having mentioned an insider by his gross natural name. I shall do so no more: and, if I should have occasion to glance at so painful a subject, I shall always call him 'that other creature.' Let us hope, however, that no such distressing occasion will arise. But, by the way, an occasion arises at this moment; for the reader will be sure to ask, when we come to the story, 'Was this other creature present?' He was *not*; or more correctly, perhaps, *it* was not. We dropped the creature—or the creature, by natural imbecility, dropped itself—within the first ten miles from Manchester. In the latter case, I wish to make a philosophic remark of a moral tendency. When I die, or when the reader dies, and by repute suppose of fever, it will never be known whether we died in reality of the fever or of the doctor. But this other creature, in the case of dropping out of the coach, will enjoy a coroner's inquest; consequently he will enjoy an epitaph. For I insist upon it, that the verdict of a coroner's jury makes the best of epitaphs. It is brief, so that the public all find time to read it; it is pithy, so that the surviving friends (if any *can* survive such a loss) remember it without fatigue; it is upon oath, so that rascals and Dr Johnsons* cannot pick holes in it. 'Died through the visitation of intense stupidity, by impinging on a moonlight night against the off hind wheel of the Glasgow mail! Deodand* upon the said wheel—two-pence.' What a simple lapidary inscription! Nobody much in the wrong but an off-wheel; and with few acquaintances; and if it were but rendered into choice Latin, though there would be a little bother in finding a Ciceronian word for 'off-wheel,' Morcellus* himself, that great master of sepulchral eloquence, could not show a better. Why I call this little remark *moral*, is, from the compensation it points out. Here, by the supposition, is that other creature on the one side, the beast of the world; and he (or it) gets an epitaph. You and I, on the contrary, the pride of our friends, get none.

But why linger on the subject of vermin? Having mounted the box, I took a small quantity of laudanum, having already travelled two hundred and fifty miles—viz., from a point seventy miles beyond London, upon a simple breakfast. In the taking of laudanum there was nothing extraordinary. But by accident it drew upon me the special attention of my assessor on the box, the coachman. And in *that* there was nothing extraordinary. But by accident, and with great delight, it drew my attention to the fact that this coachman was a monster in point of size, and that he had but one eye. In fact he had been foretold by Virgil as—

'Monstrum horrendum, informe, ingens, cui lumen ademptum.'*

He answered in every point—a monster he was—dreadful, shapeless, huge, who had lost an eye. But why should *that* delight me? Had he been one of the Calendars in the Arabian Nights, and had paid down his eye as the price of his criminal curiosity,* what right had *I* to exult in his misfortune? I did *not* exult: I delighted in no man's punishment, though it were even merited. But these personal distinctions identified in an instant an old friend of mine, whom I had known in the south for some years as the most masterly of mail-coachmen. He was the man in all Europe that could best have undertaken to drive six-in-hand full gallop over *Al Sirat*—that famous bridge of Mahomet* across the bottomless gulf, backing himself against the Prophet and twenty such fellows. I used to call him *Cyclops mastigophorus,* Cyclops the whip-bearer, until I observed that his skill made whips useless, except to fetch off an impertinent fly from a leader's head; upon which I changed his Grecian name to Cyclops *diphrélates* (Cyclops the charioter). I, and others known to me, studied under him the diphrelatic* art. Excuse, reader, a word too elegant to be pedantic. And also take this remark from me, as a *gage d'amitié**—that no word ever was or *can* be pedantic which, by supporting a distinction, supports the accuracy of logic; or which fills up a chasm for the understanding. As a pupil, though I paid extra fees, I cannot say that I stood high in his esteem. It showed his dogged honesty, (though, observe, not his discernment,) that he could not see my merits. Perhaps we ought to excuse his absurdity in this particular by remembering his want of an eye. *That* made him blind to my merits. Irritating as this blindness was, (surely it could not be envy?) he always courted my conversation, in which art I certainly had the whip-hand of him. On this occasion, great joy was at our meeting. But what was Cyclops doing here? Had the medical men recommended northern air, or how? I collected, from such explanations as he volunteered, that he had an interest at stake in a suit-at-law pending at Lancaster; so that probably he had got himself transferred to this station, for the purpose of connecting with his professional pursuits an instant readiness for the calls of his law-suit.

Meantime, what are we stopping for? Surely we've been waiting long enough. Oh, this procrastinating mail, and oh this procrastinating post-office! Can't they take a lesson upon that subject from *me*? Some people have called *me* procrastinating. Now you are witness, reader, that I was in time for *them*. But can *they* lay their hands on their hearts, and say that they were in time for me? I, during my life, have often had to wait for the post-office: the post-office never waited a minute for me. What are they about? The guard tells me that there is a large extra accumulation of foreign mails this night, owing to irregularities caused by war* and by the packet-service, when as yet nothing is done by steam.* For an *extra* hour, it seems, the post-office has been engaged in threshing out the pure wheaten correspondence of Glasgow, and winnowing it from the chaff of all baser intermediate towns. We can hear the flails going at this moment. But at last all is finished. Sound your horn, guard. Manchester, good bye; we've lost an hour by your criminal conduct at the post-office: which, however, though I do not mean to part with a serviceable ground of complaint, and one which really *is* such for the horses, to me secretly is an advantage, since it compels us to recover this last hour amongst the next eight or nine. Off we are at last, and at eleven miles an hour:* and at first I detect no changes in the energy or in the skill of Cyclops.

From Manchester to Kendal, which virtually (though not in law) is the capital of Westmoreland,* were at this time seven stages of eleven miles each. The first five of these, dated from Manchester, terminated in Lancaster, which was therefore fifty-five miles north of Manchester, and the same distance exactly from Liverpool. The first three terminated in Preston (called, by way of distinction from other towns of that name, *proud* Preston,) at which place it was that the separate roads from Liverpool and from Manchester to the north became confluent. Within these first three stages lay the foundation, the progress, and termination of our night's adventure. During the first stage, I found out that Cyclops was mortal: he was liable to the shocking affection of sleep—a thing which I had never previously suspected. If a man is addicted to the vicious habit of sleeping, all the skill in aurigation* of Apollo himself, with the horses of Aurora* to execute the motions of his will, avail him nothing. 'Oh, Cyclops!' I exclaimed more than once, 'Cyclops, my friend; thou art mortal. Thou snorest.' Through this first eleven miles, however, he betrayed his infirmity—which I grieve to say he shared with the whole Pagan Pantheon—only by short stretches. On waking up, he made an apology for himself, which, instead of mending the matter, laid an ominous foundation for coming disasters. The summer assizes were now proceeding at Lancaster: in consequence of which, for three nights and three days, he had not lain down in a bed. During the day, he was waiting for his uncertain summons as a witness on the trial in which he was interested; or he was drinking with the other witnesses, under the vigilant surveillance of the attorneys. During the night, or that part of it when the least temptations existed to conviviality, he was driving. Throughout the second stage he grew more and more drowsy. In the second mile of the third stage, he surrendered himself finally and without a struggle to his perilous temptation. All his past resistance had but deepened the weight of this final oppression. Seven atmospheres of sleep seemed resting upon him; and, to consummate the case, our worthy guard, after singing 'Love amongst the Roses,'* for the fiftieth or sixtieth time, without any invitation from Cyclops or myself, and without applause for his poor labours, had moodily resigned himself to slumber—not so deep doubtless as the coachman's, but deep enough for mischief; and having, probably, no similar excuse. And thus at last, about ten miles from Preston, I found myself left in charge of his Majesty's London and Glasgow mail then running about eleven miles an hour.

What made this negligence less criminal than else it must have been thought, was the condition of the roads at night during the assizes. At that time all the law business of populous Liverpool, and of populous Manchester, with its vast cincture of populous rural districts, was called up by ancient usage to the tribunal of Lilliputian Lancaster.* To break up this old traditional usage required a conflict with powerful established interests, a large system of new arrangements, and a new parliamentary statute.* As things were at present, twice in the year so vast a body of business rolled northwards, from the southern quarter of the county, that a fortnight at least occupied the severe exertions of two judges for its despatch.

The consequence of this was—that every horse available for such a service, along the whole line of road, was exhausted in carrying down the multitudes of people who were parties to the different suits. By sunset, therefore, it usually happened that, through utter exhaustion amongst men and horses, the roads were all silent. Except exhaustion in the vast adjacent county of York from a contested election,* nothing like it was ordinarily witnessed in England.

On this occasion, the usual silence and solitude prevailed along the road. Not a hoof nor a wheel was to be heard. And to strengthen this false luxurious confidence in the noiseless roads, it happened also that the night was one of peculiar solemnity and peace. I myself, though slightly alive to the possibilities of peril, had so far yielded to the influence of the mighty calm as to sink into a profound reverie. The month was August, in which lay my own birth-day; a festival to every thoughtful man suggesting solemn and often sigh-born thoughts.[1] The county was my own native county*—upon which, in its southern section, more than upon any equal area known to man past or present, had descended the original curse of labour in its heaviest form, not mastering the bodies of men only as of slaves, or criminals in mines, but working through the fiery will. Upon no equal space of earth, was, or ever had been, the same energy of human power put forth daily. At this particular season also of the assizes, that dreadful hurricane of flight and pursuit, as it might have seemed to a stranger, that swept to and from Lancaster all day long, hunting the county up and down, and regularly subsiding about sunset, united with the permanent distinction of Lancashire as the very metropolis and citadel of labour, to point the thoughts pathetically upon that counter vision of rest, of saintly repose from strife and sorrow, towards which, as to their secret haven, the profounder aspirations of man's heart are continually travelling. Obliquely we were nearing the sea upon our left,* which also must, under the present circumstances, be repeating the general state of halcyon repose. The sea, the atmosphere, the light, bore an orchestral part in this universal lull. Moonlight, and the first timid tremblings of the dawn, were now blending; and the blendings were brought into a still more exquisite state of unity, by a slight silvery mist, motionless and dreamy,

---

[1] 'Sigh-born:' I owe the suggestion of this word to an obscure remembrance of a beautiful phrase in Giraldus Cambrensis, viz., *suspiriosae cogitationes*.*

that covered the woods and fields, but with a veil of equable transparency. Except the feet of our own horses, which, running on a sandy margin of the road, made little disturbance, there was no sound abroad. In the clouds, and on the earth, prevailed the same majestic peace; and in spite of all that the villain of a schoolmaster has done for the ruin of our sublimer thoughts, which are the thoughts of our infancy, we still believe in no such nonsense as a limited atmosphere. Whatever we may swear with our false feigning lips, in our faithful hearts we still believe, and must for ever believe, in fields of air traversing the total gulf between earth and the central heavens. Still, in the confidence of children that tread without fear *every* chamber in their father's house, and to whom no door is closed, we, in that Sabbatic vision which sometimes is revealed for an hour upon nights like this, ascend with easy steps from the sorrow-stricken fields of earth, upwards to the sandals of God.

Suddenly from thoughts like these, I was awakened to a sullen sound, as of some motion on the distant road. It stole upon the air for a moment; I listened in awe; but then it died away. Once roused, however, I could not but observe with alarm the quickened motion of our horses. Ten years' experience had made my eye learned in the valuing of motion; and I saw that we were now running thirteen miles an hour. I pretend to no presence of mind. On the contrary, my fear is, that I am miserably and shamefully deficient in that quality as regards action. The palsy of doubt and distraction hangs like some guilty weight of dark unfathomed remembrances upon my energies, when the signal is flying for *action*. But, on the other hand, this accursed gift I have, as regards *thought*, that in the first step towards the possibility of a misfortune, I see its total evolution: in the radix,* I see too certainly and too instantly its entire expansion; in the first syllable of the dreadful sentence, I read already the last. It was not that I feared for ourselves. What could injure *us*? Our bulk and impetus charmed us against peril in any collision. And I had rode through too many hundreds of perils that were frightful to approach, that were matter of laughter as we looked back upon them, for any anxiety to rest upon *our* interests. The mail was not built, I felt assured, nor bespoke, that could betray *me* who trusted to its protection. But any carriage that we could meet would be frail and light in comparison of ourselves. And I remarked this ominous accident of our situation. We were on the wrong side of the road. But then the other party, if other there was, might also be on the wrong side; and two wrongs might make a right. *That* was not likely. The same motive which had drawn *us* to the right-hand side of the road, viz., the soft beaten sand, as contrasted with the paved centre, would prove attractive to others. Our lamps, still lighted, would give the impression of vigilance on our part. And every creature that met us, would rely upon *us* for quartering.[1] All this, and if the separate links of the anticipation had been a thousand times more, I saw—not discursively or by effort—but as by one flash of horrid intuition.

Under this steady though rapid anticipation of the evil which *might* be gathering ahead, ah, reader! what a sullen mystery of fear, what a sigh of woe, seemed to steal upon the air, as again the far-off sound of a wheel was heard! A whisper it was—a whisper from, perhaps, four miles off—secretly announcing a ruin that, being foreseen, was not the less inevitable. What could be done—who was it that could do it—to check the storm-flight of these maniacal horses? What! could I not seize the reins from the grasp of the slumbering coachman? You, reader, think that it would have been in *your* power to do so. And I quarrel not with your estimate of yourself. But, from the way in which the coachman's hand was viced between his upper and lower thigh, this was impossible. The guard subsequently found it impossible, after this danger had passed. Not the grasp only, but also the position of this Polyphemus, made the attempt impossible. You still think otherwise. See, then, that bronze equestrian statue. The cruel rider has kept the bit in his horse's mouth for two centuries. Unbridle him, for a minute, if you please, and wash his mouth with water. Or stay, reader, unhorse me that marble emperor: knock me those marble feet from those marble stirrups of Charlemagne.*

The sounds ahead strengthened, and were now too clearly the sounds of wheels. Who and what could it be? Was it industry in a taxed cart?*—was it youthful gaiety in a gig? Whoever it was, something must be attempted to warn them. Upon the other party rests the active responsibility, but upon *us*—and, woe is me! that *us* was my single self—rests the responsibility of warning. Yet, how should this be accomplished? Might I not seize the guard's horn? Already, on the first thought, I was making my way over the roof to the guard's seat.

---

[1] '*Quartering*'—this is the technical word; and, I presume, derived from the French *cartayer*, to evade a rut or any obstacle.*

But this, from the foreign mails being piled upon the roof, was a difficult, and even dangerous attempt, to one cramped by nearly three hundred miles of outside travelling. And, fortunately, before I had lost much time in the attempt, our frantic horses swept round an angle of the road, which opened upon us the stage where the collision must be accomplished, the parties that seemed summoned to the trial, and the impossibility of saving them by any communication with the guard.

Before us lay an avenue, straight as an arrow, six hundred yards, perhaps, in length; and the umbrageous trees, which rose in a regular line from either side, meeting high overhead, gave to it the character of a cathedral aisle. These trees lent a deeper solemnity to the early light; but there was still light enough to perceive, at the further end of this gothic aisle, a light, reedy gig, in which were seated a young man, and, by his side, a young lady. Ah, young sir! what are you about? If it is necessary that you should whisper your communications to this young lady—though really I see nobody at this hour, and on this solitary road, likely to overhear your conversation—is it, therefore, necessary that you should carry your lips forward to hers? The little carriage is creeping on at one mile an hour; and the parties within it, being thus tenderly engaged, are naturally bending down their heads. Between them and eternity, to all human calculation, there is but a minute and a half. What is it that I shall do? Strange it is, and to a mere auditor of the tale, might seem laughable, that I should need a suggestion from the *Iliad* to prompt the sole recourse that remained. But so it was. Suddenly I remembered the shout of Achilles, and its effect. But could I pretend to shout like the son of Peleus, aided by Pallas?* No, certainly: but then I needed not the shout that should alarm all Asia militant; a shout would suffice, such as should carry terror into the hearts of two thoughtless young people, and one gig horse. I shouted—and the young man heard me not. A second time I shouted—and now he heard me, for now he raised his head.

Here, then, all had been done that, by me, *could* be done: more on *my* part was not possible. Mine had been the first step: the second was for the young man: the third was for God. If, said I, the stranger is a brave man, and if, indeed, he loves the young girl at his side—or, loving her not, if he feels the obligation pressing upon every man worthy to be called a man, of doing his utmost for a woman confided to his protection—he will at least make some effort to save her. If *that* fails, he will not perish the more, or by a death more cruel, for having made it; and he will die, as a brave man should, with his face to the danger, and with his arm about the woman that he sought in vain to save. But if he makes no effort, shrinking, without a struggle, from his duty, he himself will not the less certainly perish for this baseness of poltroonery. He will die no less: and why not? Wherefore should we grieve that there is one craven less in the world? No; *let* him perish, without a pitying thought of ours wasted upon him; and, in that case, all our grief will be reserved for the fate of the helpless girl, who, now, upon the least shadow of failure in *him*, must, by the fiercest of translations—must, without time for a prayer—must, within seventy seconds, stand before the judgment-seat of God.

But craven he was not: sudden had been the call upon him, and sudden was his answer to the call. He saw, he heard, he comprehended, the ruin that was coming down: already its gloomy shadow darkened above him; and already he was measuring his strength to deal with it. Ah! what a vulgar thing does courage seem, when we see nations buying it and selling it for a shilling a-day: ah! what a sublime thing does courage seem, when some fearful crisis on the great deeps of life carries a man, as if running before a hurricane, up to the giddy crest of some mountainous wave, from which accordingly as he chooses his course, he describes two courses, and a voice says to him audibly—'This way lies hope; take the other way and mourn for ever!' Yet, even then, amidst the raving of the seas and the frenzy of the danger, the man is able to confront his situation—is able to retire for a moment into solitude with God, and to seek all his counsel from *him*! For seven seconds, it might be, of his seventy, the stranger settled his countenance steadfastly upon us, as if to search and value every element in the conflict before him. For five seconds more he sate immovably, like one that mused on some great purpose. For five he sate with eyes upraised, like one that prayed in sorrow, under some extremity of doubt, for wisdom to guide him towards the better choice. Then suddenly he rose; stood upright; and, by a sudden strain upon the reins, raising his horse's forefeet from the ground, he slewed him round on the pivot of his hind legs, so as to plant the little equipage in a position nearly at right-angles to ours. Thus far his condition was not improved; except as a first step had been taken towards the possibility of a second. If no more were done, nothing was done;* for the little carriage still occupied the very centre of our path, though in an altered direction. Yet even now it may not be too late: fifteen of the twenty seconds may still be unexhausted; and one almighty bound forward may avail to clear the ground. Hurry then, hurry! for the flying moments—*they* hurry! Oh hurry, hurry, my brave young man! for the cruel hoofs of our horses—*they* also hurry! Fast are the flying moments, faster are the hoofs of our horses. Fear not for *him*, if human energy can suffice: faithful was he that drove, to his terrific duty; faithful was the horse to *his* command. One blow, one impulse given with voice and hand by the stranger, one rush from the horse, one bound as if in the act of rising to a fence, landed the docile creature's fore-feet upon the crown or arching centre of the road. The larger half of the little equipage had then cleared our over-towering shadow: *that* was evident even to my own agitated sight. But it mattered little that one wreck should float off in safety, if upon the wreck that perished were embarked the human freightage. The rear part of the carriage—was *that* certainly beyond the line of absolute ruin? What power could answer the question? Glance of eye, thought of man, wing of angel, which of these had speed enough to sweep between the question and the answer, and divide the one from the other? Light does not tread upon the steps of light more indivisibly, than did our all-conquering arrival upon the escaping efforts of the gig. *That* must the young man have felt too plainly. His back was now turned to us; not by sight could he any longer communicate with the peril; but by the dreadful rattle of our harness, too truly had his ear been instructed—that all was finished as regarded any further effort of *his*. Already in resignation he had rested from his struggle; and perhaps, in his heart he was whispering—'Father, which art above, do thou finish in heaven what I on earth have attempted.' We ran past them faster than ever mill-race in our inexorable flight. Oh, raving of hurricanes that must have sounded in their young ears at the moment of our transit! Either with the swingle-bar,* or with the haunch of our near leader, we had struck the off-wheel of the little gig, which stood rather obliquely and not quite so far advanced as to be accurately parallel with the near wheel. The blow, from the fury of our passage, resounded terrifically. I rose in horror, to look upon the ruins we might have caused. From my elevated station I looked down, and looked back upon the scene, which in a moment told its tale, and wrote all its records on my heart for ever.

The horse was planted immovably, with his fore-feet upon the paved crest of the central road. He of the whole party was alone

untouched by the passion of death. The little cany carriage*—partly
perhaps from the dreadful torsion of the wheels in its recent movement, partly from the thundering blow we had given to it—as if it
sympathised with human horror, was all alive with tremblings and
shiverings. The young man sat like a rock. He stirred not at all. But
his was the steadiness of agitation frozen into rest by horror. As yet he
dared not to look round; for he knew that, if anything remained to do,
by him it could no longer be done. And as yet he knew not for certain
if their safety were accomplished. But the lady——

But the lady——! Oh heavens! will that spectacle ever depart from
my dreams, as she rose and sank upon her seat, sank and rose, threw up
her arms wildly to heaven, clutched at some visionary object in the air,
fainting, praying, raving, despairing! Figure to yourself, reader, the
elements of the case; suffer me to recal before your mind the circumstances of the unparalleled situation. From the silence and deep peace
of this saintly summer night,—from the pathetic blending of this sweet
moonlight, dawnlight, dreamlight,—from the manly tenderness of this
flattering, whispering, murmuring love,—suddenly as from the woods
and fields,—suddenly as from the chambers of the air opening in revelation,—suddenly as from the ground yawning at her feet, leaped upon
her, with the flashing of cataracts, Death the crownèd* phantom, with
all the equipage of his terrors, and the tiger roar of his voice.

The moments were numbered. In the twinkling of an eye our flying horses had carried us to the termination of the umbrageous aisle;
at right-angles we wheeled into our former direction; the turn of the
road carried the scene out of my eyes in an instant, and swept it into
my dreams for ever.*

DREAM-FUGUE

ON THE ABOVE THEME OF SUDDEN DEATH

'Whence the sound
Of instruments, that made melodious chime,
Was heard, of harp and organ; and who mov'd
Their stops and chords, was seen; his volant touch
Instinct through all proportions, low and high,
Fled and pursued transverse the resonant fugue.'

Par. Lost, B. xi.*

*Tumultuosissimamente**

Passion of Sudden Death! that once in youth I read and interpreted by the shadows of thy averted[1] signs;—Rapture of panic taking the shape, which amongst tombs in churches I have seen, of woman bursting her sepulchral bonds—of woman's Ionic* form bending forward from the ruins of her grave, with arching foot, with eyes upraised, with clasped adoring hands—waiting, watching, trembling, praying, for the trumpet's call to rise from dust for ever;—Ah, vision too fearful of shuddering humanity on the brink of abysses! vision that didst start back—that didst reel away—like a shrivelling scroll from before the wrath of fire racing on the wings of the wind! Epilepsy so brief of horror—wherefore is it that thou canst not die? Passing so suddenly into darkness, wherefore is it that still thou sheddest thy sad funeral blights upon the gorgeous mosaics of dreams? Fragment of music too stern, heard once and heard no more, what aileth thee that thy deep rolling chords come up at intervals through all the worlds of sleep, and after thirty years have lost no element of horror?

I

Lo, it is summer, almighty summer! The everlasting gates of life and summer are thrown open wide; and on the ocean, tranquil and verdant as a savannah, the unknown lady from the dreadful vision and I myself are floating: she upon a fairy pinnace, and I upon an English three-decker. But both of us are wooing gales of festal happiness within the domain of our common country—within that ancient watery park—within that pathless chase where England takes her pleasure as a huntress through winter and summer, and which stretches from the rising to the setting sun. Ah! what a wilderness of floral beauty was hidden, or was suddenly revealed, upon the tropic islands through which the pinnace moved. And upon her deck what a bevy of human flowers—young women how lovely, young men how noble, that were dancing together, and slowly drifting towards *us* amidst music and incense, amidst blossoms from forests and

---

[1] '*Averted* signs.'—I read the course and changes of the lady's agony in the succession of her involuntary gestures; but let it be remembered that I read all this from the rear, never once catching the lady's full face, and even her profile imperfectly.

gorgeous corymbi* from vintages, amidst natural caroling and the echoes of sweet girlish laughter. Slowly the pinnace nears us, gaily she hails us, and slowly she disappears beneath the shadow of our mighty bows. But then, as at some signal from heaven, the music and the carols, and the sweet echoing of girlish laughter—all are hushed. What evil has smitten the pinnace, meeting or overtaking her? Did ruin to our friends couch within our own dreadful shadow? Was our shadow the shadow of death?* I looked over the bow for an answer; and, behold! the pinnace was dismantled; the revel and the revellers were found no more; the glory of the vintage was dust; and the forest was left without a witness to its beauty upon the seas. 'But where,' and I turned to our own crew—'where are the lovely women that danced beneath the awning of flowers and clustering corymbi? Whither have fled the noble young men that danced with *them*?' Answer there was none. But suddenly the man at the mast-head, whose countenance darkened with alarm, cried aloud—'Sail on the weather-beam! Down she comes upon us; in seventy seconds she will founder!'

2

I looked to the weather-side, and the summer had departed. The sea was rocking, and shaken with gathering wrath. Upon its surface sate mighty mists, which grouped themselves into arches and long cathedral aisles. Down one of these, with the fiery pace of a quarrel from a cross-bow, ran a frigate right athwart our course. 'Are they mad?' some voice exclaimed from our deck. 'Are they blind? Do they woo their ruin?' But in a moment, as she was close upon us, some impulse of a heady current* or sudden vortex gave a wheeling bias to her course, and off she forged without a shock. As she ran past us, high aloft amongst the shrouds stood the lady of the pinnace. The deeps opened ahead in malice to receive her, towering surges of foam ran after her, the billows were fierce to catch her. But far away she was borne into desert spaces of the sea: whilst still by sight I followed her, as she ran before the howling gale, chased by angry sea-birds and by maddening billows; still I saw her, as at the moment when she ran past us, amongst the shrouds, with her white draperies streaming before the wind. There she stood with hair dishevelled, one hand clutched amongst the tackling—rising, sinking, fluttering, trembling, praying—there for leagues I saw her as she stood, raising at intervals one hand to heaven, amidst the fiery crests of the pursuing waves and the raving of the storm; until at last, upon a sound from afar of malicious laughter and mockery, all was hidden for ever in driving showers; and afterwards, but when I know not, and how I know not,

3

Sweet funeral bells from some incalculable distance, wailing over the dead that die before the dawn, awakened me as I slept in a boat moored to some familiar shore. The morning twilight even then was breaking; and, by the dusky revelations which it spread, I saw a girl adorned with a garland of white roses about her head for some great festival, running along the solitary strand with extremity of haste. Her running was the running of panic; and often she looked back as to some dreadful enemy in the rear. But when I leaped ashore, and followed on her steps to warn her of a peril in front, alas! from me she fled as from another peril; and vainly I shouted to her of quicksands that lay ahead. Faster and faster she ran; round a promontory of rock she wheeled out of sight; in an instant I also wheeled round it, but only to see the treacherous sands gathering above her head. Already her person was buried; only the fair young head and the diadem of white roses around it were still visible to the pitying heavens; and, last of all, was visible one marble arm. I saw by the early twilight this fair young head, as it was sinking down to darkness—saw this marble arm, as it rose above her head and her treacherous grave, tossing, faultering, rising, clutching as at some false deceiving hand stretched out from the clouds— saw this marble arm uttering her dying hope, and then her dying despair. The head, the diadem, the arm,—these all had sunk; at last over these also the cruel quicksand had closed; and no memorial of the fair young girl remained on earth, except my own solitary tears, and the funeral bells from the desert seas, that, rising again more softly, sang a requiem over the grave of the buried child, and over her blighted dawn.

I sate, and wept in secret the tears that men have ever given to the memory of those that died before the dawn, and by the treachery of earth, our mother. But the tears and funeral bells were hushed suddenly by a shout as of many nations, and by a roar as from some great king's artillery advancing rapidly along the valleys, and heard afar by its echoes among the mountains. 'Hush!' I said, as I bent my ear earthwards to listen—'hush!—this either is the very anarchy of strife, or else'—and then I listened more profoundly, and said as I raised my head—'or else, oh heavens! it is *victory* that swallows up all strife.'

4

Immediately, in trance, I was carried over land and sea to some distant kingdom, and placed upon a triumphal car, amongst companions crowned with laurel. The darkness of gathering midnight, brooding over all the land, hid from us the mighty crowds that were weaving restlessly about our carriage as a centre—we heard them, but we saw them not. Tidings had arrived, within an hour, of a grandeur that measured itself against centuries; too full of pathos they were, too full of joy that acknowledged no fountain but God, to utter themselves by other language than by tears, by restless anthems, by reverberations rising from every choir, of the *Gloria in excelsis.** These tidings we that sate upon the laurelled car had it for our privilege to publish amongst all nations. And already, by signs audible through the darkness, by snortings and tramplings, our angry horses, that knew no fear of fleshly weariness, upbraided us with delay. Wherefore *was* it that we delayed? We waited for a secret word, that should bear witness to the hope of nations, as now accomplished for ever. At midnight the secret word arrived; which word was—Waterloo and Recovered Christendom! The dreadful word shone by its own light; before us it went; high above our leaders' heads it rode, and spread a golden light over the paths which we traversed. Every city, at the presence of the secret word, threw open its gates to receive us. The rivers were silent as we crossed. All the infinite forests, as we ran along their margins, shivered in homage to the secret word. And the darkness comprehended it.*

Two hours after midnight we reached a mighty minster. Its gates, which rose to the clouds, were closed. But when the dreadful word, that rode before us, reached them with its golden light, silently they moved back upon their hinges; and at a flying gallop our equipage entered the grand aisle of the cathedral. Headlong was our pace; and at every altar, in the little chapels and oratories to the right hand and

left of our course, the lamps, dying or sickening, kindled anew in
sympathy with the secret word that was flying past. Forty leagues we
might have run in the cathedral, and as yet no strength of morning
light had reached us, when we saw before us the aërial galleries of the
organ and the choir. Every pinnacle of the fret-work, every station of
advantage amongst the traceries, was crested by white-robed choris-
ters, that sang deliverance; that wept no more tears, as once their
fathers had wept; but at intervals that sang together to the generations, saying—

> 'Chaunt the deliverer's praise in every tongue,'

and receiving answers from afar,

> ——'such as once in heaven and earth were sung.'*

And of their chaunting was no end; of our headlong pace was neither
pause nor remission.

Thus, as we ran like torrents—thus, as we swept with bridal rapture over the Campo Santo[1] of the cathedral graves—suddenly we
became aware of a vast necropolis rising upon the far-off horizon—
a city of sepulchres, built within the saintly cathedral for the warrior
dead that rested from their feuds on earth. Of purple granite was
the necropolis; yet, in the first minute, it lay like a purple stain upon
the horizon—so mighty was the distance. In the second minute it
trembled through many changes, growing into terraces and towers of
wondrous altitude, so mighty was the pace. In the third minute
already, with our dreadful gallop, we were entering its suburbs. Vast
sarcophagi rose on every side, having towers and turrets that, upon
the limits of the central aisle, strode forward with haughty intrusion,
that ran back with mighty shadows into answering recesses. Every
sarcophagus showed many bas-reliefs—bas-reliefs of battles—
bas-reliefs of battle-fields; of battles from forgotten ages—of battles

---

[1] *Campo Santo.*—It is probable that most of my readers will be acquainted with the
history of the Campo Santo at Pisa—composed of earth brought from Jerusalem* for a
bed of sanctity, as the highest prize which the noble piety of crusaders could ask or
imagine. There is another Campo Santo at Naples, formed, however, (I presume,) on the
example given by Pisa. Possibly the idea may have been more extensively copied. To
readers who are unacquainted with England, or who (being English) are yet unacquainted
with the cathedral cities of England, it may be right to mention that the graves within-
side the cathedrals often form a flat pavement over which carriages and horses might roll;
and perhaps a boyish remembrance of one particular cathedral, across which I had seen
passengers walk and burdens carried, may have assisted my dream.

from yesterday—of battle-fields that, long since, nature had healed and reconciled to herself with the sweet oblivion of flowers—of battle-fields that were yet angry and crimson with carnage. Where the terraces ran, there did *we* run; where the towers curved, there did *we* curve. With the flight of swallows our horses swept round every angle. Like rivers in flood, wheeling round headlands; like hurricanes that ride into the secrets of forests; faster than ever light unwove the mazes of darkness, our flying equipage carried earthly passions— kindled warrior instincts—amongst the dust that lay around us; dust oftentimes of our noble fathers that had slept in God from Créci* to Trafalgar. And now had we reached the last sarcophagus, now were we abreast of the last bas-relief, already had we recovered the arrow-like flight of the illimitable central aisle, when coming up this aisle to meet us we beheld a female infant that rode in a carriage as frail as flowers. The mists, which went before her, hid the fawns that drew her, but could not hide the shells and tropic flowers with which she played—but could not hide the lovely smiles by which she uttered her trust in the mighty cathedral, and in the cherubim that looked down upon her from the topmost shafts of its pillars. Face to face she was meeting us; face to face she rode, as if danger there were none. 'Oh baby!' I exclaimed, 'shalt thou be the ransom for Waterloo? Must we, that carry tidings of great joy to every people,* be messengers of ruin to thee?' In horror I rose at the thought; but then also, in horror at the thought, rose one that was sculptured on the bas-relief— a Dying Trumpeter. Solemnly from the field of battle he rose to his feet; and, unslinging his stony trumpet, carried it, in his dying anguish, to his stony lips—sounding once, and yet once again; proc- lamation that, in *thy* ears, oh baby! must have spoken from the battle- ments of death. Immediately deep shadows fell between us, and aboriginal silence. The choir had ceased to sing. The hoofs of our horses, the rattling of our harness, alarmed the graves no more. By horror the bas-relief had been unlocked into life. By horror we, that were so full of life, we men and our horses, with their fiery fore-legs rising in mid air to their everlasting gallop, were frozen to a bas-relief. Then a third time the trumpet sounded; the seals were taken off all pulses; life, and the frenzy of life, tore into their channels again; again the choir burst forth in sunny grandeur, as from the muf- fling of storms and darkness; again the thunderings of our horses car- ried temptation into the graves. One cry burst from our lips as the

clouds, drawing off from the aisle, showed it empty before us—
'Whither has the infant fled?—is the young child caught up to God?'
Lo! afar off, in a vast recess, rose three mighty windows to the clouds;
and on a level with their summits, at height insuperable to man, rose
an altar of purest alabaster. On its eastern face was trembling a crimson glory. Whence came *that*? Was it from the reddening dawn
that now streamed *through* the windows? Was it from the crimson
robes of the martyrs that were painted *on* the windows? Was it from
the bloody bas-reliefs of earth? Whencesoever it were—there, within
that crimson radiance, suddenly appeared a female head, and then a
female figure. It was the child—now grown up to woman's height.
Clinging to the horns of the altar,* there she stood—sinking, rising,
trembling, fainting—raving, despairing; and behind the volume of
incense that, night and day, streamed upwards from the altar, was
seen the fiery font, and dimly was descried the outline of the dreadful
being that should baptise her with the baptism of death. But by her
side was kneeling her better angel, that hid his face with wings; that
wept and pleaded for *her*; that prayed when *she* could *not*; that fought
with heaven by tears for *her* deliverance; which also, as he raised his
immortal countenance from his wings, I saw, by the glory in his eye,
that he had won at last.

5

Then rose the agitation, spreading through the infinite cathedral,
to its agony; then was completed the passion of the mighty fugue.
The golden tubes of the organ, which as yet had but sobbed and mut-
tered at intervals—gleaming amongst clouds and surges of
incense—threw up, as from fountains unfathomable, columns of
heart-shattering music. Choir and anti-choir were filling fast with
unknown voices. Thou also, Dying Trumpeter!—with thy love that
was victorious, and thy anguish that was finishing, didst enter the
tumult: trumpet and echo—farewell love, and farewell anguish—rang
through the dreadful *sanctus*.* We, that spread flight before us, heard
the tumult, as of flight, mustering behind us. In fear we looked round
for the unknown steps that, in flight or in pursuit, were gathering
upon our own. Who were these that followed? The faces, which no
man could count—whence were *they*? 'Oh, darkness of the grave!'
I exclaimed, 'that from the crimson altar and from the fiery font

wert visited with secret light—that wert searched by the effulgence
in the angel's eye—were these indeed thy children? Pomps of life,
that, from the burials of centuries, rose again to the voice of perfect
joy, could it be *ye* that had wrapped me in the reflux of panic?' What
ailed me, that I should fear when the triumphs of earth were advancing? Ah! Pariah heart within me, that couldst never hear the sound
of joy without sullen whispers of treachery in ambush; that, from six
years old, didst never hear the promise of perfect love,* without seeing aloft amongst the stars fingers as of a man's hand writing the
secret legend—'*ashes to ashes, dust to dust!*'*—wherefore shouldst
thou not fear, though all men should rejoice? Lo! as I looked back for
seventy leagues through the mighty cathedral, and saw the quick and
the dead* that sang together to God, together that sang to the generations of man—ah! raving, as of torrents that opened on every side:
trepidation, as of female and infant steps that fled—ah! rushing, as
of wings that chased! But I heard a voice from heaven, which said—
'Let there be no reflux of panic—let there be no more fear, and
no more sudden death! Cover them with joy as the tides cover the
shore!' *That* heard the children of the choir, *that* heard the children
of the grave. All the hosts of jubilation made ready to move. Like
armies that ride in pursuit, they moved with one step. Us, that, with
laurelled heads, were passing from the cathedral through its eastern
gates, they overtook, and, as with a garment, they wrapped us round
with thunders that overpowered our own. As brothers we moved
together; to the skies we rose—to the dawn that advanced—to the
stars that fled: rendering thanks to God in the highest—that, having
hid his face through one generation behind thick clouds of War,
once again was ascending—was ascending from Waterloo—in the
visions of Peace:—rendering thanks for thee, young girl! whom having overshadowed with his ineffable passion of Death*—suddenly
did God relent; suffered thy angel to turn aside his arm; and even in
thee, sister unknown! shown to me for a moment only to be hidden
for ever, found an occasion to glorify his goodness. A thousand
times, amongst the phantoms of sleep, has he shown thee to me,
standing before the golden dawn, and ready to enter its gates—with
the dreadful Word going before thee—with the armies of the grave
behind thee; shown thee to me, sinking, rising, fluttering, fainting,
but then suddenly reconciled, adoring: a thousand times has he followed thee in the worlds of sleep—through storms; through desert

seas; through the darkness of quicksands; through fugues and the persecution of fugues; through dreams, and the dreadful resurrections that are in dreams—only that at the last, with one motion of his victorious arm, he might record and emblazon the endless resurrections of his love!*

APPENDIX A

MANUSCRIPT AND OTHER MATERIAL
RELATING TO THE *CONFESSIONS OF*
AN ENGLISH OPIUM-EATER

1. *Manuscript Material*

[This passage is housed in the Wordsworth Library, Dove Cottage, Grasmere, MS 1988:192. It is the most substantive variant between the manuscript of the first instalment of the *Confessions of an English Opium-Eater* and the published version of that text in the *London Magazine* for September 1821. The passage appears in the section of the opening instalment in which De Quincey seeks to use his correspondence with the earl of Altamont to secure a loan from a Jewish moneylender (see above, p. 27). For full details, see *Works*, ii. 279–324.]

[. . .] He had accordingly, from the time that I was fifteen, corresponded with me; sometimes upon the great improvements which he had made or was meditating in the counties of M—— and Sl—— since I had been there; sometimes upon the merits of a Latin Poet; at other times suggesting subjects to me on which he wished me to write verses. One in particular I remember as being the first which I put into the hands of a certain Jew: it began with criticisms on that ode in Horace (*Qualem ministrum fulminis alitem*)* which stands 4th. I think in the 4th. book, which ode the Marquis for some reason had often urged me to translate, being dissatisfied with all the existing ones: and two years before, in travelling from Dublin to ———,* we had amused ourselves in drawing up a pompous dedication to himself with which I was to publish it. To this conversation the letter alluded. The perplexity of the Jew was infinite as he read—sometimes a quere about Ganymede,* sometimes a remark on the Roman metres, sometimes a reference to the monstrous hyperboles of the proposed Dedication.—I was far too grave from habitual melancholy, and my business with the Jew was too much a matter of anxiety with me, to leave me in much disposition for laughter: yet I was now and then obliged to bite my lips at the odd and involuntary expressions of wonder and perplexity in the Jew as at times he ejaculated suddenly to himself—'The Devil!'—and then suddenly turned to the cover of the letter to see if it really were a letter at all. However the Post-mark, Frank,* Seal, &c. all bore witness to combined to authenticate it.

[This fragment is housed in the Henry W. and Albert A. Berg Collection of the New York Public Library. It begins with familiar material from the second instalment of the *Confessions* for October 1821 (see above, p. 63). But it soon leads into an anecdote excluded from the published text concerning De Quincey's intellectual frustrations as played out in games with his eldest son William. For full details, see *Works*, ii. 325–7.]

My studies have now been long interrupted. I cannot read to myself with any pleasure, hardly with a moment's endurance. Yet I read aloud sometimes for the pleasure of others; because reading is an accomplishment of mine; and, in the slang use of the word accomplishment as a superficial and ornamental attainment, almost the only one I possess: and formerly if I had any vanity at all connected with any endowment or attainment of mine, it was with this; for I had observed that no accomplishment was so rare: players are the worst readers of all: ——— reads vilely: and M^rs ———, who is so celebrated, can read nothing well but dramatic compositions: she attempted to read a passage in Milton at Mrs Hannah More's,* and all the company thought it an oblig to admire. But nothing could be worse. Milton she cannot read sufferably.—People in general read poetry either without any passion at all, or else overstep the modesty of nature and read not like scholars.—Of late, if I have felt moved by anything in books, it has been by the grand lamentations of Samson Agonistes or the great harmonies of the Satanic speeches in Paradise Regained when read aloud by myself. A young lady sometimes comes and drinks tea with us: at her request and M's I now and then read W———'s poems to them (W. by the bye is the only Poet I ever met who could read his own verses: Blank verse he reads admirably.

This then has been the extent of my reading for upwards of 16 months. It frets me to enter those rooms of my cottage in which the books stand. In one of them, to which my little boy* has access, he has found out a use for some of them: somebody has given him a bow and arrows; God knows who: certainly not I: for I have not energy or ingenuity to invent a walking-stick. Thus equipped for action, he rears up the largest of the Folios that he can lift: places them on a tottering base; and then shoots until he brings down the enemy. He often prefers me to join him: and sometimes I consent and we are both engaged together in these intellectual labors. We build up a pile having for it's base some slender modern Metaphysician ill able (poor man!) to sustain such a weight of philosophy; upon this we place the Dutch Quartos of Des Cartes and Spinosa;* then a third story of Schoolmen* in Folio—The Master of Sentences, Suarez, Picus Mirandola,* and the Telamonian bulk of Thomas Aquinas:* and, when the whole architecture seems firm and compact, we finish our system of metaphysics by roofing the whole with Duval's enormous Aristotle.* So far there is some pleasure: building up is something: but what is that to destroying? Thus thinks at least my little companion, who now with the wrath of the Pythian Apollo* assumes his bow and arrows; plants himself in the remotest corner of the room: and prepares his fatal shafts. The bow-string twangs: flights of arrows are in the air: but the Dutch impregnability of the Bergen-op-Zooms* at the base receiving the few which reach the mark: and they recoil without mischief done: again the baffled archer collects his arrows, and again he takes his station. An arrow issues; and takes effect on a weak side of Thomas. Symptoms of dissolution appear: the cohesion of the system is loosened:—the Schoolmen begin to totter: the Stagyrite trembles:* Philosophy rocks to its centre:—and, before it can be seen whether time will do anything to heal their wounds, another arrow is planted in the schism of their ontology: the mighty structure heaves—reels—seems in suspense for one moment and then with one choral crash, to the frantic joy of the young Sagittary,* lies subverted on the floor: Kant and Aristotle, Nominalists and Realists, Doctors Seraphic or Irrefragable,* what cares he? All are at his feet: the Irrefragable has been confuted by his arrows, the Seraphic has been found mortal: and the greatest philosopher and the least differ but as to the brief noise they have made.

For nearly two years I believe that I read no book but one: and I owe it to the author,

[This fragment is housed in the Henry W. and Albert A. Berg Collection of the New York Public Library. It closes with a version of the apocalypse dream from the finale of the *Confessions* for October 1821 (see above, p. 76). But its opening section was not included in the published text, and reveals in greater detail De Quincey's struggles with 'visionary companions' and the pains of sleep. For full details, see *Works*, ii. 325–8.]

This dream at first brought tears to one who had been long familiar only with groans: but afterwards it fluctuated and grew unsteady: the passions and the scenery changed countenance: and the whole was transposed into another key. It's variations, though interesting, I must omit.

At length I grew afraid to sleep: and I shrunk from it as from the most savage torture. Often I fought with my own drowsiness and kept it aloof by sitting up the whole night and following day. Sometimes I lay down only in the dawn time: and sought to charm away the phantoms by requesting my family to sit around me and to talk: hoping thus to derive an influence from what affected me externally into my internal world of shadows: but, far from that, I infected and stained as it were the whole of my waking experience with feelings derived from sleep. I seemed indeed to live and to converse even when awake with my visionary companions much more than with the realities of life.—'Oh, X. what do you see? dear X, what is it that you see?' was the constant exclamation of M. by which I was awakened as soon as I had fallen asleep (though to me it seemed as if I had slept for years): my groans had, it seems, wakened her; and, from her account, they had commenced immediately on my falling asleep.

The following dream, as an impressive one to me, I shall close with: it grew up under the influence of that misery which I have described above as resulting from the almost paralytic incapacity to do anything towards completing my intellectual labours—combined with a belief which at the time I reasonably entertained that I should soon be called on to quit for ever this world and those for whose sake I still cling to it.

———————————— As a final specimen I cite one of a different character. The dream commenced with a music which now I often heard in dreams— a music of preparation and of awakening suspense; a music like the opening of the Coronation anthem, and which like *that* gave the feeling of a vast march—of infinite cavalcades filing off—and the tread of innumerable armies. The morning was come of a mighty day—a day of crisis and of final hope for human nature then suffering some mysterious eclipse, and laboring in some dread extremity. Somewhere, I knew not where—somehow, I knew not how—by some beings, I knew not whom—a battle, a strife, an agony was going on, was evolving like a great drama or piece of music; in which my sympathy was the more insupportable, from my confusion as to its place, its cause, its nature, and its possible issue. I, as is usual in dreams (where of necessity we make ourselves central to every movement) had the power, and yet had not the power to decide it: I had the power if I could raise myself to will it: but the weight of twenty Atlantics was upon me, or the oppression of inexpiable guilt 'deeper than ever plummet sounded'. I lay inactive. Then, like a chorus, the passion deepened:—Some greater interest was at stake, some mightier cause than ever yet the Sword had pleaded or Trumpet had proclaimed. Then came sudden alarms: hurryings to and fro: trepidations of innumerable fugitives I knew not whether from the good cause or the bad: darkness and lights, tempest and human faces: and at last, with the sense that all was lost, female faces and the smiles that were worth all the world to me, and but a moment allowed,—and clasped hands and heart-breaking partings, and then— Everlasting Farewells! and, with a sigh such as the caves of Hell sighed when the incestuous mother uttered the abhorred name of Death, the sound was reverberated—Everlasting Farewells! and again and yet again reverberated—Everlasting Farewells!

And I awoke in struggles, and cried aloud—I will sleep no more.

2. *Notice to the Reader*

[First published anonymously in the *London Magazine*, 4 (October 1821), 351. This short notice appeared as part of 'The Lion's Head', the column that prefaced each number of the *London*, and that was usually compiled by the magazine's sub-editor Thomas Hood (1799–1845), poet, essayist, and humourist. De Quincey's 'Notice' was itself prefaced by a brief introduction from Hood. 'We are not often in the habit of eulogizing our own work', he declared, '—but we cannot neglect the opportunity which the following explanatory note gives us of calling the attention of our readers to the deep, eloquent, and masterly paper which stands first in our present Number. Such Confessions, so powerfully uttered, cannot fail to do more than interest the reader. We give the following chronological explanation in the author's own words, and at his request.']

The incidents recorded in the Preliminary Confessions already published, lie within a period of which the earlier extreme is now rather more, and the latter extreme less, than nineteen years ago: consequently, in a popular way of computing dates, many of the incidents might be indifferently referred to a distance of eighteen or of nineteen years; and, as the notes and memoranda for this narrative were drawn up originally about last Christmas,* it seemed most natural in all cases to prefer the former date. In the hurry of composing the narrative, though some months had then elapsed, this date was every where retained: and, in many cases, perhaps, it leads to no error, or to none of importance. But in one instance, viz. where the author speaks of his own birth-day,* this adoption of one uniform date has led to a positive inaccuracy of an entire year: for, during the very time of composition, the *nineteenth* year from the earlier term of the whole period revolved to its close. It is, therefore, judged proper to mention, that the period of that narrative lies between the early part of July, 1802, and the beginning or middle of March, 1803.

3. *To the Editor of the London Magazine*

[First published anonymously in the *London Magazine*, 4 (December 1821), 584–6. This letter forms part of 'The Lion's Head'. Immediately preceding it is a list of proposed articles for 1822, beginning with 'The Essays of ELIA' and closing with 'The Third Part of the CONFESSIONS OF AN ENGLISH OPIUM-EATER'. The editorial commentary then states that 'in reference to the last Article, we have to lay before our Readers the following Letter'.]

SIR,

* * * * * * * * * * * * *

But to leave this subject,* and to pass to another more immediately connected with your Journal:—I have seen in the Sheffield Iris* a notice of my two papers entitled *Confessions of an English Opium-eater*. Notice of any sort from Mr Montgomery* could not have failed to gratify me, by proving

that I had so far succeeded in my efforts as to catch the attention of a distinguished man of genius: a notice so emphatic as this, and introduced by
an exordium of so much beauty as that contained in the two first paragraphs on the faculty of dreaming,* I am bound in gratitude to acknowledge as a more flattering expression and memorial of success than any
which I had allowed myself to anticipate.

  I am not sorry that a passage in Mr Montgomery's comments enables
me to take notice of a doubt which had reached me before: the passage
I mean is this: in the fourth page of the Iris, amongst the remarks with
which Mr Montgomery has introduced the extracts which he has done me
the honour to make, it is said—'whether this character,' (the character in
which the Opium-eater speaks) 'be real or imaginary, we know not.' The
same doubt was reported to me as having been made in another quarter;
but, in that instance, as clothed in such discourteous expressions, that I do
not think it would have been right for me, or that on a principle of just self-
respect, I could have brought myself to answer it at all; which I say in no
anger, and I hope with no other pride than that which may reasonably
influence any man in refusing an answer to all direct impeachments of his
veracity. From Mr Montgomery, however, this scruple on the question of
authenticity comes in the shape which might have been anticipated from
his own courteous and honourable nature, and implies no more than a
suggestion (in one view perhaps complimentary to myself) that the whole
might be professedly and intentionally a fictitious case as respected the
incidents—and chosen as a more impressive form for communicating
some moral or medical admonitions to the unconfirmed Opium-eater.
Thus shaped—I cannot have any right to quarrel with this scruple. But on
many accounts I should be sorry that such a view were taken of the narrative by those who may have happened to read it. And therefore, I assure
Mr Montgomery, in this public way, that the entire Confessions were
designed to convey a narrative of my own experience as an Opium-eater,
drawn up with entire simplicity and fidelity to the facts; from which they
can in no respect have deviated, except by such trifling inaccuracies of
date, &c. as the memoranda I have with me in London would not, in all
cases, enable me to reduce to certainty. Over and above the want of these
memoranda, I laboured sometimes (as I will acknowledge) under another,
and a graver embarrassment:—To tell nothing *but* the truth—must, in all
cases, be an unconditional moral law: to tell the *whole* truth is not equally
so: in the earlier narrative I acknowledge that I could not always do this:
regards of delicacy towards some who are yet living, and of just tenderness
to the memory of others who are dead, obliged me, at various points of my
narrative, to suppress what would have added interest to the story, and

sometimes, perhaps, have left impressions on the reader favourable to other purposes of an auto-biographer. In cases which touch too closely on their own rights and interests, all men should hesitate to trust their own judgment: thus far I imposed a restraint upon myself, as all just and conscientious men would do: in every thing else I spoke fearlessly, and as if writing private memoirs for my own dearest friends.* Events, indeed, in my life, connected with so many remembrances of grief, and sometimes of self-reproach, had become too sacred from habitual contemplation to be altered or distorted for the unworthy purposes of scenical effect and display, without violating those feelings of self-respect which all men should cherish, and giving a lasting wound to my conscience.

Having replied to the question involved in the passage quoted from the Iris, I ought to notice an objection, conveyed to me through many channels, and in too friendly terms to have been overlooked if I had thought it unfounded: whereas, I believe it is a very just one:—it is this: that I have so managed the second narrative, as to leave an overbalance on the side of the *pleasures* of opium; and that the very horrors themselves, described as connected with the use of opium, do not pass the limit of pleasure.—I know not how to excuse myself on this head, unless by alleging (what is obvious enough) that to describe any pains, of any class, and that at perfect leisure for choosing and rejecting thoughts and expressions, is a most difficult task: in my case I scarcely know whether it is competent to me to allege further, that I was limited, both as to space and time, so long as it appears on the face of my paper, that I did not turn all that I had of either to the best account. It is known to you, however, that I wrote in extreme haste, and under very depressing circumstances in other respects.*—On the whole, perhaps, the best way of meeting this objection will be to send you a Third Part* of my Confessions:[1] drawn up with such assistance from fuller memoranda, and the recollections of my only companion during those years, as I shall be able to command on my return to the north: I hope that I shall be able to return thither in the course of the next week:* and, therefore, by the end of January, or thereabouts, I shall have found leisure from my other employments, to finish it to my own satisfaction. I do not venture to hope, that it will realize the whole of what is felt to be wanting: but it is fit that I should make the effort, if it were only to meet the

---

[1] In the Third Part I will fill up an omission noticed by the *Medical Intelligencer*,* (No. 24,) viz.—The omission to record the particular effects of the Opium between 1804–12. This *Medical Intelligencer* is a sort of digest or analytic summary of contemporary medical essays, reviews, &c. wherever dispersed. Of its general merits I cannot pretend to judge: but, in justice to the writer of the article which respects myself, I ought to say, that it is the most remarkable specimen of skilful abridgement and judicious composition that I remember to have met with.

expressions of interest in my previous papers, which have reached me from all quarters, or to mark my sense of the personal kindness which, in many cases, must have dictated the terms in which that interest was conveyed.

This, I think, is what I had to say. Some things, which I might have been disposed to add, would not be fitting in a public letter. Let me say, however, generally, that these two papers of mine, short and inconsiderable as they are, have, in one way, produced a disproportionate result though but of a personal nature, by leading to many kind acts, and generous services, and expressions of regard, in many different shapes, from men of talents in London.

To these hereafter I shall look back as to a fund of pleasant remembrances. Meantime, for the present, they have rendered me a service not less acceptable, by making my residence in London, in many respects, agreeable, at a time when, on other accounts, it should naturally have been far otherwise.

     I remain, Sir,

        Your faithful friend and servant,

                X. Y. Z.

London, Nov. 27, 1821.

4. *'Appendix' to the* Confessions of an English Opium-Eater

[First published in the book version of the *Confessions of an English Opium-Eater* (London: Taylor and Hessey, 1822), 187–206. Taylor and Hessey then reprinted the 'Appendix' in the *London Magazine*, 6 (December 1822), 512–17, where it was prefaced with the following notice: 'The interest excited by the two papers bearing this title, in our Numbers for September and October, 1821, will have kept our promise of a THIRD PART fresh in the remembrance of our Readers. That we are still unable to fulfil our engagement in its original meaning, will, we are sure, be matter of regret to them, as to ourselves, especially when they have perused the following affecting narrative. It was composed for the purpose of being appended to an Edition of the CONFESSIONS, in a separate Volume, which is already before the public; and we have reprinted it entire, that our Subscribers may be in possession of the whole of this extraordinary history.' The copy-text is the book version of the 'Appendix'.]

The proprietors of this little work having determined on reprinting it, some explanation seems called for, to account for the non-appearance of a Third Part promised in the London Magazine of December last; and the more so, because the proprietors, under whose guarantee that promise was issued, might otherwise be implicated in the blame—little or much—attached to its non-fulfilment. This blame, in mere justice, the author takes wholly upon himself. What may be the exact amount of the guilt which he thus appropriates, is a very dark question to his own judgment, and not much illuminated by any of the masters in casuistry whom he has consulted on the occasion. On the one hand it seems generally agreed that a promise is binding in the *inverse* ratio of the numbers to whom it is made: for which reason it is that we see many persons break promises without scruple that are made to a whole nation, who keep their faith religiously in all private engagements,—breaches of promise towards the stronger party being committed at a man's own peril: on the other hand, the only parties interested in the promises of an author are his readers; and these it is a point of modesty in any author to believe as few as possible; or perhaps only one, in which case any promise imposes a sanctity of moral obligation which it is shocking to think of. Casuistry dismissed however,—the author throws himself on the indulgent consideration of all who may conceive themselves aggrieved by his delay—in the following account of his own condition from the end of last year, when the engagement was made, up nearly to the present time. For any purpose of self-excuse, it might be sufficient to say that intolerable bodily suffering had totally disabled him for almost any exertion of mind, more especially for such as demand and presuppose a pleasurable and genial state of feeling: but, as a case that may by possibility contribute a trifle to the medical history of Opium in a further stage of its action than can often have been brought under the notice of professional men, he has judged that it might be acceptable to some readers to have it described more at length. *Fiat experimentum in corpore vili** is a just rule where there is any reasonable presumption of benefit to arise on a large scale; what the benefit may be, will admit of a doubt: but there can be none as to the value of the body: for a more worthless body than his own, the author is free to confess, cannot be: it is his pride to believe—that it is the very ideal of a base, crazy, despicable human system—that hardly ever could have been meant to be sea-worthy for two days under the ordinary storms and wear-and-tear of life: and indeed, if that were the creditable way of disposing of human bodies, he must own that he should almost be ashamed to bequeath his wretched structure to any respectable dog.—But now to the case; which, for the sake of avoiding the constant recurrence of a cumbersome periphrasis, the author will take the liberty of giving in the first person.

Those who have read the Confessions will have closed them with the impression that I had wholly renounced the use of Opium. This impression I meant to convey: and that for two reasons: first, because the very act of deliberately recording such a state of suffering necessarily presumes in the recorder a power of surveying his own case as a cool spectator, and a degree of spirits for adequately describing it, which it would be inconsistent to suppose in any person speaking from the station of an actual sufferer: secondly, because I, who had descended from so large a quantity as 8,000 drops to so small a one (comparatively speaking) as a quantity ranging between 300 and 160 drops, might well suppose that the victory was in effect achieved. In suffering my readers therefore to think of me as of a reformed opium-eater, I left no impression but what I shared myself; and, as may be seen, even this impression was left to be collected from the general tone of the conclusion, and not from any specific words—which are in no instance at variance with the literal truth.—In no long time after that paper was written, I became sensible that the effort which remained would cost me far more energy than I had anticipated: and the necessity for making it was more apparent every month. In particular I became aware of an increasing callousness or defect of sensibility in the stomach; and this I imagined might imply a schirrous* state of that organ either formed or forming. An eminent physician,* to whose kindness I was at that time deeply indebted, informed me that such a termination of my case was not impossible, though likely to be forestalled by a different termination, in the event of my continuing the use of opium. Opium therefore I resolved wholly to abjure, as soon as I should find myself at liberty to bend my undivided attention and energy to this purpose. It was not however until the 24th of June last that any tolerable concurrence of facilities for such an attempt arrived. On that day I began my experiment, having previously settled in my own mind that I would not flinch, but would 'stand up to the scratch'—under any possible 'punishment.'* I must premise that about 170 or 180 drops had been my ordinary allowance for many months: occasionally I had run up as high as 500; and once nearly to 700: in repeated preludes to my final experiment I had also gone as low as 100 drops; but had found it impossible to stand it beyond the 4th day—which, by the way, I have always found more difficult to get over than any of the preceding three. I went off under easy sail—130 drops a day for 3 days: on the 4th I plunged at once to 80: the misery which I now suffered 'took the conceit'* out of me at once: and for about a month I continued off and on about this mark: then I sunk to 60: and the next day to —— none at all. This was the first day for nearly ten years that I had existed without opium. I persevered in my abstinence for 90 hours; i. e. upwards of half a week. Then I took —— ask me not how much: say, ye severest, what would ye have done? then I abstained again: then took about 25 drops: then abstained: and so on.

Meantime the symptoms which attended my case for the first six weeks of the experiment were these:—enormous irritability and excitement of the whole system: the stomach in particular restored to a full feeling of vitality and sensibility; but often in great pain: unceasing restlessness night and day: sleep —— I scarcely knew what it was: 3 hours out of the 24 was the utmost I had, and that so agitated and shallow that I heard every sound that was near me: lower jaw constantly swelling: mouth ulcerated: and many other distressing symptoms that would be tedious to repeat; amongst which however I must mention one, because it had never failed to accompany any attempt to renounce opium—viz. violent sternutation:* this now became exceedingly troublesome: sometimes lasting for 2 hours at once, and recurring at least twice or three times a day. I was not much surprised at this, on recollecting what I had somewhere heard or read, that the membrane which lines the nostrils is a prolongation of that which lines the stomach; whence I believe are explained the inflammatory appearances about the nostrils of dram-drinkers. The sudden restoration of its original sensibility to the stomach expressed itself, I suppose, in this way. It is remarkable also that, during the whole period of years through which I had taken opium, I had never once caught cold (as the phrase is), nor even the slightest cough. But now a violent cold attacked me, and a cough soon after. In an unfinished fragment of a letter begun about this time to ———— I find these words: 'You ask me to write the ———— ————.* Do you know Beaumont and Fletcher's play of Thierry and Theodoret?* There you will see my case as to sleep: nor is it much of an exaggeration in other features.—I protest to you that I have a greater influx of thoughts in one hour at present than in a whole year under the reign of opium. It seems as though all the thoughts which had been frozen up for a decad of years by opium, had now according to the old fable been thawed at once*—such a multitude stream in upon me from all quarters. Yet such is my impatience and hideous irritability—that, for one which I detain and write down, 50 escape me: in spite of my weariness from suffering and want of sleep, I cannot stand still or sit for 2 minutes together. 'I nunc, et versus tecum meditare canoros.'*

At this stage of my experiment I sent to a neighbouring surgeon,* requesting that he would come over to see me. In the evening he came: and after briefly stating the case to him, I asked this question:—Whether he did not think that the opium might have acted as a stimulus to the digestive organs; and that the present state of suffering in the stomach, which manifestly was the cause of the inability to sleep, might arise from indigestion? His answer was—No: on the contrary he thought that the suffering was caused by digestion itself—which should naturally go on below the consciousness, but which from the unnatural state of the stomach, vitiated by so long a use of opium, was become distinctly perceptible. This opinion was plausible: and the unintermitting nature of the suffering disposes me to think that it was true: for, if it had been any mere *irregular* affection of the stomach, it should naturally have intermitted occasionally, and constantly fluctuated as to degree. The intention of nature, as manifested in the healthy state, obviously is—to withdraw from our notice all the vital motions, such as the circulation of the blood, the expansion and contraction of the lungs, the peristaltic* action of the stomach, &c.; and opium, it seems, is able in this as in other instances to counteract her purposes.—By the advice of the surgeon I tried *bitters*:* for a short time these greatly mitigated the feelings under which I laboured: but about the forty-second day of the experiment the symptoms already noticed began to retire, and new ones to arise of a different and far more tormenting class: under these, but with a few intervals of remission, I have since continued to suffer. But I dismiss them undescribed for two reasons: 1st, because the mind revolts from retracing circumstantially any sufferings from which it is removed by too short or by no interval: to do this with minuteness enough to make the review of any use—would be indeed '*infandum renovare dolorem*,'* and possibly without a sufficient motive: for 2dly, I doubt whether this latter state be any way referable to opium—positively considered, or even negatively; that is, whether it is to be numbered amongst the last evils from the direct action of opium, or even amongst the earliest evils consequent upon a *want* of opium in a system long deranged by its use. Certainly one part of the symptoms might be accounted for from the time of year (August): for, though the summer was not a hot one, yet in any case the sum of all the heat *funded* (if one may say so) during the previous months, added to the existing heat of that month, naturally renders August in its better half the hottest part of the year: and it so happened that the excessive perspiration, which even at Christmas attends any great reduction in the daily quantum of opium—and which in July was so violent as to oblige me to use a bath five or six times a day, had about the setting in of the hottest season wholly retired: on which account any bad effect of the heat might be the more unmitigated. Another symptom, viz. what in my ignorance I call internal rheumatism (sometimes affecting the shoulders, &c., but more often appearing to be seated in the stomach), seemed again less probably attributable to the opium or the want of opium than to the dampness of the house[1] which I inhabit, which had about that time attained its maximum—July having been, as usual, a month of incessant rain in our most rainy part of England.

[1] In saying this I mean no disrespect to the individual house,* as the reader will understand when I tell him that, with the exception of one or two princely mansions and some few inferior ones that have been coated with Roman cement, I am not acquainted with any house in this mountainous district which is wholly water-proof. The architecture of books, I flatter myself, is conducted on just principles in this county: but for any other architecture—it is in a barbarous state; and, what is worse, in a retrograde state.

Under these reasons for doubting whether opium had any connexion with the latter stage of my bodily wretchedness—(except indeed as an occasional cause, as having left the body weaker and more crazy, and thus predisposed to any mal-influence whatever),—I willingly spare my reader all description of it: let it perish to him: and would that I could as easily say, let it perish to my own remembrances: that any future hours of tranquillity may not be disturbed by too vivid an ideal of possible human misery!

So much for the sequel of my experiment: as to the former stage, in which properly lies the experiment and its application to other cases, I must request my reader not to forget the reasons for which I have recorded it: these were two: 1st, a belief that I might add some trifle to the history of opium as a medical agent: in this I am aware that I have not at all fulfilled my own intentions, in consequence of the torpor of mind—pain of body—and extreme disgust to the subject which besieged me whilst writing that part of my paper; which part, being immediately sent off to the press (distant about five degrees of latitude), cannot be corrected or improved. But from this account, rambling as it may be, it is evident that thus much of benefit may arise to the persons most interested in such a history of opium—viz. to opium-eaters in general—that it establishes, for their consolation and encouragement, the fact that opium may be renounced; and without greater sufferings than an ordinary resolution may support; and by a pretty rapid course[1] of descent.*

[1] On which last notice I would remark that mine was *too* rapid, and the suffering therefore needlessly aggravated: or rather perhaps it was not sufficiently continuous and equably graduated. But, that the reader may judge for himself—and above all that the opium-eater, who is preparing to retire from business, may have every sort of information before him, I subjoin my diary:

FIRST WEEK		SECOND WEEK		THIRD WEEK	
Drops of Laud.		Drops of Laud.		Drops of Laud.	
Mond. June 24	130	Mond. July 1	80	Mond. July 8	300
—25	140	—2	80	—9	50
—26	130	—3	90	—10	
—27	80	—4	100	—11	Hiatus in
—28	80	—5	80	—12	MS.
—29	80	—6	80	—13	
—30	80	—7	80	—14	76

FOURTH WEEK		FIFTH WEEK	
Drops of Laud.		Drops of Laud.	
Mond. July 15	76	Mond. July 22	60
—16	73½	—23	none
—17	73½	—24	none
—18	70	—25	none
—19	240	—26	200
—20	80	—27	none
—21	350		

To communicate this result of my experiment—was my foremost purpose. 2dly, as a purpose collateral to this, I wished to explain how it had become impossible for me to compose a Third Part in time to accompany this republication: for during the very time of this experiment, the proof sheets of this reprint were sent to me from London: and such was my inability to expand or to improve them, that I could not even bear to read them over with attention enough to notice the press errors, or to correct any verbal inaccuracies. These were my reasons for troubling my reader with any record, long or short, of experiments relating to so truly base a subject as my own body: and I am earnest with the reader that he will not forget them, or so far misapprehend me as to believe it possible that I would condescend to so rascally a subject for its own sake, or indeed for any less object than that of general benefit to others. Such an animal as the self-observing valetudinarian—I know there is: I have met him myself occasionally: and I know that he is the worst imaginable *heautonti-moroumenos*;* aggravating and sustaining, by calling into distinct consciousness, every symptom that would else perhaps—under a different direction given to the thoughts—become evanescent. But as to myself, so profound is my contempt for this undignified and selfish habit, that I could as little condescend to it as I could to spend my time in watching a poor servant girl—to whom at this moment I hear some lad or other making love at the back of my house. Is it for a Transcendental Philosopher to feel any curiosity on such an occasion? Or can I, whose life is worth only 8½ years' purchase, be supposed to have leisure for such trivial employments?—However, to put this out of question, I shall say one thing, which will perhaps shock some readers: but I am sure it ought not to do so, considering the motives on which I say it. No man, I suppose, employs much of his time on the phenomena of his own body without some regard for it; whereas the reader sees that, so far from looking upon mine with any complacency or regard, I hate it and make it the object of my bitter ridicule and contempt: and I should not be displeased to know that the last indignities which the law inflicts upon the bodies of the worst malefactors might hereafter fall upon it. And, in testification of my sincerity in saying this, I shall make the following offer. Like other men, I have particular

---

What mean these abrupt relapses, the reader will ask perhaps, to such numbers as 300–350, &c.? The *impulse* to these relapses was mere infirmity of purpose: the *motive*, where any motive blended with this impulse, was either the principle of '*reculer pour mieux sauter*;'* (for under the torpor of a large dose, which lasted for a day or two, a less quantity satisfied the stomach—which, on awaking, found itself partly accustomed to this new ration): or else it was this principle—that of sufferings otherwise equal those will be borne best which meet with a mood of anger; now, whenever I ascended to any large dose, I was furiously incensed on the following day, and could then have borne any thing.

fancies about the place of my burial: having lived chiefly in a mountainous region, I rather cleave to the conceit that a grave in a green church yard amongst the ancient and solitary hills will be a sublimer and more tranquil place of repose for a philosopher than any in the hideous Golgothas* of London. Yet if the gentlemen of Surgeons' Hall* think that any benefit can redound to their science from inspecting the appearances in the body of an opium-eater, let them speak but a word, and I will take care that mine shall be legally secured to them—i. e. as soon as I have done with it myself. Let them not hesitate to express their wishes upon any scruples of false delicacy, and consideration for my feelings: I assure them they will do me too much honour by 'demonstrating' on such a crazy body as mine: and it will give me pleasure to anticipate this posthumous revenge and insult inflicted upon that which has caused me so much suffering in this life. Such bequests are not common: reversionary benefits contingent upon the death of the testator are indeed dangerous to announce in many cases: of this we have a remarkable instance in the habits of a Roman prince—who used, upon any notification made to him by rich persons that they had left him a handsome estate in their wills, to express his entire satisfaction at such arrangements, and his gracious acceptance of those loyal legacies: but then, if the testators neglected to give him immediate possession of the property, if they traitorously 'persisted in living' (*si vivere perseverarent*,* as Suetonius expresses it), he was highly provoked, and took his measures accordingly.—In those times, and from one of the worst of the Caesars, we might expect such conduct: but I am sure that from English surgeons at this day I need look for no expressions of impatience, or of any other feelings but such as are answerable to that pure love of science and all its interests which induces me to make such an offer.

Sept. 30*th*, 1822.

5. *'General Preface' to* Selections Grave and Gay

[This passage is taken from the 'General Preface' to De Quincey's own edition of his works, *Selections Grave and Gay*, 14 vols. (Edinburgh: Hogg, 1853–60), vol. i, pp. v–xix. In the 'Preface', De Quincey divides his writings into three main categories. The first contains that class of composition 'which proposes primarily to amuse the reader; but which, in doing so, may or may not happen occasionally to reach a higher station, at which the amusement passes into an impassioned interest'. The second contains that class of papers 'which address themselves purely to the understanding as an insulated faculty; or do so primarily'. These De Quincey calls 'by the general name of ESSAYS'. The third class is much smaller than the other two, and aims much higher. It is comprised only of the *Confessions of an English Opium-Eater* and *Suspiria de Profundis*.

Finally, as a third class, and, in virtue of their aim, as a far higher class of compositions . . . I rank *The Confessions of an Opium-Eater*, and also (but more emphatically) the *Suspiria de Profundis*. On these, as modes of impassioned prose ranging under no precedents that I am aware of in any literature, it is much more difficult to speak justly, whether in a hostile or a friendly character. As yet, neither of these two works has ever received the least degree of that correction and pruning which both require so extensively; and of the *Suspiria* not more than perhaps one-third has yet been printed. When both have been fully revised, I shall feel myself entitled to ask for a more determinate adjudication on their claims as works of art. At present I feel authorised to make haughtier pretensions in right of their *conception* than I shall venture to do, under the peril of being supposed to characterise their *execution*. Two remarks only I shall address to the equity of my reader. First, I desire to remind him of the perilous difficulty besieging all attempts to clothe in words the visionary scenes derived from the world of dreams, where a single false note, a single word in a wrong key, ruins the whole music; and, secondly, I desire him to consider the utter sterility of universal literature in this one department of impassioned prose; which certainly argues some singular difficulty, suggesting a singular duty of indulgence in criticising any attempt that even imperfectly succeeds. The sole Confessions, belonging to past times, that have at all succeeded in engaging the attention of men, are those of St Austin and of Rousseau.* The very idea of breathing a record of human passion, not into the ear of the random crowd, but of the saintly confessional, argues an impassioned theme. Impassioned, therefore, should be the tenor of the composition. Now, in St Augustine's *Confessions* is found one most impassioned passage,—viz., the lamentation for the death of his youthful friend in the 4th Book;* one, and no more. Further, there is nothing. In Rousseau there is not even so much. In the whole work there is nothing grandly affecting but the character and the inexplicable misery of the writer.

6. *Letter to Emily De Quincey*

[This letter from De Quincey to his youngest daughter Emily (1833–1917) dates from September or October 1856, and is only extant in A. H. Japp, *Thomas De Quincey: His Life and Writings* (New York: Scribner, Armstrong, 1877), ii. 109–13, and (London: Hogg, 1890), 386–90. In the following selection, De Quincey talks candidly about his expansion of the 1821 *Confessions*, and the key differences between the text in its original and revised forms.]

[. . .] Volume v. is on the point of closing, viz., 'THE CONFESSIONS.' It is almost rewritten; and there cannot be much doubt that here and there it is enlivened, and so far improved. To justify the enormous labour it has cost me, most certainly it *ought* to be improved. And yet, reviewing the volume as a *whole*, now that I can look back from nearly the end to the beginning, greatly I doubt whether many readers will not prefer it in its original fragmentary state to its present full-blown development. But if so, why could I not have felt this objection many weeks since, when it would have come in time to save me what has proved an exhausting labour? The truth is, I *did* feel it; but what countervailed the objection was secretly the following awkward dilemma:—A doubt had arisen whether, with my own horrible recoil from the labour of converging and unpacking all hoards of MSS., I could count upon bringing together enough of the 'Suspiria' (yet unpublished) materially to enlarge the volume. If not, this volume (standing amongst sister volumes of 320 to 360 pp.) would present only a beggarly amount of 120 pp. Upon which arose this dilemma—Either the volume must be strengthened by the addition of papers altogether alien, which to me was eminently disagreeable, as breaking up the unity of the volume—or else, if left in the slenderness of figure, would really to *my* feeling involve us in an act that looked very like swindling. How could 7s. 6d. be reasonably charged to the public for what obviously was but a third part in bulk of the other volumes? But could not the price for this anomalous volume have been commensurately lessened? No. Mr H.,* the publisher, who knows, of course, so much more than I do about such cases, assures me that nothing so much annoys the trade as any interruption of the price scale upon a series of volumes. Such being the case, no remedy remained but that I should *doctor* the book, and expand it into a portliness that might countenance its price. I should, however, be misleading you if any impression were left upon your mind that I had eked out the volume by any wiredrawing process: on the contrary, nothing has been added which did not originally belong to my outline of the work, having been left out chiefly through hurry at the period of first, *i.e.*, original, publication in the autumn of 1821. [. . .] As a further reason for reading it I must mention, that as a book of *amusement* it is undoubtedly improved; what I doubt is, whether also as a book to *impress*. [. . .] Here again, as in thousands of similar cases, is a conflict—is a call for a choice—between an almost *extempore* effort, having the faults, the carelessness, possibly the graces, of a fugitive inspiration—this on the one side, and on the other a studied and mature presentation of the same thoughts, facts, and feelings, but without the same benefit from extemporaneous excitement.

7. *'Preface'* to the **Confessions of an English Opium-Eater**

[This passage is taken from the 'Prefatory Notice' in De Quincey's *Selections Grave and Gay*, 14 vols. (Edinburgh: Hogg, 1853–60), vol. v, pp. xi–xv. It was first published in 1856 in the revised version of the *Confessions of an English Opium-Eater*, and features De Quincey's thoughts on his revisions to the original text of 1821, as well as on Ann of Oxford Street, who still haunted his dreams after more than half a century. For more detail, see *Works*, ii. 100–2.]

When it had been settled that, in the general series of these republications, the 'Confessions of an English Opium-Eater' should occupy the Fifth Volume, I resolved to avail myself most carefully of the opening thus made for a revision of the entire work. By accident, a considerable part of the Confessions (all, in short, except the Dreams) had originally been written hastily; and, from various causes, had never received any strict revision, or, *virtually*, so much as an ordinary verbal correction. But a great deal more was wanted than this. The main narrative should naturally have moved through a succession of secondary incidents; and with leisure for recalling these, it might have been greatly inspirited. Wanting all opportunity for such advantages, this narrative had been needlessly impoverished. And thus it had happened, that not so properly correction and retrenchment were called for, as integration of what had been left imperfect, or amplification of what, from the first, had been insufficiently expanded.

With these views, it would not have been difficult (though toilsome) to re-cast the little work in a better mould; and the result might, in all reason, count upon the approbation at least of its own former readers. Compared with its own former self, the book must certainly tend, by its very principle of change, whatever should be the *execution* of that change, to become better: and in my own opinion, after all drawbacks and allowances for the faulty exemplification of a good principle, it *is* better. This should be a matter of mere logical or inferential necessity; since, in pure addition to everything previously approved, there would now be a clear surplus of extra matter—all that might be good in the old work, and a great deal beside that was new. Meantime this improvement has been won at a price of labour and suffering that, if they could be truly stated, would seem incredible. A nervous malady, of very peculiar character, which has attacked me intermittingly for the last eleven years, came on in May last, almost concurrently with the commencement of this revision; and so obstinately has this malady pursued its noiseless, and what I may call sub-terraneous, siege, since none of the symptoms are externally manifested, that, although pretty nearly dedicating myself to this one solitary labour, and not intermitting or relaxing it for a single day, I have yet spent, within a very few days, six calendar months upon the re-cast of this one small volume. [. . .]

[T]he case of poor Ann the Outcast formed not only the most memorable and the most suggestively pathetic incident, but also *that* which, more than any other, coloured—or (more truly I should say) shaped, moulded and remoulded, composed and decomposed—the great body of opium dreams. The search after the lost features of Ann, which I spoke of as pursued in the crowds of London, was in a more proper sense pursued through many a year in dreams. The general idea of a search and a chase reproduced itself in many shapes. The person, the rank, the age, the scenical position, all varied themselves for ever; but the same leading traits more or less faintly remained of a lost Pariah woman, and of some shadowy malice which withdrew her, or attempted to withdraw her, from restoration and from hope. [. . .]

November, 1856.

APPENDIX B

MANUSCRIPT AND OTHER MATERIAL
RELATING TO *SUSPIRIA DE PROFUNDIS*

Manuscript Material

I

[This manuscript is held in the Henry W. and Albert A. Berg Collection, New York Public Library. A version of it was published in A. H. Japp, *The Posthumous Works of Thomas De Quincey*, 2 vols. (London: Heinemann, 1891–3), i. 4–5). As was so often the case, however, Japp altered the manuscript with several unauthorized additions of his own.]

1. The dreadful infant   *There* was the glory of innocence made perfect in power: there was the dreadful beauty of infancy that had seen God
2. Foundering ships*
3. The Archbishop and Controller of Fire
4. God that didst promise—Count the leaves in Vallambrosa*
5. But if I submitted with resignation,—not the less I searched for the unsearchable—
                    sometimes in Arabian deserts
                    Sometimes on the Sea—and then No 6.
6. That ran before us in malice
7. Morning of Execution
8. Daughter of Lebannon*
9. Kyrie Eleison*
10. Peroration
11. The Nursery in Arabian deserts
12. The Halcyon calm—and the Coffin
     Faces Angels' faces!
13. At that word, or that thought or that image
14. Oh Apothanate!* that hatest Death and cleansest from the pollution of sorrow
15. Who is this woman that for some months has followed me up and down—Her face I cannot see for she keeps for ever behind me—But I guess who it is.
16. Cagot and Cressida*

Fallentis semita vitae*—that course of life which, like a path trodden only by an infant, disguises dies away from unconsciousness, and beguiles the sense of its own fluctuation

II

[This section is in two parts. The first is a transcription of a manuscript fragment held in the New York Public Library. The second is taken from Japp, *Posthumous Works*. De Quincey closed the third instalment of *Suspiria de Profundis* with 'Levana and Our Ladies of Sorrow', 'The Apparition of the Brocken', and 'Savannah-la-Mar' (see above, pp. 138–50). His original intention, however, appears to have been to include another, separate essay entitled 'The Dark Interpreter', which was to have been inserted immediately following 'Levana and Our Ladies of Sorrow'. If De Quincey had been able to follow through on this design, the appearance of the Dark Interpreter in both 'The Apparition of the Brocken' and 'Savannah-la-Mar' would have been more fully intelligible. The manuscript in the New York Public Library refers to 'our Ladies of Sorrow', and gives the order of the closing dream episodes as 'THE DARK INTERPRETER, THE APPARITION OF THE BROCKEN, AND SAVANNAH-LA-MAR'. The manuscript of 'The Dark Interpreter' has been lost, but a version exists in Japp, *Posthumous Works*, i. 7–9.]

(i)
New York Public Library
Thomas De Quincey miscellaneous personal file
Manuscripts and Archives Division

FINALE TO PART I
THE DARK INTERPRETER, THE APPARITION OF THE BROCKEN,
AND SAVANNAH-LA-MAR

You have heard reader in the Vision which describes our Ladies of Sorrow, and particularly in the dark admonition of Madonna, to her wicked sister that hateth and tempteth, what sort of dark uses may lie concerted in moral convulsions; not the uses hypocritically vaunted by theatrical resignation which affronts the majesty of God that ever and in all things loves the truth—sincerity that is erring to piety that cants—upright sincerity even if it errs. Rebellion which is as the sin of witchcraft is more pardonable in his sight than speechifying resignation, listening with complacency to its own self-conquests. Show always as much neighbourhood as thou canst, to grief in a person who occupies a station of grief which will be but little endeavour if thy grief is great. Such resignation being self-delusion and resting, however nobly, on no basis of real grief. As it is the contrary of life, and the just condition to gruesome gallantry in a hollow grief. But God who sees thy efforts in secret will slowly strengthen those efforts and make that to be a real deed bearing tranquillity for thyself, which at first was but a feeble wish breathing homage to *him*.

In after life when from 20 to 24 on looking back to those struggles of my childhood, I used to wonder exceedingly that a child could be exposed to struggles on such a scale. But two views unfolded upon me as my experience widened, which took away that wonder. The first was—the vast scale upon which the sufferings of children are found everywhere expanded in the realities of life. The generation of infants, which you see is but part of those who belong to it; were born in it and make, the world over, not one half of it. The missing half, more than an equal number to those of any age that are now living—have perished by every kind of torments. Three thousand children per annum, that is three hundred thousand per century, that is, (omitting Sundays) about ten every day, pass to heaven through flames[1]—in this very island of Great Britain. And of those who survive to reach maturity what multitudes have fought with fierce pangs of hunger, cold, and nakedness!—When I came to know all this, then reverting my eye to *my* struggle, I said oftentimes—'It was nothing.' Secondly, in watching the infancy of my own children, I made another discovery:—It is well known to mothers, to nurses, and also to philosophers—that the tears and lamentations of infants, during the year or so when they have no *other* language of complaint, run through a gamut that is as inexhaustible as the cremona of Paganini.* An ear but moderately learned in that language cannot be deceived as to the rate and *modulus** of the suffering which it indicates. A fretful or peevish cry cannot by any efforts make itself impassioned. The cry of impatience, of hunger, of irritation, of reproach, of alarm, are all different—different as a chorus of Beethoven from a chorus of Mozart.* But if ever you saw an infant suffering for an hour as sometimes the healthiest does under some attack of the stomach which has the tiger grasp of the oriental cholera*—then you will hear moans that address to their mothers an anguish of supplication for aid such as might storm the heart of Moloch.* Once hearing it, you will not forget it. Now it was a constant remark of mine,—after any storm of that nature (occurring suppose once in 2 months) that always on the following day—when a long long sleep had chased away the darkness and the memory of the darkness from the little creature's brain, a sensible expansion had taken place in the intellectual faculties of attention, observation, and animation. It renewed the case of our great modern poet, who on listening to the raving of the midnight storm and the crashing which it was making in the mighty woods, reminded himself that all this hell of trouble

'Tells also of bright calms that shall succeed.'*

[1] Three thousand children are annually burnt to death in the nations of England and Scotland, chiefly through the *carelessness* of parents. I shudder to add another and darker cause, which horror too accounts for the figure.*

Pain driven to agony, or grief driven to frenzy, is essential to the ventilation of profound natures. A sea, which is deeper than any that Count Massigli[1] measured, cannot be searched and torn up from its sleeping depths without a levanter or a monsoon. A nature, which is profound in excess but also introverted and abstracted in excess, so as to be in peril of wasting itself in interminable reverie, cannot be awakened sometimes without afflictions that go

(ii)

Japp, *Posthumous Works*, i. 7–9

Suffering is a mightier agency in the hands of nature, as a Demiurgus* creating the intellect, than most people are aware of.

The truth I heard often in sleep from the lips of the Dark Interpreter. Who is he? He is a shadow, reader, but a shadow with whom you must suffer me to make you acquainted. You need not be afraid of him, for when I explain his nature and origin you will see that he is essentially inoffensive; or if sometimes he menaces with his countenance, that is but seldom: and then, as his features in those moods shift as rapidly as clouds in a gale of wind, you may always look for the terrific aspects to vanish as fast as they have gathered. As to his origin—what it is, I know exactly, but cannot without a little circuit of preparation make *you* understand. Perhaps you are aware of that power in the eye of many children by which in darkness they project a vast theatre of phantasmagorical figures moving forwards or backwards between their bed-curtains and the chamber walls. In some children this power is semi-voluntary—they can control or perhaps suspend the shows; but in others it is altogether automatic. I myself, at the date of my last confessions, had seen in this way more processions—generally solemn, mournful, belonging to eternity, but also at times glad, triumphal pomps, that seemed to enter the gates of Time—than all the religions of paganism, fierce or gay, ever witnessed.* Now, there is in the dark places of the human spirit—in grief, in fear, in vindictive wrath—a power of self-projection not unlike to this. Thirty years ago, it may be, a man called Symons committed several murders in a sudden epilepsy of planet-struck fury. According to my recollection, this case happened at Hoddesdon, which is in Middlesex.* 'Revenge is sweet!' was his hellish motto on that occasion, and that motto itself records the abysses which a human will can open. Revenge is *not* sweet, unless by the mighty charm of a charity that seeketh not her own it

---

[1] Count Massigli* (an Austrian I believe in the Imperial Service) about 60 years ago attempted to fathom many parts of the Mediterranean and the Atlantic: If I remember rightly, he generally found the bottom within less than an English mile.

has become benignant. And what he had to revenge was woman's scorn. He had been a plain farm-servant; and, in fact, he was executed, as such men often are, on a proper point of professional respect to their calling, in a smock-frock, or blouse, to render so ugly a clash of syllables. His young mistress was every way and by much his superior, as well in prospects as in education. But the man, by nature arrogant, and little acquainted with the world, presumptuously raised his eyes to one of his young mistresses. Great was the scorn with which she repulsed his audacity, and her sisters participated in her disdain. Upon this affront he brooded night and day; and, after the term of his service was over, and he, in effect, forgotten by the family, one day he suddenly descended amongst the women of the family like an Avatar of vengeance. Right and left he threw out his murderous knife without distinction of person, leaving the room and the passage floating in blood.

The final result of this carnage was not so terrific as it threatened to be. Some, I think, recovered; but, also, one, who did *not* recover, was unhappily a stranger to the whole cause of his fury. Now, this murderer always maintained, in conversation with the prison chaplain, that, as he rushed on in his hellish career, he perceived distinctly a dark figure on his right hand, keeping pace with himself. Upon *that* the superstitious, of course, supposed that some fiend had revealed himself, and associated his superfluous presence with the dark atrocity. Symons was not a philosopher, but my opinion is, that he was too much so to tolerate that hypothesis, since, if there was one man in all Europe that needed no tempter to evil on that evening, it was precisely Mr Symons, as nobody knew better than Mr Symons himself. I had not the benefit of his acquaintance, or I would have explained it to him. The fact is, in point of awe a fiend would be a poor, trivial *bagatelle* compared to the shadowy projections, *umbras* and *penumbras*,* which the unsearchable depths of man's nature is capable, under adequate excitement, of throwing off, and even into stationary forms. I shall have occasion to notice this point again. There are creative agencies in every part of human nature, of which the thousandth part could never be revealed in one life.

III

[This reverie is produced from two different sources, and seems to correspond to the dream episode De Quincey entitled 'Who is this woman that for some months has followed me up and down', and that he lists as number fifteen in his catalogue of material to be included in 'Suspiria' (see above, p. 242). The first part of the reverie is extant only in Japp. The second part of the reverie is a manuscript held in the Wordsworth Library.]

(i)

Japp, *Posthumous Works*, i. 16–17

In my dreams were often prefigurements of my future, as I could not but read the signs. What man has not some time in dewy morn, or sequestered eve, or in the still night-watches, when deep sleep falleth on other men but visiteth not his weary eyelids—what man, I say, has not some time hushed his spirit and questioned with himself whether some things seen or obscurely felt, were not anticipated as by mystic foretaste in some far halcyon time, post-natal or ante-natal he knew not; only assuredly he knew that for him past and present and future merged in one awful moment of lightning revelation. Oh, spirit that dwelleth in man, how subtle are *thy* revelations; how deep, how delirious the raptures thou canst inspire; how poignant the stings with which thou canst pierce the heart; how sweet the honey with which thou assuagest the wound; how dark the despairs and accusings that lie behind thy curtains, and leap upon us like lightning from the cloud, with the sense as of some heavenly blazoning, and oftentimes carry us beyond ourselves!

It is a sweet morning in June, and the fragrance of the roses is wafted towards me as I move—for I am walking in a lawny meadow, still wet with dew—and a wavering mist lies over the distance. Suddenly it seems to lift, and out of the dewy dimness emerges a cottage, embowered with roses and clustering clematis; and the hills, in which it is set like a gem, are tree-clad, and rise billowy behind it, and to the right and to the left are glistening expanses of water. Over the cottage there hangs a halo, as if clouds had but parted there. From the door of that cottage emerges a figure,* the countenance full of the trepidation of some dread woe feared or remembered. With waving arm and tearful uplifted face the figure first beckons me onward, and then, when I have advanced some yards, frowning, warns me away. As I still continue to advance, despite the warning, darkness falls: figure, cottage, hills, trees, and halo fade and disappear; and all that remains to me is the look on the face of her that beckoned and warned me away.

(ii)

Wordsworth Library, Dove Cottage, Grasmere, MS 2002.1.14

seemed—not that I fancied such a thing when she was gone I thought it not but with her look I seemed to read it—as tho' we two had been together—and had together entered from troubled gulphs—struggled together, suffered together was it as lovers torn asunder by calamity was it as combatants forced by bitter necessity into bitter feud when we only in all the world yearned for peace together—Oh what a searching as if she being in the spiritual sort of condition—abstracted from flesh remembered things that I could *not* remember. Oh how I shuddered as the sweet, sunny eyes in the sweet sunny morning of June, as the month that was 'very angelical' half opens to the summer day that was 'very angelical' seemed reproachfully to challenge in me recollections of things passed thousands of years ago (old indeed, yet that were made new again for us because now first it was that we met again)—Oh heavens—it came over me as doth the raven o'er the infected house*—as from a bed of violets swept the saintly odor of corruption. I had a shocking glimpse revealed—glory in darkness—as

of that gorgeous vegetation, that hid the sterilities of the grave in the trop-ics of summer—of that profound beauty which slept side by side with my sister's coffin in the month of June*—of those saintly swells that rose from infinite distance. I know not whether from or to my sister. Could this be a memorial of that nature? Are the dusky and distant stages of life—thus dimly connected and the connexion hidden but suddenly revealed for a flash.

This lady—for years appeared to me in dreams. In that considering the electric character of *my* dreams, and that they were far less a lake reflecting the heavens above than some pencil of a mighty artist—Da Vinci or Michelangelo* that cannot in simplicity copy but comments in freedom whilst reflecting in fidelity: but a change in this appearance *was* remark-able. She oftentimes after 3 years had passed she appeared in summer dawn—window. It was a window that opened on a balcony. This feature only gave a distinction a refinement to the truth of the cottage which else was a rural simplicity. Spirit of Peace, dove like dawn—that slept upon this cottage—that were not broken by

Ah reader!—you will think this, which I am going to say, too near too holy for recital. But not so. The deeper a woe touches me in heart so much the more I have to recite it. The world disappears: In graves I seek only the grand reliques of a world—Memorials of a love that has departed has been—records of a sorrow that has its greyness covered with verdure—Monuments of a wrath that has been reconciled of fear that is atoned in stealth—convulsions of a storm that is gone by. What I am going to say is the most like a superstitious thing that I ever shall say. And I have reason to think that every man who is not a villain once in his life must be supersti-tious. It is a tribute which he pays to human frailty—which tribute if he will not pay—which frailty if he will not consent to share, then also he shall not have anything of it's strength.—

The face of this Hebe* haunted me for 3 years in a way that I must faintly attempt to explain not as is the usual musing of such faded words in degree but in kind. It is little to say that it was the sweetest face, with the most peculiar expression of sweetness, that I had or *have* seen. That was much: but that was earthly. There was something more terrific behind than this: yet that was not the word: terror looks to the future; and this perhaps did; but not primarily. Chiefly it looked to some unknown past, and was for that reason awful: yes awful that was the word; it had the character of the grave about it. Never on any of those heavenly sunny mornings that now are buried in an endless grave did I descend to that breakfast room but my earliest salutation was to *her*: that ever, as the looks of pictures do, pursued me round the room: and oftentimes with a subtle checking of grief as if sorrow had been or would be hers.

It is in this sweet May time.

Oh yes she was—but as if she had been—as if it were her original character to have been the Aurora* of a heavenly clime—and then suddenly of whom for a thousand years Paradise had received no report—that then again she entered the gates of Paradise not less innocent—but broken with a woe that no man could read—that she travelled back to her early joy— yet now no longer the joy that is sublime in joy—but the joy that now is the resurrection from abysses of memories polluted into anguish— Somewhere—Oh where? In some far distant world—oh world where dost thou lurk—

past the drops of blood—All was peace and the deep silence of untroubled solitude—only in the lovely lady was a sign of horror that had slept under deep ages of frost in her heart—but now rose with the rushing of wings to her face. Could it be supposed that one life—so pitiful a thing—was what moved her care. Oh no: it was, it seemed, as if this poor wreck of a life happened to be that one which determined a fate or determined a bias of some ten thousand others. Nothing less—nothing so abject as one poor 50 years—nothing less than a century of centuries—could have stirred the horror that rose to her lovely lips—as she waved me off from the cottage.

Oh reader 5 years after I saw that sweet face in reality: saw it in the flesh: saw that pomp of womanhood: saw that cottage: saw a thousand times that lovely dawn: heard the cooing of the solitary dove in the solitary morning: saw the peace and also the horror which warned me off from that cottage still rings thro' the dreams of five and twenty years.

as if sorrow had been or were to be between us two—Is that the clause?

IV

[This manuscript is held in the Rosenbach Museum and Library, Philadelphia, EL3\.D426c\MS.]

Whatever were the impelling principle to the publication of the Opium Confessions, whether motive that was distinctly contemplated, or impulse that was obscurely felt,—there will remain a perfectly separate question as to the practical result. For a conscientious man will grieve over those consequences from his acts which he never could have designed, and will charge upon himself those seductions which he had not even suspected.

Here then opens an admissible occasion for measuring the extent of my power by laying bare the world of mischief which I have caused; and secondly the finest excuse possible for resuming my enchanter's wand in order that I may exorcise the evil spirits which I have evoked. Listening to others, as Coleridge for instance,* I ought first to be horror struck at the havock which my revelations have produced; and next, under the coercion of conscience, I ought to find the necessity for redressing this havock by revelations still more appalling. There in 1822 is your bane: here in 1845 is your antidote. Oh stratagems of vanity!—but I reject both. I have neither done the evil in past times with which I am charged; nor am I at present seeking to repair it. The first is not a fact: the second is not a possibility.

I remember at this moment with laughter the case of a man on a sick bed, who was deploring to his Confessor the awful mischief likely to affect his own and future generations from an infidel book that he had published. But the kind-hearted father entreated him to take comfort upon the ground that, except for a stray trunk-maker or so, and a few vagabond pastry-cooks,* no man to his own certain knowledge had ever bought a copy. Whereupon the sinner leaped out of bed; and, being a member of the 'fancy',* he proceeded to floor the Confessor as a proper reward for his insulting consolations.

For my own part, I cannot in a literal sense appropriate the benefit of the good father's suggestion. It is past all denying that in 1822 very many people (trunk-makers not included) did procure copies, and cause copies to be multiplied, of the Opium Confessions.* But I have yet to learn that any one of these people was inoculated by me, or could have been, with a first love for a drug so notorious as opium.* Teach opium-eating!—Did I teach wine-drinking? Did I reveal the mystery of sleeping? Did I inaugurate the infirmity of laughter?

Yet still I may have sharpened the attention, or I may have pointed a deeper interest, to this perilous medicine. But these cases, rare accidents perhaps in a world where comparatively so few can be left to their own free choice in matters of daily habit, are such slight undulations upon the face of society as we see arising on the sea from the passing of a steam-boat: they subside almost immediately into the mighty levels around them. In any ten cases of this nature five will probably cure themselves by original defect of natural preconformity to the drug: four others by coercion of circumstances barring all means of procuring opium. The opium-eater goes to sea; to jail; to the hulks;* to a hospital: or he is ordered off on a march. And in any of these cases the chain is broken violently. But then for the one case remaining? As to *that*, there is reason to think, from the vast diffusion of opium in all its forms, that any individual temptation must have been the *causa occasionalis* only and not the *causa sine quâ non** of such a habit. A man has read a description of the powers lodged in opium; or, which is still more striking, he has found these powers heraldically emblazoned in some magnificent dream due to that agency. This by accident has been his own introduction to opium-eating. But, if he never *had* seen the gorgeous description or the gorgeous dream, he would (fifty to one) have tried opium on the recommendation of a friend for tooth-ache, which is as general as the air, or for ear-ache, or (as Coleridge) for rheumatism:* and thus, without either description or dream, he would have learned the powers of opium on the surer basis of his own absolute experience.

Consequently I deny the opening to any large range of mischief; and not believing in any mischief caused by my Confessions, equally I deny the opening to any compensating power of deterring men from opium. My faith is—that no man is likely to adopt opium or to lay it aside in consequence of anything he may read in a book: a book may suggest it; but, in default of the book, every day's intercourse with men and every day's experience of pain would have made the same suggestion.

V

[The following three manuscript fragments are held in the Wordsworth Library, Dove Cottage, Grasmere, MS 2002.44.5.]

(i)

-migrations, and unrelentingly evades his evasions. One of these is—to lurk in the shape of a pomegranate. The princess lies in wait for the event which she foresees. The pomegranate swells, opens, splits: the seeds, which she knows to be roots of evil, rapidly she swallows; but one, only one, before it could be arrested, rolls away into a river. It is lost: it is irrecoverable: she has triumphed, but she must perish: already she feels the flames mounting up which are to consume her; and she calls for water hastily, not to deliver herself (for that is impossible) but nobly forgetting her own misery, that she may prevent that destruction of her brother mortal which had been the original object for hazarding her own.—Yet why go to Arabian fictions? Even in our daily life is exhibited in proportions far more gigantic that tendency to swell and amplify itself into mountains of darkness which exists oftentimes in germs that are imperceptible. An error in human choice, an infirmity in the human will, though it were at first less than a mote, though it should swerve from the right line by an interval less than any thread

> 'That ever spider twisted from her womb',*

sometimes begins to swell, to grow, to widen its distance *rapidly*, travels off into boundless spaces remote from the true centre, spaces incalculable and irretraceable, until hope seems extinguished and return impossible. Such was the course of my own Opium career. Such is the history of human errors every day. Such was the original sin of the Greek theories on Deity, which could not have been healed but by putting off their own nature, and kindling into a new principle—absolutely undiscoverable, as I contend, for the Grecian intellect.

(ii)

Oftentimes an echo goes as it were to sleep: the series of reverberations has died away. Suddenly a second series awakens: this also subsides: then a third wakens up. So of actions done in youth. After great tumults all is quieted. You dream that they are over. In a moment, in the twinkling of an eye, on some fatal morning in middle life—the far off consequences come back upon you. And you say to yourself, 'Oh, heavens, if I had 50 lives—this crime would reappear as Pelion upon Ossa.* So was it with my affliction. Left to natural peace I might have conquered it: *Verschmerzen*,* to charm it down by the mere suffering of grief—to hush it by endurance—that was the natural policy—that was the natural process. But behold! A new form of sorrow arises; and the two multiply together. And the worm which was beginning to fall asleep is roused again to pestilential fierceness.

(iii)

We stretch out our

We after a time becoming too sadly convinced that this is simply hopeless, next we say—If she will not come to me, then I will go to her. There is a gulph fixed which childhood rarely can pass. But we link our wishes with whatsoever would waft us gently over. We stretch out our hands and say—Sister, lend us thy help—and plead for us with God, that we may pass over without much agony.

Had he said 'I found the room filled {text cut away}: but when he {remaining text cut away}.

VI

[The following nine manuscript fragments are held in the Henry W. and Albert A. Berg Collection, New York Public Library.]

(i)

So passed away one out of three that made my nursery companions; and so did my acquaintance commence with mortality. Yet in fact I knew little more of it than that Jane had disappeared. She had gone away; but perhaps she would come back. This case was hardly more of an introduction to that gloomy vision than one which since occurred with my daughter M. when 2 years old. She had a wounded bird, which had already cost her some tears. And at night when going to bed she came into my study, begging that I would watch the bird through the night and above all things that I would '*mend*' it (oh record of my habits!) with laudanum (or as she pronounced it trisyllabically with yoddĕnum.) The bird and I passed the night together: for then I was too apt to sit up all night. Neither of us was gay; but of the two the bird had the advantage. In the morning, and after breakfast, when little M. was like a rose in June* and carolling with excess of happiness, but I and the bird were exhausted and sad, it occurred to us—that every one of the party—little M. in the first place the bird and I in the second, and lastly the grown-up women of the family and also in the 4th the tea-kettle M. I believe thought secretly that M. might be the better for going out into the morning air. It was a sunny day in April: we lived at that time in lovely Grasmere: and behind the house we had an orchard—not unsung by great poets.* The bird, that could not have escaped, was placed upon a stone-step which connected one of the many inequalities in a mountain orchard with some higher range. It too evidently drooped; and would not eat; from which I augured a sad result. Yet it seemed to enjoy the morning scene.

(ii)

Mystery unfathomable of Death! Mystery unapproachable of God!— Destined it was, from the foundations of the worlds, that each mystery should make war upon the other: once that the lesser mystery should swallow up for a moment a *limbus** of the greater; and that woe is past: once that the greater mystery should swallow up for ever the whole vortex of the lesser; and that glory is yet to come. After which man, that is the Son of God, shall lift up his eyes for ever—saying 'Behold! there were two mysteries; and one is not; and there is but one mystery that survives for ever!'

(iii)

Great changes summon to great meditations. Daily we see the most joyous of events take a coloring of solemnity from the mere relation in which they stand to an uncertain future: the birth of a child, heir to the greatest expectations and welcomed clamorously by the sympathy of myriads, speaks to the more reflecting in an under tone of monitory sadness were it only as a tribute to the frailty of human expectations: and a marriage-day, of all human events the most lawfully festal, yet needs something of effort to chase away the boding sadness which settles unavoidably upon any new career the promise is but new hopes have created new dangers; and responsibilities contracted perhaps with rapture

(iv)

Turn a screw—tighten a linch-pin—which is not to disease but perhaps to exalt the mighty machinery of the brain—and the Infinities appear, before which the tranquillity of man unsettles, the gracious forms of life depart, and the ghostly enters. So profoundly is this true, that oftentimes I have said of my own tremendous experience in the region, destined too certainly I fear finally to swallow up intellect and the life of lifes in the heart unless God of his mercy fetches me away by some sudden death—that Death, considered as an entrance to this ghostly world, is but a postern gate by comparison with the heaven-aspiring vestibule thro' which this world of the Infinite introduces the ghostly world.

(v)

If things, that have fretted us, had not some art for retiring into secret oblivion,—what a hell would life become!—Now, understand how in some nervous derangements this horror really takes place. Some things that had sunk into utter forgetfulness, others that had faded in visionary power— all rise as gory phantoms from the dust: the field of our earthly combats, that should by night have settled into peace, is all alive with hosts of resurrections—cavalries that sweep in gusty charges—columns that thunder from afar—arms gleaming thro' clouds of sulphur.*

(vi)

If an eternity (Death suppose) is as vast as a star, yet the most miserable of earthly blocks not 4 feet square will eclipse—masque—hide it from centre to circumference. And so it really is. Incredible as it might seem apart from experience, the dreadful reality of Death is utterly withdrawn from us because itself dwindles to an apparent mote, and the perishing non-reality thickens into a darkness as massy as a rock.

(vii)

Suspiria. Ah reader rise to what—whether you refuse it or not as the reality of realities—is assuredly the reality of dreams,—linking us to a far vaster cycle in which the love and the languishing—the ruin and the horror—of this world are but moments, but elements, in an eternal circle. The cycle stretches from an East that is forgotten to a West that is but conjectured.

The mere fact of your own individual calamity is a life—the tragedy is a nature; the hope is but as a dim augury written on a flower.[1]

(viii)

For every one of us, male or female, there is a year of crisis—a year of solemn and conscious transition, a year in which the light-hearted sense of the *irresponsible* ceases to gild the heavenly dawn. A year there is, settled by no law or usage, for me perhaps the 18th, for you the 17th, for another the 19th, within the gates of which, underneath the gloomy archway of which, sits a phantom of yourself.

(ix)

Oh eternity with outstretched wings that broodest over the secret truths in whose roots lie the mysteries of man—his whence his whither—have I searched thee and struck a right *key* on thy dreadful organ.

[1] I allude to the *signatures* of nature.

APPENDIX C

MANUSCRIPT AND OTHER MATERIAL
RELATING TO 'THE ENGLISH MAIL-COACH'

1. *Manuscript Material*

[This passage is housed in the National Library of Scotland, MS 4789. It is one of the most substantive variants between the manuscript versions of 'The Vision of Sudden Death' and the published version of that text in *Blackwood's Magazine* for December 1849. The passage is a footnote that De Quincey appended in manuscript to the sentence, 'And the only new element in the man's act is not any element of extra immorality, but simply of extra misfortune' (see above, p. 199). For full details, see *Works*, xvi. 463–89.]

If a father, visiting without warning his son an Oxford student, should find him at a gaming table, he would naturally be entitled to argue from this *act* of gambling as from a *habit* of gambling: since there could be no reasonable licence for presuming any act, in which by chance he should detect his son, to be one contradicting the whole tenor of that son's ordinary life. The laws of probability would not allow of such construction. And yet by possibility the case might really be of that exceptional and improbable character. It is the limited vision of man, and the necessity of his adhering to the laws of probability, which would coerce an earthly father into error in such circumstances. But a heavenly father not limited in vision, not tied to laws of likelihood, is under no such coercion. And it is therefore deliberately to load God with the infirmities of man, when we allow ourselves to think that a man's intoxication has any separate horror in it from the accident of his dying under that intoxication. This in effect to suppose that God would anthropomorphically judge an act—not by its intrinsic qualities or tendencies—but by its scenical position, as a dramatic incident calculated for stage effects.

[This passage is housed in the Wordsworth Library, Dove Cottage, Grasmere, MS 1989: 161.44. References to 'mounting the box' and the use of the phrase 'too late' suggest that this is a discarded passage from 'The Vision of Sudden Death'. The most likely point for insertion is following the line '. . . the mail was not even yet ready to start' (see above, p. 202).]

But how came I to run any risk?

At my birth, among the fairies that honored that event by their presence, was one—an excellent creature—who said, 'The gift, which I bring for the young child, is this: among the dark lines in the woof of his life I observe one which indicates a trifle of procrastination as lying amongst his frailties: and from that frailty I am resolved to take out the sting. My gift therefore is—that, if he must always seem in danger of being too late, he shall very seldom really be so in fact. All his errors in that respect shall not through his whole life cost him 10 guineas. Now then I trust to have taken the sting out of that infirmity.' Upon which up jumped a wicked old fairy, vexed at not having received a special invitation to the natal festivity, who said—'*You*'ll take the sting out, will you? But now, Madam, please to see me put it back again. *My* gift is—that, if seldom actually in danger of being too late, he shall always be in fear of it. Not often completing the offence, he shall for ever be suffering its penalties.' Yes, reader, so she said; and so it happened. The curse, which she imposed, I could not evade. My only resource was—to take out my revenge in affronting her. On this occasion I whispered to her, whilst mounting the box,—'Well, old girl, here I am; and, *as usual*, quite in time.' That word—'*as usual*'—must I knew be wormwood to her heart: so I repeated it, saying—'Your malice, old can- kered lady, is defeated; defeated, you see, *as usual*.' 'Certainly my son'—was her horrid reply—'You are in time; and generally you are so. But it grieves me know that for the last half hour you have been suffering horrid tor- ments of mind.'

[This passage is housed in the National Library of Scotland, MS 21239. Remarkably, it appears to be an account of what De Quincey did following the near-fatal collision between a small gig and the mail-coach he was driv- ing. For full details, see *Works*, xvi. 458–9.]

When we reached the inn at Preston, what was it that I proceeded to do? Never trouble yourself reader to be angry, when I tell you that I had the baseness to think (or at least to speak) chiefly on the subject of cold beef and port wines. There is not much to be said in defence of such conduct, but there is always something to be said in defence of any possible conduct. I had travelled 250 miles, by Patterson (the great authority of those days)*—fasting from everything but tea, a trifle of opium, and (as Falstaff observes of himself) from sin.* But this is secondary matter: the first is—that in the recent event which at the time, and soon not long afterwards struck me with horror—so profound there was in fact a funeral and a fes- tival of joy: being on the very brink of the 1st, we issued into the second.

2. '*Preface*' to '*The English Mail-Coach*'

[This passage is taken from the 'Explanatory Notices' in De Quincey's *Selections Grave and Gay*, 14 vols. (Edinburgh: Hogg, 1853–60), vol. iv,

pp. xii–xiv. It was first published in 1854 in a volume entitled *Miscellanies,*
Chiefly Narrative, and features De Quincey's thoughts on how the law of
association shapes the dreaming mind, as well as on the relationship
between the various parts of 'The English Mail-Coach', and its connection
to *Suspiria de Profundis*. For full details, see *Works*, xx. 29–35.]

This little paper, according to my original intention, formed part of the
'Suspiria de Profundis,' from which, for a momentary purpose, I did not
scruple to detach it, and to publish it apart, as sufficiently intelligible even
when dislocated from its place in a larger whole. To my surprise, however,
one or two critics, not carelessly in conversation, but deliberately in print,
professed their inability to apprehend the meaning of the whole, or to follow the links of the connection between its several parts. I am myself as
little able to understand where the difficulty lies, or to detect any lurking
obscurity, as those critics found themselves to unravel my logic. Possibly
I may not be an indifferent and neutral judge in such a case. I will therefore
sketch a brief abstract of the little paper according to my own original
design, and then leave the reader to judge how far this design is kept in
sight through the actual execution.

Thirty-seven years ago, or rather more, accident made me, in the dead
of night, and of a night memorably solemn, the solitary witness to an
appalling scene, which threatened instant death in a shape the most terrific
to two young people, whom I had no means of assisting, except in so far as
I was able to give them a most hurried warning of their danger; but even
that not until they stood within the very shadow of the catastrophe, being
divided from the most frightful of deaths by scarcely more, if more at all,
than seventy seconds.

Such was the scene, such in its outline, from which the whole of this
paper radiates as a natural expansion. This scene is circumstantially narrated in Section the Second, entitled, 'The Vision of Sudden Death.'

But a movement of horror, and of spontaneous recoil from this dreadful
scene, naturally carried the whole of that scene, raised and idealised, into
my dreams, and very soon into a rolling succession of dreams. The actual
scene, as looked down upon from the box of the mail, was transformed into
a dream, as tumultuous and changing as a musical fugue. This troubled
dream is circumstantially reported in Section the Third, entitled, 'Dream-
Fugue on the Theme of Sudden Death.' What I had beheld from my seat
upon the mail; the scenical strife of action and passion, of anguish
and fear, as I had there witnessed them moving in ghostly silence; this
duel between life and death narrowing itself to a point of such exquisite
evanescence as the collision neared; all these elements of the scene blended,
under the law of association, with the previous and permanent features of
distinction investing the mail itself: which features at that time lay—1st, in

velocity unprecedented; 2dly, in the power and beauty of the horses; 3dly, in the official connection with the government of a great nation; and, 4thly, in the function, almost a consecrated function, of publishing and diffusing through the land the great political events, and especially the great battles during a conflict of unparalleled grandeur. These honorary distinctions are all described circumstantially in the FIRST or introductory section ('The Glory of Motion'). The three first were distinctions maintained at all times; but the fourth and grandest belonged exclusively to the war with Napoleon; and this it was which most naturally introduced Waterloo into the dream. Waterloo, I understand, was the particular feature of the 'Dream-Fugue' which my censors were least able to account for. Yet surely Waterloo, which, in common with every other great battle, it had been our special privilege to publish over all the land, most naturally entered the Dream under the license of our privilege. If not—if there be anything amiss—let the Dream be responsible. The Dream is a law to itself: and as well quarrel with a rainbow for showing, or for *not* showing, a secondary arch. So far as I know, every element in the shifting movements of the Dream derived itself either primarily from the incidents of the actual scene, or from secondary features associated with the mail. For example, the cathedral aisle derived itself from the mimic combination of features which grouped themselves together at the point of approaching collision—viz., an arrow-like section of the road, six hundred yards long, under the solemn lights described, with lofty trees meeting overhead in arches. The guard's horn, again—a humble instrument in itself—was yet glorified as the organ of publication for so many great national events. And the incident of the Dying Trumpeter, who rises from a marble bas-relief, and carries a marble trumpet to his marble lips for the purpose of warning the female infant, was doubtless secretly suggested by my own imperfect effort to seize the guard's horn, and to blow a warning blast. But the Dream knows best; and the Dream, I say again, is the responsible party.

EXPLANATORY NOTES

ABBREVIATIONS

Coleridge,
  Biographia Literaria   Samuel Taylor Coleridge, *Biographia Literaria*, ed. James Engell and Walter Jackson Bate, 2 vols. (Princeton: Princeton University Press, 1983).

Coleridge, *Letters*   *Collected Letters of Samuel Taylor Coleridge*, ed. Earl Leslie Griggs, 6 vols. (Oxford: Clarendon Press, 1956–71).

Gray   Samuel Frederick Gray, *A Supplement to the Pharmacopoeia: being a treatise on pharmacology in general* (London: Underwood, 1821).

Hayter   Alethea Hayter, *Opium and the Romantic Imagination* (London: Faber, 1968).

Hogg   James Hogg, *De Quincey and his Friends* (London: Sampson Low, Marston and Company, 1895).

Jordan   *De Quincey to Wordsworth*, ed. John E. Jordan (Berkeley: University of California Press, 1963).

Morrison   *The English Opium-Eater: A Biography of Thomas De Quincey* (London: Weidenfeld and Nicolson, 2009).

OED   *Oxford English Dictionary.*

Symonds   'De Quincey and His Publishers: The Letters of Thomas De Quincey to His Publishers', ed. Barry Symonds (Unpublished Ph.D. thesis. University of Edinburgh, 1994).

Woodhouse   'Richard Woodhouse's *Cause Book*: The Opium-Eater, the Magazine Wars, and the London Literary Scene in 1821', ed. Robert Morrison, *Harvard Library Bulletin*, 9 (1998), pp. i–xxiv, 1–43.

Works   *The Works of Thomas De Quincey*, gen. ed. Grevel Lindop, 21 vols. (London: Pickering and Chatto, 2000–3).

Unless otherwise noted, all references to the Bible are to the King James Version; all references to classical sources are to the Loeb editions; and all references to Shakespeare are to *The Riverside Shakespeare*, gen. eds. G. Blakemore Evans and J. J. M. Tobin, 2nd edn. (Boston: Houghton Mifflin, 1997).

CONFESSIONS OF AN ENGLISH OPIUM-EATER

3 *'decent drapery'*: Edmund Burke (1729–97), Whig politician and eminent conservative political philosopher, *Reflections on the Revolution in France* (1790), ed. L. G. Mitchell (Oxford: Oxford University Press, 2009), 77:

'But now all is to be changed. All the pleasing illusions, which made power gentle, and obedience liberal, which harmonized the different shades of life, and which, by a bland assimilation, incorporated into politics the sentiments which beautify and soften private society, are to be dissolved by this new conquering empire of light and reason. All the decent drapery of life is to be rudely torn off.'

3 *demireps*: Henry Fielding (1707–54) offers a vivid description of a 'demirep' in *Tom Jones* (1749), ed. John Bender and Simon Stern (Oxford: Oxford University Press, 1998), 718: 'a demirep; that is to say, a woman who intrigues with every man she likes, under the name and appearance of virtue; and who, though some over-nice ladies will not be seen with her, is visited (as they term it) by the whole town; in short, whom everybody knows to be what nobody calls her'. 'Demirep' is a contraction of '*demi*-monde *rep*utation'. The 1821 Dove Cottage manuscript reveals that De Quincey originally wrote 'Demireps Prostitutes, Adventures, or Swindlers' (*Works*, vol. ii, pp. xii, 285).

French literature: De Quincey is thinking especially of Jean-Jacques Rousseau (1712–78), Swiss-born philosopher, educationalist, and political theorist whose writings inspired the leaders of the French Revolution. In his famous *Confessions* (1782–9), Rousseau embarks on an intimate and innovative exploration of his own dreams, preoccupations, desires, and delusions. Perhaps, too, De Quincey has in mind Charles Pinot Duclos (1704–72), historian and writer, *Les Confessions du Comte de **** (1741).

the German: De Quincey's most obvious target is Johann Wolfgang von Goethe (1749–1832), poet, philosopher, playwright, and novelist. In *The Sorrows of Young Werther* (1774), Goethe candidly describes the highly wrought emotional responses of a young man who is ravaged by his hopeless love for a married woman, and who finally puts a bullet through his head.

many months . . . concluded on taking it: later, De Quincey told rather a different story: 'in 1821', he states, '. . . I went up to London avowedly for the purpose of exercising my pen, as the one sole source then open to me for extricating myself from a special embarrassment, (failing which case of dire necessity, I believe that I should never have written a line for the press)' (*Works*, xi. 261).

Humbly to express | A penitential loneliness: William Wordsworth (1770–1850), *The White Doe of Rylstone* (1815), 176–7: 'humbly would express | A penitential loneliness'. During one of their first walks together, Wordsworth read De Quincey the opening section of *The White Doe*. It was, De Quincey wrote nearly half a century later, 'an incident most memorable to myself' (Jordan, 48).

4 *one celebrated man . . . greatly exceeded me in quantity*: Samuel Taylor Coleridge (1772–1834), critic, philosopher, and poet. His opium consumption was public knowledge. The wife of Coleridge's doctor, for example, reported that she saw him drink 'a large wine glass full' of

laudanum (a solution of opium dissolved in alcohol). Astonished, she explained to him 'what the medicine was, as she imagined he had made a mistake'. But there was no mistake. 'Very soon afterwards', she added, 'he drank off another glass full. And before he left the house he had emptied a half pint bottle in addition' (Woodhouse, 14).

untwisted . . . the accursed chain which fettered me: De Quincey claimed on numerous occasions to have given up the drug. He never did. In his revised *Confessions* of 1856, he remarks that for over forty years he has performed 'manoeuvres the most intricate, dances the most elaborate, receding or approaching, round my great central sun of opium' (*Works*, ii. 244).

doubts of casuistry: De Quincey himself defined casuistry as 'the science of cases, or of those special varieties which are for ever changing the face of actions as contemplated in general rules' (*Works*, xi. 350).

5 *the eloquent and benevolent . . . late under-secretary of state*: these are, in order: William Wilberforce (1759–1833), British politician and the acknowledged leader of the Clapham Saints, a group of evangelical Christians who successfully campaigned for the abolition of slavery; De Quincey's mother was closely allied with the Clapham Saints. Dr Isaac Milner (1750–1820), natural philosopher, Dean of Carlisle, and close friend of Wilberforce; 'Dean Milner had ruined his own activities by eating opium', De Quincey remarked in 1831 (*Works*, viii. 14). Thomas Erskine, first Baron Erskine (1750–1823), Whig lawyer and Lord Chancellor; De Quincey thought him 'the greatest of modern advocates' (*Works*, xii. 72). Coleridge (the 'philosopher'). John Hiley Addington (1759–1818) served as Under Secretary of State for Home Affairs from 1812 until his death; his brother, Henry Addington, Viscount Sidmouth (1757–1844), was Prime Minister, 1801–4, and Home Secretary, 1812–21. The Addington family is mentioned in several letters to De Quincey written by his mother and sister Jane between 1812 and 1816 (Woodhouse, 37).

Mr———: Charles Lloyd (1775–1839), poet and novelist, was De Quincey's Lake District neighbour and close friend, though De Quincey criticized his 'sensibility' as 'eminently *Rousseauish*—that is, it was phys-ico-moral'. In his 1856 revision to this passage, De Quincey forgot Lloyd. He identified the last person on the list as 'Samuel Taylor Coleridge', and wondered about the identity of 'Mr Dash, the philosopher'. But the 1821 Dove Cottage manuscript confirms that 'M^r C' is 'the philosopher', and that the last person on the list is 'Mr C. Ll.' (*Works*, xi. 197; ii. 97, 287).

druggists . . . London . . . opium: De Quincey may have been purchasing 'small quantities of opium' in 'widely remote quarters of London' in order to conceal how much of the drug he was consuming.

view to suicide: opium was the weapon of choice for many suicides. Fanny Imlay (1794–1816), the half-sister of Mary Shelley (1797–1851), killed herself with it, and De Quincey himself recounted the suicide of a young Lake District student, who 'took a dose, such as he had heard would be sufficient', lay down with his 'face upturned to the heavens', and 'slipped quietly away'. De Quincey himself was blamed for many deaths. 'Pray, is it true, my dear Laudanum, that your "Confessions" have caused about fifty unintentional suicides?', asks Christopher North, the fictive editor of *Blackwood's Magazine*. 'I should think not', replies the Opium Eater. 'I have read of six only; and they rested on no solid foundation' (*Works*, xi. 163; cited in Morrison, 230).

5 *known demand of the evening*: cf. Charles Kingsley (1819–75), *Alton Locke* (1850), chapter 12:

'Yow goo into druggist's shop o' market-day, into Cambridge, and you'll see the little boxes, doozens and doozens, a' ready on the counter; and never a ven-man's wife goo by, but what calls in for her pennord o' eleva-tion, to last her out the week'. . . .

'But what is it?'

'Opium, bor' alive, opium!'

lowness of wages . . . ale or spirits: 'Laudanum was cheaper than beer or gin, cheap enough for even the lowest-paid worker' (Hayter, 33).

That those eat now . . . now eat the more: De Quincey parodies Thomas Parnell (1679–1718), Irish poet and essayist, 'The Vigil of Venus', 1–2: 'Let those love now, who never lov'd before, | Let those who always lov'd, now love the more'. Parnell's poem is a translation of 'Pervigilium Veneris', thought to date from the fourth century, and generally attributed to Tiberianus.

Awsiter: John Awsiter (1734–68), *An Essay on the Effects of Opium, Considered as a poison. With the most rational method of cure, deduced from experience* (London: Kearsley, 1763).

6 *Mead*: Richard Mead (1673–1754), physician and bibliophile, *A Mechanical Account of Poisons* (London: South, 1702), 136: Mead devotes 'Essay the Fourth' to 'Opium', where he observes that 'they who take a moderate dose' of the drug, 'especially not long accustomed to It, are so transported with the pleasing Senses it induces, that They are, as they oftentimes express themselves in Heaven'.

(φωναντα συνετοισι): Pindar (*c*.520–after 446 BC), greatest lyric poet of ancient Greece, *Olympian Odes*, ii. 82–6: '[sayings] that speak to those who understand'.

'whose talk is of oxen': adapted from Ecclesiasticus 38: 25: 'How can he get wisdom that holdeth the plow, and that glorieth in the goad; that driveth oxen, and is occupied in their labours, and whose talk is of bullocks?'

7 *Humani nihil a se alienum putat*: Terence (*c*.195–*c*.159 BC), Roman comic dramatist, *Heauton Timoroumenos* (*The Self-Tormentor*), 77: 'I am a man, I hold that what affects another man affects me.'

third exception: William Hazlitt (1778–1830), critic and essayist, who wrote brilliantly on politics, poetry, painting, and the theatre. His *Essay on the Principles of Human Action* (1805) is his lone philosophical work.

Though De Quincey and Hazlitt were both early admirers of Coleridge and Wordsworth, and fellow contributors to the *London Magazine*, they 'thought poorly of each other', declared Bryan Waller Procter. 'Hazlitt pronounced verbally that the other would be good only "whilst the opium was trickling from his mouth"' (cited in Morrison, 225).

criticism and the Fine Arts: Hazlitt had recently gathered his lectures and essays on literature and the fine arts into books such as *The Round Table* (1817), *Characters of Shakespeare's Plays* (1817), *Lectures on the English Poets* (1818), and *Table Talk* (1821).

Kant: Immanuel Kant (1724–1804), German philosopher, best known for the *Critique of Pure Reason* (1781), the *Critique of Practical Reason* (1788), and the *Critique of Judgement* (1790).

David Ricardo: David Ricardo (1772–1823), economist and MP, was a close friend of the philosopher and economist James Mill (1773–1836) and the utilitarian philosopher Jeremy Bentham (1748–1832). His most important works are *Essay on the Influence of a Low Price of Corn on the Profits of Stock* (1815) and *Principles of Political Economy and Taxation* (1817).

inner eye: cf. Wordsworth, *The Prelude* (1805), v. 474–7: 'And yet no vulgar fear, | Young as I was, a child not nine years old, | Possessed me, for my inner eye had seen | Such sights before'.

existing professors . . . I know only one: De Quincey excepts his closest friend, John Wilson (1785–1854), leading contributor to *Blackwood's Magazine*, and Professor of Moral Philosophy at the University of Edinburgh, 1820–51.

Scottish Professors: At various points in his writings, De Quincey spoke slightingly of Thomas Reid (1710–96), Professor of Moral Philosophy at Glasgow; Adam Smith (1723–90), Professor of Moral Philosophy at Glasgow; and Thomas Brown (1778–1820), Professor of Moral Philosophy at Edinburgh. But De Quincey is thinking especially of Dugald Stewart (1753–1828), champion of the Scottish 'common sense' school of philosophy, and Professor of Moral Philosophy at Edinburgh. De Quincey 'thinks very meanly of Dugald Stewart, who has no originality or grasp of mind in him—who constantly misunderstands & misquotes writers, from taking their opinions at secondhand from others, and then falling foul of them'. In a December 1821 letter, De Quincey condemned himself 'for having uttered a needless truth about Scotch Professors' in the *Confessions*: 'that it *is* a truth, makes it of course the more unwelcome' (Woodhouse, 8; Symonds, 131).

8 *My father died . . . four guardians*: Thomas Quincey died on 18 July 1793, less than a month before De Quincey's eighth birthday. The four guardians were: Thomas Belcher, a merchant; James Entwhistle, a rural magistrate; Henry Gee, a Lincolnshire banker and 'the wisest of the whole band'; and the Revd Samuel Hall (1749–1815), who took the most active part in De Quincey's upbringing (Morrison, 18).

8 *one of my masters*: Revd Nathaniel Morgan, headmaster of Bath Grammar School, which De Quincey attended from 1796 to 1799.

'and a ripe and good one': William Shakespeare (1554–1616), *Henry VIII*, IV. ii. 51: 'He was a scholar, and a ripe and good one'.

a blockhead: Revd Edward Spencer, headmaster of Winkfield (now Wingfield) School in Wiltshire. De Quincey was a student there from 1799 to 1800.

respectable scholar . . . great school . . . ancient foundation: Charles Lawson (d. 1807) was the High Master of Manchester Grammar School, which Hugh Oldham (*c*.1450–1519) founded in 1515.

9 —— *College, Oxford*: Brasenose College.

sacrifice to the graces: in Greek mythology, the three Graces were Aglaia (Brightness), Euphrosyne (Joyfulness), and Thalia (Bloom). Collectively they were frequently taken as goddesses of beauty or charm. To 'sacrifice to the graces' is to render oneself agreeable.

Sophocles: (*c*.495–406 BC), Greek dramatist best known for *Oedipus the King*.

'Archididascalus': 'headmaster'.

income . . . college . . . sent thither immediately: under the terms of his father's will, De Quincey was to receive £150 a year once he turned 21 years old. As he did throughout his adult life, De Quincey seems to have been looking for an advance on this money.

opposition to his will: Henry Gee 'lived at a distance'. De Quincey's wish to leave Manchester Grammar School brought him into direct confrontation with his mother and his guardian Samuel Hall. 'Must you govern me or must I govern you?', Mrs Quincey demanded of him. 'I see no use in repeating the same things, or all the new ones in the world, if you only say the old one, that you are miserable' (cited in Morrison, 60).

woman of high rank: Susan Watson (*c*.1770–1828), a close friend of the De Quincey family, inherited approximately £300,000 at the death of her father, Colonel Henry Watson (*c*.1738–86). In 1792, she married George Evans, fourth Baron Carbery (1766–1804), an Irish peer and politician.

10 *double letter*: a letter of two sheets of paper, the postage on which would have cost double. Postage was paid by the recipient.

remark of Dr Johnson's . . . sadness of heart: Samuel Johnson (1709–84), critic, poet, lexicographer, and man of letters, 'No. 103. *Saturday, 5 April 1760*', in *The Idler*, ed. W. J. Bate, John Bullitt, and L. F. Powell (New Haven: Yale University Press, 1963), 314: 'There are few things not purely evil, of which we can say, without some emotion of uneasiness, "this is the last." Those who never could agree together, shed tears when mutual discontent has determined them to final separation; of a place which has been frequently visited, tho' without pleasure, the last look is taken with heaviness of heart.'

the head-master's house: De Quincey stayed as a boarder in Charles Lawson's home at 3, Long Millgate.

the ancient towers of ———: the fifteenth-century collegiate church of St Mary. It became Manchester Cathedral in 1847. The 'ancient towers' which De Quincey saw in 1802 have since been reconstructed.

'drest in earliest light': Percy Shelley (1792–1822), *The Revolt of Islam*, v. xliii. 6–8: 'the summit shone | Like Athos seen from Samothracia, dressed | In earliest light'.

11 *'pensive citadel'*: Wordsworth, 'Nuns fret not', 3: 'And students with their pensive citadels'.

eighteen years ago: in fact, just over nineteen years ago—from July 1802 when he fled Manchester, to the autumn of 1821 as he wrote the *Confessions*.

a picture of the lovely ———: Sarah Seymour (née Alston), Duchess of Somerset (1631–92), created scholarships at Brasenose College, Oxford, and St John's College, Cambridge, to support poor students from Hereford, Marlborough, and Manchester Grammar School. In 1856, De Quincey added that tradition in the school held that the picture 'was a copy' from Anthony Van Dyck (1599–1641), Flemish painter (*Works*, ii. 157).

12 *Of Atlantean shoulders . . . mightiest monarchies*: John Milton (1608–74), *Paradise Lost*, ii. 306–7.

Salisbury plain: a plateau-like area in Wiltshire covering about 300 square miles.

contretems: French, and more commonly, 'contretemps'. It literally means 'against the time'; thus, an inopportune or embarrassing situation.

Seven Sleepers: the legend of the Seven Sleepers of Ephesus is extant in several different versions. According to the story, the Roman emperor Decius (*c*. AD 201–51) persecuted seven Christian soldiers, who concealed themselves in a cave and fell into a miraculous sleep. They awoke 230 years later.

étourderie: a careless mistake, a mishap.

13 *'with Providence my guide'*: Milton, *Paradise Lost*, xii. 646–7: 'The world was all before them, where to choose | Their place of rest, and Providence their guide'.

a favourite English poet: Wordsworth.

12mo. volume . . . nine plays of Euripides: duodecimo or twelve*mo* indicates 'the size of a book, or of the page of a book, in which each leaf is one-twelfth of a whole sheet' (*OED*). Euripides (*c*.484–406 BC), Greek dramatist and, according to De Quincey, 'the most Wordsworthian of the Athenian poets'. In his 1856 *Confessions*, De Quincey expanded this passage to remark that he was carrying 'an odd volume, containing about one-half of Canter's "Euripides"'. Wilhelm Canter of Utrecht (1542–75), Greek scholar and textual critic, published his famous edition of Euripides at Antwerp in 1571. It ran to over 800 pages and was often reprinted (*Works*, xi. 500; ii. 158).

13 *other personal accounts*: De Quincey initially hoped to summon the courage to introduce himself to Wordsworth, who lived in Dove Cottage in Westmorland, and who with Coleridge had published *Lyrical Ballads* in 1798. But he soon thought better of it. The principle of 'veneration . . . was by many degrees too strong' in him for any face-to-face meeting at this point, and he detested the thought of appearing before the poet as a 'homeless vagrant' (*Works*, ii. 147, 139).

B———: Bangor.

'*Not to know them, argues one's self unknown*': adapted from Milton, *Paradise Lost*, iv. 830: 'Not to know me argues your selves unknown.'

14 *noli me tangere*: 'touch me not': from John 20: 17. The words are spoken by Christ to Mary Magdalene in the garden after his resurrection.

ὁι πολλοι: 'the many'; i.e., the common people.

Bishop of ———: William Cleaver (1742–1815), Master of Brasenose College, Oxford, as well as bishop of Bangor (1800) and then St Asaph (1806).

high road to the Head: Holyhead, just off the west coast of Anglesey island, was (and still is) an important port for travel to and from Ireland.

Isle of Man: located in the Irish Sea off the north-west coast of England.

15 *hips, haws*: De Quincey's autobiographical accounts seem often to have literary precedents. Cf. Tobias Smollett (1721–71), *The Adventures of Peregrine Pickle* (1751), ch. 98: 'such was the resolution conspicuous in him, even at such a tender age, that after his small finances were exhausted, he persisted in his design; and, because he would not make his wants known, actually subsisted for several days on hips, haws and sloes, and other spontaneous fruits which he gathered in the woods and fields'. 'Hips' are rose hips. 'Haws' are hawthorn berries.

Shrewsbury: county town of Shropshire, on the English–Welsh border.

16 *Llan-y-styndw (or some such name)*: De Quincey almost certainly stayed at the farm now known as 'Glanllynnau', which lies on the main road between Afonwen and Criccieth (Morrison, 70).

prize-money . . . English man of war: the navies of warring countries routinely captured each other's ships as 'prizes', and sailors—based on rank—shared the value of the vessels they seized. A 'man of war' was the term used for a ship of any size that was ready for combat. The young Welshman had probably not been paid what he considered his lawful share of some prize, and so had asked De Quincey to write a letter to the War Office stating the particulars of the case.

'*gentle blood*': commonplace; see Shakespeare, *Henry VI, Part I*, iv. i. 43–4: 'like a hedge-born swain | That doth presume to boast of gentle blood'.

17 *Methodists*: Methodism was an eighteenth-century religious movement founded by John Wesley (1703–91) that sought to reform the Church of England from within. The name 'Methodism' was given contemptuously on account of the methodic strictness with which Wesley observed religious duties. The Methodists broke from the Church of England in 1795. The movement enjoyed great popularity in early nineteenth-century Wales, where it was spearheaded by leaders such as Thomas Charles (1755–1814).

Caernarvon: properly, 'Caernarfon', in north-western Wales, opposite Anglesey island.

Greek Sapphics or Alcaics: sapphics and alcaics are lyric metres invented by, respectively, the Greek poetess Sappho (*c.*610–*c.*570 BC) and the Greek poet Alceus (*c.*620–*c.*580 BC).

Shelley . . . his notions about old age: Percy Shelley, *The Revolt of Islam*, II. xxxiii. 1–8: 'old age . . . is . . . cold and cruel, and is made | The careless slave of that dark power which brings | Evil, like blight on man'.

upwards of sixteen weeks: from, approximately, November 1802 to March 1803.

18 *hunger-bitten*: cf. Job 18: 12: 'His strength shall be hunger-bitten'; and Wordsworth, *The Prelude*, ix. 511–12: 'And when we chanced | One day to meet a hunger-bitten Girl'.

19 *Cromwell . . . different quarter of London*: Oliver Cromwell (1599–1658), English solider and statesman who led Parliamentary forces in the English Civil Wars. De Quincey draws on Edward Hyde, first Earl of Clarendon (1609–74), statesman and historian, *History of the Rebellion and Civil Wars in England* (1702–4), ed. Paul Seaward (Oxford: Oxford University Press, 2009), 386: Cromwell 'never had the same serenity of mind he had been used to, after he refused the crown', but grew 'much more apprehensive of danger to his person', and 'rarely lodged two nights together in one chamber, but had many furnished and prepared, to which his own key conveyed him . . . when he had a mind to go to bed'.

esculent: edible.

Blue-beard room of the house: in the famous fairy tale, Bluebeard forbids his wife to enter one room in his castle, which turns out to contain the bodies of the wives he has previously murdered.

Mr ——: in his 1856 *Confessions*, De Quincey reveals that his shady attorney 'called himself, on most days of the week, by the name of Brunell, but occasionally . . . by the more common name of Brown' (*Works*, ii. 195).

Tartarus: the nethermost part of the underworld, where the most notorious sinners were punished and tormented in the afterlife.

20 *(a periphrasis . . . reader's taste)*: put plainly, De Quincey means that Brown is unscrupulous.

'laying down': to give up as too expensive.

20 *'cycle and epicycle, orb in orb'*: Milton, *Paradise Lost*, viii. 84.

Dr Johnson . . . wall-fruit as he could eat: Hester Lynch Piozzi (1740–1821), *Anecdotes of the Late Samuel Johnson* (London: Cadell, 1786), 103: 'I have heard him protest that he never had quite as much as he wished of wall-fruit, except once in his life, and that was when we were all together at Ombersley'. 'Wall-fruit' is fruit from trees which are grown against a protective garden- or house-wall.

'the world was all before us': Milton, *Paradise Lost*, xii. 646.

house . . . well-known part of London: in his 1856 revisions, De Quincey added that the house stood 'at the north-west corner of Greek Street, being the house on that side the street nearest to Soho Square'. It was number 38. The house has since been demolished (*Works*, ii. 201).

21 *'Sine Cerere,' &c.*: 'Without bread and wine love grows cold' (in full, 'Sine Cerere et Libero friget Venus'). The line appears famously in Terence (see above, p. 264), *Eunuchus*, IV. v. 6.

could not have been an impure one: The evidence suggests the opposite. De Quincey was almost certainly indulging his taste for brothels in Manchester six months before he arrived in London as a runaway, and in Liverpool only a few months after he returned from London he regularly visited prostitutes: 'go to the same fat whore's as I was at the last time;— give her 1ˢ and a cambrick pocket handkerchief;—go home miserable' (Morrison, 60, 82; *Works*, i. 46).

more Socratico: in the manner of the Greek philosopher Socrates (470–399 BC), who spoke freely with anybody anywhere.

Catholic: universal, free from prejudice. Cf. Charles Lamb, *Elia and the Last Essays of Elia*, ed. Jonathan Bate (Oxford: Oxford University Press, 1987), 196: 'I bless my stars for a taste so catholic, so unexcluding'.

22 *watchmen*: before professional police forces, watchmen kept 'watch and ward in all towns from sunset to sunrise' (*OED*).

23 *curse of a father . . . supernatural power*: De Quincey perhaps alludes to the story of Jacob, who fraudulently obtains a blessing from his father in Genesis 27: 11–12: 'And Jacob said . . . I shall seem to him as a deceiver, and I shall bring a curse upon me, and not a blessing.'

to chace—to haunt—to way-lay: De Quincey echoes Wordsworth, 'She was a Phantom of Delight', 10: 'To haunt, to startle, and way-lay'.

24 *'too deep for tears'*: Wordsworth, 'Ode: Intimations of Immortality', 206.

late Majesty's household: the household of George III (1738–1820), king of Great Britain and Ireland, reigned 1760–1820.

1ol.: 'l.' is an abbreviation for the Latin *libra*, meaning pound.

soliciting: 'to conduct (a lawsuit, etc.) as a solicitor; to transact or negotiate in the capacity of a law-agent' (*OED*).

25 *any clue for recovering me*: contrary to the impression he creates here, at some point toward the middle of his truancy, De Quincey himself

contacted his guardian, Samuel Hall. '[A]s you have hitherto persisted in rejecting the wishes of your guardians', Hall responded curtly, '. . . you cannot be surprised to hear that they have no new proposition to make' (cited in Morrison, 74).

except once for a few hours: De Quincey passed through London in the summer of 1800.

To this same Jew: in his 1856 revisions, De Quincey gave the moneylender's name as 'Mr Dell', and noted that 'like all other Jews with whom I have had negotiations, he was frank and honourable in his mode of conducting business' (*Works*, ii. 206).

26 *siege of Jerusalem . . . Second Temple*: the First Temple of Jerusalem was completed in 957 BC and destroyed by the Babylonians in 587/6 BC. The Second Temple was completed in 515 BC, and destroyed in AD 70, when the Roman army sacked Jerusalem.

perches: 'a measure of length used especially for land, fences, walls, etc. varying locally but later standardized at 5½ yards, 16½ ft' (*OED*).

Doctor's Commons: the college of doctors of canon and civil law. From 1565 until 1858, it was located in Paternoster Row, near St Paul's Cathedral. It contained the registry of wills.

second son of ———: Thomas Quincey. His first son, De Quincey's elder brother William, had died in 1797.

materialiter . . . formaliter: 'materially' and 'formally'. De Quincey jokes that he found himself considered as a material object, counterfeiting himself considered as an object of thought, or idea. The contrast goes back to Aristotle, and received notable expression in St Thomas Aquinas, *Disputed Questions on the Virtues*, ed. E. M. Atkins and Thomas Williams (Cambridge: Cambridge University Press, 2005), 130: 'We can consider the object . . . from the point of view of either (i) of its form or (ii) of its matter. (i) The *formal* element in an object is that by which it is related to the relevant capacity or disposition; (ii) the *material* element is what this is grounded in'.

Earl of ———: Howe Peter Browne (1788–1845), Irish peer and Vice-Admiral of Jamaica, was Earl of Altamont from 1800 to 1809, when he became the second Marquess of Sligo. He and De Quincey knew each other in Bath and travelled to Ireland together in the summer of 1800. He subscribed to Coleridge's newspaper *The Friend* (1809–10) and was a boon companion of Lord Byron (1788–1824).

Eton: Eton College was established in 1440–1, and is located across the River Thames from Windsor. Altamont was educated at Eton and Jesus College, Cambridge.

Marquis of ———: John Browne (1756–1809), Irish peer and politician, was the father of De Quincey's friend the Earl of Altamont, and Marquess of Sligo from 1800 until his death.

27 *M—— and Sl——*: Mayo and Sligo.

27 *he wished me to write verses*: the 1821 Dove Cottage manuscript contains an expanded version of this passage (see above, Appendix A, p. 223).

28 *Gloucester Coffee-house*: located in Piccadilly, it was a regular stop for mail-coaches travelling to West Country towns such as Bath and Bristol.

30 *Roman poet*: Juvenal (*c.* AD 55–in or after 127), *Satires*, x. 22: 'The traveller with empty pockets will sing in the face of the robber'.

the murdered person was Steele: John Cole Steele was murdered on Hounslow Heath on 6 November 1802, only a few months before De Quincey found himself on the same heath. It was a particularly brutal killing, as James Harmer (1777–1853), lawyer and politician, recorded in *Murder of Mr Steele* (London: Lewis and Hamblin, 1807), 7: 'Mr Hughes proved that he found the body in a ditch, by a clump of trees; and a strap round the neck, which was *drawn very tight*, with marks of a violent blow on the back part of the head; the witness also found the shoes about 50 yards off'. No charges were laid at the time, but four years later John Holloway and Owen Haggerty were found guilty and executed for killing Steele, though the evidence against them was 'very questionable', as De Quincey himself observed in his 1856 revisions (*Works*, ii. 210).

lavender plantation in that neighbourhood: Harmer, 6: 'Mr Steele left town on 5th November, 1802, for Feltham, where he had a small house and lavender nursery'.

Lord of my learning and no land beside: adapted from Shakespeare, *King John*, I. i. 137: 'Lord of thy presence and no land beside'.

Lord ————: Lord Altamont.

31 *Parad. Regained*: slightly altered from Milton, *Paradise Regained*, ii. 455–6.

Pote's: Joseph Pote (1704–1787) ran a well-known bookshop and a small boardinghouse in Eton. When he died, the business passed to his son Thomas.

University of ————: Cambridge.

'Ibi omnis effusus labor!': Virgil (70–19 BC), *Georgics*, iv. 491–2: 'There all my labour was spent in vain.'

the Earl of D ————: John Otway Cuffe, second Earl of Desart (1788–1820), Irish peer and politician, was still Viscount Castle Cuffe when De Quincey visited him at Eton. He succeeded to the Earldom in 1804, and matriculated the following year at Christ Church, Oxford.

32 *an author*: Thomas Quincey, *A Short Tour in the Midland Counties of England; performed in the summer of 1772. Together with an account of a similar excursion, undertaken September 1774* (1775).

'mother English': cf. Coleridge, *Biographia Literaria* (1817), ii. 30: 'It is true, that of late a great improvement in this respect is observable in our most popular writers. But it is equally true, that this recurrence to plain sense, and genuine mother English, is far from being general.'

M. W. Montague: Lady Mary Wortley Montagu (1689–1762), poet, essayist, and traveller, is best known for her *Embassy Letters* (1763).

'good man's table': De Quincey has in mind Shakespeare, *As You Like It*, II. vii. 115: 'If ever sate at any good man's feast'.

Otway . . . eating too rapidly: Thomas Otway (1652–85), dramatist and poet, celebrated for his blank-verse tragedy, *Venice Preserved* (1682). De Quincey recollects the description of Otway's death in Samuel Johnson, *Lives of the Poets* (1779–81); ed. Roger Lonsdale, 4 vols. (Oxford: Clarendon Press, 2006), ii. 26: 'He went out, as is reported, almost naked, in the rage of hunger, and finding a gentleman in a neighbouring coffee-house, asked him for a shilling. The gentleman gave him a guinea; and Otway going away bought a roll, and was choaked with the first mouthful.'

33 *my intimacy with some of his relatives*: Lord Desart and Lord Altamont were cousins.

34 —————— *in* —*shire*: St John's Priory in Cheshire.

35 *Magdalen*: Mary Magdalen was healed by Jesus of evil spirits (Luke 8: 2), and is traditionally considered a reformed prostitute (Luke 7: 36–50).

in the next Number. ED.: The first instalment of the *Confessions* ended here. These words were added by either John Taylor (1781–1864) or James Hessey (1785–1870), co-editors of the *London*.

36 *years . . . far asunder . . . common root*: cf. Wordsworth, *The Prelude*, xi. 326–8: 'So feeling comes in aid | Of feeling, and diversity of strength | Attends us, if but once we have been strong.'

therefore to —————: Dove Cottage in Grasmere, where Wordsworth lived from 1799 to 1808.

wings of a dove . . . fly for comfort: Psalm 55: 6: 'O that I had wings like a dove; *for then* would I flee away and be at rest.'

second birth of my sufferings began: De Quincey lived in Dove Cottage from 1809 until 1820, and thereafter intermittently until 1835, when the landlord finally forced his removal.

Orestes: in Greek mythology, Orestes is the son of Agamemnon, king of Mycenae, and his wife, Clytemnestra. When Agamemnon returns from the siege of Troy he is killed by Aegisthus, Clytemnestra's lover. Orestes avenges his father's death by killing both Aegisthus and Clytemnestra. He is haunted by the Furies for his violent actions. His sister Electra comforts him.

φίλον ὕπνου θελγήτρον ἐπίκουρον νόσου: Euripides, *Orestes*, 211: 'O Sleep, precious enchantment and ally against sickness!' (*Euripides: Orestes and Other Plays*, ed. Robin Waterfield (Oxford: Oxford University Press, 2009), 53).

Eumenides: literally, the 'kindly minded ones', an ironically euphemistic name for 'the Furies', as the Greeks dreaded to call these fearful goddesses by their real name.

36 *beloved M.*: De Quincey's wife, Margaret Simpson (*c.*1796–1837). De Quincey began to court her in 1813. Their son William was born in 1816. They were married in 1817.

37 ἡδὺ δούλευμα. *Eurip. Orest.*: Euripides, *Orestes*, 221: 'I welcome the menial task.'

'sleep no more!': Shakespeare, *Macbeth*, II. ii. 38.

ἀναξάνδρων Ἀγαμέμνων: Homer (flourished ninth or eighth century BC), *Iliad*, i. 442: 'Agamemnon, lord of men'.

ὄμμα θεῖσ' ἔισω πέπλων. Euripides, *Orestes*, 280: 'Why have you covered your head with your robes?' (*Euripides: Orestes and Other Plays*, ed. Waterfield, 56).

mistress of that very house: slightly misleading. As he wrote the *Confessions*, De Quincey was still renting Dove Cottage (and so Margaret was still its 'mistress'). But from 1820 through 1825, she and the children were in fact living three miles away at Fox Ghyll cottage.

38 *my entrance at college*: De Quincey matriculated at Worcester College, Oxford, on 17 December 1803. For most of his time as an undergraduate, he lived on staircase 10 in the front quad, at a cost of 6 guineas a year.

manna or of Ambrosia, but no further: manna is the bread that miraculously fell from heaven as food for the Israelites in the wilderness (Exodus 16: 31). Ambrosia is the meat of the gods in Greek mythology. De Quincey is not being entirely truthful when he claims that he knew little of opium before he actually took it. He was almost certainly given the drug as a young child suffering from ague. He had read several literary descriptions of its powers. He may well have discussed the drug with Lady Carbery (see above, p. 266), whose father made his vast fortune smuggling Bengal opium into China.

duller spectacle . . . has not to show: De Quincey parodies Wordsworth, 'Composed Upon Westminster Bridge', 1: 'Earth has not any thing to shew more fair'.

'the stately Pantheon,': Wordsworth, 'Power of Music', 3. The Pantheon, located on the south side of Oxford Street, contained assembly rooms built for the entertainment of the gentry.

39 *Charles II . . . Kings should disdain to die, and only disappear*: misquoted from Thomas Flatman (1637–88), 'On the Much Lamented Death of Our Late Sovereign Lord King Charles II. Of Blessed Memory. A Pindarique Ode', 21–5:

> But *Princes* (like the wondrous *Enoch*) should be free
> From Death's unbounded Tyranny,
> And when their Godlike Race is run,
> And nothing glorious left undone,
> Never submit to Fate, but only Disappear'.

Charles II (1630–85), king of Great Britain and Ireland, reigned 1660–85.

revulsion: 'recovery, restoration'; 'a sudden violent change of feeling' (*OED*).

inner spirit: cf. Wordsworth, 'Though narrow be that Old Man's cares', 6–7: 'The region of his inner spirit teems | With vital sounds, and monitory gleams.'

world within me: cf. De Quincey in his 1823 *London Magazine* examination of the 'literature of power': 'When I am thus suddenly startled into a feeling of the infinity of the world within me, is this power? or what may I call it?' (*Works*, iii. 71).

φαρμαχον νήπενθες: Homer, *Odyssey*, iv. 220–1: 'a drug to quiet all pain and strife'.

l'Allegro . . . Il Penseroso: companion poems by Milton probably written in 1631 and describing, respectively, 'The Cheerful Man' and 'The Melancholy Man'.

40 *anti-mercurial*: De Quincey is punning. 'Mercurial' can apply both to a person who is lively or quick-witted, and to a laxative such as calomel. 'Anti-mercurial' is thus grave, as well as—like opium—constipative.

travellers in Turkey: De Quincey is thinking primarily of François Baron de Tott (1733–93), *Memoirs of the Turks and the Tartars* (1784), 'with its vivid picture of the addicts of Constantinople repairing every evening to the Market of the Opium Eaters where, reclining on sofas under the shade of arbours, they took their evening dose and then walked home in stately abstracted happiness' (cited in Hayter, 28).

ex cathedra: literally, 'from the chair'; that is, speaking with the authority of the office or position (rather than, for example, from reasoned argument or empirical evidence).

satiric author: unidentified.

'By . . . the list of bankrupts': the *London Gazette* was published on Tuesdays and Saturdays, and contained public notices, records of official appointment, and names of bankrupts.

rather dear; which also I grant: De Quincey's acknowledgement that opium is 'rather dear' is surprising, given that in the first instalment of the *Confessions* he declared that 'work-people' bought the drug because it was cheaper than 'ale or spirits' (see above, p. 5).

Buchan's Domestic Medicine: William Buchan (1729–1805), physician and author of the phenomenally popular *Domestic Medicine*. Between its first publication in 1769 and its last issue in 1871, there were at least 142 separate English-language editions.

41 *meo periculo*: 'at my risk'; i.e., on my own authority.

proof spirit . . . so much opium: laudanum typically contained anywhere from 45 to 60 per cent pure alcohol (Morrison, 162–5).

42 *'ponderibus librata suis'*: Ovid (43 BC–AD 17), *Metamorphoses*, i. 13: 'poised by its own weight'.

42 *Athenaeus ... complexion of character*: Athenaeus (*fl.* AD 200), Greek grammarian and author, *The Deipnosophists* ('Intellectuals at Dinner'), ii. 6 (37E): 'And Philochoros says that those who drink not only reveal who they themselves are, but even through starting free discussion uncover each of the others'.

majestic intellect: cf. Wordsworth, *The Prelude*, xi. 143–5: 'now all eye | And now all ear, but ever with the heart | Employed, and the majestic intellect'.

the alpha and the omega: the first and last letters of the Greek alphabet.

the brilliant author of 'Anastasius': Thomas Hope (1769–1831) is best known as an art collector, connoisseur, and furniture designer. But he also produced a romantic novel, *Anastasius; or, Memoirs of a Greek Written at the Close of the Eighteenth Century* (1819), which he published anonymously in three volumes, and which was initially thought to be the work of Lord Byron. De Quincey noted in 1856 that *Anastasius* was 'a book both of high reputation and of great influence amongst the leading circles of society' (*Works*, ii. 230). In the passage from the novel cited by De Quincey, Hope writes, 'I resolved to renounce the slow poison, of whose havock my neighbour presented so woeful a specimen; and, in order not even to preserve a memento of the sin I abjured, presented him, as a reward for his advice, with the little golden receptacle of the pernicious drug which I used to carry. He took the bauble without appearing sensible of the gift; while I, running into the middle of the square, pronounced, with outstretched hands, against the execrable market where insanity was sold by the ounce' (i. 232–3).

43 *materia medica*: a branch of medical science concerned with the sources, properties, and preparation of drugs.

I have met with one person: untraced. Previous editions have identified this surgeon as John Abernethy (1764–1831), but I can find no evidence that he was addicted to opium.

primâ facie: 'at first sight'.

44 *drunk upon green tea*: cf. Coleridge in 1804 on the character of Sir Thomas Browne (1605–82), physician and author: 'Does the whimsical Knight give us thus a dish of strong green Tea, & call it an *opiate*?' (Coleridge, *Letters*, ii. 1083).

numerous pictures of Turkish opium-eaters: see above, p. 275.

to excite and stimulate the system: in the heated late eighteenth-century debates about the effects of opium, some medical professionals, inspired by Dr John Brown (1735–88), believed that it was a stimulant. But others, led by William Cullen (1710–90), held that it was a sedative. In the opening decades of the nineteenth century, medical opinion swung increasingly in favour of the Cullenites, but here De Quincey sides decisively with the 'Brunonians'.

exhibition ... to speak medically: in medical terms, an exhibition is 'the administration of a remedy' (*OED*).

45 *Duke of* ———— . . . *'Next Friday . . . to be drunk'*: Charles Howard, eleventh Duke of Norfolk (1746–1815), politician celebrated for his conviviality and eccentricity. In 1856, De Quincey noted that his authority for this reference was Sir George Beaumont (1753–1827), 'an old familiar acquaintance of the duke's', as well as a painter, patron of the arts, and close friend of Wordsworth (*Works*, ii. 224).

laudanum negus, warm, and without sugar: 'negus' is 'made from wine (usually port or sherry) mixed with hot water, sweetened with sugar and sometimes flavoured' (*OED*).

seldom drank laudanum . . . once in three weeks: De Quincey's account of his opium consumption as an undergraduate may well be inaccurate. 'So early even as his Oxford days, De Quincey, we are told, was incapable of steady application without large doses of opium', wrote Richard Lynch Cotton (1794–1880), Provost of Worcester College. Coleridge's recollections of De Quincey as an undergraduate paint an even grimmer picture. During one of their first meetings the two men discussed opium. De Quincey 'utterly denied' he had a problem. 'But', insisted Coleridge, 'I fear that I had even then to *deter* perhaps not to forewarn' (cited in Morrison, 133, 132).

Grassini: Josephina Grassini (1773–1850), Italian contralto, sang in London from 1804 to 1806, and again in 1814. She was noted for her acting talent, powerful singing voice, and great beauty, which brought her many lovers.

tyranny of the violin: De Quincey's condemnation of the violin is somewhat unexpected, given his publisher James Hogg's claim that 'his favourite instrument was the violin'. 'Hundreds of times I must have heard him dwell with impassioned force upon the *capacity* of the violin as a musical instrument', Hogg declared. De Quincey's 'favourite expression on the subject' was ' "there is an *infinity* about the violin" ' (Hogg, 185).

Andromache, at the tomb of Hector: in the Homeric story, Andromache was the wife of the great Trojan warrior Hector, who was slain by Achilles. Perhaps De Quincey saw Grassini as Andromache in *Achilles at the Siege of Troy* (1798), a recent opera by the Italian composer Domenico Cimarosa (1749–1801). Cf. De Quincey's assessment with an anonymous reviewer's who also saw Grassini during these years: 'Grassini had *pathos* indeed, both of voice and deportment: but she was always pathetic; and, in many parts of her respective characters, which required very different expressions, could neither divest her voice, her looks, nor her action, of that air of affliction or melancholy dignity, which she so finely personified' (*La Belle Assemblée*, 2 (February 1807), 103).

fine extravaganza . . . in Twelfth Night: Shakespeare, *Twelfth Night*, 1. i. 1–7:

> If music be the food of love, play on,
> Give me excess of it; that surfeiting,
> The appetite may sicken, and so die.

That strain again, it had a dying fall;
O, it came o'er my ear like the sweet sound
That breathes upon a bank of violets,
Stealing and giving odor.

45 *Religio Medici of Sir T. Brown*: Sir Thomas Browne, *Religio Medici* (1642),
part 2, section 9 in *Sir Thomas Browne: Selected Writings*, ed. Geoffrey
Keynes (London: Faber, 1968), 80: 'Whosoever is harmonically composed
delights in harmony; which makes me much distrust the symmetry of
those heads which disclaime against all Church musicke. For my selfe, not
only from my obedience but my particular genius, I doe imbrace it; for
even that vulgar and Taverne Musicke, which makes one man merry,
another mad, strikes me into a deepe fit of devotion, and a profound contemplation of the first Composer; there is something in it of Divinity more
than the eare discovers. It is an Hieroglyphicall and shadowed lesson of
the whole world, and [the] Creatures of God.'

46 *Weld . . . Canada . . . Indian women*: Isaac Weld (1774–1856), Irish topo-
graphical writer, *Travels Through the States of North America and the Provinces
of Upper and Lower Canada, During the Years 1795, 1796, and 1797*, 2 vols.
(London: Stockdale, 1799), ii. 288: Native American women, Weld asserts,
'speak with the utmost ease, and the language, as pronounced by them,
appears as soft as the Italian. They have, without exception, the most delicate harmonious voices I ever heard, and the most pleasing gentle laugh
that it is possible to conceive. I have oftentimes sat amongst a group of
them for an hour or two together, merely for the pleasure of listening to
their conversation, on account of its wonderful softness and delicacy.'

Marinus in his life of Proclus: Proclus (AD 412–85), the last major Greek
philosopher, was chair of the Academy of Athens and a Neoplatonic
Idealist who taught that thoughts constitute reality, while concrete 'things'
are mere appearances. His successor at the Academy, Marinus of Flavia
Neapolis, wrote his biography.

no labours that I rested from: cf. Revelation 14: 13: 'they may rest from their
labours, and their works do follow them'.

47 *all the markets . . . on a Saturday night*: cf. Hogg, 199: 'De Quincey . . . told
me of his solitary walks at night, his studies of the working poor in and
around Drury Lane and St Giles's, and his close knowledge of the concen-
trated misery of these quarters of London. . . . Clare Market was one of
his favourite hunting-grounds. Sometimes, also, I think, but not so frequently, the region of the New Cut, at Lambeth.'

quartern loaf: 'a loaf made of a quarter of flour; a four-pound loaf' (*OED*).
Cf. *The Times*, 12 April 1804, p. 4, col. A: 'The price of Bread continued
the same as last week, viz. 8½d. the quartern loaf of wheaten, and 7d.
household' ('d.' is an abbreviation for the Latin *denarius*, meaning pence).

48 *bee . . . the soot of chimneys*: in 1856, De Quincey elaborated on this reference. 'In the large capacious chimneys of the rustic cottages throughout

the Lake district,' he observed, 'you can see up the entire cavity from the seat which you occupy, as an honoured visiter, in the chimney corner. There I used often to hear (though not to see) bees. Their murmuring was audible, though their bodily forms were too small to be visible at that altitude. On inquiry, I found that soot (chiefly from wood and peats) was useful in some stage of their wax or honey manufacture' (*Works*, ii. 227).

seeking ambitiously for a north-west passage: De Quincey's reference is highly topical. Following the Napoleonic Wars, several European countries redoubled their exploratory efforts in the Arctic. There were a number of British expeditions, including those led by John Franklin (1786–1847), John Ross (1777–1856), and William Edward Parry (1790–1855).

terrae incognitae: unknown or unexplored lands.

the cave of Trophonius: a celebrated oracle in Greece. It was believed that, when people went to the cave to consult the oracle, a mysterious force dragged them violently inside. When the same force eventually expelled them, their looks were melancholy and pale. Cf. Coleridge in the famous letter from 'Chapter 13' of *Biographia Literaria*, i. 302: *'Be assured, however, that I look forward anxiously to your great book on the* CONSTRUCTIVE PHILOSOPHY, *which you have promised and announced: and that I will do my best to understand it. Only I will not promise to descend into the dark cave of Trophonius with you, there to rub my own eyes.'*

49 *the great town of L* ————: Liverpool. De Quincey is in Everton at the home of Mr and Mrs Best, family friends who lived at 9 Middle Lane (now Everton Terrace).

Behmenism, quietism: Behmenists followed the writings of Jakob Böhme (1575–1624), German Christian mystic best-known for *The Great Mystery* (1623). Quietism is a doctrine of Christian spirituality that holds that our soul attains perfection by withdrawing from outward activities into a passive state in which God's will enters us and we are absorbed into the Divine.

Sir H. Vane, the younger: Sir Henry Vane the Younger (1613–62), skilled politician and committed republican, was executed by Charles II. He wrote several books of theology, including the mystical *Retired Man's Meditations* (1655), which De Quincey undoubtedly has in mind here.

with its sorrows and its graves left behind: De Quincey's reference to the 'sorrows' and 'graves' of Liverpool evokes his knowledge of the city as a key centre in the British slave trade, which he condemned categorically: 'of the kidnapping, murdering *slave-trade*, there cannot be two opinions'. De Quincey also has in mind William Roscoe (1753–1831), politician and historian, whose anti-slavery poem 'Mount Pleasant' is similarly set above Liverpool and parallels De Quincey's reverie in striking ways (*Works*, x. 4; Robert Morrison, 'De Quincey on "Mount Pleasant": William Roscoe and *Confessions of an English Opium-Eater*', *Notes and Queries*, 52 (2005), 54–6).

49 *typify the mind and the mood which then swayed it*: cf. Wordsworth, *The Prelude*, xiii. 66–70: 'A meditation rose in me that night | Upon the lonely Mountain when the scene | Had passed away, and it appeared to me | The perfect image of a mighty mind.'

the tumult, the fever, and the strife: De Quincey echoes John Keats (1795–1821), 'Ode to a Nightingale', 23: 'the weariness, the fever, and the fret'.

Oh! just, subtle, and mighty opium!: De Quincey models this apostrophe on Sir Walter Raleigh (*c.*1554–1618), adventurer and author, *The History of the World* (London: Burre), 1614), 669: 'O eloquent, just, and mighty Death! whom none could advise, thou hast persuaded; what none hath dared, thou hast done; and whom all the world hath flattered, thou only hast cast out of the world and despised.'

'the pangs that tempt the spirit to rebel': Wordsworth, dedicatory poem prefacing *The White Doe of Rylstone*, 36.

Wrongs unredress'd, and insults unavenged: Wordsworth, *The Excursion* (1814), iii. 374.

50 *Phidias and Praxiteles*: Phidias (*fl. c.*490–430 BC) and Praxiteles (*fl.* 370–330 BC), the two greatest Greek sculptors.

Babylon and Hekatómpylos: in the fifth century BC, Babylon was one of the world's most magnificent cities. The ancient Egyptian city of Thebes was also known as Hekatómpylos (meaning 'the hundred-gated') to distinguish it from the Greek city of Thebes, which was known as Heptápylos ('the seven-gated').

'from the anarchy of dreaming sleep': Wordsworth, *The Excursion*, iv. 87.

'dishonours of the grave': De Quincey might have several different sources in mind: Shakespeare, *The Rape of Lucrece*, 197–8: 'O shame to knighthood, and to shining arms! | O foul dishonour to my household's grave!'; Thomas Flatman, 'On the Death of the Truly Valiant George Duke of Albemarle. Pindarique Ode', 160–1: 'That Sanctuary shall thee save | From the dishonours of a Regal Grave'; or George Wither (1588–1667), *Salt Upon Salt*, 1605–6: 'Who, in those *Flatt'ries*, much more pleasure have | That send them with dishonour to the *Grave*'.

Bodleian: the main library of the University of Oxford, founded in 1602 by Sir Thomas Bodley (1545–1613).

frailer vessels . . . bed-makers: according to 1 Peter 3: 7, when compared with men, women are the frailer or 'weaker vessels'. Bed-makers were college servants, and a byword for women of easy virtue. Cf. Hastings to Marlow in Oliver Goldsmith (1730–74), *She Stoops to Conquer* (1773), Act II: 'In the company of women of reputation I never saw such an idiot, such a trembler . . . If you could but say half the fine things to them that I have heard you lavish upon the barmaid of an inn, or even a college bed-maker'. By including 'bed-makers' in a list of 'frailer vessels' he had 'once possessed', De Quincey hints at his sexual activities during his undergraduate days.

six o'clock matins: Oxford students began their day with attendance at chapel.

tintinnabulous: 'characterized by or pertaining to bell-ringing' (*OED*).

51 *Kant, Fichte, Schelling*: For Immanuel Kant, see above, p. 265. Johann Gottlieb Fichte (1762–1814) and Friedrich Wilhelm Joseph von Schelling (1775–1854) were both disciples of Kant, and major figures in the development of German Idealism.

a cottage: Dove Cottage in Grasmere (see above, p. 268).

honi soit qui mal y pense: 'evil be to him who thinks evil'. The phrase is the motto of the Most Noble Order of the Garter.

'house-keeper': De Quincey vigorously denied it, but it seems likely that this housekeeper was Margaret Simpson, his future wife. 'The observation which offended [De Quincey] . . . was on persons marrying below their station in life, which he himself had done, having married his housekeeper whom he mentions in his *Confessions* under this name' (Woodhouse, 2).

my private fortune: when De Quincey turned 21, he inherited £2,600. In 1812, some of this fortune remained, though it was fast disappearing.

esquire . . . distinguished honour: legally speaking, the designation 'esquire' applies to a variety of more or less distinguished people, including the younger sons of peers, the eldest sons of knights, judges, military officers, and Justices of the Peace. De Quincey, as the son of a merchant, has no right to the title.

X. Y. Z.: De Quincey's favourite signature, and one he published under in both the *London Magazine* and *Blackwood's*.

Custos Rotulorum: 'the principal Justice of the peace in a county' (*OED*).

in the straw: in childbed.

'particular Madeira': Madeira is a wine from the Portuguese island of Madeira. Cf. Walter Scott (1771–1832), *The Antiquary* (1816), ed. David Hewitt (Edinburgh: Edinburgh University Press, 1995), 136: 'I, in the meanwhile, without any divining rod, will shew you an excellent venison pasty, and a bottle of London particular Madeira.'

medical advice from Anastasius: see above, p. 276.

52 *'particularly . . . five-and-twenty ounces of laudanum'*: see above, p. 40.

a very melancholy event: the death of Wordsworth's youngest daughter Catharine (1808–12). De Quincey was particularly close to her, and deeply distressed when he received the news in June 1812. 'Oh that I might have seen my darling's face once again!' he wrote to Dorothy Wordsworth (1771–1855). Later, he described his 'fierce . . . convulsion of grief . . . on receiving that heart-shattering news', and how 'for more than two months running' he slept every night upon Catharine's grave (Jordan, 263; *Works*, xi. 237).

53 *à force d'ennuyer*: 'from sheer boredom'.

53 *pandiculation*: what is 'vulgarly called yawning', as De Quincey puts it in his 1856 revisions (see *Works*, ii. 231).

Eudaemonist: the theory that the highest ethical goal is happiness. Cf. De Quincey in his essay on 'The Last Days of Immanuel Kant': 'Ethics, braced up into stoical vigour by renouncing all effeminate dallyings with *Eudaemonism*' (*Works*, vi. 397).

The Porch . . . followers of Zeno: Zeno of Citium (*c.*335–263 BC), Greek Stoic philosopher who lectured in the Stoa Poikile (Painted Colonnade) in Athens. The Portico Library in Manchester opened in 1806 as a news-room and private subscription library, and still occupies its original site in Mosley Street (see Grevel Lindop, 'De Quincey and the Portico Library', *Bulletin of the John Rylands University Library of Manchester*, 76 (1994), 179–86).

Stoic philosophy: a school of thought which emphasizes the control of the passions, and which sees goodness as indifferent to both joy and grief.

Eclectic philosopher: a philosopher who chooses doctrines from various schools of thought.

'sweet men . . . to give absolution': adapted from Geoffrey Chaucer (*c.*1342–1400), 'General Prologue' to *The Canterbury Tales*, 221–2: 'Ful swetely herde he confessioun, | And plesaunt was his absolucioun.'

opium that has not been boiled: to prepare opium for consumption, it needs to be boiled and filtered to remove the impurities. Samuel Frederick Gray (1766–1828), naturalist and pharmacologist, published a new and improved edition of his *Supplement to the Pharmacopoeia* in 1821 (the same year as De Quincey published his *Confessions*), and in it he offers very helpful advice on the preparation of the drug. 'Rub . . . opium with a pint of boiling water, for ten minutes, and pour off the solution,' Gray instructs; 'repeat this a second and third time; mix the liquors and expose them to the air in a broad flat vessel, for two days, then strain through linen, and evaporate' (187).

54 *'with a snow-white beard . . . pernicious drug'*: De Quincey quotes again from Thomas Hope's novel *Anastasius*.

Lent or Ramadan: Christian and Muslim fasts. Lent is the forty weekdays from Ash Wednesday to Easter, and commemorates Christ's fasting and temptation in the wilderness. Ramadan is the ninth month of the Islamic year, and is observed as sacred with fasting practised daily from dawn to sunset.

lustrum: a period of five years.

This year: De Quincey is exaggerating. His 'year' can have been no more than about five months, from December 1815 to April 1816 (Morrison, 175–7).

water . . . jewellers: the 'water' of a gem is the degree of its lustre and trans-parency.

55 *twenty-five drops . . . one grain of opium*: as different chemists used different methods to prepare opium, and different lots of raw opium differed considerably in potency, so estimates vary on the number of drops to be derived from one grain of opium. Cf. John Redman Coxe (1773–1864), *The American Dispensatory* (Philadelphia: Carey and Lea, 1831), 676: '18 drops of laudanum, will about equal one grain of opium'; or Anonymous, *The Day, a Journal of Literature, Fine Arts, Fashions* (Glasgow: Finlay, 1832), 130: '30 drops of laudanum, or one grain of opium'.

νυχθημερον: twenty-four hours; literally, 'for a night and a day'. De Quincey may be thinking of 2 Corinthians 11: 25: 'a night and a day I have been in the deep'.

That moveth altogether, if it move at all: Wordsworth, 'Resolution and Independence', 84.

sea-port about forty miles distant: as De Quincey makes clear in 1856, the Malay is almost certainly heading towards either Whitehaven or Workington, both ports on the coast of Cumbria in north-west England (*Works*, ii. 234).

young girl born . . . amongst the mountains: in 1856, De Quincey identifies the young girl as Barbara Lewthwaite. Cf. Wordsworth, 'The Pet Lamb', 13: ''Twas little Barbara Lewthwaite, a Child of beauty rare' (*Works*, ii. 274–8).

56 *impassable gulph fixed*: cf. Luke 16: 26: 'between us and you there is a great gulfe fixed'.

Adelung's Mithridates: Johann Christoph Adelung (1732–1806), German philologist and librarian, *Mithridates, oder allgemeine Sprachenkunde* (*Mithridates, or General Linguistics*, 1806–17). The book is a kind of universal dictionary in which Adelung affirms the relation of Sanskrit and the major European languages. He derives his title from Mithridates (134–63 BC), king of Pontus, who was reputed to be able to speak all of the twenty-two dialects within his kingdom.

the Iliad: epic poem on the Trojan War traditionally ascribed to the ancient Greek poet Homer (see above, p. 274).

57 *Struggles through Life . . . advanced age*: John Harriott (1745–1817), magistrate and a founder of the Thames police, *Struggles through Life, exemplified in the various travels and adventures in Europe, Asia, Africa and America*, 3 vols. (London: Longman, 1815), iii. 392: 'I have seen extraordinary effects from opium abroad, and heard much of its potency as a drug, at home,' Harriott remarks; 'I was consequently surprised at its inefficacy with myself.'

a country surgeon: perhaps Richard Scambler (d. 1820), an apothecary and physician based in Ambleside who attended the Wordsworth family, as well as Coleridge and De Quincey.

my projected medical treatise on opium: one of De Quincey's many facetious promises. He did not produce a medical treatise on opium.

57 *accounts in any Eastern traveller or voyager*: for example, John Hawkesworth
(*c*.1720–73), *An Account of the Voyages Undertaken . . . by Commodore
Byron, Captain Wallis, Captain Carteret, and Captain Cook*, 3 vols.
(London: Strahan and Cadell, 1773), iii. 754: 'It is well known, that to run
a muck in the original sense of the word, is to get intoxicated with opium,
and then rush into the street with a drawn weapon, and kill whoever comes
in the way.'

intercalary: 'an insertion between the original or ordinary members of a
series' (*OED*). De Quincey uses the phrase here to signify one year of happiness interpolated between several years of sorrow.

58 *a solid and a liquid shape*: purified opium was 'left soft for pills, or hard for
powdering'. De Quincey most often drank opium as laudanum, but on
occasion he consumed it in solid shape. 'He usually . . . was drunk dead
drunk at an early hour', John Gibson Lockhart (1794–1854) observed of
De Quincey, '—for he drank all he could get and between glasses kept
munching opium pills' (Gray, 187; cited in Morrison, 174).

East India and Turkey: commentators frequently discussed how opium differed depending on its place of origin. East Indian opium is 'smooth like
an extract, totally soluble in water, and the solution is precipitated by acet-
ate of barytes, by which the solution of Turkey opium is not altered'. East
Indian opium is also 'considered weaker than that of Turkey' (Gray, 188).

French surgeon inoculated himself lately with cancer: in 1808, Jean Louis
Alibert (1768–1837), French dermatologist and court physician, allowed
himself to be injected with tumour tissue from a breast cancer patient.

English one, twenty years ago, with plague: John Parkin, *Epidemiology*
(London: Churchill, 1873), 53: 'Mr White, an English surgeon . . . inoculated himself with the pus taken from the bubo of a plague-patient, during
the stay of the British forces in Egypt'.

a third . . . with hydrophobia: in 1856, De Quincey added that this third
person was 'also English', and a 'surgeon at Brighton' (*Works*, ii. 236). See
John Eric Erichsen, *The Science and Art of Surgery* (Philadelphia: Lea,
1881), 259: 'White, of Brighton, disbelieving in the contagion of the disease, inoculated himself with the saliva of a rabid dog with impunity'.
Hydrophobia is another name for rabies.

cottage . . . valley . . . any town: Dove Cottage, in the vale of Grasmere, is
eighteen miles north-west of Kendal.

witty author . . . 'a cottage with a double coach-house': there are in fact two
witty authors, as the line appears in both Coleridge, 'The Devil's
Thoughts', 21; and Robert Southey (1774–1843), historian, biographer,
essayist, and Poet Laureate, 'The Devil's Walk', 37.

59 *And at the doors . . . Indolence*: adapted from James Thomson (1700–48),
Scottish poet, *The Castle of Indolence*, I. xliii. 5–9.

Mr ———: in the 1856 *Confessions*, De Quincey identifies this man as
Thomas Clarkson (1760–1846), anti-slavery campaigner best known for

his *History of the Rise, Progress and Accomplishment of the Abolition of the African Slave-Trade* (1808). From 1796 to 1804, Clarkson lived in the Lake District at Eusemere House, where he hosted Coleridge and Wordsworth.

fee-simple: full possession.

St Thomas's day: 21 December, the shortest day of the year.

Johnson . . . bellum internecinum . . . Hanway . . . disparage it: tea was the subject of a literary skirmish between Samuel Johnson and Jonas Hanway (1712–86), philanthropist and merchant, best remembered for his *Essay on Tea* (1756). Johnson loved tea. Hanway thought it unhealthy. Johnson's 'defence of tea against Mr Jonas Hanway's violent attack upon that elegant and popular beverage, shews how very well a man of genius can write upon the slightest subject,' reported Johnson's biographer James Boswell (1740–95). 'Mr Hanway wrote an angry answer to Johnson's review of his *Essay on Tea*, and Johnson, after a full and deliberate pause, made a reply to it' (Boswell, *Life of Johnson*, ed. R. W. Chapman (Oxford: Oxford University Press, 2008), 222). 'Bellum internecinum' is an 'internecine war' or a 'war of extermination'.

60 *'a double debt to pay'*: Oliver Goldsmith, *The Deserted Village*, 229–30: 'The chest contrived a double debt to pay, | A bed by night, a chest of drawers by day.'

see one such: perhaps a misprint for 'see one on such'.

à parte ante, and à parte post: 'in front' and 'at the back'; that is, without beginning or end. The terms were commonly used in Christian arguments about eternity.

Aurora's . . . Hebe's: Aurora is the goddess of the dawn. Hebe is the goddess of youth, and a cupbearer to the gods.

personal beauty: De Quincey was deeply hurt by the Wordsworths' unkind treatment of Margaret, and spoke always in praise of her personal attractiveness. In 1817, Dorothy Wordsworth wrote with disdain (and probably a little jealousy) that De Quincey 'utter'd in raptures of the beauty, the good sense, the simplicity, the "angelic sweetness" of Miss Sympson, who to all other judgments appeared to be a stupid, heavy girl, and was reckoned a Dunce at Grasmere school' (cited in Morrison, 181).

61 *pleasing both to the public and to me?*: De Quincey was very sensitive about his personal appearance. Dorothy Wordsworth wrote that 'his person is *unfortunately* diminutive'. When Richard Woodhouse (1788–1834) read the *Confessions*, he pictured De Quincey as 'a tall, thin, pale, gentlemanly looking, courtier like man'. But when the two men met, he found De Quincey 'a short, sallow-looking person, of a very peculiar cast of countenance, & apparently much an invalid' (Jordan, 229; Woodhouse, 5).

ten categories of my condition: in *Categories*, Aristotle (384–322 BC) proposes ten fundamental types of predicates: substance, quantity, quality, relation, place, time, posture, dress, action, and passion.

61 *farewell—a long farewell to happiness*: De Quincey adapts Shakespeare, *Henry VIII*, III. ii. 351: 'Farewell? a long farewell to all my greatness!'

Iliad of woes: one of De Quincey's favourite phrases. He borrows from Cicero, *Letters to Atticus*, VIII. xi. 3: 'this vast impending Iliad of evils'; and Edmund Burke, 'Letters on a Regicide Peace' in *The Writings and Speeches of Edmund Burke*, ix, ed. R. B. McDowell (Oxford: Clarendon Press, 1991), 276: 'It opens another Iliad of woes to Europe.'

as when . . . earthquake and eclipse: Percy Shelley, *The Revolt of Islam*, v. xxiii. 8–9.

62 *further reduction causes intense suffering*: De Quincey's account differs markedly from the evidence of modern pharmacology, which insists that withdrawal from opiates is 'uncomfortable' or 'extremely uncomfortable', but that it only lasts about one week and is 'not life threatening' (see Theodore Dalrymple, *Romancing Opiates* (New York: Encounter Books, 2006), 20–7).

63 *'in medias res'*: Horace (65–8 BC), *Ars poetica*, 148: 'into the story's midst'.

acmé: highest point.

attainment . . . it was with this: cf. Woodhouse, who heard De Quincey read and was decidedly unimpressed: 'He reads with too inward a voice,' Woodhouse complained; 'he dwells much upon the long vowels (this he does in his conversation, which makes it resemble more a speech delivered in a debating society than the varitonous discourse usually held among friends); he ekes out particular syllables, has generally much appearance of intensity' (Woodhouse, 8–9).

——— *reads vilely: and Mrs* ———: in 1856, De Quincey identified these 'players' as John Philip Kemble (1757–1823), actor and manager of the Drury Lane and Covent Garden theatres; and his sister Sarah Siddons (1755–1831), great tragic actress. He added too that 'neither Coleridge nor Southey is a good reader of verse. Southey is admirable almost in all things, but not in this. Both he and Coleridge read as if crying, or at least wailing lugubriously' (*Works*, ii. 252–3).

overstep the modesty of nature: De Quincey borrows from Shakespeare, *Hamlet*, III. ii. 17–19: 'Suit the action to the word, the word to the action, with this special observance, that you o'erstep not the modesty of nature.'

Sampson Agonistes . . . Paradise Regained: Milton published his biblical tragedy *Samson Agonistes* and his brief epic *Paradise Regained* in the same volume in 1671.

A young lady . . . drinks tea with us: possibly Sophia Lloyd (d. 1830), the wife of Charles Lloyd (see above, p. 263). Elsewhere De Quincey notes that Sophia and her mother came 'frequently' to Dove Cottage 'on summer evenings to drink tea with me' (*Works*, xi. 197).

M.'s . . . W———*'s*: 'M' is 'Margaret'. 'W' is 'Wordsworth'.

Mathematics . . . philosophy . . . insupportable to me: cf. De Quincey in an 1818 letter to his mother: 'My ambition was, that by long and painful labour, combining with such faculties as God had given me, I might become the intellectual benefactor of my species', as both 'the first founder of true Philosophy', and 'the re-establisher in England (with great accessions) of Mathematics' (cited in Morrison, 184).

64 *Spinosa's . . . De emendatione humani intellectûs*: Benedict de Spinoza (1632–77), Dutch-Jewish philosopher who did not complete his *Tractatus de Intellectus Emendatione* (*Treatise on the Correction of the Understanding*).

friend in Edinburgh . . . Mr Ricardo's book: David Ricardo (see above, p. 265) published his most important work, *Principles of Political Economy and Taxation*, in 1817. John Wilson (see above, p. 265) is almost certainly the friend in Edinburgh who sent the volume to De Quincey, undoubtedly in the hope that he would review it for *Blackwood's*.

65 *'Thou art the man!'*: 2 Samuel 12: 7: 'And Nathan said to David, Thou art the man.'

Scotchman of eminent name . . . want of encouragement: John Leslie (1766–1832), Scottish physicist and mathematician, wrote in the 'Preface' to his *Elements of Geometry, and Plane Trigonometry* (1820) that his 'original design was to exhibit, within the compass perhaps of five volumes, the Elements of Mathematic Science in their full extent, including the principles and application of the Higher Calculus. But, after due reflection, I have abandoned that aspiring project. There is unfortunately very little incitement to the publication of abstract works in this country' (see Robert Morrison, 'The "Scotchman of eminent name" in De Quincey's *Confessions of an English Opium-Eater*', *Notes and Queries*, 46 (1999), 45–7).

mercantile and senatorial cares: Ricardo was a member of the Stock Exchange and an MP.

à priori: from first principles; from what is already known.

'the inevitable eye': adapted from Wordsworth, 'When to the Attractions of the Busy World', 82: 'an inevitable ear'.

Prolegomena to all future Systems of Political Economy: De Quincey takes his title from Immanuel Kant's *Prolegomena to all Future Metaphysics* (1783).

66 *Circean*: in Greek myth, Circe is a sorceress who uses incantations and drugs to change humans into brutes. She transformed the companions of Odysseus into swine, but Odysseus himself, protected by a herb, defied her powers and procured the release of his men. Cf. John Keats, 'Lamia', i. 115: 'Ravish'd, she lifted her Circean head'.

exasperate: 'to embitter, intensify' (*OED*).

67 *Roman centurion over his soldiers*: see Matthew 8: 8–9: 'The Centurion answered. . . . For I am a man under authority, having soldiers under me:

and I say to this man, Go, and he goeth: and to another, Come, and he cometh.'

67 *Oedipus . . . Priam . . . Tyre . . . Memphis*: Oedipus is the legendary king of Thebes. Priam is the last king of Troy. Tyre was the chief city of the Phoenicians. Memphis was the capital of ancient Egypt.

Midas turned all things to gold: Midas, a legendary king, was granted his wish that all he touched turn to gold. When his food became gold he almost starved to death.

sympathetic ink: 'invisible ink'; that is, invisible until treated with heat, chemical, or special light.

depths below depths: De Quincey adapts Milton, *Paradise Lost*, iv. 76–7: 'And in the lowest deep a lower deep | Still threatening to devour me'.

68 *a near relative of mine*: De Quincey's mother, Elizabeth Quincey (*c*.1749–1846).

twice in modern books: there seems little doubt that the two books De Quincey has in mind are *Biographia Literaria* (1817) by Coleridge, and *Arcana Coelestia* (1749–56) by Emanuel Swedenborg (1688–1772). See Georges Poulet, 'Timelessness and Romanticism', *Journal of the History of Ideas*, 15 (1954), 20.

dread book: Revelation 20: 12: 'and another book was opened, which is *the book* of life: and the dead were judged out of those things which were written in the books, according to their works'. De Quincey follows Coleridge, *Biographia Literaria*, i. 114: 'if the intelligent faculty should be rendered more comprehensive, it would require only a different and apportioned organization, *the body celestial* instead of *the body terrestrial*, to bring before every human soul the collective experience of its whole past existence. And this, this, perchance, is the dread book of judgement.'

no such thing as forgetting possible to the mind: cf. De Quincey in conversation in 1828: 'Is such a thing as *forgetting* possible to the human mind? . . . Is not every impression it has once received reproducible?' (cited in Morrison, 260).

common light of day: cf. Wordsworth, 'Ode: Intimations of Immortality', 76: 'And fade into the light of common day'.

69 *Livy*: Livy (*c*.59 BC–AD 17), Roman historian, author of *A History of Rome from its Foundations* (*Ab urbe condita libri*).

Consul Romanus: this reference famously reappears in Joris-Karl Huysmans (1848–1907), *Against Nature* (1884), trans. Margaret Mauldon, ed. Nicholas White (Oxford: Oxford University Press, 2009), 68: 'De Quincey, after smoking a little opium, would, on hearing the words "Consul Romanus," conjure up entire pages of Livy, would watch the consuls solemnly processing and the stately array of the Roman armies beginning their march.'

period of the Parliamentary War: the English Civil Wars (1642–51), fought between the Parliamentarians and the supporters of the monarchy.

memoirs which survive those unquiet times: De Quincey undoubtedly has in mind the writings and memoirs of prominent Civil War figures such as Thomas May (1595–1650), man of letters; Lucy Hutchinson (1620–81), wife of the Parliamentarian solider John Hutchinson (1615–64); Edmund Ludlow (*c*.1617–92), radical republican; John Rushworth (*c*.1612–90), historian; and Bulstrode Whitelocke (1605–75), republican lawyer.

Charles I: Charles I (1600–49), king of Great Britain and Ireland, reigned 1625–49. His quarrels with Parliament provoked the Civil Wars and led to his execution.

certain day in August, 1642: the Civil Wars began on 22 August 1642.

Marston Moor . . . Newbury . . . Naseby: the battle of Marston Moor (2 July 1644) was the first major defeat for the Royalists. There were two battles at Newbury, the first (20 September 1643) won by Parliamentary forces, and the second (27 October 1644) by Royalist forces. At the battle of Naseby (14 June 1645), the Royalists were soundly defeated.

George IV: George IV (1762–1830), king of Great Britain and Ireland, reigned 1820–30. He was king when De Quincey wrote his *Confessions*.

'sweeping by': from Milton, *Il Penseroso*, 97–8: 'Sometime let Gorgeous Tragedy | In scepter'd pall come sweeping by.'

paludaments: Roman military cloaks, fastened at one shoulder with a brooch or clasp.

Paulus or Marius: Lucius Aemilius Paullus Macedonicus (229–160 BC) was consul twice, and led the Roman forces to victory in the Third Macedonian War (171–168 BC). Gaius Marius (157–86 BC) was consul seven times, and one of the greatest Roman generals.

crimson tunic hoisted on a spear: De Quincey probably has in mind Plutarch (AD 46–after 119), *Life of M. Brutus*, xl. 5: 'As soon as it was day, a scarlet tunic, the signal for battle, was displayed before the camps.' Cf. Shakespeare, *Julius Caesar*, v. i. 14: 'Their bloody sign of battle is hung out'.

alalagmos: in 1856, De Quincey himself defined 'alalagmos' as 'expressing collectively the gathering of the Roman war-cries—*Alála, alála!*' (*Works*, ii. 258).

Piranesi's Antiquities of Rome . . . Dreams: Giovanni Battista Piranesi (1720–78), Italian architect and artist famous for his engravings of Rome, as seen in volumes such as *Le Antichità romane* (*Roman Antiquities*, 1756). The plates which De Quincey calls his *Dreams* were in fact his *Carceri d'Invenzione* (*Imaginary Prisons*, 1745), which depict ancient Roman ruins transformed into surreal dungeons filled with mysterious instruments of torture.

71   *The appearance . . . under a cerulean sky. &c. &c.*: Wordsworth, *The Excursion*, ii. 834–51.

Dryden: John Dryden (1631–1700), dramatist, critic, and Poet Laureate best known for his support of Charles II in *Absolom and Achitophel* (1681), and his satiric abuse of fellow playwright Thomas Shadwell in

Mac Flecknoe (1682). The source of De Quincey's anecdote has not been traced; see V.H.C., 'De Quincey on Meat and Dreams' in *Notes and Queries*, 11th ser., 1 (1910), 88. But the anecdote was repeated many times following its appearance in the *Confessions*. Cf. Maturin Murray Ballou (1820–95), *Genius in Sunshine and Shadow* (Boston: Ticknor, 1887), 73–4: 'It is well known that Dryden resorted to singular aids as preparatory to literary composition; being in the habit of first having himself bled and then making a meal of raw meat. The former process, he contended, rendered his brain clear, and the latter stimulated his imagination.'

71 *Fuseli*: Henry Fuseli (1741–1825), Swiss-born painter famous for his nude figures, and for his macabre fantasies in works such as *The Nightmare* (1781). Cf. Allan Cunningham (1784–1842), *The Lives of the Most Eminent British Painters, Sculptors, and Architects*, 6 vols. (London: Murray, 1829–33), ii. 338: 'Two meals a-day were all he ventured on—he always avoided supper—the story of his having supped on raw pork-chops that he might dream his picture of the Nightmare has no foundation.'

Shadwell: Thomas Shadwell (*c.*1640–92), playwright and Poet Laureate, whose heavy drinking and opium addiction were common knowledge. Dryden lampooned Shadwell in *Mac Flecknoe* for his 'mighty mug of potent ale' (121) and his crown of poppies (126).

Homer: Homer, *Odyssey*, iv. 220–1: 'At once she cast into the wine of which they were drinking a drug to quiet all pain and strife, and bring forgetfulness of every ill.'

objective: 'This word,' De Quincey observes in his revised *Confessions*, 'so nearly unintelligible in 1821, so intensely scholastic, and, consequently, when surrounded by familiar and vernacular words, so apparently pedantic, yet, on the other hand, so indispensable to accurate thinking, and to *wide* thinking, has since 1821 become too common to need any apology' (*Works*, ii. 260).

last Lord Orford . . . rest of my person: Horace Walpole, fourth Earl of Orford (1717–97), letter-writer, connoisseur, and author of *The Castle of Otranto* (1764), generally regarded as the first Gothic novel. The source of the quotation has not been traced. But cf. Edward Bulwer-Lytton (1803–73), 'My Novel; or, Varieties in English Life (Part XXI)', *Blackwood's Magazine*, 71 (1852), 592: 'Horace Walpole said that "his stomach would survive all the rest of him" '.

some part of my London life: in 1856, De Quincey was more specific: 'the searching for Ann amongst fluctuating crowds' brought on these nightmares of the human face (*Works*, ii. 260).

72 *Ganges . . . Euphrates*: the Ganges in northern India is the holy river of the Hindus. The Euphrates is the largest river in western Asia, and in its lower portion it helped to define the region known as Mesopotamia, one of the cradles of civilization.

officina gentium: 'workshop of peoples'.

73 *Brama . . . Vishnu . . . Seeva*: three major Hindu deities: Brahmā is the creator; Vishnu is the preserver; Śiva is the destroyer.

Isis and Osiris: two of the most important deities of ancient Egypt. Osiris was a god of fertility. His wife was Isis, whose magical powers brought her dead husband back to life. Cf. Milton, *Paradise Lost*, i. 476–82:

> After these appear'd
> A crew who under Names of old Renown,
> *Osiris, Isis, Orus* and thir Train
> With monstrous shapes and sorceries abus'd
> Fanatic *Egypt* and her Priests, to seek
> Thir wand'ring Gods disguis'd in brutish forms
> Rather than human.

ibis: a wading bird sacred to the ancient Egyptians.

children . . . at my bed-side: De Quincey dates this dream 'May 1818', but it clearly haunted him for months. 'Children', in any event, could not have stood at his bedside in May 1818 because at that time the De Quinceys had only one child, William. Their second child, Margaret, was not born until 5 June 1818, and of course it would have been some time before she was able to stand beside her brother.

74 *caeteris paribus*: 'the rest being equal'.

May . . . Easter Sunday: De Quincey dates this dream 'June 1819', but then describes events which take place on an Easter Sunday in May. Neither month can be correct, however, as Easter Sunday can only fall in March or April.

75 *the grave of a child*: Catharine Wordsworth (see above, p. 281).

first fruits of resurrection: 1 Corinthians 15: 20–1: 'But now is Christ risen from the dead, *and* become the first fruits of them that slept. For since by man *came* death, by man *came* also the resurrection of the dead.'

twinkling of an eye: 1 Corinthians 15: 51–2: 'We shall not all sleep, but we shall all be changed, in a moment, in the twinkling of an eye, at the last trumpet.'

76 *Coronation Anthem*: the celebrated anthem 'Zadok the Priest' was composed by George Frederick Handel (1685–1759) for the 1727 Coronation of George II (1683–1760), king of Great Britain, reigned 1727–60. De Quincey may have had the anthem in mind because he was in London on 19 July 1821, when the Coronation of George IV took place.

'Deeper than ever plummet sounded': Shakespeare, *The Tempest*, V. i. 54–7: 'I'll break my staff, | Bury it certain fadoms in the earth, | And deeper than did ever plummet sound | I'll drown my book.'

incestuous mother . . . name of death: Milton, *Paradise Lost*, ii. 787–9; x. 602.

'I will sleep no more!': see above, p. 274.

78 *William Lithgow . . . Malaga is overpoweringly affecting*: William Lithgow (1582–*c*.1645), Scottish traveller and author, was arrested at Malaga in southern Spain in the autumn of 1620 on suspicion of spying on English ships. He was kept in irons, and then tortured on the rack, an episode he describes in *The Totall Discourse, of the Rare Adventures, and painefull Peregrinations of long nineteene Years Travayles, from Scotland, to the most Famous Kingdomes in Europe, Asia, and Africa* (London: Okes, 1632), 462: 'Thus being hoised, to the appointed height, the Tormentor descended below, and drawing down my Legs, through the two sides of the three-planked Rack, he tied a Cord about each of my ancles: And then ascending upon the Rack, he drew the Cords upward, and bending forward with main force, my two knees, against the two planks; the sinews of my hams burst asunder, and the lids of my knees being crushed, and the Cords made fast, I hung so demained, for a large hour.'

James I: James I (1566–1625), king of Scotland (as James VI), reigned 1567–1625; and king of England, reigned 1603–25.

Edinburgh surgeon . . . Valerian: George Bell (1777–1832) attended De Quincey in Edinburgh in late 1820, and prescribed 'ammoniated tinc-ture of Valerian', which was given to patients who suffered from 'a debility of the nervous system'. The tincture was easy to make: 'Take of Valerian root, four ounces; Aromatic spirit of ammonia, two pints. Macerate for fourteen days, and strain.' What is more, it was 'of great use in nervous disorders . . . some recommend it as procuring sleep, particularly in fever, even when opium fails' (see Robert Morrison, ' "An Edinburgh surgeon of great eminence" in De Quincey's *Confessions of an English Opium-Eater*', *Notes and Queries*, 46 (1999), 47–8).

Jeremy Taylor . . . born as to die: in 1856, De Quincey realized that 'the exact passage moving' in his mind was not from Jeremy Taylor (1613–67), Anglican clergyman and author, but from Francis Bacon (1561–1626), statesman, philosopher, and writer, in his 'Essay on Death': 'It is as natural to die as to be born; and to a little infant perhaps the one is as painful as the other' (*Works*, ii. 266).

79 *With dreadful . . . arms*: Milton, *Paradise Lost*, xii. 644.

SUSPIRIA DE PROFUNDIS

81 *SUSPIRIA DE PROFUNDIS*: 'sighs from the depths', De Quincey bor-rows from Psalm 130: 1: 'Out of the depths have I cried unto thee, O Lord.'

object of that work . . . human dreams: De Quincey makes a different claim in the *Confessions* themselves: 'the object was to display the marvellous agency of opium, whether for pleasure or for pain' (see above, p. 77).

talk is of oxen . . . dream of oxen: see above, p. 264.

Daguerreotype, &c.: Louis-Jacques-Mandé Daguerre (1787–1851), French physicist and painter who in 1839 invented the first practical form of pho-tography, known as the daguerreotype.

82 *fleshly torpor*: cf. Wordsworth in the 'Preface' to *Lyrical Ballads* (1800) in
   William Wordsworth: The Major Works, ed. Stephen Gill (Oxford: Oxford
   University Press, 2000), 599: 'For a multitude of causes, unknown to
   former times, are now acting with a combined force to blunt the discrim-
   inating powers of the mind, and unfitting it for all voluntary exertion to
   reduce it to a state of almost savage torpor.'

   fierce condition of eternal hurry: cf. De Quincey in his 1852 essay on 'Sir
   William Hamilton': the 'principle of contagion' that now exists in society
   has arisen in part because of the railways, 'which are not only swift in
   themselves, but the causes of swiftness in everything else; so that very
   soon, I am convinced, out of pure, blind sympathy with railway trains,
   men will begin to trot through the streets' (*Works*, xvii. 151).

   How much solitude, so much power: cf. Wordsworth, *The Prelude*, ii. 78: 'The
   self-sufficing power of solitude'; or Southey, 'The Poet's Pilgrimage to
   Waterloo', 1. xxi. 3: 'The Power divine which dwells in solitude'.

83 *praemissis praemittendis*: literally, 'with those things sent on ahead that
   should be sent on ahead'; thus, 'putting first what must be put first'.

   synthetic order: as opposed to analytic order.

   sine qua non: absolute requirement.

84 *striking incident in a modern novel*: the incident has not been traced; it may
   well be De Quincey's invention.

   Holy Office: the Congregation of the Holy Office of the Inquisition was
   established in 1542 by Pope Paul III (1468–1549). It was charged with
   eradicating Protestantism, and maintaining the integrity of the Catholic
   faith.

85 *to warn other opium-eaters*: De Quincey has changed his tune. 'The moral
   of the narrative is addressed to the opium-eater,' he wrote at the end of the
   Confessions. '. . . If he is taught to fear and tremble, enough has been
   effected' (see above, p. 78).

   (being the same) . . . he is not the same: cf. Wordsworth on his childhood self
   in *The Prelude*, ii. 28–33:

> so wide appears
> The vacancy between me and those days,
> Which yet have such self-presence in my mind
> That, sometimes, when I think of them, I seem
> Two consciousness, conscious of myself
> And of some other Being.

86 *in extenso*: at full length.

87 *recreant indorser of a bill*: see below, p. 315.

   English lakes . . . in search of the picturesque: De Quincey alludes here to
   the enormously popular *Tour of Dr Syntax in Search of the Picturesque*
   (1812), which featured the verse of William Combe (1742–1823) and the

illustrations of Thomas Rowlandson (1757–1827), and which contained an account of a tour through the English Lakes.

87 *'by the virtue of his oath'*: see the *Irish Jurist*, 4 (1852), 202: 'When a witness is examined it is not an uncommon thing to say, "by the virtue of the oath which you have taken." We all know that this does not add to the obligation of the witness.'

Keswick . . . postilions . . . Westmoreland: Keswick is a town at the north end of Derwent Water, below the peak of Skiddaw, in the historic county of Cumberland. Westmorland is a historic county of north-western England, bounded on the north and west by Cumberland. A postilion is a person who rides as a guide on the near horse of one of the pairs of horses pulling a carriage.

fly down hills . . . without locking: cf. De Quincey in 1839: 'The descent into Patterdale is much above two miles; but such is the propensity for flying down hills in Westmoreland, that I have found the descent accomplished in about six minutes' (*Works*, xi. 114). 'Locking' prevents a wheel from turning to the left or the right, and thus slows a vehicle as it descends a hill.

fiery race: cf. Shakespeare, Sonnet 51, 9–11: 'Then can no horse with my desire keep pace; | Therefore desire (of perfect'st love being made) | Shall neigh (no dull flesh) in his fiery race.'

lets down the glasses: 'A pane of glass, *especially* the window of a coach' (*OED*).

τὸ brevity: brevity itself.

caduceus: a staff encircled by two snakes with a pair of wings at the top. In Greek mythology, it was carried by Hermes, messenger of the gods. Later the caduceus was adopted as a symbol of the physician.

Cheapside: in De Quincey's day, a bustling centre of shops in the City of London near St Paul's Cathedral. De Quincey's father was a linen draper in Cheapside in the 1770s. Cf. Charles Dickens, Junior (1837–96) a century later in his *Dictionary of London* (London: Dickens, 1879), 48: 'Cheapside . . . may boast of being the busiest thoroughfare in the world, with the sole exception perhaps of London-bridge.'

88 *Valerius Flaccus . . . 'viridantem floribus hastas' . . . halberts*: Valerius Flaccus (*fl.* first century AD), epic poet, *Argonautica*, vi. 136. De Quincey's own translation is accurate.

89 *My father was a merchant*: Thomas Quincey (see above, p. 265).

Cicero . . . Ethics . . . wholesale: Cicero, *On Duties*, i. 151: 'Trade, if it is on a small scale, is to be considered vulgar; but if wholesale and on a large scale, importing large quantities from all parts of the world and distributing to many without misrepresentation, it is not to be greatly disparaged.'

small-beer: inferior or weak beer. Cf. Shakespeare, *Othello*, II. i. 160: 'To suckle fools and chronicle small beer'.

ménage: household.

90 *'Give me neither poverty nor riches'*: Agur's—not Agar's—prayer in Proverbs 30: 8: 'Remove far from me vanity, and lies; give me neither poverty, nor riches.'

Marcus Aurelius: Marcus Aurelius (AD 121–80), Roman emperor, celebrated for his *Meditations* on Stoic philosophy. Book I includes an account of the blessings of his early life.

horrid pugilistic brothers: De Quincey had three brothers. Only the eldest William (see above, p. 271) was a bully.

The first who died was Jane: De Quincey echoes Wordsworth, 'We Are Seven', 49: 'The first that died was little Jane'.

91 *She was three and a half, I two and a half*: in fact, Jane Quincey (1786–90) was a year younger than De Quincey.

sad perplexity: cf. Wordsworth, 'Lines Written a Few Miles Above Tintern Abbey', 60–1: 'With many recognitions dim and faint, | And somewhat of a sad perplexity'.

maternal grandmother: Sarah Penson, whose only daughter was De Quincey's mother, died on 16 January 1790, aged 69 years.

forced me to revolt . . . violence: later, of course, De Quincey developed a deep fascination with violence, as seen most clearly in his terror fiction and his essays 'On Murder Considered as One of the Fine Arts'.

large town . . . rural seclusion: De Quincey was born in Manchester, but when very young moved first to a place outside the city limits known as 'The Farm', and then in 1791 to a much larger house about a mile outside Manchester called 'Greenhay' (Morrison, 9–10).

three innocent little sisters for playmates: De Quincey's playmates were Elizabeth (who was two years older), Mary (a year older), and Jane.

92 *A boy . . . could have viewed as an offence*: De Quincey almost certainly recounts the death of his youngest son Julius (1829–32), who was 'a boy of rather more than 3 years old' when he died one night 'in his mother's arm'. De Quincey's wife Margaret, however, died five (not seven) years after Julius's death (Morrison, 272–3, 295).

93 *Dr Percival*: Thomas Percival (1740–1804) was a physician and a key figure in the cultural circles of Enlightenment Manchester. His children's book, *A Father's Instructions* (1775–1800), was a favourite with De Quincey.

Condorcet, D'Alembert: Marie-Jean-Antoine-Nicolas de Caritat, marquis de Condorcet (1743–94), and Jean Le Rond d'Alembert (1717–83) were leading figures of the French Enlightenment. Both excelled in philosophy and mathematics.

Charles White . . . human skull . . . human species: Charles White (1728–1813) was Manchester's leading surgeon for nearly six decades. His *Account of the Regular Gradation in Man, Animals, and Vegetables* (1799) was written to 'prove that the human being was connected by a regular series of links with the brute; *i.e.* that the transition from the African skull to that of the ape, in some species or other, was not more abrupt than from the European to the African', as De Quincey remarked in 1834 (*Works*, x. 11). See Peter J. Kitson, 'The Strange Case of Dr White and Mr De Quincey: Manchester, Medicine and Romantic Theories of Biological Racism', *Romanticism*, 17/3 (2011), 278–87.

93 *hydrocephalus*: a disease characterized by an accumulation of cerebrospinal fluid within the cranial cavity. It is typically accompanied by an enlargement of the skull and forehead, and an atrophy of the brain. De Quincey was obsessed with the condition. Elizabeth, however, is much more likely to have died from cerebrospinal meningitis (Morrison, 14).

Pillar of fire: Exodus 13: 21: 'And the Lord went before them by day in a pillar of a cloud, to lead them the way, and by night in a pillar of fire, to give them light to go by day and night.'

shadow of death: Job 10: 21: 'Before I go *whence* I shall not return, *even* to the land of darkness and the shadow of death'.

94 '*If God should make another Eve*': Milton, *Paradise Lost*, ix. 911: 'Should God create another Eve'.

'*Creature . . . amiable, or sweet*': Milton, *Paradise Lost*, ix. 897–9.

'*Loss of thee!*': Milton, *Paradise Lost*, ix. 912–16.

John Paul . . . restoration to innocence: Johann Paul Friedrich Richter (1763–1825), German novelist and humourist who wrote under the pen name Jean Paul. 'From every sort of vice and infirmity he drew nutriment for his philosophic mind,' De Quincey wrote enthusiastically. 'It is to the honour of John Paul, that in this, as in other respects, he constantly reminds me of Shakespeare' (*Works*, iii. 26). It is not clear which passage in Richter's work De Quincey has in mind here.

95 '*Love . . . in thee was most intense*': Wordsworth, 'Tribute to the Memory of the Same Dog', 29–30: 'For love, that comes to all; the holy sense, | Best gift of God, in thee was most intense'.

as much above eight years as I above six: Elizabeth Quincey was born in 1783 and she died on 2 June 1792, two and a half months before De Quincey turned 7.

ex officio: by virtue of the office.

Speech of Alhadra in Coleridge's Remorse: Coleridge, *Remorse*, IV. iii. 78–9.

96 *sleeping the sleep . . . no awaking*: cf. Psalm 13: 3: 'O Lord my God: lighten mine eyes, lest I sleep *the sleep* of death.'

caeteris paribus: see above, p. 291.

profoundly affecting . . . other parts of the year: see above, pp. 74–5.

97 *involutes . . . abstract shapes*: De Quincey's 'involutes' are strikingly similar to Wordsworth's 'spots of time', for both concepts are rooted in childhood memory, and involve emotions and material objects that have become inextricably combined.

guard: fireguard.

disciples plucking the ears of corn: see, for example, Matthew 12: 1: 'Jesus went on the Sabbath day through the corn, and his Disciples were an hungered, and began to pluck the ears of corn.'

98 *Palm Sunday . . . Jerusalem*: 'Palm Sunday', or 'Passion Sunday', is the Sunday before Easter, and commemorates Christ's triumphal entry into Jerusalem.

Delphi: the ancient Greeks regarded Delphi as the centre of the world. The town lies 100 miles north-west of Athens, along the slopes of Mount Parnassus, and is the site of the famous oracle of Apollo.

Memnonian: Memnon, king of the Ethiopians, was commemorated near Thebes in Egypt by a colossal stone statue, which was said to give forth musical sounds when touched by the rays of the rising sun.

99 *Aeolian intonation*: in the epics of Homer, Aeolus is the controller of the winds. De Quincey probably has in mind the sound produced by an Aeolian harp, a stringed instrument that makes music when the wind blows across it.

Sarsar wind of death: from the Arabic 'çarçar', 'a cold wind' (*OED*). Cf. Southey, *Thalaba the Destroyer* (1801), i. 476–7: 'The Sarsar can pierce through, | The Icy Wind of Death.'

Φυγὴ μονου προς μονον. Plotinus (AD 205–70), the greatest of the Neoplatonist philosophers of Graeco-Roman antiquity, *Enneads*: VI. ix. 11: 'escape in solitude to the solitary'. Plotinus espoused the idea that the individual soul is able, both by intellect and by mystical intuition, to raise itself to union with the Supreme and Absolute Reality.

final notes . . . course of the narrative: these 'final notes' were never written.

100 *like a guilty thing*: De Quincey quotes Shakespeare, *Hamlet*, I. i. 148. Wordsworth quotes these same words in 'Ode: Intimations of Immortality', 150. De Quincey probably also has in mind Milton, *Paradise Lost*, ix. 784–5: 'Back to the Thicket slunk | The guilty Serpent'.

'Everlasting Jew!' . . . than our own: in Christian legend, a man taunts Christ on the way to the Crucifixion. As punishment, he is fated to roam the earth until the Day of Judgement. The name 'Ahasuerus' was first given to the man in 1602 in a German pamphlet entitled *Kurze Beschreibung und Erzählung von einem Juden mit namen Ahasverus* (*A Brief Description and Narration Regarding a Jew Named Ahasuerus*).

101 *experience . . . illuminate the hour of death*: perhaps De Quincey got his wish. As death came upon him, he threw up his arms, as if in great surprise, and exclaimed distinctly, 'Sister! sister! sister!' (Morrison, 394).

beautiful boy . . . same complaint: De Quincey's eldest son William died on 25 November 1834. He was 18. An autopsy took place twenty-eight hours after death. Under the scalp was 'a large mass of olive-green coloured matter', and under the skull-cap were 'thin layers of similar green-coloured matter, interspersed with some bloody spots'. De Quincey described

William as 'the crown and glory of my life' (Morrison, 288–9; *Works*, xx. 269).

101 *the church*: St Ann's church in Manchester, where De Quincey's guardian Samuel Hall preached. De Quincey was baptized there. His sister Elizabeth is buried there.

St Paul . . . always read at burials: 1 Corinthians 15: 42–3.

present illustrious Laureate: Wordsworth became Poet Laureate in 1843, following the death of Southey.

102 *The Excursion . . . a beloved object*: Wordsworth, *The Excursion*, iv. 153–61:

> For who could sink and settle to that point
> Of selfishness; so senseless who could be
> As long and perseveringly to mourn
> For any object of his love, removed
> From this unstable world, if he could fix
> A satisfying view upon that state
> Of pure, imperishable, blessedness,
> Which reason promises, and holy writ
> Ensures to all believers?

'We shall be changed': 1 Corinthians 15: 51: 'Behold, I show you a mystery: we shall not all sleep, but we shall all be changed'.

103 *ashes to ashes . . . dust to dust*: part of the funeral service in the Book of Common Prayer. The words are derived from Genesis 18: 27, where Abraham describes himself as 'but dust and ashes'; see too, Job 30: 19.

104 *a slight defect in my eyes*: De Quincey suffered from myopia, which by the time he began his career at Oxford was 'so marked' that he was 'rumoured to be a bit of a Jacobin because he failed to "cap" the Master of his college . . . when he met him, only from sheer inability to recognize him by sight' (Hogg, 233).

105 *young children . . . might yet meet the sooner*: see Matthew 18: 1–6.

man's mind . . . during his infancy: cf. Wordsworth, 'My heart leaps up when I behold', 7: 'The Child is father of the Man'.

106 *inosculate*: unite, join.

107 *lilies . . . arrayed, or . . . ravens . . . feed their young*: De Quincey adapts Luke 12: 24–7.

'communion undisturbed': Wordsworth, *The Excursion*, iv. 83–6: 'thou, who didst wrap the cloud | Of infancy around us, that thyself, | Therein, with our simplicity awhile | Might'st hold, on earth, communion undisturbed'.

Agrippa's mirror: Heinrich Cornelius Agrippa (1486–1535), German philosopher and occultist, *Three Books of Occult Philosophy*, ed. Donald Tyson (St Paul, Minn.: Llewellyn, 2004), 17: the 'vital spirit' of the air, declares Agrippa, 'receives into itself, as if it were a divine looking glass, the species of all things, as well natural, as artificial', and thus 'affords matter for divers strange dreams and divinations'.

hereafter I will convince you of this truth: De Quincey does not return to the subject.

108 *the very dimmest of his truths!*: the first instalment of *Suspiria* ended here.

Death of Wallenstein . . . Piccolomini: *The Death of Wallenstein* is a drama by the German writer and literary theorist Johann Christoph Friedrich von Schiller (1759–1805). Coleridge translated the play in 1800. Like De Quincey's Gothic romance *Klosterheim* (1832), *Wallenstein* is set in Germany during the Thirty Years War. Albrecht von Wallenstein (1583–1634) is commanding general of the armies of the Holy Roman Empire. Ottavio Piccolomini (1599–1656) is his Lieutenant-General. The 'younger Piccolomini' is Ottavio's son Max Piccolomini, a fictional character introduced by Schiller.

'Was verschmerzte nicht der mensch?': cf. Coleridge, *The Death of Wallenstein* (London: Longman and Rees, 1800), 130: 'This anguish will be wearied down'. In a footnote, however, Coleridge acknowledges that this is 'a very inadequate translation of the original. . . . LITERALLY . . . I shall *grieve down* this blow, of that I'm conscious; | What does not man grieve down?'

the shafts of Apollo: the most widely influential of all Greek gods, Apollo carried a bow and arrows, and was a superb archer.

109 *'dislimn'*: Shakespeare, *Antony and Cleopatra*, IV. xiv. 10–11: 'The rack dislimns, and makes it indistinct | As water is in water.'

pensive tenderness: cf. Wordsworth, *The Excursion*, IV. 742–3: 'in every grove | A gay or pensive tenderness prevailed'.

composing-stick: a tray of adjustable width that a printer holds in one hand and sets type into with the other.

110 * * *: it is not known what was removed from the text at this point.

* *: it is not known what was removed from the text at this point.

111 *ubi Caesar, ibi Roma*: 'where Caesar is, there is Rome'.

112 *Mr Alston*: Washington Allston (1779–1843), American painter and poet, *The Dead Man Revived by Touching the Bones of the Prophet Elisha* (1811–14). Allston was a good friend of Coleridge, and painted famous portraits of him in 1806 and 1814. De Quincey also knew Allston, and undoubtedly saw *The Dead Man Revived* when he visited him in London (Morrison, 170). The painting is not an altarpiece.

nympholepsy: 'passion supposedly inspired in men by nymphs; an ecstasy or yearning' (*OED*). Cf. De Quincey in his January 1839 article on Wordsworth, where he refers to 'the sort of "nympholepsy" which had seized upon me' (*Works*, xi. 43).

Obeah: 'a kind of sorcery, witchcraft, or folk medicine originating in West Africa and mainly practised in the English-speaking areas of the Caribbean' (*OED*).

112 *distinguished writers . . . Edgeworth . . . Belinda*: Maria Edgeworth (1767–1849), Anglo-Irish novelist and children's writer, incorporates Obeah into the plot of her social novel *Belinda* (1801). Other 'distinguished writers' who refer to Obeah include Thomas Campbell in *The Pleasures of Hope* (1799) and Percy Shelley in *Peter Bell the Third* (1819).

Three-finger'd Jack: in the folklore of Jamaica, Jack Mansong is a slave turned outlaw who terrorized the island in 1780–1, and who was said to carry a small Obeah bag which made him invincible. He became the hero of several stage melodramas in Britain.

113 *'On the sublime attractions of the grave'*: Wordsworth, *The Excursion*, iv. 235–8: 'With only such degree of sadness left | As may support longings of pure desire; | And strengthen love, rejoicing secretly | In the sublime attractions of the grave'.

the Erl-king's Daughter: De Quincey draws on the Danish legend of the Erl-King, a seductive but malevolent fairy. Johann Wolfgang von Goethe (see above, p. 262) used the legend in his *Der Erlkönig*, which Matthew 'Monk' Lewis (1775–1818) translated into English in his *Tales of Wonder*, 2 vols. (London: Bulmer, 1801), i. 51–2. De Quincey quotes from the opening stanzas of Lewis's translation. Lewis followed his translation from Goethe with a second poem from the Danish entitled 'The Erl-King's Daughter' (i. 53–5).

114 *one of my guardians . . . accomplished scholar*: De Quincey's guardian Samuel Hall (see above, p. 265).

a present from Leicestershire: perhaps the present was from a relative, as one report of dubious authenticity asserts that De Quincey's paternal grandfather was at the head of a family of nearly two dozen children, and that he lived in Ashby-de-la-Zouche in Leicestershire, a county in the East Midlands.

little cousin of mine, Emma H———: perhaps Emma's last name is 'Hodgson', as the British philosopher Shadworth Hodgson (1832–1912) was a relative of the De Quincey family. De Quincey's three daughters called him 'cousin' (Morrison, 376).

ἐπώνυμος: 'appropriately named'.

115 *ego et rex meus*: 'I and my king'.

116 *where this paper is proceeding*: De Quincey is writing either in lodgings at 71 Clerk Street in Edinburgh; or at Mavis Bush Cottage in Lasswade, seven miles outside Edinburgh.

'Iraeque leonum . . . nocte rudentum': Virgil, *Aeneid*, vii. 15–16: 'hinc exaudiri gemitus iraeque leonum | vincla recusantum et sera sub nocte rudentum' ('Hence could be heard the angry growls of lions chafing at their bonds and roaring in midnight hours'. In the *Aeneid*, the sounds are described as coming, not from Tartarus (see above, p. 269) as De Quincey claims, but from the palace of Circe, the wicked enchantress who turned men into beasts.

caveae: cages for wild beasts.

117 *'Blessed . . . they shall obtain mercy'*: Matthew 5: 7.

ague: in De Quincey's day, a well-established, if vague, medical term usually associated with acute or violent fevers.

ab urbe condita: 'From the Founding of the City', the title of Livy's monumental history of Rome (see above, p. 288).

118 *vis medicatrix*: healing power.

'Kilcrops': fairy or demon changelings substituted for genuine children. Southey suggests they do not exist in his poem 'The Killcrop', 119–20: 'Trust me, thou art mistaken, 'tis no Killcrop: | See how he smiles! Poor infant: give him me.'

119 *coup-de-main*: 'assault' or 'blow'.

the least in heaven: see Matthew 11: 11.

120 *'On the Intimations of Immortality in Childhood'*: Wordsworth, 'Ode: Intimations of Immortality'.

St Matthew, chap. xxi., and v. 15 . . . v. 16: 'And when the chief Priests and Scribes saw the wonderful things that he did, and the children crying in the temple, and saying, Hosanna to the son of David, they were sore displeased, And said until him, Hearest thou what these say? And Jesus saith unto them, Yea, have ye never read, Out of the mouth of babes and sucklings thou hast perfected praise?'

Sanhedrims: the supreme Jewish legislative and judicial court.

lovely sketch . . . by Mr Wordsworth: see Wordsworth, 'Water Fowl', especially 10–17:

> Their jubilant activity evolves
> Hundreds of curves and circlets, to and fro,
> Upward and downward, progress intricate
> Yet unperplexed, as if one spirit swayed
> Their indefatigable flight. 'Tis done—
> Ten times, or more, I fancied it had ceased;
> But lo! the vanished company again
> Ascending.

Apollonius: Apollonius of Perga (*c*.240–*c*.190 BC), ancient Greek mathematician, known as 'the Great Geometer', and celebrated for his treatise on *Conics*.

121 *kaleidoscope*: De Quincey's fellow *Blackwood's* writer David Brewster (1781–1868) invented the kaleidoscope in 1816.

least: perhaps a misprint for 'last'.

122 *Vatican . . . Bodleian . . . Bibliothéque du Roi*: three of the world's greatest book collections: the Vatican Library in Rome; the Bodleian Library at the University of Oxford; and the Bibliothèque du Roi, which is now the Bibliothèque Nationale (the National Library of France).

122 *incestuous . . . lurking in the future*: in Greek mythology, Oedipus, the king of Thebes, unwittingly kills his father and marries his mother, who commits suicide when the truth becomes known.

123 *Brutus and a thousand years of impossibilities*: according to the medieval English chronicler Geoffrey of Monmouth (d. 1155) in *The History of the Kings of Britain*, the eponymous founder and first king of Britain was Brutus of Troy, who was descended from the mythical Trojan hero Aeneas, and who settled Britain after conquering a race of giants.

124 *universal sea*: cf. Wordsworth, 'Processions', 25–7: 'Old Cham, the solar Deity, who dwells | Aloft, yet in a tilting vessel rode, | When universal sea the mountains overflowed'.

knocked away the 'shores': a 'shore' is 'a piece of timber or iron set obliquely against the side of . . . a ship in dock . . . as a support when it is in danger of falling or when undergoing alteration or repair' (*OED*).

Beza's Latin Testament: Theodore Beza (1519–1605), French theologian and educator, succeeded John Calvin (1509–64) as leader of the Protestant Reformation. His Latin translation of the New Testament is a crucial source for the King James Version of the Bible (1611).

great chapter of St Paul: 1 Corinthians 15.

bravura: a dazzling display of skill.

Alcaics and Choriambics: Greek metres (see above, p. 269) used in both Greek and Latin poetry.

125 *Delphi*: see above, p. 297.

yellow admirals: a term 'applied to naval captains retired as rear admirals in H.M. Fleet without being attached to a particular squadron (red, white, or blue)' (*OED*).

stretch to the crack of doom: Shakespeare, *Macbeth*, IV. i. 117: 'What, will the line stretch out to th' crack of doom?'

126 *caitiff*: 'wretch' or 'villain'.

Stationers' Company: a printers' guild founded in 1556. The hall of the Stationers' Company kept a register of all copyrights. Books sometimes carried warnings that unauthorized copiers would be prosecuted.

'scena': 'a composition consisting largely of recitative of a dramatic and impassioned character' (*OED*).

counterpanes: bedspreads.

127 *'star-y-pointing'*: Milton, 'On Shakespeare', 1–4: 'What needs my Shakespeare for his honour'd Bones, | The labour of an age in piled Stones, | Or that his hallow'd reliques should be hid | Under a Star-y-pointing Pyramid?'

Arabian Nights . . . some old magician: *The Thousand and One Nights*, or *The Arabian Nights' Entertainment*, a collection of oriental stories of uncertain date and authorship. The first European translation was by the Frenchman

Antoine Galland (1646–1715), and appeared under the title *Les Mille et Une Nuits* (1704–17). The tale De Quincey has in mind has not been identified.

zenana: harem.

Bagdat . . . Tigris: Baghdad lies on the banks of the Tigris River, in the heart of ancient Mesopotamia.

128 *the ticking of a death-watch*: 'the popular name of various insects which make a noise like the ticking of a watch, supposed by the ignorant and superstitious to portend death' (*OED*).

Caesar: Julius Caesar (*c*.100–44 BC), celebrated Roman statesman, general, and dictator. His major writings are on *The Gallic War* and *The Civil Wars*.

'foremost man of all this world': Shakespeare, *Julius Caesar*, IV. iii. 22.

homeward road . . . reveries which besieged me: De Quincey walked the single main road from the open country near Greenhay to Samuel Hall's home in Salford, a distance of almost two miles (*Works*, xix. 32).

'Into what depth thou see'st, | From what height fallen': Milton, *Paradise Lost*, i. 91–2: 'into what Pit thou seest | From what highth fall'n'.

129 *accidents of the press . . . have thus been lost*: De Quincey planned to end the second instalment of *Suspiria* with 'Levana and Our Ladies of Sorrow', which he had relied on as his 'main artillery' for the number. But his editor Blackwood insisted that there was not enough room in the April issue, and deferred 'Levana' to the third instalment (Morrison, 340–1).

jury-mast: 'a temporary mast put up in place of one that has been broken or carried away' (*OED*).

130 *Euripides*: in Greek mythology, Medea is an enchantress who helps Jason steal the Golden Fleece. Later, at Corinth, Jason deserts Medea, and in her fury she murders her children in their nursery. De Quincey's reference is to Euripides, *Medea*, 1271–8.

the frost of death: cf. Percy Shelley, *The Revolt of Islam*, IX. xxiii. 5–6: 'Lo, Winter comes!—the grief of many graves, | The frost of death, the tempest of the sword'.

'Him that sate thereon': Milton, 'At a Solemn Music', 8: 'To Him that sits thereon'.

that live only to languish in tears.: the second instalment of *Suspiria* ended here.

131 *masculine reader . . . female reader*: when De Quincey published *Confessions of an English Opium-Eater* in 1821, he could confidently expect that the vast majority of his readers were men who had received an education steeped in Greek and Latin literature. But magazine audiences expanded enormously over the course of his career, and by mid-century women— very few of whom would have received a classical education—formed an increasingly large proportion of his readership. Cf. De Quincey in 1853:

'An attention to the unlearned part of an audience, which 15 years ago might have rested upon pure courtesy, *now* rests upon a basis of absolute justice' (*Works*, xviii. 4).

131 *dragomans*: interpreters.

Cowper . . . or a sofa: William Cowper (1731–1800) opens his long, introspective poem *The Task* (1785) with a mock-Miltonic account of the origins of the sofa.

Pisistratus: Peisistratus (b. 6th century BC, d. 527 BC), tyrant of ancient Athens.

132 *Dr Whately . . . archbishop of Dublin*: Richard Whately (1787–1863), *Elements of Rhetoric*, second edition (London: Murray, 1828), 3: 'the invention of printing is too obvious not to have speedily followed, in a literary nation, the introduction of a paper sufficiently cheap to make the art available'. De Quincey reviewed *Elements of Rhetoric* for *Blackwood's* in 1828 (*Works*, vi. 155–89).

133 *Hermes Trismegistus*: literally, 'Hermes the Triple-Greatest', the messenger god of classical Greece who was associated with escorting the dead out of the world. He is the reputed author of a variety of philosophical, astrological, and quasi-scientific tracts now designated as Hermetic writings.

Sicilian river Arethusa . . . English river Mole: the Alpheus River in Greece disappears and re-emerges several times before emptying into the Ionian Sea, which its waters were said to pass beneath before rising again in the fountain of Arethusa near Syracuse, Sicily. The Mole River flows northwards across the county of Surrey to join the Thames at Hampton Court, west of London. It was said during its course to pass underground. De Quincey is perhaps thinking of Edmund Spenser (*c*.1552–99), *The Faerie Queene*, IV. xi. 291–2: 'And Mole, that like a nousling Mole doth make | His way still under ground, till Thamis he overtake'.

Agamemnon of Aeschylus . . . Phoenissae of Euripides: Aeschylus (525–456 BC) is the earliest Greek tragic poet. His *Agamemnon* concerns the great Greek king of that name who is murdered by his vengeful wife Clytemnestra (see above, p. 273). The *Phoenician Women*, by Euripides, is set at Thebes and centres on the mutual slaughter of the two sons of Oedipus.

Western Empire: the western half of the Roman Empire broke up in the late fifth century AD.

134 *'my Cid' . . . Coeur de Lion . . . Sir Tristrem . . . Lybaeus Disconus*: the twelfth-century epic poem *El cantar de mío Cid* (*The Song of the Cid*) recounts the adventures of Rodrigo Díaz de Vivar (*c*.1043–99), Spanish military hero. Richard the Lionheart (1157–99), king of England, reigned 1189–99, was the subject of several chivalric romances. *Sir Tristrem* is a verse romance of the late thirteenth century, based on the tale of Tristan and Iseult, and closely associated with the tradition of courtly love. *Libeaus Desconus* is a fourteenth-century verse romance treating the subject of the 'Fair Unknown', and sometimes attributed to Thomas Chestre.

more elaborate chemistry of our own days: De Quincey may be recalling Henry Richard Vassall Fox, third Baron Holland (1773–1840), who in a letter of 7 February 1797 observed that 'in the ruins of Herculaneum were found several hundred ancient manuscripts in scrolls, but so burnt that, to the eye of an inobservant person, they seem little more than ashes. An ingenious man invented a method of unrolling the scrolls, and at the same time preserving the letters' (see *Works*, vii. 315–16).

thaumaturgy: magic. Cf. De Quincey in his 1834–5 essay on Coleridge, where he points out that he read in the 'same track as Coleridge,—that track in which few of any age will ever follow us, such as German metaphysicians, Latin schoolmen, thaumaturgic Platonists, religious Mystics' (*Works*, x. 293).

Paracelsus . . . from its combustion: Paracelsus (1493–1541), German-Swiss alchemist and physician, discussed 'the resuscitation of natural things' in Book VI of *De Natura Rerum*; see his *Hermetic and Alchemical Writings*, ed. Arthur Edward Waite, 2 vols. (London: Elliott, 1894), i. 148: 'mortified things are not dead and compelled to continue in death, but can be brought back and resuscitated and vitalised by man, according to natural guidance and rule'.

doubles: a sharp turn or reversal.

Erictho . . . Pharsalia, lib. vi. or vii.: Lucan (AD 39–65), Roman poet, whose historical epic *Pharsalia* recounts the civil war between Julius Caesar and Pompey. Erichtho is a Thessalian sorceress introduced in Book VI, where she uses her powers of necromancy to foretell the outcome of the impending battle.

135 *Phoenix*: a mythical bird, said to perish in the flames of a funeral pyre only to resurrect itself from its own ashes.

regressus: cf. Coleridge in *Biographia Literaria*, i. 284: 'the self-consciousness may be the modification of a higher form of being, perhaps of a higher consciousness, and this again of a yet higher, and so on in an infinite regressus'.

Dr Faustus: a widely travelled German necromancer or astrologer who died about 1540, and who passed into legend as the man who sold his soul to the devil in exchange for power and knowledge. His story inspired the play *The Tragicall History of Dr Faustus* (1604) by Christopher Marlowe (1564–93), and *Faust* (Part 1, 1808; Part 2, 1832) by Goethe.

well-known passage in Prometheus: Aeschylus, *Prometheus Bound*, 89–90. In the drama, Prometheus steals fire from the gods and gives it to humans. Zeus punishes him by chaining him to a rock and sending an eagle to eat out his liver, which constantly replaces itself.

136 *diplomata*: 'an original document as a matter of historical investigation or literary study' (*OED*, which cites this example from De Quincey).

lady . . . of unusually great age: De Quincey's mother, Elizabeth Quincey (see above, p. 288). She was about 70 years old when De Quincey published his *Confessions* in 1821, and around 95 when *Suspiria* appeared in 1845.

136 *she had become religious to asceticism*: Elizabeth Quincey's religious views were 'precisely those' of 'the Clapham Saints', a group of evangelical Christians that campaigned for the abolition of the slave trade, and that promoted missionary work at home and abroad (*Works*, xix. 273).

twinkling of an eye: see above, p. 291.

destined Apostle on his road to Damascus: Acts 22: 6–12: Saul of Tarsus (AD *c*.10–*c*.67), later St Paul, was a bitter enemy of Christianity. Jesus appeared to him 'in a great light' on the road to Damascus, and converted him to a life of service in the Christian church.

138 *Levana*: the Roman goddess of newborn babies. Her name (from the Latin *levare* 'to lift') derives from the tradition of the mother placing her new-born child on the ground, and of the father picking it up to show that he accepts it as his own, and does not intend to harm it. De Quincey draws from St Augustine, *City of God*, iv. 11. He also has in mind Jean Paul Richter (see above, p. 296), who in 1807 published *Levana; or, the Doctrine of Education* (London: Bell, 1876), 75: 'The first part of this work treats at large of the budding, the second and third of the blossoming, season of childhood,' Richter declares. '. . . May LEVANA, the motherly goddess who was formerly entreated to give a father's heart to fathers, hear the prayer which the title of this book addresses to her.'

139 *covet any man's ox nor his ass*: see Exodus 20: 17.

Wordsworth . . . day and night: Wordsworth, 'Conclusion. To ———', 9–11: 'Life flies: now every day | Is but a glimmering spoke in the swift wheel | Of the revolving week.'

Euclid . . . universally . . . genus: Euclid (*fl.* 300 BC), the most significant mathematician of the ancient world, is celebrated for his treatise on geom-etry, the *Elements*.

world: perhaps a misprint for 'word'.

on the foundation: on a scholarship.

I speak of what I know: De Quincey's good friend Lord Westport was a student at Eton (see above, p. 271), and at one point De Quincey's mother thought seriously of sending him there. But the thought seems genuinely to have frightened De Quincey. 'You may judge of the Discipline of the School', he told his mother, 'when I tell you that a week ago they beat an old Porter (in defiance of the Masters, some of whom were standing by and hardly trying to prevent them) with such brutality that his life I hear, is despaired of.—My situation, as a Boy on the foundation would be still more miserable' (Morrison, 45–6).

140 *Graces are three*: see above, p. 266.

Parcae are three: the three 'Fates', anthropomorphized by the Greeks and Romans as spinners, one of whom measures, one of whom spins, and one of whom cuts the thread of life.

Furies are three: Alecto, Megaera, and Tisiphone, the goddesses of retribution.

Muses were but three: the Muses—usually nine in number—were patrons of the arts and sciences.

harp and timbrel, by dulcimer and organ: a 'timbrel' is like a tambourine; a 'dulcimer' is a stringed instrument played with hammers. De Quincey recalls Job 21: 12: 'They take the timbrel and harp, and rejoice at the sound of the organ.'

telegraphed: signalled, either with a semaphore (an apparatus for visual signalling), or with an electric telegraph (used in Britain from the 1830s onwards).

141 *She stood in Rama . . . not unmarked in heaven*: Matthew 2: 16–18. Herod (73–4 BC), king of Judaea, slaughtered the children of Bethlehem shortly before his own death.

the Czar: Nicholas I (1796–1855), Russian emperor, whose youngest daughter, Grand Duchess Alexandra, married on 28 January 1844 and died on 10 August of the same year. She was diagnosed with tuberculosis shortly before her wedding day, and died, at 19, after going into labour three months prematurely.

Ganges . . . Nile . . . Mississippi: the great rivers of, respectively, India, Egypt, and America.

142 *Pariah*: originally, a member of the lowest caste in South India; more generally, a social outcast.

English criminal . . . Norfolk island: the most desperate criminals from the British convict settlements in Australia were sent to Norfolk Island in the south-western Pacific Ocean, 1,000 miles north-east of Sydney. The prison—notorious for the brutality of its punishments—closed in 1855.

143 *tents of Shem*: Genesis 9: 27.

Cybèle: an ancient oriental and Graeco-Roman deity known as 'Mother of the Gods'. Her priests worshipped her with bloody cultic ceremonies. In art she often appeared with a mural crown and veil. Cf. Milton, *Arcades*, 21–2: 'the towered Cybele, | Mother of a hundred gods'.

as near as a Greek word could come: De Quincey's notion of the sublime was fundamentally indebted to Christian mysteries such as the idea of sin and the infinity of God. 'All the moral theories of antiquity were utterly disjoined from religion,' he insisted in 1846. '. . . It is the anachronism of unconsciously reflecting back upon the ancient religions of darkness, and as if essential to *all* religions, features that never were suspected as possible, until they had been revealed in Christianity' (*Works*, xv. 348).

Eumenides: see above, p. 273.

144 *it rehearses or prefigures their course*: De Quincey makes no attempt to follow this plan.

THE APPARITION OF THE BROCKEN: according to the manuscript in the New York Public Library, before this dream episode on 'The Apparition of the Brocken', De Quincey intended to insert a separate prefatory essay on 'The Dark Interpreter' (see above, Appendix B, pp. 243–6).

144 *Whitsunday*: or Pentecost Sunday, is celebrated on the seventh Sunday after Easter, and commemorates the descent of the Holy Spirit on the Apostles. It was a traditional time for baptisms, and became known as 'White Sunday' (Whitsunday) because of the white clothing worn by the newly baptized.

Brocken of North Germany: the highest peak in the Harz Mountains.

145 *'Spectre of the Brocken'*: an atmospheric phenomenon that occurs when the shadow of a person standing on the Brocken is cast by the sun upon the adjacent clouds. An optical illusion causes the observer's shadow to appear enormously enlarged.

Sir David Brewster's 'Natural Magic': De Quincey is indebted to David Brewster (see above, p. 301), *Letters on Natural Magic: Addressed to Sir Walter Scott* (London: Murray, 1834), 128: 'From the earliest periods of authentic history, the Brocken has been the seat of the marvellous. On its summits are still seen huge blocks of granite called the Sorcerer's Chair and the Altar. A spring of pure water is known by the name of the Magic Fountain, and the Anemone of the Brocken is distinguished by the title of the Sorcerer's Flower. These names are supposed to have originated in the rites of the great Idol Cortho, whom the Saxons worshipped in secret on the summit of the Brocken, when Christianity was extending her benignant sway over the subjacent plains.'

Lady Echo of Ovid: in Greek mythology, the nymph Echo hides from Narcissus, and is only able to repeat back to him portions of what he calls to her. When she finally does reveal herself, Narcissus rejects her, and she pines away to bodiless invisibility (see Ovid, *Metamorphoses*, iii. 358–401).

Coleridge . . . failed to see the phantom: Coleridge ascended the Brocken twice: once on Monday, 13 May 1799 (the day after Whitsunday); and again on Sunday, 24 June 1799. On both occasions he failed to see the spectre. See Coleridge, *Letters*, i. 504: 'On the first day of May all the Witches dance here at midnight & those who go may see their own Ghosts walking up & down.'

'And art thou . . . that which he pursues': Coleridge, 'Constancy to an Ideal Object', 25–32. In the published version, the last two lines read, 'The enamoured rustic worships its fair hues, | Nor knows, he *makes* the shadow, he pursues!' De Quincey, however, is working from a 'corrected copy', though it is not clear whether he means a corrected copy of the printed text, or a corrected manuscript version.

147 *Judaea (on the Roman coins)*: the Roman emperor Vespasian (AD 9–79) struck special coins to commemorate the capture and destruction of Jerusalem by his son Titus (39–81). The coins showed Judea as a woman sitting sorrowfully beneath a palm tree (see Paul Mallinson, 'De Quincey's Ann in Judea', *Notes and Queries*, 27 (1980), 505–7).

the Danube: the second longest river in Europe, it rises in Germany, flows through eight other countries, and empties into the Black Sea.

parhelion: 'a bright spot in the sky, often associated with a solar halo and often occurring in pairs on either side of the sun . . . a mock sun' (*OED*).

Phantasus: in Graeco-Roman mythology, Hypnos, the god of sleep, has three sons. The first, Morpheus, brought human shapes to the dreamer. The other two, Phobetor and Phantasus, sent animals and inanimate things, respectively.

148 *'And . . . hail, ran along upon the ground'*: see Psalm 105: 32 and Exodus 9: 23–4. First performed in 1739, *Israel in Egypt* is one of the most celebrated oratorios of George Frederick Handel (see above, p. 291).

Greek chorus . . . not quite understood by critics: 'One great error which remains to be removed, is the notion that the chorus either did support, or was meant to support the office of a moral teacher,' De Quincey wrote in 1840. 'The chorus simply stood on the level of a sympathizing spectator, detached from the business and interests of the action; and its office was to guide or to interpret the sympathies of the audience' (*Works*, xi. 501).

Savannah-la-Mar: a coastal town and port on the south-western shore of Jamaica. It was destroyed by a hurricane in 1780.

Pompeii: ancient Italian city near Naples destroyed by the violent eruption of Mount Vesuvius in AD 79.

149 *Fata-Morgana*: a mirage periodically observed in the Strait of Messina between Italy and Sicily, and named after Morgan le Fay, a fairy enchantress of Arthurian romance.

jubilates: a joyous song. In the Vulgate, 'jubilate' ('rejoice') is the first word of Psalm 100.

clepsydra: water-clock.

150 *sanctus*: Isaiah 6: 3: 'Sanctus, sanctus, sanctus' ('Holy, holy, holy'). The words are spoken or sung before the administration of the sacrament at Holy Communion or Mass.

END OF PART I: the third instalment of *Suspiria* ended here.

151 *Mozart or Beethoven*: Wolfgang Amadeus Mozart (1756–91), Austrian composer. Ludwig van Beethoven (1770–1827), German composer.

'male and female created he them': Genesis 1: 27.

'in to-day already walks to-morrow': Coleridge, *The Death of Wallenstein*, v. i. 102.

152 *a part*: perhaps a misprint for 'in part'.

retiarius: a gladiator who fought with a net designed to trap his opponent.

154 *a banker . . . to his house*: Henry Gee, a banker, lived in Lincolnshire (see above, p. 265).

155 *Facit indignatio versum*: Juvenal (see above, p. 272), *Satires*, i. 79: 'indignation will inspire my poetry'.

'Te nimis . . . insector Satyrae reboante flagello': 'You, too stern one, who destroys the covenants of a sacred table, I harry with satire's resounding lash.'

155 *'mea saeva querela . . . hybernâ nocte procellam'*: 'My fierce complaint
alights on wax-plugged ears which will not hear the wintry night's
tempest.'

stylites: the Stylites were solitary ascetics, especially prominent in the
East Mediterranean Christian world of the fourth and fifth centuries.
They lived on platforms placed on top of pillars (from the Greek *stylos*),
and were thus venerated as exemplary critics of the luxurious excesses
of their age.

156 *a great public school*: De Quincey has misremembered the date. He entered
Bath Grammar School in late 1796, when he was 11 years old (see above,
p. 266).

bracing intercourse . . . English classical school: De Quincey's claim is surprising given the anxiety he felt at the possibility of attending Eton (see
above, p. 306).

small private schools . . . masters: De Quincey is thinking especially of
Winkfield School in Wiltshire, where he was a student for one year (see
above, p. 266).

areopagus: the supreme tribunal of Athens.

graduation: De Quincey means his formal entry into the school, rather
than his formal departure from it.

Mordecai the Jew: see Esther 6: 2–11. Mordecai is one of the chief ministers of King Ahasuerus, reigned 486–465 BC. He saves the king from an
assassination attempt. In response, Ahasuerus 'delighteth to honour'
Mordecai.

157 *no male relatives but . . . those in India*: De Quincey's uncle Thomas Penson
(d. 1835) was the brother of his mother, and a lieutenant in Bengal in the
service of the East India Company.

Sophocles: see above, p. 266.

aposiopesis: 'a rhetorical artifice, in which the speaker comes to a sudden
halt, as if unable or unwilling to proceed' (*OED*, which cites this example
from De Quincey).

158 *illness affecting my head*: the root of this illness seems to be De Quincey's
powerful identification with his sister Elizabeth, and his ongoing grief
over her death. 'At present I doubt whether in reality anything very serious
had happened,' he acknowledged in 1853. 'In fact, I was always under a
nervous panic for my head; and certainly exaggerated my internal feelings
without meaning to do so; and this misled the medical attendants' (*Works*,
xix. 95).

159 *public school of ancient foundation*: Manchester Grammar School, which
De Quincey entered on 9 November 1800 (see above, p. 266).

literature of my native land: De Quincey is thinking especially of his reading of the 1798 *Lyrical Ballads* of Wordsworth and Coleridge. It was, he
later remarked, 'the greatest event in the unfolding of my own mind'
(*Works*, x. 287).

my guardians . . . £200 per annum: De Quincey tells a very different story in his *Confessions* (see above, p. 26).

160 *I did not condescend to answer*: De Quincey did in fact respond to some of the critics who questioned the veracity of his *Confessions*, most notably in his 'Letter to the Editor of the *London Magazine*' (see above Appendix A, pp. 227–30). Cf. also the evening when fellow *London* contributor Charles Lamb (1775–1834) began 'a sort of playful attack' on him about the *Confessions*, and 'added something in a jeering but good humoured way' about Ann and Oxford Street (Woodhouse, 22).

twenty-two years . . . objection . . . notice it: De Quincey refers to William Maginn (1794–1842), reckless Irish satirist and key *Blackwood's* contributor. In 1824 (not 'twenty-two' but twenty-one years before the publication of *Suspiria*) Maginn viciously attacked De Quincey and his 'ultra-lying' *Confessions* in the first issue of the *John Bull Magazine*, 21–4. For example, in the *Confessions* De Quincey calls his wife Margaret his 'beloved . . . Electra'. 'The truth of the business is', Maginn sneered in response, 'that this Electra . . . was his servant-maid long before he married her.' De Quincey's claim, however, that he had not 'condescend[ed] to notice' Maginn's abuse is untrue, for he had already discussed the episode in an 1841 *Tait's Magazine* article, where he describes his feelings on first reading Maginn's attack: 'upwards I looked to the clouds, downwards to the earth, for vengeance. I trembled with excessive wrath . . . had I possessed forty thousand lives, all, and every one individually, I would have sacrificed in vindication of her that was thus cruelly libelled' (*Works*, xi. 294).

inter alia: 'among other things'.

161 *a disreputable attorney in London*: Mr Brunell | Brown (see above, p. 269).

young Earl of A———t: the Earl of Altamont (see above, p. 271).

Oxford Street . . . could be so situated: Maginn, *John Bull Magazine*, 1 (1824), 24: 'Now, we happen to know Oxford-street well, and must be permitted to doubt the existence, in that quarter, of such a house and household. . . . We must humbly request from Quincy the *number* of the house in which he, and his friend Ann, used to spend their evenings.'

162 *the Herod being dead*: Herod (see above, p. 307) was notorious for his cruelty. Maginn died in August 1842, two and a half years before *Suspiria* began to appear.

solatium: compensation for loss, suffering, or injured feelings.

Sus. per coll.: *Suspendatur per collum*: 'Let him be hanged by the neck'.

Newgate: the main prison in London from the thirteenth till the nineteenth century.

same affliction that Gibbon . . . dreaded so much: not the same affliction, in fact. Edward Gibbon (1737–94), scholar and historian, closed the first volume of his celebrated *History of the Decline and Fall of the Roman Empire* (1776–88) with two chapters that dealt sceptically with the rise of Christianity, and then defended himself against charges of irreligion in his masterly *Vindication of some Passages in the Fifteenth and Sixteenth Chapters* (1779). It was this *Vindication* that he did not wish to see published together with the *History*, as he made clear in his posthumously published *Memoirs*; see John Holroyd, first Earl of Sheffield (1741–1821), *Miscellaneous Works of Edward Gibbon . . . with Memoirs of his Life and Writings*, 3 vols. (Dublin: Wogan, White, Chambers, 1796), i. 153: 'I would not print this Vindication in quarto, lest it should be bound and preserved with the history itself.'

162 *Old Bailey*: London's central criminal court.

163 *attorney's having at least found his way to Australia*: that is, as a transported criminal.

yard-arm to yard-arm: to fight at close proximity.

fierce as famine and hungry as the grave: De Quincey echoes James Thomson (see above, p. 284), 'Winter', 393: 'Cruel as death, and hungry as the grave!'

half-a-crown . . . a shilling: a crown was 5 shillings.

164 *and I wished to * * **: it is not known what was removed from the text at this point.

caravanserai: in Eastern countries, a large quadrangular inn with a court in the middle.

165 *her Majesty's coronation*: Queen Victoria's coronation was on 28 June 1838.

166 *Agrippina*: Agrippina the Elder (14 BC–AD 33) was the wife of Germanicus Caesar (15 BC–AD 19), and the mother of the emperor Caligula (AD 12–41). The Roman historian Tacitus (AD 56–*c.*120) celebrates her beauty and spirit in his *Annals*, I. xxxiii: Agrippina's 'temper was not without a hint of fire, though purity of mind and wifely devotion kept her rebellious spirit on the side of righteousness'.

168 *'a pearl richer than all his tribe'*: Shakespeare, *Othello*, V. ii. 347–8.

169 *'open sesame!'*: the magic password that opens and shuts the door of the robbers' den in the tale of 'Ali Baba and the Forty Thieves' in *The Arabian Nights' Entertainment* (see above, pp. 302–3).

170 *Ayah*: Hindu nurse or maidservant employed by European families living in India and other parts of South Asia.

'THE ENGLISH MAIL-COACH'

173 *Oxford, Mr Palmer, M.P. for Bath*: De Quincey matriculated at Worcester College, Oxford, in 1803. He left five years later without taking a degree. In 1784, John Palmer (1742–1818), a theatre manager in Bath and Bristol, and William Pitt (1759–1806), then Chancellor of the Exchequer, arranged the first trial mail-coach run. It was highly successful, and other mail-coach routes were quickly established. Palmer became Comptroller General of the Post Office in 1786. He was MP for Bath, 1801–7.

Lady Madeline Gordon: De Quincey has his facts confused, though understandably. John Palmer was married first to Sarah Mason, and then, in November 1786, to a Miss Pratt (d. 1807). Their eldest son, Charles Palmer (1777–1851), was MP for Bath, 1808–26, 1830–7. Lady Madelina Gordon (*c.*1772–1847) was the fourth child of Alexander Gordon, fourth Duke of Gordon (1743–1827), and Jane Maxwell (*c.*1748–1812). Her second husband was Charles Fyshe Palmer (1769–1842), MP for Reading, 1818–37. Thus, for a considerable period of time, there were two MPs named Charles Palmer: one was the eldest son of the postal reformer; the other was the second husband of the Duke of Gordon's daughter.

Galileo . . . satellites of Jupiter: Galileo (1564–1642), Italian mathematician, astronomer, and physicist. He discovered four of Jupiter's satellites in 1610. He did not marry.

174 *Trafalgar . . . Salamanca . . . Vittoria . . . Waterloo*: decisive British victories in the Napoleonic Wars. Horatio Nelson (1758–1805) destroyed the French fleet in the Battle of Trafalgar (1805). Arthur Wellesley (1769–1852), later the Duke of Wellington, won dramatic battles at Salamanca (1812) and Vitoria (1813). Napoleon (1769–1821) was finally defeated at Waterloo (1815).

Te Deums: a Christian Latin hymn sung on occasions of public thanksgiving, and often at morning prayer in the Church of England. The opening words are 'Te Deum laudamus' ('We praise thee, O Lord').

intermitting communication with Oxford . . . fellows: De Quincey himself was only intermittently in Oxford during his years as an undergraduate, and sometimes was absent for six months together (Morrison, 114). A 'fellow' is the name given to the 'incorporated members' of an Oxford college (*OED*).

Act: an old name for Trinity (summer) term at Oxford, and derived from the 'act' or thesis submitted for a degree.

going down: it is 'up' to Oxford, and 'down' to all other towns and cities.

175 *four inside people . . . Charles II*: Charles II (1630–85), reigned 1660–85. Traditionally, mail-coaches carried four passengers on the inside and three (including the driver) on the outside.

delf ware: cheap glazed earthenware, originally from Delft in Holland. It is much coarser than porcelain.

attaint: 'to infect with corruption, poison, etc.' (*OED*).

assizes: sessions of the superior courts held periodically in each county of England for the purpose of administering criminal and civil justice.

delirium tremens: 'a species of delirium induced by excessive indulgence in alcoholic liquors' (*OED*).

salle-à-manger: dining room.

maxim . . . same logical construction: De Quincey's free translation of the Roman legal phrase 'De non apparentibus et non existentibus eadem est lex'.

176 *'raff'*: persons of the lowest class.

'Snobs' ... *'nobs'*: a 'snob' was 'a shoemaker or cobbler'; as a piece of university slang, a 'snob' also meant 'any one not a gownsman; a townsman'. A 'nob' was 'a person of some wealth or social distinction' (*OED*).

Great wits jump: a proverbial phrase meaning 'men of great minds arrive independently at the same conclusions'. Cf. Laurence Sterne (1713–68) in *Tristram Shandy* (1759–67), ed. Ian Campbell Ross (Oxford: Oxford University Press, 1998), 132: 'GREAT wits jump: for the moment Dr *Slop* cast his eyes upon his bag ... the very same thought occurred.'

celestial intellect of China: De Quincey is punning. One of the names for China is 'Tien Chan' ('Celestial Empire').

177 *George III ... Lord Macartney*: in 1792, George III (1738–1820) appointed George Macartney, Earl Macartney (1737–1806), as first British emissary to Peking (now Beijing). De Quincey's anecdote, however, is fictitious. He embellished it from a single sentence in Sir George Staunton (1737–1801), *An Authentic Account of an Embassy from the King of Great Britain to the Emperor of China*, 3 vols. (London: Nicol, 1797), ii. 343: 'When a splendid chariot intended as a present for the Emperor was unpacked and put together, nothing could be more admired; but it was necessary to give directions for taking off the box; for when the mandarines found out that so elevated a seat was destined for the coachman ... they expressed the utmost astonishment that it should be proposed to place any man in a situation *above* the Emperor.'

the emperor: Ch'ien-lung (1711–99), fourth emperor of the Ch'ing dynasty, reigned 1735–96.

hammer-cloth: 'a cloth covering the driver's seat or "box" in a state or family coach' (*OED*).

first lord of the treasury: in England, the Prime Minister.

flowery people: one of the Chinese names for China is 'Chung Hwa Kwoh' ('Middle Flowery Kingdom').

checkstrings ... jury-reins: a 'checkstring' is 'a string by which the occupant of a carriage may signal to the driver to stop' (*OED*). A 'jury-rein' is a 'temporary rein'.

Fo, Fo ... Fi, Fi: there is no Chinese God 'Fo, Fo', but De Quincey may be playing on 'Fu Xi', the name of the first of China's mythical emperors.

Ca ira: properly 'Ça ira' ('That will succeed'). The expression, many times repeated, comprised about half the words of a revolutionary song that later became the official song of the French Revolution. It is said to have originated on 5 October 1789 when the French mob marched to Versailles to bring the King and royal family to Paris.

178 *chief seats in synagogues*: Matthew 23: 6: 'And love the uppermost rooms at feasts, and the chief seats in the Synagogues'.

Aristotle's, Cicero's: Aristotle was the author of the *Nicomachean Ethics*, and founded the Peripatetic school of philosophy. Cicero wrote several ethical treatises, of which the most noted is the *De Officiis*.

Euclid . . . five shillings to sixpence: for Euclid, see above, p. 306. Formerly, in British currency, a shilling was worth twelve pence.

bills . . . noters and protesters: De Quincey's reference is to a 'bill of exchange' such as an IOU for a loan. When a bill came due, the debtor either had to pay, or to face the possibility of imprisonment. Bills were negotiable. A 'protested' bill meant that someone had refused to accept it, in which case the bill was 'noted' as worthless. De Quincey knew all about this process, and on at least three occasions was jailed for debt.

posse: 'posse comitatus' (literally, 'the power of the county') is a legal term for the band of assistants which may be summoned by a sheriff.

179 *snakes in Von Troil's Iceland*: De Quincey is wrong. He thought the laconic chapter on snakes appeared in Uno Von Troil (1746–1803), *Letters on Iceland* (London: Richardson, 1780). But it is actually in Niels Horrebow (1712–60), *The Natural History of Iceland* (London: Linde, 1758), 91: '*Concerning snakes*. No snakes of any kind are to be met with throughout the whole island.'

parliamentary rat: an MP who leaves his own party and joins the opposition.

Exeter . . . Devonport: Exeter is in Devon in south-western England. Devonport is either the district of Devonport (known as 'Plymouth Dock' until 1824) in the city of Plymouth in Devon; or the city of Devonport on the northern coast of Tasmania, Australia.

Jack: 'Jack Tar' was a common nickname for men of the Royal Navy.

forbidden seat: in his 1854 revisions, De Quincey appended a lengthy footnote to this passage. 'The very sternest code of rules was enforced upon the mails by the Post-office,' he begins. 'Throughout England, only three outsides were allowed, of whom one was to sit on the box, and the other two immediately behind the box; none, under any pretext, to come near the guard' (see *Works*, xvi. 726).

laesa majestas: 'violated majesty'; a crime committed against the sovereign power in a state.

boot: 'The receptacle for luggage or parcels under the seats of the guard and coachman' (*OED*).

'Jam proximus ardet | Ucalegon': Virgil, *Aeneid*, ii. 311–12. The lines are taken from the description, given by Aeneas to Dido, of the destruction of Troy: 'Even now the spacious house of Deiphobus has fallen, as the fire-god towers above; even now his neighbour Ucalegon blazes.'

way-bill: the list of passengers booked on the coach.

180 *crane-neck quarterings*: urgent manoeuvres to remove vehicles from the path of oncoming traffic. The crane-neck was a curved iron rod diagonally

connecting the back and front axles of a cart. It pivoted to allow turning in the smallest possible space.

180 *attainder*: the deprivation of the rights of a person convicted of a felony and sentenced to death or outlawry. The blood of the attainted person was regarded as corrupted, and the person could neither inherit land nor pass it on to an heir.

benefit of clergy: formerly under English law, all persons in holy orders, and ultimately all persons who could read, might, by pleading 'benefit of clergy', be exempted from criminal punishment at the hands of a secular judge. The right survived for some offences until 1827.

Quarter Sessions: a general court held quarterly by the Justices of the Peace of each county, and having jurisdiction over all but the highest crimes.

having authority: De Quincey invokes Matthew 7: 29: 'For he taught them as one having authority, and not as the scribes.'

levied upon the hundred: charged to the hundred, 'a subdivision of a county or shire, having its own court' (*OED*).

lying poached: De Quincey is punning on 'poached eggs', usually produced with boiling water, but here the result of being 'poached' ('stamped down with the feet') by horses' hoofs.

Napoleon . . . Desaix, never were uttered at all: Louis-Charles-Antoine Desaix de Veygoux (1768–1800), French military hero killed at the Battle of Marengo in northern Italy. When Napoleon heard of his death, he is reported to have said, 'Alas! it is not permitted to me to weep' (John Gibson Lockhart, *The History of Napoleon Buonaparte*, ed. J. Holland Rose (London: Oxford University Press, 1916), 154).

Vengeur . . . Cambronne . . . 'La Garde . . . pas': Richard Howe, Earl Howe (1726–99), commanded the British fleet in the 'Glorious First of June' victory of 1794, capturing six French ships and sinking a seventh, the *Vengeur*, which was reported to have gone down with her streamers flying and her crew all shouting, 'Vive la République'. Pierre Cambronne (1770–1842), French general, commanded Napoleon's Old Guard, which was decimated at the Battle of Waterloo. His 'vaunt' was 'The Guards die, but do not surrender'. He later denied using the phrase.

the repartees of Talleyrand: Charles-Maurice, prince de Talleyrand-Périgord (1754–1838), diplomat and statesman noted for his wit and remarkable capacity for political survival.

181 *à fortiori*: with greater reason or more convincing force.

Holyhead . . . Shrewsbury and Oswestry: for Holyhead, see above, p. 268. Shrewsbury and Oswestry are in Shropshire, a county in western England that borders on Wales.

Tallyho or Highflier: 'Tally-ho' was 'originally, the proper name given to a fast day-coach between London and Birmingham, started in 1823' (*OED*). A 'Highflier' was another fast stagecoach.

tombs of Luxor: Luxor is on the east bank of the Nile. It includes part of the ruins of ancient Thebes, and is rich in tombs with hieroglyphic inscriptions.

jacobinical: the Jacobins were extreme democrats in the French Revolution, and so called because they held their meetings in the former convent of the Jacobin friars in Paris.

'which they upon the adverse faction wanted': Shakespeare, *Richard III*, v. iii. 12–13: 'Besides, the King's name is a tower of strength, | Which they upon the adverse faction want.'

182 *cat might look at a king*: James Davies, 'Proverbs, ancient and modern', *Quarterly Review*, 125 (1868), 231: ' "A cat may look at a king" is but a modern way of putting the Greek adage, "You're nothing sacred" '.

Brummagem: a contemptuous name for Birmingham.

very fine story . . . elder dramatists: Thomas Heywood (*c*.1573–1641), actor and playwright, *The Royal King and the Loyal Subject*, v. v. De Quincey, however, probably knew the story from its inclusion by Charles Lamb in his *Specimens of the English Dramatic Poets* (1808), where it appears under the title 'Noble Traitor' (*The Works of Charles and Mary Lamb*, ed. E. V. Lucas, 7 vols. (London: Methuen, 1903–5), iv. 88–9).

10th of Edward III chap. 15: Edward III (1312–77), king of England, 1327–77. No such statute exists.

183 *fifty miles in the hour . . . York . . . London*: fifty miles an hour for four hours would almost cover the distance from London to York, but no train in mid-Victorian England could travel this fast.

Non magna loquimur . . . magna vivimus: in his 1854 revision, De Quincey translated this phrase as 'we do not make verbal ostentation of our grandeurs, we realise our grandeurs in act, and in the very experience of life'.

Nile nor Trafalgar: at the Battle of the Nile (1798), the English fleet under Nelson routed the French under Napoleon. For Trafalgar, see above, p. 313.

184 *Marlborough Forest*: Marlborough is in Wiltshire, and on the old high road between London and Bath.

185 *excelled myself in personal advantages*: De Quincey was highly conscious of his personal appearance (see above, p. 285).

Ulysses . . . accursed bow . . . suitors: in Homer, *Odyssey*, xxi–xxii, Ulysses slays the suitors of his wife, Penelope, using his magic bow.

mais oui donc: 'but of course'.

'Say, all our praises' . . . 'Say, all our roses . . . engross': Alexander Pope (1688–1744), 'Epistle to Allen Lord Bathurst', 249: 'But all our praises why should lords engross?'

186 *Jovian*: Jove, also called Jupiter, was the chief Roman god.

silver turrets: in 1854, De Quincey appended a footnote to this phrase. 'As one who loves and venerates Chaucer for his unrivalled merits of tenderness, of picturesque characterisation, and of narrative skill,' he writes, 'I noticed with great pleasure that the word *torrettes* is used by him to designate the little devices through which the reins are made to pass. This same word, in the same exact sense, I heard uniformly used by many scores of illustrious mail-coachmen, to whose confidential friendship I had the honour of being admitted in my younger days.' De Quincey seems to have in mind Chaucer, 'The Knight's Tale', 2152 (*Works*, xvi. 732).

187 *ex abundanti*: 'out of an abundance'.

guardianship of Chancery: the Court of Chancery was the court of equity under the Lord High Chancellor. It was abolished in 1873.

Mr Waterton: Charles Waterton (1782–1865), naturalist, best known for *Wanderings in South America* (1825).

cayman: or 'caiman', Central and South American reptiles related to alligators.

the crocodile . . . is to be ridden: De Quincey refers to Waterton's account of crocodile riding in *Wanderings in South America*: 'By the time the Cayman was within two yards of me, I saw he was in a state of fear and perturbation; I instantly dropped the mast, sprung up, and jumped on his back, turning half round as I vaulted, so that I gained my seat with my face in the right position. I immediately seized his legs, and, by main force, twisted them on his back; thus they served me for a bridle. . . . Should it be asked, how I managed to keep my seat, I would answer,—I hunted some years with Lord Darlington's fox hounds' (cited in Grevel Lindop, 'De Quincey and the Cursed Crocodile', *Essays in Criticism*, 45 (1995), 130). De Quincey may also have in mind Percy Shelley, 'The Mask of Anarchy', 24–5: 'Like Sidmouth, next, Hypocrisy | On a crocodile rode by.'

188 *rose in June*: cf. Wordsworth, 'Strange Fits of Passion I have Known', 5–6: 'When she I loved was strong and gay, | And like a rose in June'.

driving four-in-hand: driving a coach drawn by four horses.

sorrowful admonition, upwards to heaven: in 1854, De Quincey deleted the rest of this paragraph, a deep cut of over 1,000 words that removed one of the most celebrated passages of the 1849 version.

190 *kraken*: a vast mythical sea-monster.

monokeras: the Greek form of 'monoceros', a unicorn. It is not clear which one-horned animal De Quincey has in mind, but it may be the rhinoceros.

shield that embalms it: the lion and the unicorn are heraldic symbols of the United Kingdom, and appear on the royal coat of arms.

Spenser . . . our elder poets: Edmund Spenser (see above, p. 304), *The Faerie Queene*, I. iii. 5–7.

Warwick . . . lion called Wallace: in 1825, George Wombwell (1777–1850) staged two fights between a lion and a number of dogs in the 'Old Factory Yard' in the suburbs of Warwick. The first fight involved a lion named

Nero, who 'was merely a sufferer' and 'never struck a blow' (*The Times*, 28 July 1825, p. 2, cols. D–E). In the second contest, however, a lion named Wallace mauled the dogs: 'Wombwell has, notwithstanding the strong expression of public indignation which accompanied the exposure of the lion Nero to the six dogs, kept his word with the lovers of cruel sports. . . . He matched his "Wallace," a fine lion, cubbed in Scotland, against six of the best dogs that could be found. . . . In the 1st round . . . [Wallace] clapped his paw upon poor *Ball*, took *Tinker* in his teeth, and deliberately walked round the stage with him as a cat would with a mouse' (*The Times*, 1 August 1825, p. 3, col. E).

Southey: Southey and De Quincey were Lake District neighbours and, for a few years, spent a good deal of time together (Morrison, 151).

poor-rates: government measures for relief or support of the poor.

191 *baubling schooner*: De Quincey probably has in mind Shakespeare, *Twelfth Night*, v. i. 54: 'A baubling vessel was he captain of'.

Soult . . . Majesty's coronation . . . Manchester: Nicolas-Jean de Dieu Soult, duc de Dalmatie (1769–1851) was commander of French armies in the Peninsular War (1808–14). After Napoleon's defeat, he became a royalist and represented the French government at the Coronation of Queen Victoria. He visited Manchester on 21 July 1838, as described in *The Times*, 23 July 1838, p. 6, col. B: after touring various parts of the city, the marshal and his party 'proceeded to the Union Club House, where an elegant collation was provided . . . On his arrival here he was warmly greeted by the members of the club, and an address from the Chamber of Commerce was presented to him, to which he promised to return a written answer.'

en flagrant delit.: from the Latin *flagrante delicto*, 'in flagrant transgression'.

Albuera . . . bloodiest of recorded battles: in May 1811, Soult was defeated with heavy losses at Albuera in south-western Spain. It was one of the fiercest battles of the Napoleonic Wars. In the weeks that followed, however, Soult spoke confidently of his own troops, and contemptuously of the British: 'A month has not elapsed since your arms were crowned with triumph on the plains of Albuera, and since the enemy trembled at the thunder of your artillery,' he told his forces. 'Discomfited, they fled, and left their cannon and their standards in your possession. Soon you shall have another opportunity of displaying your valour, if the English will venture to give it you; and, with another glorious and decisive victory, you shall terminate the war in the Peninsula' (*The Times*, 5 July 1811, p. 4, col. A).

at that time . . . General Post-Office: Lombard Street is in the City of London, and the centre of the money market. In 1829, the Lombard Street post office was replaced by a new post office in St Martin's le Grand, just north of St Paul's Cathedral.

attelage: equipage, team of horses.

192 *One heart . . . English blood*: cf. De Quincey in his 1831 *Blackwood's* essay on Samuel Parr: 'If ever, in this world, a nation had one heart and one soul, it was the British nation in the spring of 1803' (*Works*, viii. 92).

193 *Badajoz . . . Salamanca*: the Duke of Wellington stormed Badajoz in south-western Spain in 1812. He took Salamanca later that same year (see above, p. 313).

an American writer: untraced; possibly De Quincey's invention.

the Tiber: the second longest river in Italy. It flows through the city of Rome.

194 *Barnet*: originally a village in Hertfordshire; now a borough of Greater London.

glasses: see above, p. 294.

195 *Every joy . . . grief, to some*: cf. William Cowper's description of the postman in *The Task*, iv. 13–15: 'messenger of grief | Perhaps to thousands, and of joy to some'.

Courier . . . gazette: *The Courier* was a London evening paper established in 1792. 'The gazette' is 'one of the three official journals entitled the *London Gazette*, the *Edinburgh Gazette*, and the *Dublin Gazette*, issued by authority twice a week, and containing lists of government appointments and promotions . . . and other public notices' (*OED*).

fey: doomed or fated to die.

196 *Bengal lights*: 'a kind of firework producing a steady and vivid blue-coloured light, used for signals' (*OED*).

Talavera: on 27–8 July 1809 the Duke of Wellington (then Sir Arthur Wellesley) routed the French at Talavera in central Spain, but suffered heavy casualties and was forced to retreat soon afterwards.

23d Dragoons . . . one in four survived: in his account of the English charge, De Quincey may be drawing in part on William Francis Patrick Napier (1785–1860), *History of the War in the Peninsula* (1828–40), 6 vols. (London: Marne, 1892), ii. 175–6: 'Sir Arthur Wellesley immediately ordered Anson's brigade of cavalry, composed of the 23rd Light Dragoons and the 1st German Hussars, to charge the head of these columns; and this brigade, coming on at a canter, and increasing its speed as it advanced, rode headlong against the enemy, but in a few moments came upon the brink of a hollow cleft, which was not perceptible at a distance. The French, throwing themselves into squares, opened their fire; and Colonel Arenstchild, commanding the Hussars, an officer whom forty years' experience had made a master of his art, promptly reined up at the brink, exclaiming, in his broken English, "I will not kill my young mans." The English blood was hotter. The 23rd, under Colonel Seymour, rode wildly down into the hollow, and men and horses fell over each other in dreadful confusion. . . . Those who were not killed or taken made for Bassecour's Spanish division, and so escaped, leaving behind 207 men and officers, or about half the number that went into action.'

197 *aceldama*: Acts 1: 19: 'field of blood'.

    poor woman, kissed me.: the first instalment of 'The English Mail-Coach' ended here.

    ultimate object . . . Dream-Fugue: cf. De Quincey in 1838, when he described the dream finale in the *Confessions* as 'the real object of the whole work' (*Works*, x. 265).

198 *'That which should be most sudden'*: Suetonius (AD 69–after 122), *Lives of the Caesars*, i. 87: 'The day before his murder, in a conversation which arose . . . as to what manner of death was most to be desired, he had given his preference to one which was sudden and unexpected.'

    'From lightning . . . sudden death . . . deliver us': from 'The Litany' in the Book of Common Prayer.

199 *words or acts*: as De Quincey makes plain in his 1854 revisions, he means 'final' words or acts.

    simply of extra misfortune: in manuscript, De Quincey appended a footnote on gambling and intoxication to this passage (see above, Appendix C, p. 256).

    Βιαθανατος . . . Βιαιος: respectively, 'violent death' and 'violent'. De Quincey draws in this discussion on John Donne (1572–1631) and his casuistic defence of suicide, Βιαθανατος.

200 *twinkling of an eye*: see above, p. 291.

    lâcheté: cowardice.

201 *That dream . . . of lying down before him*: cf. De Quincey in the 1856 *Confessions*, where he describes the 'languishing impotence . . . most of us have felt in the dreams of our childhood when lying down without a struggle before some all-conquering lion' (*Works*, ii. 170).

    'Nature . . . all is lost': Milton, *Paradise Lost*, ix. 782–4: 'Earth felt the wound, and nature from her seat | Sighing through all her works gave signs of woe, | That all was lost.'

202 *Manchester post-office . . . considerably past midnight*: in 1854, De Quincey dramatically expanded the opening of this paragraph. 'The incident,' he writes, 'so memorable in itself by its features of horror, and so scenical by its grouping for the eye, which furnished the text for this reverie upon *Sudden Death*, occurred to myself in the dead of night, as a solitary spectator, when seated on the box of the Manchester and Glasgow mail, in the second or third summer after Waterloo. I find it necessary to relate the circumstances, because they are such as could not have occurred unless under a singular combination of accidents. In those days, the oblique and lateral communications with many rural post-offices were so arranged, either through necessity or through defect of system, as to make it requisite for the main north-western mail (*i.e.*, the *down* mail), on reaching Manchester, to halt for a number of hours; how many, I do not remember; six or seven, I think; but the result was, that, in the ordinary course, the mail recommenced its journey northwards about midnight. Wearied with

the long detention at a gloomy hotel, I walked out about eleven o'clock at night for the sake of fresh air; meaning to fall in with the mail and resume my seat at the post-office. The night, however, being yet dark, as the moon had scarcely risen, and the streets being at that hour empty, so as to offer no opportunities for asking the road, I lost my way; and did not reach the post-office until it was considerably past midnight' (*Works*, xvi. 740–1).

202 *Westmorland*: see above, p. 294.

mail was not even yet ready to start: De Quincey may have intended to insert a passage here on his habit of procrastination, which he calls one of 'the dark lines in the woof of his life' (see above Appendix C, pp. 256–7).

jus dominii . . . jus gentium: legal terms meaning, respectively, 'the law of ownership' and 'the law of nations'.

gas being a great ally of morality: the first street lighting using coal-gas was installed in Westminster, London, in 1814.

Effendi: 'a Turkish title of respect' (*OED*).

Stamboul: an ancient city first known as Byzantium, capital of the Byzantine Empire; then, Constantinople, capital of the Ottoman Empire; now Istanbul, the largest city in Turkey.

203 *Chrysippus . . . salt . . . for a soul*: Chrysippus (*c.*280–*c.*206 BC), Greek philosopher who regarded animals as created solely for the use of man. According to Cicero, *De Natura deorum*, II. lxiv. 160, Chrysippus held that 'its soul was given it to serve as salt and keep it from putrefaction'. De Quincey attributes the converse of this view to him.

son of Othman: a Turk; the Ottoman dynasty ruled Turkey from 1300 to 1922.

Dr Johnsons: Samuel Johnson published two well-known examinations of epitaphs: 'Essay on Epitaphs' (1740) and 'A Dissertation on Epitaphs Written by Pope' (1756).

Deodand: a fine charged against the owner of an object that has caused injury or death.

Morcellus: Stefano Antonio Morcelli (1737–1822), Italian antiquary and expert on Latin inscriptions, *De stilo Inscriptionum Latinarum* (1780).

204 *Virgil . . . 'Monstrum . . . lumen ademptum'*: Virgil, *Aeneid*, iii. 658: 'a monster awful, shapeless, huge, bereft of light'. The reference is to the Cyclops Polyphemus. The Cyclopes had only one eye in the centre of the forehead, and even this eye Polyphemus had lost in his battle with Odysseus (Homer, *Odyssey*, ix).

Calendars . . . Arabian Nights . . . curiosity: Calendars belonged to a religious order of Dervishes. The three Calendars in *The Arabian Nights' Entertainment* were princes in disguise. Each tells the story of how he lost his right eye. Only the third 'paid down his eye as the price of his criminal curiosity'.

Al Sirat . . . Mahomet: according to Muslim tradition, 'Al Sirat' is the bridge swinging over Hell, leading from Earth to Paradise. It was narrower than a hair and sharper than a sword. The righteous will pass safely; the wicked will fall into the abyss.

diphrelatic: 'relating to the driving of a chariot' (*OED*).

gage d'amitié: 'pledge of friendship'.

205 *irregularities caused by war*: De Quincey seems confused about the date of the accident. In his 1854 revisions, he states that it occurred 'in the second or third summer after Waterloo' (see above, p. 321). But here he points out that 'there is a large extra accumulation of foreign mails' because of the war.

packet-service . . . nothing is done by steam: the 'packet-service' was the boats that ran at regular intervals between two ports for the conveyance of mail. Steam travel was still approximately ten years away, for the first locomotive ran from Darlington to Stockton in September 1825.

eleven miles an hour: cf. De Quincey in his 1833 *Tait's Magazine* essay on Hannah More: 'In the year 1809 . . . even the Bristol mail, the swiftest in the kingdom, did not then perform much above seven miles an hour' (*Works*, ix. 333–4).

Kendal . . . Westmoreland: in 1849 Appleby was still the county town, though Kendal had long been the real commercial and administrative centre of Westmorland.

206 *aurigation*: 'The action or art of driving a chariot or coach' (*OED*).

Apollo . . . horses of Aurora: the horses of the dawn, which pulled the chariot of the Greek sun-god Apollo.

'Love amongst the Roses': presumably John Colston Doyle (d. 1813), *Love Among the Roses: as sung with the greatest applause by Mr Sinclair at the Theatre Royal Covent Garden in the revived opera of the Lord of the Manner* (London: Dale, *c*.1812).

Lilliputian Lancaster: Lancaster was the county town, but it was much smaller than Manchester and Liverpool. De Quincey draws on Jonathan Swift (1667–1745) in *Gulliver's Travels* (1726), where the Lilliputians are only 6 inches tall.

new parliamentary statute: in 1798, the Lancashire Sessions Act empowered the Lancashire justices to hold a Court of Annual General Session. In 1838, however, four Lancashire boroughs, including Manchester and Liverpool, secured separate courts of quarter sessions.

207 *York from a contested election*: prior to the 1832 Reform Bill, the number of constituencies in Yorkshire was small, and for each constituency there was only one voting centre. As there were few borough members, the vast majority of the electors were obliged to flock together from different parts of the county to record their vote.

Giraldus Cambrensis . . . suspiriosae cogitationes: Giraldus Cambrensis (*c*.1146–*c*.1223), historian, whose works include *Itinerarium Cambriae*

(1191; *Itinerary of Wales*) and *De rebus a se gestis* (*c.*1204–5; *Concerning the Facts of My History*). The phrase has not been traced in his works.

207 *my own birth-day . . . my own native county*: De Quincey was born on 15 August 1785 in Manchester.

nearing the sea upon our left: De Quincey is nearing Preston, which is located at the lowest bridging point of the Irish Sea estuary, on the north bank of the River Ribble.

208 *radix*: root.

209 *'Quartering' . . . rut or any obstacle*: De Quincey's etymology is wrong. The 'quarters' were the four parts into which the width of the road was divided by the two wheel ruts and the central track of the horses. 'Quartering' involved moving the vehicle out of the ruts to drive on the 'quarters' (see above, pp. 315–16).

Charlemagne: Charlemagne (742–814), king of the Franks, reigned 768–814.

a taxed cart: an open two-wheeled cart used for trade purposes, on which reduced road-tax was paid.

210 *shout of Achilles . . . Peleus, aided by Pallas*: Achilles is the greatest Greek warrior. The subject of the *Iliad* is the 'wrath of Achilles'. Peleus is the king of the Myrmidons, and the father of Achilles. Pallas, or Pallas Athena, is the Greek goddess of war. De Quincey refers to Homer, *Iliad*, xviii. 217–19: 'There [Achilles] stood and shouted, and from afar Pallas Athene called out; but among the Trojans he roused unspeakable confusion.'

211 *If no more were done, nothing was done*: cf. Lucan, *Pharsalia*, ii. 657: '[Caesar] . . . thought nothing done while anything remained to do'.

212 *swingle-bar*: or 'swingletree', a pivoted crossbar to which the horses' traces were fastened.

213 *cany carriage*: De Quincey echoes Milton, *Paradise Lost*, iii. 438–9: 'where Chineses drive | With Sails and Wind thir canie Waggons light'.

crownèd: in the National Library of Scotland manuscript of 'The Vision of Sudden Death', De Quincey instructs the compositor on the importance 'to the rhythmus' of the word '*crowned*'. It 'should be read, and therefore should be printed, as a dissyllable—crownéd' (*Works*, xvi. 481).

swept it into my dreams for ever: in one manuscript fragment related to 'The Vision of Sudden Death', De Quincey appears to describe what he did following the collision between the mail-coach and the gig (see above Appendix C, p. 257).

Par. Lost, B. xi: Milton, *Paradise Lost*, xi. 558–63.

214 *Tumultuosissimamente*: 'most tumultuously'.

Ionic: Vitruvius (*fl.* first century BC), Roman architect and engineer, in writing of the origin of the different orders of architecture, observed that the Greeks shaped the Ionic column in imitation of 'the delicacy and ornaments of a woman' (*De architectura*, iv. 1).

215 *corymbi*: a cluster of grapes or berries.

the shadow of death?: a familiar biblical phrase: see, for example, Job 38: 17: 'Have the gates of death been opened unto thee? or hast thou seen the doors of the shadow of death?'

heady current: De Quincey recalls Shakespeare, *Henry V*, i. i. 33–4: 'Never came reformation in a flood | With such a heady currance'.

217 *Gloria in excelsis*: Luke 19: 38: 'Glory to God in the highest'.

darkness comprehended it: cf. John 1: 5: 'And the light shineth in darkness, and the darkness comprehended it not.'

218 *'Chaunt the deliverer's . . . earth were sung'*: Wordsworth, 'Siege of Vienna raised by John Sobieski', 11–14: 'Chant the Deliverer's praise in every tongue! | The Cross shall spread, the Crescent hath waxed dim; | He conquering, as in joyful Heaven is sung, | HE CONQUERING THROUGH GOD, AND GOD BY HIM.'

Campo Santo at Pisa . . . Jerusalem: 'Campo Santo' is, literally, 'holy field'. The Campo Santo at Pisa was built 1278–83 and, according to legend, on the site where the Crusaders placed soil they had brought back from the Holy Land.

219 *Créci*: the English defeated the French at the Battle of Crécy in 1346.

tidings of great joy to every people: cf. Luke 2: 10: 'And the Angel said unto them, "Fear not: for behold, I bring you good tidings of great joy, which shall be to all people." '

220 *horns of the altar*: in the Old Testament, sacrifices were placed upon the horns of the altar (see Exodus 29: 12). The horns were also clasped by those seeking sanctuary (1 Kings 1: 50).

sanctus: literally, 'holy'. De Quincey has in mind Revelation 4: 8: 'Holy, holy, holy, Lord God Almighty, which was, and is, and is to come.'

221 *six years old . . . promise of perfect love*: De Quincey is thinking in particular of the death of his sister Elizabeth. 'About the close of my sixth year, suddenly the first chapter of my life came to a violent termination,' he writes in his *Autobiographic Sketches* (1853); 'that chapter which, even within the gates of recovered Paradise, might merit a remembrance. "*Life is Finished!*" was the secret misgiving of my heart' (*Works*, xix. 3).

'ashes to ashes, dust to dust!': see above, p. 298.

the quick and the dead: cf. Acts 10: 42: 'it is he which was ordained of God to be the Judge of the quick and the dead'.

passion of Death: cf. Wordsworth, 'The Force of Prayer', 42–3: 'A solace she might borrow | From death, and from the passion of death'.

222 *victorious arm . . . his love!*: cf. Milton, *Paradise Lost*, x. 633–7:

> At one sling
> Of thy victorious arm, well-pleasing Son,
> Both Sin, and Death, and yawning grave at last

Through chaos hurled, obstruct the mouth of hell
For ever, and seal up his ravenous jaws.

APPENDIX A: *CONFESSIONS OF AN ENGLISH OPIUM-EATER*

223 *Qualem ministrum fulminis alitem*: Horace (see above, p. 286), *Odes*, IV. iv. 1: 'Like the winged bearer of the lightning'.

Dublin to ———: Westport House in County Mayo. De Quincey made the journey in August 1800 with the Earl of Altamont and his son, Lord Westport.

Ganymede: in Greek mythology, the beautiful boy who was abducted either by the gods or by Zeus. He is mentioned in Horace, *Odes*, IV. iv.

Frank: to mark a letter with the signature or official sign of a person who is entitled to free postage. As a member of the House of Lords, the Earl of Altamont enjoyed this privilege.

224 *Mrs Hannah More's*: Hannah More (1745–1833), playwright, poet, novelist, and religious writer, whose strong piety drew her to the society of the Evangelicals, where she became a close friend of William Wilberforce and of De Quincey's mother. De Quincey himself knew More 'tolerably well' (*Works*, ix. 325).

my little boy: William De Quincey (see above, p. 274) was born in November 1816, so at this time he was about 4 years old.

Des Cartes and Spinosa: René Descartes (1596–1650), French mathematician, scientist, and philosopher. For Spinosa, see above, p. 287.

Schoolmen: the 'schoolmen' are the major philosophers of the thirteenth and fourteenth centuries, and include figures such as Joannes Duns Scotus (*c*.1266–1308) and William Ockham (*c*.1285–1347).

Master of Sentences, Suarez . . . Mirandola: Peter Lombard (*c*.1100–60), bishop of Paris, whose *Four Books of Sentences* earned him the title 'Master of the Sentences'. Francisco Suárez (1548–1617), Spanish philosopher and theologian, whose works include *Metaphysical Disputations*. Giovanni Pico della Mirandola (1463–94), Italian philosopher and scholar, best known for his *Oration on the Dignity of Man*.

Telamonian bulk of Thomas Aquinas: in Greek myth, Telamon was the king of Salamis and the father of 'the Greater Ajax' (or 'Telamonian Ajax'), who was at the siege of Troy, and who is usually represented as colossal in size. St Thomas Aquinas (1225–74), Italian theologian and the greatest of the medieval philosophers.

Duval's enormous Aristotle: Guillaume Du Val (1572–1646) published a folio edition of the complete works of Aristotle at Paris in 1619.

Pythian Apollo: Pythia was the priestess of Apollo at Delphi. Under his inspiration, she gave oracles to those who consulted her. Apollo was frequently depicted with a bow and arrows.

225 *Bergen-op-Zooms*: Bergen op Zoom is a town located in the south-western Netherlands. It was occupied during the Napoleonic Wars by the French, who repulsed British attacks so often that the town became a byword for impregnability. Elsewhere De Quincey explains that 'a "*Bergen-op-Zoom*" ' is a person 'impregnable to all sense or argument' (*Works*, vi. 319).

the Stagyrite trembles: Aristotle was born in Stagira, Chalcidice, Greece, and was commonly known as 'the Stagyrite'.

Sagittary: an archer.

Kant . . . Doctors Seraphic or Irrefragable: for Immanuel Kant, see above, p. 265. In medieval theology, Realists and Nominalists disagreed on the question of whether general types were real or figments of the mind. 'Doctor Seraphicus' is the name given to St Bonaventure (1221–74), Italian theologian. Alexander of Hales (*c.*1185–1245), theologian and philosopher, was known as 'Doctor Irrefragable' ('Impossible to Refute').

227 *memoranda . . . drawn up . . . last Christmas*: in December 1820, De Quincey was in Edinburgh and preparing an 'Opium article' for *Blackwood's Magazine*.

the author speaks of his own birth-day: 15 August 1785.

subject: there is no indication of what subject, if any, was discussed earlier in the letter.

Sheffield Iris: the *Iris* for 23 October 1821 reviewed the *Confessions*.

Mr Montgomery: James Montgomery (1771–1854), hymn writer and poet who edited the *Sheffield Iris* from 1794 to 1825.

228 *the faculty of dreaming*: Montgomery opens his review by observing that 'Man leads a double life on earth:—he inhabits a world of reality by day, and a world of imagination by night. A third of human existence would be lost, if the blank space of sleep were not filled up with pictured fancies that amuse the brain in dreams.'

229 *writing private memoirs for my own dearest friends*: some of De Quincey's friends, however, knew nothing of the experiences he described in the *Confessions*. Charles Lloyd, for example, asked Thomas Noon Talfourd, 'Is it not very singular that we should have associated with him for several years pretty confidentially, & should never have heard him allude to one of these adventures?' (cited in Morrison, 212).

very depressing circumstances in other respects: years later De Quincey recollected the circumstances under which he wrote the *Confessions*: 'I began to view my unhappy London life—a life of literary toils, odious to my heart—as a permanent state of exile from my Westmoreland home. My three eldest children, at that time in the most interesting stages of childhood and infancy, were in Westmoreland; and so powerful was my feeling (derived merely from a deranged liver) of some long, never-ending separation from my family, that at length, in pure weakness of mind, I was obliged to relinquish my daily walks in Hyde Park and Kensington Gardens, from the misery of seeing children in multitudes, that too forcibly recalled my own' (*Works*, x. 262).

229 *Third Part*: De Quincey did not write this 'third part'.

Medical Intelligencer: a review of the *Confessions* appeared in the *Medical Intelligencer*, 2 (October 1821), 613–15.

in the course of the next week: in fact, it was just over a month later, on 29 December, that De Quincey left London and returned to the Lakes.

231 *Fiat experimentum in corpore vili*: 'Let trial be made on a worthless body'.

232 *schirrous*: 'indurated; covered with hard excrescences' (*OED*).

eminent physician: probably George Darling (*c*.1780–1862).

'*stand up to the scratch*' . . . '*punishment*': 'fancy' (that is, boxing) slang: 'endure bravely, regardless of injuries'.

conceit: confidence.

233 *sternutation*: sneezing.

write the ——— ———: almost certainly the 'Third Part' of the *Confessions*.

Thierry and Theodoret: *Thierry and Theodoret* is now attributed to Francis Beaumont (*c*.1585–1616), John Fletcher (1579–1625), and Philip Massinger (1583–1640). In the tragedy, Thierry is drugged with a poison that permanently prevents him from falling asleep, a condition he laments at v. ii. 63–8:

> The eyes of heaven
> See but their certain motions, and then sleep;
> The rages of the ocean have their slumbers,
> And quiet silver calms; each violence
> Crowns in his end a peace; but my fixed fires
> Shall never, never set!

old fable been thawed at once: De Quincey has in mind Sir John Mandeville (*fl.* fourteenth century), the reputed author of a collection of travellers' tales from around the world. De Quincey, however, almost certainly draws the reference from Joseph Addison (1672–1719), 'No. 254' in *The Tatler*, ed. Donald F. Bond, 3 vols. (Oxford: Clarendon Press, 1987), iii. 289–90: Addison prints 'an Extract of Sir *John's* journal' in which words freeze in the air until a thaw brings 'a Volley of Oaths and Curses'.

'*I nunc, et versus tecum meditare canoros*': Horace, *Epistles* II. ii. 76: 'Now go, and thoughtfully con melodious verses.'

a neighbouring surgeon: perhaps Richard Scambler (see above, p. 283).

234 *peristaltic*: 'peristalsis' is 'the propulsive movement of the gastrointestinal tract and other tubular organs . . . consisting of coordinated waves of contraction and relaxation of the circular muscle' (*OED*).

bitters: an alcoholic solution of bitter bark or herbs used as a mild tonic.

'*infandum renovare dolorem*': adapted from Virgil, *Aeneid*, ii. 3: 'Infandum, regina, iubes renovare dolorem' ('Beyond all words, O queen, is the grief thou bidst me revive').

the individual house: De Quincey was then living at Fox Ghyll (see above, p. 274).

235 *ordinary resolution . . . pretty rapid course of descent*: this account of withdrawal from opium is much more in line with the evidence of modern pharmacology (see above, p. 286).

236 *reculer pour mieux sauter*: to draw back in order to make a better jump forward.

heautontimoroumenos: 'heauton timoroumenos' ('the self-tormentor'). The Roman dramatist Terence uses the phrase for the title of a play that De Quincey quotes in the *Confessions* (see above, p. 264).

237 *hideous Golgothas*: Golgotha, a skull-shaped hill in Jerusalem, was the site of the crucifixion of Christ. It is mentioned in all four Gospels. London burial grounds in the early nineteenth century were notoriously overcrowded.

Surgeons' Hall: a reference to doctors and surgeons in general; their headquarters was the Hall of the Royal College of Surgeons in Lincoln's Inn Fields.

si vivere perseverarent: De Quincey reference is to the Roman emperor Caligula, and a story told of him by Suetonius in *Lives of the Caesars*, iv. 38: 'he accused them of making game of him by continuing to live after such a declaration, and to many of them he sent poisoned delicacies'.

238 *Rousseau*: as the opening paragraph of the *Confessions of an English Opium-Eater* makes plain, De Quincey did not admire the *Confessions* of Jean-Jacques Rousseau (see above, p. 3).

death of his youthful friend in the 4th Book: St Augustine (354–430), *The Confessions*, trans. and ed. Henry Chadwick (Oxford: Oxford University Press, 2008), 59: 'So I boiled with anger, sighed, wept, and was at my wits' end. I found no calmness, no capacity for deliberation. I carried my lacerated and bloody soul when it was unwilling to be carried by me. I found no place where I could put it down. There was no rest in pleasant groves, nor in games or songs, nor in sweet-scented places, nor in exquisite feasts, nor in the pleasures of the bedroom and bed, nor, finally, in books and poetry. Everything was an object of horror, even light itself.'

239 *Mr H.*: James Hogg (1806–88), and his son James Hogg, junior, were the publishers of *Selections Grave and Gay*.

APPENDIX B: *SUSPIRIA DE PROFUNDIS*

242 *Foundering ships*: perhaps this dream episode is related to the opening two movements of the 'Dream Fugue' in 'The English Mail-Coach',

where a 'fairy pinnace' lies in the path of 'an English three-decker' (see above, p. 214).

242 *Count the leaves in Vallambrosa*: cf. Milton, *Paradise Lost*, i. 302–3: 'Thick as autumnal leaves that strew the brooks | In Vallombrosa'.

Daughter of Lebannon: De Quincey published 'The Daughter of Lebannon' at the close of the 1856 *Confessions* (*Works*, ii. 266–70).

Kyrie Eleison: 'Lord, have mercy'.

Apothanate: presumably derived from the Greek, 'to die' or 'one must die'.

Cagot and Cressida: cf. Hogg, 174–5: 'Of all the subjects which exercised a permanent fascination over De Quincey, I would place first in order Thuggism in India and the Cagots of Spain and France. . . . The Cagots— the lepers of France and Spain—excited his deep pity. Many times he would draw word-pictures to me of the sad, touching scenes which must have been witnessed by half-scared worshippers—the wistful, wasting figures preparing to enter church by the Cagots' door'.

Fallentis semita vitae: Horace, *Epistle*, I. xviii. 103: 'a secluded journey along the pathway of a life unnoticed'.

244 *which horror too accounts for the figure*: De Quincey presumably refers to those parents who deliberately harmed their children.

cremona of Paganini: Niccolò Paganini (1782–1840), Italian composer and virtuoso violinist. Cremona, in northern Italy, is celebrated as the home of a series of famous violin makers, including Andrea Amati (*c*.1520–*c*.1578) and Antonio Stradivari (*c*.1644–1737).

modulus: pattern or structure.

Beethoven . . . Mozart: see above, p. 309.

oriental cholera: the most virulent outbreaks of cholera in the nineteenth century were in southern Asia.

Moloch: an ancient god to whom child sacrifices were made. Cf. Leviticus 18: 21: 'And thou shalt not let any of thy seed pass through *the fire* to Molech'.

'Tells also of bright calms that shall succeed': Wordsworth, 'I dropped my pen; and listened to the Wind', 12–14: 'The prophecy,—like that of this wild blast, | Which, while it makes the heart with sadness shrink, | Tells also of bright calms that shall succeed.'

245 *Count Massigli*: untraced.

Demiurgus: in Platonic philosophy, 'Demiurge' is the name for the Creator of the world.

my last confessions . . . ever witnessed: in his 1821 *Confessions*, De Quincey refers to 'vast processions' that 'passed along in mournful pomp' (see above, p. 67).

Symons . . . Hoddesdon . . . Middlesex: Hoddesdon is in Hertforshire (not Middlesex), and the murderous rampage De Quincey has in mind happened in 1807, thirty-eight (not 'thirty') years before he published

Suspiria. But De Quincey has most of the other facts correct. Thomas Simmons, a young man 'about twenty' with 'a ferocious and ungovernable temper', worked for a time in the family of a Mr Boreham, who had a wife and four daughters, as well as a servant named Elizabeth Harris. Simmons paid his addresses to Harris, but she rejected him on the advice of the eldest Miss Boreham. Dismissed from the family, Simmons was 'heard to vow vengeance'. A short time later he broke into the Boreham house and viciously stabbed four people, killing two of them, including a Mrs Hammerstone, who was at the house 'in consequence of an invitation to spend the evening with the family'. Simmons was apprehended and incarcerated in the 'Hertford Gaol', where he told the chaplain that 'after he had stabbed those whom he had murdered, and was in pursuit of Elizabeth Harris, he heard something, as it were, flutter behind him, and follow him in his pursuit; and when he overtook her, he felt himself unable to strike as he intended, and the knife fell from his hand'. For full details, see 'Murders at Hoddesdon', *The Times*, 23 October 1807, p. 2, col. E.

246 *umbras . . . penumbras*: an 'umbra' is a full shadow; a 'penumbra' is a partial shadow.

247 *that cottage emerges a figure*: De Quincey is undoubtedly dreaming of Dove Cottage and his wife Margaret. That house, he wrote in 1840, 'by ties personal and indestructible', has been 'endeared . . . to my heart so unspeakably beyond all other houses, that even now I rarely dream through four nights running, that I do not find myself (and others beside) in some one of those rooms' (*Works*, xi. 181).

248 *raven o'er the infected house*: Shakespeare, *Othello*, IV. i. 20–1: 'O, it comes o'er my memory, | As doth the raven o'er the infectious house'.

my sister's coffin in the month of June: see above, p. 296.

Da Vinci or Michelangelo: foremost figures of the Renaissance: Leonardo da Vinci (1452–1519), Italian painter, architect, and engineer. Michelangelo (1475–1564), Italian painter, architect, and poet.

Hebe: see above, p. 285.

249 *Aurora*: see above, p. 285.

250 *Coleridge for instance*: De Quincey is responding to comments by Coleridge such as the one recorded in James Gillman, *The Life of Samuel Taylor Coleridge* (London: Pickering, 1838), 250: 'Oh, may the God to whom I look for mercy through Christ, shew mercy on the author of the "Confessions of an Opium Eater", if, as I have too strong reason to believe, his book has been the occasion of seducing others into this withering vice through wantonness.'

trunk-maker . . . and . . . pastry-cooks: the paper from unsold books was proverbially used for lining trunks or pie-dishes.

a member of the 'fancy': boxing fraternity.

copies . . . of the Opium Confessions: in book form, the *Confessions* sold very well. The first edition of 1822 appeared in a print run of 1,000 copies.

A second edition of 1,000 copies was published later that same year. A third edition of another 1,000 copies appeared at the end of 1823 (Morrison, 222).

250 *inoculated by me . . . notorious as opium*: contrary to De Quincey's assertions, the evidence strongly suggests that many readers were tempted to try opium after reading the *Confessions*. The 1824 edition of the *Family Oracle of Health*, for example, announced that the 'use of opium has been recently much increased by a wild, absurd, and romancing production, called the *Confessions of an English Opium-Eater*. We observe, that at some late inquests this wicked book has been severely censured, as the source of misery and torment, and even of suicide itself, to those who have been seduced to take opium by its lying stories about celestial dreams, and similar nonsense' (Morrison, 211).

251 *hulks*: ships used as prisons.

causa occasionalis . . . causa sine quâ non: 'opportune cause' and 'necessary cause'.

(as Coleridge) for rheumatism: the first time Coleridge is known to have taken opium was in 1791 during an attack of rheumatism (Hayter, 191).

252 *'That ever spider twisted from her womb'*: Shakespeare, *King John*, IV. iii. 128.

Pelion upon Ossa: according to Greek and Roman myth, Ossa and Pelion are the mountains which the earth-born Giants piled on top of each other in their attempt to storm Mount Olympus.

Verschmerzen: see above, p. 299.

253 *little M. . . . like a rose in June*: De Quincey's eldest daughter Margaret (see above, p. 291) was 2 in June of 1820. In 'The English Mail-Coach', De Quincey states that Fanny of the Bath Road was also like a 'rose in June', a quotation he draws from Wordsworth's 'Strange Fits of Passion' (see above, p. 318).

orchard—not unsung by great poets: see Wordsworth in poems such as 'The Green Linnet', 1–3: 'The May is come again:—how sweet | To sit upon my Orchard-seat! | And Birds and Flowers once more to greet'.

limbus: edge or border.

254 *clouds of sulphur*: cf. Percy Shelley, *The Wandering Jew*, 670–1: 'What clouds of sulphur seemed to rise! | What sounds were borne upon the air!'

APPENDIX C: 'THE ENGLISH MAIL-COACH'

257 *Patterson (the great authority of those days)*: Daniel Paterson (1738–1825), *A new and accurate description of all the direct and principal cross roads in Great Britain* (1771). The eighteenth and final edition appeared in 1829.

(as Falstaff observes of himself) from sin: De Quincey seems to have in mind Shakespeare, *1 Henry IV*, V. iv. 162–5: 'I'll follow, as they say, for reward. He that rewards me, God reward him! If I do grow great, I'll grow less, for I'll purge and leave sack, and live cleanly as a nobleman should do.'

American Literature

British and Irish Literature

Children's Literature

Classics and Ancient Literature

Colonial Literature

Eastern Literature

European Literature

Gothic Literature

History

Medieval Literature

Oxford English Drama

Poetry

Philosophy

Politics

Religion

The Oxford Shakespeare

A complete list of Oxford World's Classics, including Authors in Context, Oxford English Drama, and the Oxford Shakespeare, is available in the UK from the Marketing Services Department, Oxford University Press, Great Clarendon Street, Oxford OX2 6DP, or visit the website at www.oup.com/uk/worldsclassics.

In the USA, visit www.oup.com/us/owc for a complete title list.

Oxford World's Classics are available from all good bookshops. In case of difficulty, customers in the UK should contact Oxford University Press Bookshop, 116 High Street, Oxford OX1 4BR.

	Late Victorian Gothic Tales
JANE AUSTEN	Emma
	Mansfield Park
	Persuasion
	Pride and Prejudice
	Selected Letters
	Sense and Sensibility
MRS BEETON	Book of Household Management
MARY ELIZABETH BRADDON	Lady Audley's Secret
ANNE BRONTË	The Tenant of Wildfell Hall
CHARLOTTE BRONTË	Jane Eyre
	Shirley
	Villette
EMILY BRONTË	Wuthering Heights
ROBERT BROWNING	The Major Works
JOHN CLARE	The Major Works
SAMUEL TAYLOR COLERIDGE	The Major Works
WILKIE COLLINS	The Moonstone
	No Name
	The Woman in White
CHARLES DARWIN	The Origin of Species
THOMAS DE QUINCEY	The Confessions of an English Opium-Eater
	On Murder
CHARLES DICKENS	The Adventures of Oliver Twist
	Barnaby Rudge
	Bleak House
	David Copperfield
	Great Expectations
	Nicholas Nickleby
	The Old Curiosity Shop
	Our Mutual Friend
	The Pickwick Papers